TRAXEN
SVESTI FATED MATES   BOOK 6
WAVY MARTIN

Catalyst Publishers

P.O. Box 1232

Aliquippa, PA 15001

publisherscatalyst@gmail.com

Author website: wavymartin.com

Other books by
Wavy Martin

Svesti Fated Mates Series

Vared

Devik

Ash'n

Ronan

Karid

Table of Contents

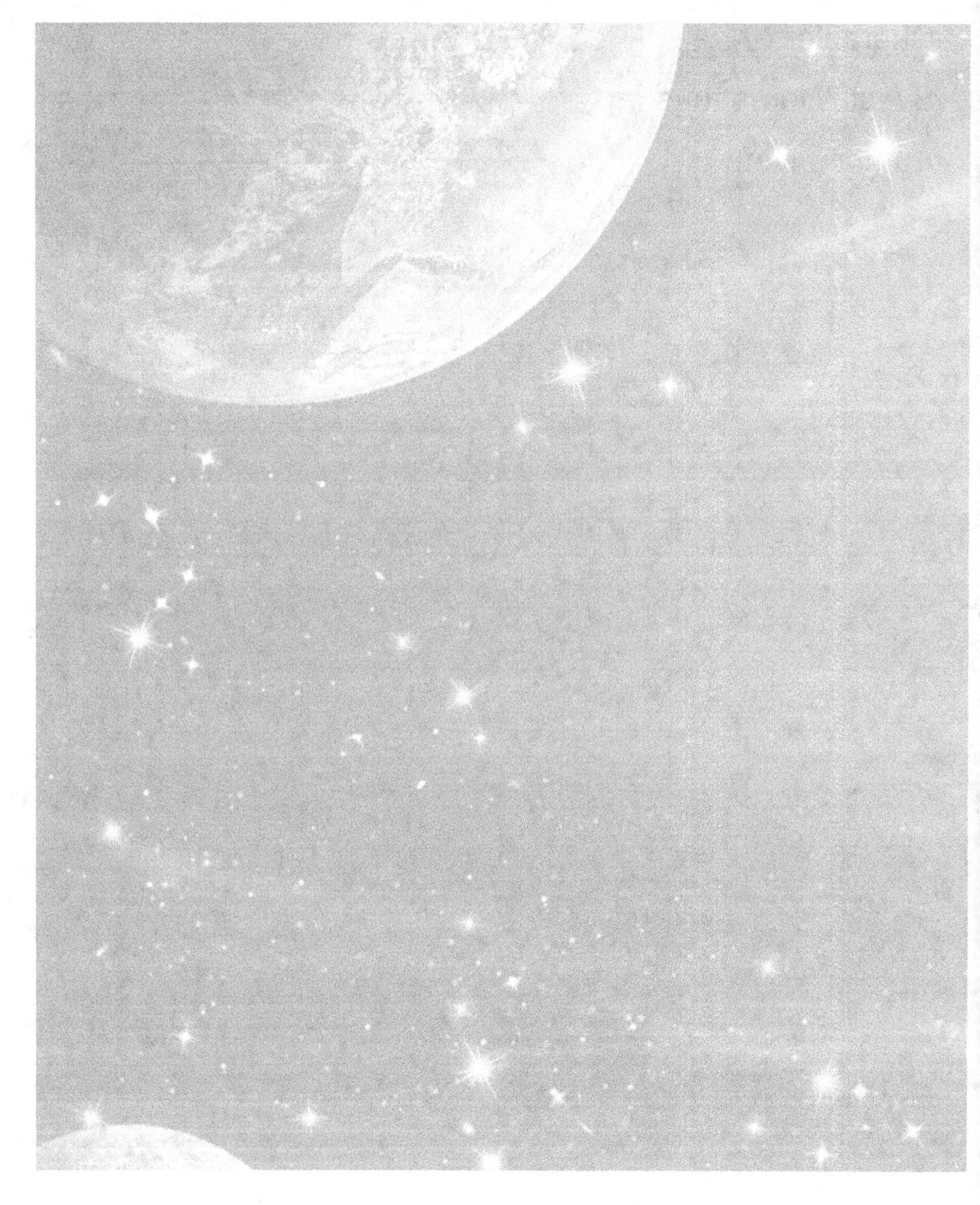

Prologue

All dates mentioned use Earth's calendar.

The Svesti, an alien warrior race, have guarded Earth's region of space from the Zuvgran since the early 1900s. Ruled by an Emperor, the Zuvgran invade worlds, kill the elderly, the very young, and some of the males. Those left living become unwilling slaves or subjects for medical experiments. The Zuvgran strip conquered worlds of their natural resources and move on. They attack anyone believed weaker, so ships or colonies are unsafe as well.

Zuvgran who disagree with the Emperor's expansionist policies or the pervasive cruelty to other species find ways to escape or aid others. Unfortunately, there are far too few of them and they are without the resources to do more.

In the early 2000s, the Zuvgran released a devastating virus on Costonia, the Svesti home world. The virus killed eighty percent of the Svesti females, as well as all female young, and rendered the remainder infertile. It's now 2037 and Svesti scientists discover the first biologically compatible beings—human females.

Ruled by a King and a Council representing their twelve Houses, the Svesti also worship a deity called the Goddess. The Svesti culture mixes old world gentility with superior technology. With their toned bodies clad in tight black pants and leather, most Svesti males tend toward over-protectiveness and a fierce sense of loyalty.

A divided Svesti Council creates discord on Costonia. Some want to invade Earth and take whatever females they want, while others believe any young born of a Svesti-human couple would no longer be Svesti. However, King Traxen Sovex wants to open up negotiations with Earth to receive willing human females for breeding or troth contracts.

A troth contract is similar to a short-term marriage. A breeding contract, now called a birthing contract, is specifically for the bearing of Svesti young. True mating, where the Svesti experience the biological urge to bite their partner and mate for life, supersedes both contracts. Fated mate bonds, where it is believed the Goddess blessed a couple by gifting them the one being in the universe who is their other half, were last recorded over a century ago. Upon meeting the first human females, the bonds begin to spark again and offer hope of lasting love and companionship for the Svesti.

King Sovex sent Commander Vared Durek of the **Invictus**, a space cruiser holding 3,000 warriors, to Earth and initiate first contact. Durek's long-time best friends serve on the **Invictus** as well—Lieutenant Karid Wurvez, head tactical officer; Lieutenant Devik Tolvex, head security officer; and Healer Ash'n Rivezt, head healer.

Durek initiated first contact with six countries based the size of their territory or influence after initial research of Earth revealed humans continue to be fragmented in their joint leadership. Each country convinced or ordered one woman to take the two-month trip to Costonia, live there and gather information for fourteen months, then return home. True to human nature, Earth's leaders instructed the women to focus on Svesti military capabilities, weaponry, and technology.

Earth's leaders allowed the Svesti to believe the women volunteered to be part of a Choosing at the King's Court, where they would choose a male for a breeding or troth contract. The women discovered the truth while traveling in space and didn't take the news well. Despite the rocky beginning and being unwittingly manipulated by Earth's leaders, the Svesti and the human females found common ground and proceeded to work together.

Talia Sullivan, the American President's secretly appointed Ambassador, worked with the Svesti on a fair treaty. During their travel to Costonia, Commander Durek, his trusted friends, and the women realized a Svesti traitor traveled onboard the **Invictus** and communicated with a Svesti noble on the home world. In a temporary alliance with the Zuvgran, these traitors attempted to kill human fertility via another virus. What the traitors didn't know was that the Zuvgran constructed the virus to also kill Svesti male fertility. Fortunately, with the help of the human physician and botanist/biochemist, Natasha Petrov and Lin Chang respectively, the Svesti developed a vaccine to protect humans and Svesti before the virus spread and both races suffered a slow genocidal attack.

About a month and a half into the trip, Durek received word from the **Defiant**, the ship they left to protect the space near Earth, that Earth's leaders publicly proclaimed the Svesti kidnapped the six women. Those same leaders called for increased military funding and gave the appearance of gearing up for war.

Talia developed an idea to get the correct information to Earth. King Sovex approved the plan and allocated resources. When all was said and done, King Sovex named Durek and Talia the Svesti Co-Ambassadors to Earth.

Despite the ongoing efforts of the loyal Svesti and women, the traitors remain unidentified. Based on information they did know, Durek sent Wurvez and another warrior, Grulen Jevax, on a secret mission.

Along the way, the **Invictus** received a distress call about a mine collapse on Talonka Six. While there assisting, Natasha met a Svesti-Zuvgran hybrid, Ronan d'Olorg, and became aware of a measles variant spreading across planets. Ronan and his adopted Zuvgran father, Largon d'Ayen, rescue Zuvgran hybrid younglings and help relocate to hidden colonies those few Zuvgran who wish to escape the Emperor's cruelty. King Sovex offered temporary sanctuary on Costonia for the hybrid younglings and his assistance in finding a permanent safe location so they can all be together.

The Zuvgran captured Natasha and Ronan on their return from distributing vaccines to the hidden colonies. The pair discovered Wurvez already imprisoned at the same location. The Svesti rescued all of them shortly thereafter and they rejoined the **Invictus**, which now carried the hybrid younglings and their caretakers. The group subsequently arrived safely at Costonia. Four of the human females formed fated mate bonds before reaching the planet.

The Zuvgran destroyed Jevax's ship not long after Wurvez became a prisoner and his status remains a mystery.

- Wavy

Chapter 1

90 years earlier
October 15, 1947 (Earth calendar)
Trezoura (capital city of the planet Costonia)

The four-year-old Svesti youngling held tightly to his mother's hand in the overwhelming crowd surrounding the palace. Wide brown eyes gazed in wonder at the larger-than-life hologram of King Aldis Sovex and his mate looking down on everyone. The chatter of the onlookers quieted as with a wide smile showing his fangs, the king greeted his subjects.

"The Goddess has blessed Queen Arinna and I with a son and heir. I present to you Prince Raxus Sovex of House Davelk." The king turned to his mate, gently took the young from her arms, and held him high while his tail wound around her waist. The young male's lavender eyes blinked sleepily.

Happy exclamations and cheers rose from the streets. The youngling winced as his mother's hand tightened as she pulled him away and weaved through the throng.

"That should have been you," she said through clenched teeth. "Your destiny was to be the heir and future king."

"I don't understand, Mother," he said as she abruptly stopped.

"Estra, there you are. Grissa and I have been looking for you both."

The youngling smiled when he saw his father holding his sister.

"Hello, Father. Did you see the King and Queen and their young?"

"I did, my son. The newest Sovex looked to be hale and healthy. A good omen for our world."

"Mother said it should have been me, but I don't know what she means." His mother squeezed his fingers. "Ow. That hurts."

His father's face fell.

"No, my son, it is not your destiny to be king. Your mother misspoke."

"How dare you correct me in front of my son?" His mother spoke harshly.

Concern filled his father's face. "Estra, we discussed this many times. I doubt Aldis even knows of your existence."

"I do not wish to discuss this with you. Our breeding contact has ended." His mother's lips pinched, and she looked like she sucked on a **wimma**.

"Allow me to escort you and the children to your parents' home, Estra."

The youngling felt the tension between his parents during the quiet walk through the crowd and flitter ride to his grandparents' estate. His mother held his sister while his father piloted the vehicle. Once they arrived, she handed Grissa to their nanny, Fridia, and sent them to the nursery.

Fridia smiled and took his hand.

"Come, you can tell me all about your trip while I change Grissa. Was it exciting?"

He told his nanny about all the people and the announcement. He kept silent about his mother's words and his father's reaction. While Fridia settled Grissa for a nap, he snuck out of the nursery to see if Cook had a snack for him. He stilled when he heard his father.

"It is time, sir. Estra's delusions worsen, and she infects our son with her fantasies. I must insist on raising my younglings elsewhere while she receives treatment from mind healers."

His grandfather sighed heavily. "I had hoped that Grissa's birth would help."

"I as well, sir. However, the younglings are better off with me until Estra faces reality. If Fridia wishes, she may continue as their nanny in my household."

"When will you take the children?"

"Tomorrow would be best."

"I will make the arrangements for Estra's care, and the younglings will be ready for you." Sadness filled his grandfather's voice. "Will you allow us to see them occasionally?"

"Of course. I have no desire to keep their family from them. I sincerely hope that Estra progresses quickly and can keep contact with them, too."

As he ran back to the nursery, the young male angrily wiped tears from his face. He loved his father and grandfather, but he did not understand why they talked of his mother the way they did.

Later that night, his mother came to them in the nursery.

"I will be going away for a while. It will be up to you, my young male, to watch over Grissa." Her smile seemed off, but she hugged him tightly and whispered in his ear. "Tell no one about your destiny to be king, my son. It is our secret."

He nodded and clasped his thin arms around her neck inhaling her scent.

"Will you be okay, Mother?"

A genuine smile graced her lips as she combed his hair with extended claws.

"I shall be fine. So will you. I will see you soon."

It was many months before he and Grissa visited their mother in the facility where she lived. They spoke of his schooling, his friends, and other topics as others listened and watched, but each time she embraced him tightly and whispered the same words to him. When questioned by his father and others, he never told them the secret, so they allowed him to visit her monthly.

As an adult, he continued to call on her and during their walks in the gardens, she told him of his fate. They discussed politics and plans to have him lead Costonia. She never left the facility and died there when the Zuvgran virus shattered their world. On her deathbed, he vowed to the Goddess that he would see that his mother's belief in his destiny became reality.

6 months earlier
December 4, 2036 (Earth calendar)

Undisclosed location (the planet Costonia)

Silently, the Svesti noble's luxury speedster landed in a clearing. Dianthia, Costonia's moon, illuminated his path to the large rectangular building in the middle of the woods. Robe swishing, he entered the structure after his guards and suppressed a smile at the waiting crowd. Their chatter quieted as he climbed the stairs to the dais.

"My fellow Svesti, I am honored by your presence here this evening. Earlier today, Traxen Sovex commanded the **Invictus** to travel to a planet named Earth, initiate first contact, and negotiate for female humans. He hopes a treaty for troth and breeding contracts with the species can be arranged." Pausing, he listened as his audience growled and watched tails flick in agitation.

"We are a proud warrior race with a long, august history living by the honorable tenets of the Goddess. Sovex minimizes our concern that dilution of our gene pool with another species will render our descendants as something other than Svesti. Breeding with humans may lift their species up but can only drag our race down. They have not yet achieved space flight beyond their solar system. They are ignorant of the wider galaxies of the universe. Their bodies are small and weak." The growls grew louder.

"Under Raxus Sovex's rule, the Svesti suffered the loss of our precious females." He bowed his head and silence reigned. Lifting his eyes, he scanned the crowd.

"Thirty years later, we still don't have a cure for the Zuvgran virus. Rather than concentrating our efforts on artificial womb or cloning technology to rebuild our female population, Traxen Sovex chooses instead to have us breed with a lesser species. The Goddess blessed the Svesti with intelligence, courage, and might. We are her chosen. It is our sacred duty to maintain the integrity of the genes she bestowed upon us." Cheers of "Always Svesti" echoed within the room. After a few moments, he gestured for silence.

"Remain vigilant to identify those who would derail our course. Prepare to act when called upon. Your commitment to our cause is unparalleled. I continue to be humbled by your request that I lead us to our destined future. I pledge to do my best to return the Svesti to its rightful trajectory." Chants of his last name rose and filled the space.

His guards stayed by his side as he walked among the crowd and shared greetings. The noble hid his satisfied grin and maintained a pleasant, but solemn, countenance as he spoke with his followers.

You were correct, Mother. I am destined to be king.

1 month earlier
May 26, 2037 (Earth calendar)
Millus (planet just outside the Costonian system)

The luxury speedster landed near the center of what had once been a centuries old fighting pit before the Zuvgran invaded Millus decades prior. The Svesti joined the fight to remove the Zuvgran and push them back out of the solar system, but the damage had been done. Only two days travel from Costonia, the lifeless world served as a somber reminder of the Zuvgran's lack of regard for the planets they plunder and why the Svesti remained diligent in protecting other species.

Accompanied by two warriors, the Svesti noble descended from the ship curling his lip at the brown sand swirling from the landing. The dust settled quickly in the still air. The yellow moon above provided the only illumination, but its brightness highlighted the Zuvgran waiting for the noble.

He gestured to the warriors to remain behind and he approached the Zuvgran confidently. One Zuvgran stepped forward, his horns gleaming in the moonlight. **Crek. They are ugly animals.**

"The Emperor sends his greetings."

"I hoped he would attend this meeting."

"He is a busy male. This meeting is beneath him."

The noble's eyes narrowed at the deliberate slight.

"Perhaps he should consider maintaining congenial relations with the future king of Costonia."

"I will relay your suggestion, Svesti."

"I was disappointed at the events on Theron. Your people did not perform to my expectations."

The Zuvgran snorted. "Hired help. Perhaps your people should have taken care of it yourselves."

"We agreed I would inform you when the females would be at the space station, and you would ensure they were infected with the virus. I kept my end of the agreement. Did you? My understanding is only one human was kidnapped and subsequently rescued." The noble's lips twisted in disgust.

"Our lab was destroyed. The Emperor is not pleased."

"Your lab is not my concern. Whether or not you upheld your agreement is."

"The records were destroyed with the lab. It is unknown whether the female was infected." The Zuvgran's face registered his displeasure at admitting a possible failure.

"I see. Perhaps I should take care of it myself. Do you have the virus?"

The noble's face hardened when one of the other Zuvgran swiftly approached and spoke quietly to their leader.

"We have an issue," the Zuvgran said.

"Which is?"

"We are not alone here. Did you send others?" Distrust laced his voice.

"Of course not. I do not spy on my allies."

"We will wait together, then."

Several minutes later, three additional Zuvgran dragged a struggling Svesti into the pit. They forced the reddish bronze male to his knees. The noble's eyes widened when he recognized the Svesti.

"Is he one of yours?"

"No. He's loyal to Sovex."

"You **crekkin'** traitor. The king will have you executed," Karid Wurvez, the head tactical officer of the **Invictus**, said angrily.

"Who else is with you?" demanded the Zuvgran.

"No one."

"Where is your ship?"

"Hidden."

The Zuvgran nodded and one of the others punched Wurvez in the jaw. Blood droplets arched before falling into the dust.

"Try again. How did you know we would be here?"

"I didn't." Wurvez received a kick to the stomach. He bent over as far as he could and coughed.

"Keep him," said the noble. "Question him as you like. All I ask is you inform me of what you discover and he never returns to Costonia."

"You don't want him?" The Zuvgran sounded surprised.

"Consider him a gift from me to you. The virus?"

"I do not have it."

The noble growled. "Get it to me and I'll ensure it's done."

The Zuvgran studied the noble, then nodded. "I will pass along your request to the Emperor."

"It's not a request. It's the completion of our original agreement."

Wurvez growled low. "I will see you dead, traitor."

The noble crouched in front of Wurvez and drew an extended claw along the prisoner's jawline leaving a trail of blood in its wake.

"It is good that you are already kneeling in front of the future king. Too bad you won't live long enough to do it again."

Wurvez bared his fangs and spit on the noble. "You will never be king."

The noble backhanded him. "Watch how you speak to me." He stood and faced the Zuvgran. "We're done. Contact me when you are ready to uphold your end."

The Zuvgran dipped his chin, then ordered his warriors to take Wurvez.

The noble walked away without looking back. When he rejoined the waiting Svesti warriors, the one who questioned him earlier spoke.

"We are not taking the Svesti, sir?"

"No. It is not the Goddess' will."

"I know you're not a warrior—" The noble grabbed his throat, his claws pricking the male's neck.

"What was that?"

"Currently." The male choked out the word. His breathing calmed when the noble released him. "I only meant that those of us who remain in the warrior ranks have difficulty seeing a Svesti at a Zuvgran's non-existent mercy, regardless of our beliefs."

"It is not easy for me either. I do not wish any of us to have Svesti blood on our hands if there is a way to avoid it. We are brethren. However, we cannot have our brother impeding our plans. The best option is to leave him to the Zuvgran."

The warrior lowered his eyes. "As you command, sir."

"Exactly."

How did Wurvez know I was on Millus? And why is he alone?

When they entered the speedster, the noble ordered, "Scan for nearby Svesti ships. If you find any, contact the Zuvgran and relay its position."

How much does Sovex know?

Less than fifteen minutes later, the Svesti warrior approached the noble.

"Sir, we think there may be a cloaked vessel within the asteroid field. There was a shift of the rocks in one section that did not appear to be normal drift."

"Did you notify the Zuvgran?"

"Yes, sir. They've deployed some fighters."

"Good. Let them take care of it." The Svesti noble tapped his tablet and a holographic image of the asteroids appeared.

He watched as the fighters peppered the suspected area with their weapons.

Moments later, an orange flash of light exploded and debris scattered within the field. The warrior said, "Scans indicate a ship was destroyed. Survivors unlikely."

The noble smiled. "Take us back to Costonia." **No witnesses left. Perfect.**

"As you command."

Chapter 2

Present day

June 24, 2037 (Earth calendar)

Invictus (Svesti space cruiser)

Dressed in what she considered her MI6 uniform—white button-down shirt, black suit, and comfortable black shoes, Rachel Llewellyn brushed her short, blonde hair and picked lint from her slacks. The last time she wore this outfit was when she first arrived on the **Invictus** almost three months ago. **So much has changed since then. I don't even know if I'm still an agent. I'm not sure I want to be after they lied and secretly offered me up for a breeding or troth contract with aliens. Knowing my boss, he probably still expects me to spy and report on Svesti**

military capabilities and politics. A loyal agent with over a decade of experience should have been treated with more respect.

The only person on the space cruiser who knew Rachel's real occupation was Talia Sullivan. **Well, I guess she's Talia Durek now that she and the Commander became fated mates.** Talia, formerly the United States Ambassador of Interplanetary Relations, now carried a new Svesti title of Co-Ambassador to Earth—a job she shared with her mate, Vared. Everyone else thought Rachel worked in security. She smirked. **Maybe I should see if Costonia has an agency like MI6. I might have considered Interpol, but interplanetary ops would be a huge step in upward mobility.**

Looking in the reflective viewer, Rachel's blue eyes framed by light brown lashes dispassionately noted her need for a haircut. Her fine hair no longer wisped along her nape but fell almost to her shoulders. Not bothering with makeup, she packed her toiletries and placed them in her suitcase. Her society mother would be horrified at Rachel's lack of mascara or lipstick—the subject of more than one argument in thirty-three years. A small smile graced Rachel's lips at the thought of her mother in a tizzy because Rachel chose to meet royalty without makeup.

She hesitated briefly before deciding to pack the knives and sheaths she had purchased on the space station Theron. While she would rather strap them to her body, being armed when she met the king of Costonia in the wee hours of the morning would be counterproductive.

Moving her suitcase near the others by the door to her quarters, she cast a final look around to ensure she remembered all her belongings. Despite a traitor onboard targeting the six human women during their trip, she enjoyed her time on the **Invictus**, and her imminent departure left her melancholy.

When she opened her door, Lieutenant Devik Tolvex, the head security officer, waited in the darkened corridor with a maglev.

"I'll get your bags." He lifted them easily onto the maglev to join other luggage and boxes.

"Where's Emmy?" Emmy Norton, an Australian hacker, recently became Devik's fated mate.

"She's packing up her computer gear." His nostrils flared and he turned. "Here she is now."

"Tell me again why Vared wanted to leave at four in the morning?" Emmy complained as she patted Devik's tail winding around her waist.

"Both he and the king believe it is best if you females arrive before members of the court show up for the day. You will enjoy your first hours on Costonia much more if you don't have to deal with them." Devik's fangs gleamed against his caramel bronze skin.

"Where's everyone else?" Rachel asked.

"Vared and Talia went to the shuttle earlier with Natasha, Ronan, and Largon. Ash'n and Lin picked up Ava to go to the med bay and will meet us there."

Rachel nodded and walked beside the maglev thinking about the people Devik mentioned. Natasha Petrov, a Russian physician, met Ronan d'Olorg, a Svesti-Zuvgran hybrid, on Talonka Six when he needed a healer to help younglings hidden in a refuge there. Natasha recognized they were suffering from a variant of Earth's measles, but no one knew how the outbreak originally started.

Largon d'Ayen, a Zuvgran warrior, raised Ronan from the age of five after the Emperor ordered Ronan's family taken. The two males rescued many Zuvgran hybrid children from lives of slavery. They also helped relocate Zuvgran who disagreed with the Emperor's expansionist policies and pervasive cruelty to other species. The Svesti king, Traxen Sovex, offered to assist Largon and Ronan in finding a permanent location for all the younglings. The **Invictus** spent the last portion of their travel picking up almost six hundred beings from various planets—most of them children. **It's been wonderful to watch the Svesti warriors interact with the kids. They haven't had any children born on their world for thirty years after the Zuvgran-engineered virus decimated the Svesti female population.**

Natasha and Ronan became fated mates after they were rescued from a Zuvgran lab on a planet called Millus. While they were there, they discovered Karid Wurvez in a cell nearby. Rachel liked Karid. They worked together on a training program for the warriors, as well as attempted to flush out the traitor. **It's been a week and a half and Karid won't interact with anyone. I don't know what the Zuvgran did to him, but I hope he talks to someone soon. Everyone is worried about him.**

Lin Chang, a petite Chinese botanist, surprised Rachel when she became fated mates with Ash'n Rivezt, the ship's main healer. None of the women suspected the two were seeing each other. Ava Taylor, a Canadian, was a feisty redhead and an exceptional chef, but she'd been out of sorts for a while. **She only told us last night that she and Karid were dating. Pain filled her eyes when she said he wouldn't see her.**

Shaking her head to dispel her thoughts, Rachel smiled at the group waiting for them outside the med bay. They exchanged small talk on the way to Shuttle Bay Bravo. While the males loaded their belongings, she boarded the spacecraft with the other women. Taking a seat next to Ava, she fastened the safety restraints, leaned back, and crossed her ankles in front of her. **Since the Invictus will remain in orbit around the planet, it will be a little while before we get through the atmosphere. Maybe I can get a short nap in before we arrive. It's too bloody early.**

Vared piloted the craft with Talia sitting next to him, while Rachel continued to rest in the back with everyone else until their final approach to the Svesti home world. Ash'n activated a viewscreen so they could watch their arrival to the planet. Pale yellow light on the horizon pierced the darkness as Costonia grew larger on the screen.

"I can't wait to see the flora growing in its natural habitat." Lin bounced in her seat next to Ash'n.

"Where are we going?" asked Rachel. **I probably should have asked the question before we left.**

"Trezoura, our capital city. You'll be guests at the palace," said Devik.

"Even us?" Emmy looked at her mate. "We're not going to your home?"

"We'll visit my brothers and father later, but for now, we have a room here." Devik smiled.

"Will our presence create problems for the king?" Largon asked with a frown.

"Possibly, but I doubt he'll care. Traxen does what he believes is right." Ash'n grinned.

"You call the king by his first name?" Ava's forehead wrinkled over her green eyes.

"Traxen is only a few years older than Vared and was still at the Warrior Academy when our group arrived. He spent time with his cousin, which meant he also befriended us. It continues to irk him when we use his title." Devik chuckled. "He is a good male. Much more even-keeled than Vared."

Along with the other women, Rachel softly laughed. They all knew about the commander's temper.

"We're approaching the palace now."

"Oh," exclaimed Lin. "It doesn't even look like a building is there." **She's so tiny next to Ash'n.**

"Most of our structures integrate with nature." His shoulders straightened as Ash'n beamed.

"That's wonderful." Lin bounced in her seat before leaning on Ash'n. Her small hands wrapped around his elbow. "You'll have to show me everything." He kissed the top of her head.

Rachel's lips pressed together when she saw Ava looking despondent before the redhead schooled her expression. **All these happy couples. Ava and I are the only single women left, but I bet she feels more lonely with Karid not being here than I do without a partner at all.**

Vared landed the shuttle in a designated area on the palace roof. Rachel took in the surroundings as she followed the group down the ramp. The king awaited them with two older males and one female. The two additional males standing behind the welcoming Svesti looked to be guards. Several others discreetly entered the ship with a maglev. **Most likely palace staff. The guards don't appear concerned.**

King Sovex shared his cousin's golden bronze skin and lavender eyes but stood several inches taller than most Svesti, putting him over seven feet tall. Rachel, at almost six feet, felt short in comparison. A black silk shirt hugged his impressive muscular torso and a short beard outlined his strong jawline. His long, dark brown hair appeared to be wavy even as it was captured in a single thick braid. **Bloody hell. The pictures I saw of him when I researched on my tablet did not do him justice. That male is fucking hot.**

The king smiled, his fangs gleaming white.

"Welcome to Costonia. I am King Traxen Sovex of House Davelk." He gestured to the others. "This is Canaan Durek of House Ruxila, main agricultural advisor. Lady Narilla Rivezt of House Yula, main medical advisor. And Ril'n Xeliv of House Fresida, my admin."

Xeliv smiled and nodded, while Canaan hugged Talia and his son Vared. Ash'n embraced and touched tails with Lady Narilla, his grandmother, who was delighted to meet Lin. While those with family chatted amongst themselves, the king greeted everyone personally. Not only did he extend respectful warrior's clasps of the forearms to the Svesti males, but he also bestowed the same courtesy to Ronan and Largon.

As Sovex shook hands with each woman and exchanged pleasantries, an itch on Rachel's neck warned her someone watched them. Casually, she turned her head and saw one of the palace servants pause the maglev laden with suitcases he was supposed to be pushing. Keeping her gaze on him from the corner of her eye, she placed herself protectively between him and the women. He rested a caramel bronze hand on the maglev and bent as if he were picking something up, but his eyes faced their group. When he straightened and continued into the palace, she mentally catalogued his average height for a Svesti along with his dark hair and eyes. **Attractive, but not too attractive. Blends into the background. I wonder if he's part of the traitor's contingent.**

Sniffing, she detected the smell of oud, cherries, and almonds. She turned back to find the source of the woody fragrance. King Sovex stood in front of her. **Is that his natural scent? If I could bottle it, I'd be rich back on Earth.**

"Lady Rachel." The king shook her hand. "It is a pleasure to meet you. Vared has spoken of your impressive sparring abilities." Tingling sensations traveled up her arm at his touch.

"King Sovex, it is an honor to be here." She smiled and dipped her chin toward their hands. "I see you've learned a typical Earth greeting."

"Merix Hunnek instructed me."

"The warrior in charge of the aquiponics area on the **Invictus**?"

"He's an old family friend. He comm'd and warned me to treat all of you well." He lifted a shoulder and grinned. "I'm not sure why he would believe I would do otherwise."

"How long have you known him?"

"Since I was a youngling."

She laughed. "That explains it. Sometimes people who remember when we were young and stupid like to remind us of it."

Twinkling lavender eyes gazed down on her and her heart stuttered. **Bloody hell. Don't tell me I'm attracted to the king.**

"Come, let's escort you all to your quarters and we can meet after you have time to rest." Traxen walked beside her as the group moved inside.

Rachel mentally filed her observations—doors, guards, cameras and their locations, corridors, stairs and lifts, and more. Their rooms occupied the majority of the third floor in the east wing. Her quarters sat on the nearest end of the hall next to Ava's.

"Please relax and settle in. Morning meals await you in your rooms. I invite you to join me for midday meal in the royal private quarters. If you require anything before then, please comm Xeliv and he will take care of it," the king said. "For your safety, guards are posted, and I ask that you remain in this section until then.”

“Are you expecting trouble?” asked Talia.

“Not necessarily. However, as the first human females visiting our planet, the more curious males may seek you out and interrupt your rest.” Soft chatter followed his statement as everyone nodded.

Rachel opened her door and glanced around the living area. Beautifully decorated in clean lines and shades of blue, silver, and white with native plants in pots, it evoked a sense of elegant comfort. She checked out the bedroom and hummed at the cobalt furnishings with hints of yellow. Her suitcases sat at the foot of the large bed. The huge sanitary facility sported a large bathtub similar to what was on the **Invictus**. A small kitchen area led to a balcony overlooking a courtyard. Perusing the area, she realized the wings of the palace enclosed the gardens. **Smart security measure. Limits outside access to the balconies.**

She inhaled deeply enjoying the scents of the flora and her shoulders relaxed. Taking off her blazer and placing it on the railing, she stretched to loosen other muscles. She gathered her blazer and went back inside to find the food. She munched happily on some fruit and **pertiza**—a creamy yellow substance similar to yogurt but sweeter.

Finished with her breakfast, she headed to the bedroom to unpack. **I still don't know what I'm going to do when I get back to Earth, but for now, catching the Svesti traitors is my priority. I need to protect the other women.**

Chapter 3

"I plan on spending the morning with Ash'n and getting to know my new granddaughter."

Traxen smiled at Lady Narilla's excited words. A faint blush tinged her bronze cheeks while laugh lines bracketed her mouth and shining blue eyes. Almost two decades older than a century, and only her silver hair truly hinted at her age.

"We'd love that." Lady Lin grinned and gestured for Lady Narilla to precede her into their room. **The human female looks like a tiny doll next to Ash'n. Not sure how that works, but they both seem very happy.**

"Then we will see you at midday meal."

"If you have no need of me, I think I'll visit with Vared and Talia." His uncle Canaan's brown eyes twinkled as he slapped Traxen's shoulder. "It's been too long since I've been in the presence of my son."

"Of course. Until later." Traxen wished he could join them, but other duties beckoned.

"Largon. Ronan. Might I have a word with you both before I take my leave?"

"Would you like to come in?" Lady Natasha gestured to the quarters assigned to Ronan and her. "Or would you prefer to use Largon's room?"

"If that's acceptable. If not, we can speak elsewhere."

"Join us, please," said Ronan. **It is still odd to see Svesti skin in gray.**

The older of the two royal guards, Bavin Hossix, cleared his throat.

"I need to check the room first." Hossix motioned to Madix Previv, the other guard, to maintain his position.

Traxen bit back his frustration at being treated as less than a warrior who could protect himself. Even after three years, the restrictions chafed at Traxen, but it wasn't his guard's fault. **So much changed when Father died.**

As they waited, Traxen watched the rest of the group enter their quarters. Lady Rachel stood in the doorway of her own scanning the interior before she stepped forward. Her tall, lithe body with its feminine curves radiated a quiet, contained power. Her scent reminded him of quality leather, **wimma**, and **valli**. **She looks as good from the back as she does the front.**

"All clear, Sire." His guard exited Ronan and Lady Natasha's quarters.

"Thank you, Hossix. Please remain in the corridor. Xeliv, feel free to report to your duties later than usual. We had a much earlier start today than normal."

"No need, Your Highness. I will be at my desk when I should be."

"As you will." Hossix and Previv took positions in the corridor guarding the door as Traxen entered the living area with his guests.

"Is there a problem, Your Majesty?" Largon asked after everyone was seated on the sofas.

"Please dispense with the formalities in private and call me Traxen. No problem, but an offer."

"Go on."

"There is a tract of land sitting between Canaan's House and my own that we believe would be a good location for the younglings to settle permanently. It's close enough to Trezoura to be convenient but far enough away to be private."

"You're offering permanent sanctuary on Costonia?" Ronan leaned forward and rested his elbows on his knees, his silver eyes searching Traxen's face. Lady Natasha squeezed Ronan's thigh, her face brightening.

"Yes. House Davelk and House Ruxila would share in the expenses. We would build to your specifications and ensure the needs of those who live there are met."

Largon's green eyes narrowed. The older male appeared relaxed, but Traxen saw his gray skin flex as his biceps tightened.

"And in return?"

"The younglings live safe from Zuvgran persecution. Ronan is family and you are Ronan's family. You do not need to earn your place on Costonia with anything more." Traxen smiled and shrugged. "However, I would be remiss if I didn't mention I am aware you have sympathetic beings on various worlds. If and when you feel our interests are sufficiently aligned, I would be willing to discuss how best to utilize said contacts for our mutual benefit."

Largon leaned back and laughed.

"You want access to our network."

Traxen met his gaze solemnly. "I would appreciate such access, but I will not demand it."

Ronan's eyes darted between the two other males before coming to rest on Largon. **He will follow the Zuvgran's lead. Good to know.**

"Ronan and I will discuss it. Before entering such negotiations, I would like to see the younglings settled."

"I understand your priority remains with the younglings—as it should. After midday meal, we will take you to the site. If it is acceptable, I will arrange temporary housing nearby so the younglings can move off the **Invictus** while the plans are drawn up and construction takes place."

"Can all of us go? I think the other women will have some valuable input into what might be needed for the children," Lady Natasha said.

"Their suggestions are welcome." Ronan's tail caressed his mate's calf. "They did a wonderful job providing for the younglings on short notice."

"I, too, value their thoughts," said Largon.

"I will make the arrangements." Traxen stood. "I will see you at midday meal."

"Let me walk with you." Largon looked at Ronan and Natasha. "I will be in my room if you need me." As they exited, he muttered while shaking his head, "They won't need me. Young love." The guards fell into step behind them. Traxen chuckled and Largon bared his fangs.

"You think I'm joking, but you'll see. My sense of smell is nowhere as sophisticated as Svesti, but being around four new fated mate couples, even I can scent them. It's a wonder any of them get anything useful done."

Traxen halted in front of Largon's door.

"You don't fool me. You are pleased for them."

Largon smiled. "True. Despite my teasing, I've never seen Ronan filled with such joy. I obviously don't know the others as well, but their happiness is obvious."

"I'm glad. Their bonds give me hope for our species."

"I've only met the human females on the **Invictus**, but if they are a good representation of their race, your hope is not misplaced." Largon extended his arm and Traxen gripped his forearm with a warrior's clasp. "Thank you, Traxen, for providing sanctuary for our younglings."

"Thank you, Largon, for saving so many." Traxen released his clasp. "Midday meal?"

"We will be there."

Traxen swallowed his sigh when Marek Tolvex of House Vramel entered his office. As a Council member and Devik's father, Marek irritated him on a regular basis. Cold and angry much of the time, he also spoke first and engaged his brain later—sometimes. **I know Devik said Marek used to be different before the virus. It's sad the male hasn't healed. If it weren't for Devik's older brothers, Devik might not have grown into the steadfast male he is today.**

"What brings you here today, Councilman?"

"Sire. I wish to discuss rumors I'm hearing that you are allowing Zuvgran to live on Costonia." Marek's lips thinned as he took a seat.

Traxen sat back in his chair and eyed the older male.

"Where have you heard these rumors?"

"Here and there." Marek waved a hand.

"I'm listening."

Marek's forehead wrinkled.

"I don't understand."

"You said you wished to discuss the rumors. What did you want to say?" Traxen kept his face courteously impassive as Marek realized the king did not confirm or deny the rumors.

"We cannot have Zuvgran on our planet. It's unsafe."

"Hmm."

"You would endanger our entire species by having such untrustworthy beings here." Marek's face darkened. "Your fitness to rule would be questioned."

"Are all Svesti trustworthy?"

"I beg your pardon?"

"Is every Svesti on Costonia trustworthy?"

"Most are. Some not so much."

"But, in your eyes, every Zuvgran is untrustworthy. Therefore, those who share our values cannot exist. If I judge individuals, rather than race, I am unfit to rule. Do I understand you correctly?"

The furrows in Marek's forehead deepened as he considered Traxen's words.

"Uh…"

Traxen pressed a hidden button, rose to his feet, and gestured for Marek to stand.

"Thank you for sharing your thoughts with me, Marek. I appreciate it. Xeliv will see you out."

The door opened and Xeliv said, "Councilman Tolvex, please follow me."

Traxen blew out a breath when he was alone again. Traitors targeted the human females while on the **Invictus** and he knew a Svesti noble ordered the events. According to his Spymaster, Marek could be the one they sought, but Traxen didn't see it. Marek didn't think strategically and spoke more than he thought. While he might be involved, he would not be the leader, nor would he be trusted with any sensitive information. **We'll root out the traitors and keep the females safe.**

The large group in the royal private dining room enjoying midday meal surrounded Traxen. With fifteen of them present, the normally silent space felt full in a way he missed. Laughter and happy conversation swirled around him as they waited for dessert to be served. Lady Reena, the head cook, chose to serve the fruit and cream-filled pastries herself. He smiled as Lady Ava perked up and spoke with Lady Reena about the meal.

"Mmm, this is so good. What is it? It tastes similar to a spicy pear." Lady Emmy licked her lips.

"**Valli**," answered her mate.

"I don't remember having it on the ship."

"**Valli** trees grow too tall to grow in an aquiponics area," said Vared. "We stocked the fruit when we left the planet, but we ran out before we reached Earth."

"The king requested a **valli** dessert as well as the **wimma** refreshment today," Lady Reena said with a smile. "I am glad you like it."

"The **wimma** drink tastes similar to Earth's limeade. It's a summer favorite of mine." Lady Ava took a sip of the citrusy concoction.

"We'll have to work off this meal with some training." The blue pattern on Lady Rachel's loose shirt enhanced the color of her eyes above her grin. The human females groaned.

"Please not today, Rachel," said Lady Emmy with a mock glare. "I think we can skip a day or two."

"Have you arranged somewhere to train?" Devik asked.

Lady Rachel shook her head.

"Not yet."

"I will try to get some space in the royal guards' training area."

"What type of training?" asked Traxen.

"Rachel teaches us self-defense moves," answered Natasha. "I know one of them probably saved my life on Straxis."

"She also worked with Karid on a training program for our warriors to counter moves smaller species may use," said Vared.

"Interesting. I would like to see this training program."

"When will we visit the site?" asked Largon.

"Whenever everyone is ready."

"I'd like to freshen up first." Talia rose from her seat. "And get my tablet so I can keep track of our ideas."

"I'll send you a copy of my notes." Lady Emmy tapped on her tablet with a flourish. "Done."

"Canaan, please escort our guests to their quarters. We can leave in a half hour. Vared, ready the **Invictus** shuttle."

Chairs shuffled as people stood. Traxen waited until they left before exiting for his bedroom. A short-sleeved shirt, uniform pants, and boots replaced his dressier clothing. After donning a weapons harness with some of his trusty knives and a blaster, he felt better able to protect the females if it became necessary.

While he walked to the east wing, he thought about midday meal. The females formed a close-knit unit even though they met only a few short lunars ago. The four couples exuded contentment. Before today, he had only interacted with Talia and Lady Natasha via comms, but all of the human females seemed intelligent, caring, and full of humor.

Lady Ava appeared quiet and stressed, while Lady Rachel's eyes and ears seemed to follow every movement and word. **I'd like to hear her impressions of Costonia. I have the feeling she doesn't miss much.**

Reaching the others, he smiled at how different they all were. Skin tones, hair and eye colors, body shapes, and even voice ranges made the human females appealing—each in their own way. However, Lady Rachel drew his interest as a male. **I shouldn't act on it. If she does decide to pursue a troth or birthing contract, many nobles would argue I used my position to be one of the first. Appearances matter. That doesn't mean I can't enjoy getting to know her, though.**

His tail swayed as he inhaled. **Crek. Her mesmerizing scent tests my willpower.**

Chapter 4

Rachel took her usual seat on the shuttle and strapped in. The king lowered himself beside her, his elbows brushing her biceps as he adjusted his seat restraints. His thigh next to hers emanated heat and warmed her skin. Despite her height, she felt small and feminine next to him. His natural scent made her want to lick his neck or any other body part in her vicinity. **Damn, he really does smell good.**

"Did you enjoy midday meal?" He leaned toward her, his hot breath near her ear. Shivers ran down her spine. **Shit. Is there nothing unappealing about this guy?**

"Yes, Your Majesty. You're in for a treat when Ava starts cooking. She's been able to recreate a number of Earth recipes with Svesti ingredients."

"Please call me Traxen." His fangs gleamed against his golden bronze skin. "I'm looking forward to trying Lady Ava's treats. Previv tells me his brother mentioned something called cookies." He dipped his head toward his younger guard.

"Call me Rachel." She studied the guard as the shuttle began moving. "Related to Talen Previv?"

"Yes. Madix Previv is one of our youngest Svesti now."

"And he's a Royal Guard? That's quite an achievement."

"Yes. Talen began training him as a youngling. Madix excelled at the Warrior Academy and subsequent training for his current position." He paused. "Talen and I were in the same Academy cohort and have been friends ever since."

"Really? All the women like Talen. Ava is especially close to him. I think she considers him an older brother."

"I'm not surprised. Talen is a natural caretaker. You'd never know he is also a formidable warrior."

"I saw him in action in Theron. I trust him to have my back any day."

Traxen sat back and his tail wrapped around his ankle.

"I hear you are a ferocious warrior as well."

She shrugged.

"I work in security. Protection is what I do."

"Do many females on Earth choose similar careers?"

"Women choose the same careers that men do. However, some professions are still male-dominated, such as the military, law enforcement, and security."

"Do you worry about getting hurt?" Rachel tensed at his question and pinned him with a narrow-eyed stare.

"Do you?"

The low rumble of his chuckle set her insides quivering.

"Fair point." He tilted his head. "Svesti have always been protective of females, but it's even more prevalent since the virus."

"I can understand that. However, for humans, our male to female ratio is close to even. Many human women will chafe at overprotective behavior and perceive it as doubting their abilities." She frowned. "On Earth, women still deal with misogynistic behavior more often than we should have to. I admit sometimes it makes us overreact."

"No doubt all of us will have to adjust to cultural differences."

The shuttle landed and everyone disembarked. Rachel took in their idyllic surroundings before taking a good look at the monstrosity before them.

"Oh my god. Please don't tell us you want the kids to live in that. It's like the creepiest haunted house ever," exclaimed Lin with a shudder.

The Svesti laughed as the women faces displayed varying degrees of shock. Even Ronan and Largon looked appalled.

"Some distant ancestor of ours built this. It has sat empty for many decades," Vared said with a smile.

"We will finally have a legitimate reason to demolish it," Traxen said. "The site itself is perfect. There's a nearby water source and lots of land." He glanced at Largon and Ronan. "Just tell us what you want and we'll build it."

Canaan waved his hand toward the left.

"I was thinking temporary quarters for everyone over there. The land is already cleared and far enough away to discourage the younglings from investigating the construction site regularly."

Largon nodded. Talia spun in a slow circle.

"You'll want classrooms so the children can receive a proper education. And a large library." Talia tapped on her tablet.

"A huge kitchen with plenty of storage. The dining area should have smaller tables around the edges for those who need it quieter, not just cafeteria-style tables and seating," Ava chimed in.

"An infirmary or onsite clinic. They shouldn't have to wait for proper medical care," said Natasha.

"I agree." Lady Narilla's tail swayed. A light breeze stirred her silver hair. **I hope I age as well as she has.**

"Playgrounds and training areas for physical education," Rachel added.

"Gardens and a greenhouse so you can grow your own food and teach the kids about nature." Lin's eyes shone.

Rachel noticed Emmy chewing her lower lip.

"Emmy? Is there anything you'd like to see?"

Emmy squared her shoulders and gripped Devik's hand tightly.

"I spent a lot of time in group homes as a kid. I hated the dormitory nature of them. No privacy. Nothing that was just yours."

"What do you think would be better, **milara**?" Devik's tail circled her waist with his quiet question and pulled her closer.

"Lots of bedrooms. Maybe two or four kids in each. And plenty of bathrooms. I really didn't like communal showers."

"Herrah told me she wanted lots of natural light after living in the caverns for so long," Ronan said.

"Oh, recreation areas spread throughout the building. Not sure if should be by different activities or age groups or not, but none of the kids should have to travel too far to interact with others," Ava suggested.

"We'll need to have offices for records and visitors." Ronan clasped Natasha's hand.

"Perhaps an underground level for the storage, including the kitchen supplies," Ash'n said.

"You'll have to decide if you want flitter access on the roof or in a separate area away from the building," Canaan said.

"I'm concerned about security and storage. We'll need quite a lot for five hundred younglings and their caregivers." Largon's brows drew together.

"Maybe design something similar to the palace." Rachel gestured with her hands. "I didn't see much of it, but it seems the wings surround a central garden area. What if you had the main playgrounds, training areas, and smaller gardens in the center? You could put the bedrooms facing that area with the recreation areas, libraries, etc. on the public-facing walls. The first floor could have the kitchen, dining area, clinic, offices, maybe even some classrooms. Just don't put balconies on the bedrooms like the palace or you'll have younglings sneaking out that way." She smirked.

"These are really good ideas." Talia kept tapping on her tablet.

"It's much more difficult planning for a large number of younglings from the beginning. For so many solars, we basically worked around whatever was there." Largon sighed.

"I think you're making an excellent start." Traxen smiled. "You have a good group with solid ideas. There is plenty of land, so you can build as much as you need. Once you think you have a general idea of what you want and how to lay out the building, we can get the architects involved. In the meantime, Canaan and I will arrange temporary housing and for the demolition of that." He pointed at the ugly building. "I'd like to get the younglings on the planet as soon as possible."

"This new beginning needs a proper name," Lady Narilla said. "Let's walk and see more of the area."

As they circled the building, everyone made suggestions—some better than others. However, none of them seemed right to Rachel and no one could agree on any of them anyway.

"Phoenix House," said Talia suddenly.

"Oh, I like that," breathed Emmy.

Rachel nodded with a smile. "I think that might be the one." The other women agreed.

Traxen asked, "What does it mean?"

"In human mythology, a phoenix is an immortal bird that rises from the ashes of its previous incarnation in a burst of flame symbolizing hope and renewal," Talia explained. "They're usually depicted as very large and colorful."

Largon and Ronan looked at each other, then smiled.

"Phoenix House it is," said Largon.

Traxen's comm chimed and he stepped away to answer it. Rachel watched him from the corner of her eye and saw him frown before he returned to the group.

"I have to return to the palace for a meeting. I apologize for cutting our outing short."

"I think we've seen enough for now." Largon began walking back to the shuttle with the others joining him.

"I took pictures, too." Emmy held up her tablet.

"We can always return at a later time," said Ronan.

"Thank you for your understanding." Traxen's tail flicked before stilling. "Unfortunately, Xeliv tells me many in the Court are aware of your presence which means I must request you attend a Court evening meal tonight." He glanced at everyone. "It's a formal occasion. I had hoped we could avoid it for a few more days."

Seated on the shuttle, Talia asked, "Do you want our clan markings on display or hidden?"

"On display, if you don't mind."

"Ladies?"

"I have to dress up?" complained Emmy.

"Yes, **milara**. You look even more beautiful when you do. Besides, I want all the males to know you're mine." Devik's teal eyes darkened.

"I would hate to have to eviscerate someone so soon after returning home." Vared's fangs flashed, and Talia slapped his pec.

"Try to rein in your temper. Remember your new position as Co-Ambassador." Traxen grinned when Vared growled.

"If you require assistance choosing suitable garments, I am happy to help," Lady Narilla offered. "We should have time to synthesize gowns if needed."

"Gowns?" Ava groaned. Rachel laughed at her friend's unhappy face.

"You'll survive."

"You'd better stick by me, Rachel. I don't have a mate to run interference and you're a badass." Ava stuck out her tongue.

"You've got it."

"If you know who will be present, we would appreciate you sending us their names, pictures, and some basic information about them so we can make a good impression." Talia looked at Traxen.

"Good idea, Co-Ambassador. I'll have Xeliv take care of that."

Just like prepping for a mission. Feels familiar.

Rachel set up her tabletop comm in the living area. Xeliv delivered it earlier with the information that the women could contact Earth weekly for now between certain hours. Silently debating, she restlessly tapped on her thigh. Disgusted with herself, she initiated the call to Earth. **It's better to know what they're thinking now so I can make a decision.**

After being routed through several intermediaries, she finally connected with her boss. His jowly face tensed, and his lips tightened when he saw her.

"Llewellyn."

"Sir."

"Is this line secure?"

"From the Zuvgran, most likely. From the Svesti, probably not, since I'm utilizing their relays."

He grunted. "What do you have for me?"

"Nothing."

His watery hazel eyes squinted, and his lips thinned further.

"Nothing?"

"Other than the military might of pretty much all the alien species I've encountered thus far significantly outweighs anything Earth can put together, I have nothing."

"I expected better intel than that from you."

"I expected to be treated as a valuable asset, not chattel." Although she was royally pissed, Rachel kept her voice even.

"You are a valuable asset. That's why you're there."

"I am here because I have a womb and a certain DNA strand. My training and experience seem to have been secondary considerations in your decision-making process. You certainly did not share pertinent information with me when offering me this assignment."

"Would you have taken the assignment if you had known the truth?"

"We'll never know because you concealed it from me and lied."

"You took an oath in service to the Crown." Redness creeped up his face from his neck. **You wanker, trying to use the oath I gave in good faith as a reason to refute responsibility.**

"That oath did not include being pimped out."

"That conclusion is insulting."

"I agree. For both of us."

"Will you do your duty? My understanding is the Svesti are not requiring you to enter a troth or breeding contract."

"No thanks to any of Earth's leaders."

"Well?"

"I haven't decided what I am going to do. I told you the truth. Even if Earth combined all their military into one, it would be no match for these species with their technology and numbers."

"Learn what allies we can cultivate. Intergalactic politics. You know the drill."

"In my opinion, the Svesti are not a threat."

"We need to know our options."

"And if I choose to resign?"

"It would be a shame if your father's political career derailed because of a scandal."

Frost coated Rachel's voice.

"Did you just threaten my family?"

"I will do what is necessary to protect Earth and country."

Rachel leaned forward and stared at the man who she had always believed had her back. She clenched her teeth.

"Let me be clear. Should any harm come to my family, the secrets I will reveal will embarrass the Crown and you personally."

"You wouldn't dare."

"Wouldn't I? I imagine I could convince King Sovex to allow me to send a planetwide transmission similar to the one Earth experienced recently. If you want to come after me personally, feel free. It'll be a few months before anyone can hitch a ride to Costonia. Leave my family alone or scorched earth will be my new modus operandi."

"This discussion has deteriorated. I trained you better than this. I hoped you would replace me when I retire."

"That carrot will not work for me. The difference between you and me is I have retained my moral center." **Even after everything the agency put me through after Jonathan's betrayal.**

"We can discuss this after you've had a chance to calm down and be reasonable. How do I contact you?"

"You don't. You can consider this my resignation."

"You can't resign."

"I just did."

"Reconsider."

"Goodbye."

Rachel disconnected the comm, then typed out the sequence to contact her father and received his voicemail.

"Father. Watch your back. MI6 made threats against our family in an attempt to have me do their bidding. Tell Mother I met a king. That will make her happy."

Finished warning her family, she stood and paced. Remembering her former partner and lover turned traitor, she recognized the parallels between the situations. **In both instances, my government asked for more than they should. I took down Jonathan for them. He deserved it for betraying me and our country. But I refuse to be part of hurting the Svesti. Maybe I should tell them the truth.**

Torn between loyalty to her country and her moral integrity, she wanted to throw or hit something. Tapping her portable comm, she drew in a deep breath as she waited for an answer.

"Devik? I need access to a training area. Now."

Chapter 5

Traxen passed his admin's desk on the way to his own office.

"Xeliv, I don't want to be interrupted for the next hour. Oh, please comm our guests with the Court attendees' profiles for tonight's evening meal."

"As you will, Sire."

"Thank you."

Traxen locked his door before pressing a hidden lever near floor-to-ceiling wooden shelves, then sat in his chair. The bookcase slid soundlessly on its tracks and his Spymaster entered the room via the secret passageway. Traxen dipped his chin at the average-looking caramel bronze male dressed in servant's clothing.

"Sire."

"Spymaster. Have a seat and tell me what you have."

"The word is out about your early morning guests. Rumblings in the Court about having Zuvgran in the palace. There is much curiosity about the females, but no mention of fated mate bonds or the younglings."

"All expected. I'm slightly surprised at the last."

"All the mates have kept their clan markings covered as far as I can tell."

"Tolvex visited me earlier about the rumors of Zuvgran settling on Costonia."

"Where did he get the information?"

"He did not enlighten me." Traxen stood and grabbed a water pouch from a small cooling unit. He held it out to his

Spymaster who shook his head. He kept it for himself taking a sip as he sat back down. "I still do not see him as the ringleader."

"I agree. I'm still investigating Hil'n Glopiz of House Nuxar, Pluvi Frulix of House Srotix, and Yistax Minnet of House Troliv."

"All three usually disagree with my decisions. Frulix argues every dissenting point even if they conflict with each other, and any one of them is intelligent enough to lead a coup."

"All of them were off-world when Wurvez was captured, although I've since discovered that Tolvex spent his time on **Rapture**. My contacts confirm his presence."

"The pleasure ship? Marek Tolvex?" Traxen smirked.

"He's still male."

"I concede your point." Traxen paused. "My guests will be attending evening meal tonight with the Court. I instructed the couples to display their clan markings."

"I will be sure to be there. I can't wait to see the reactions." The male grinned.

"As this persona?" Traxen waved at the servant's garb.

"No, I think tonight wastrel Ari Zunnax will make an appearance."

"I spoke with Largon and Ronan. I believe once the younglings are settled satisfactorily in their new home they will be open to using their network to aid us against the Zuvgran emperor."

"That would be helpful." His Spymaster paused. "I believe one of the human females noticed me this morning."

"Dressed as you are?"

"Yes. The tall one."

"Lady Rachel." Traxen's tail swayed. "She has a background in security. It is possible."

"Is she aware of the traitor?"

"Yes, all of the females are. Vared said she worked with Wurvez to narrow the suspect list on the **Invictus**."

"My instincts tell me her experience is greater than simple security."

"Noted. Have we heard from the Wing Raiders about their mission to Rumaska? With the success of the new star drive, we need more bremmite."

"They're making arrangements to visit the planet and gathering intel about the mine owners. I suggested they also obtain information on other ore or goods available for purchase. Females rule the planet and other sources say they subjugate males—to what degree, I do not know yet. I have every confidence Captain Makai's crew will find the information we need to arrange a purchase contract."

"I hope so. Their Ruling Commission refused to speak with me at all because I'm male. I want more information before I decide which female will negotiate for us." Traxen frowned. "Anything else?"

"No."

"Then get out of my office so I can pretend to work." Traxen followed his Spymaster to the bookcase. "I don't say it often enough, but I appreciate your service to Costonia."

"Your grandfather rescued me from an untenable situation as a child and gave me what I needed to succeed. I can never repay your family enough."

"Maybe when we have more human females on Costonia, you will find one and settle into a life that does not rely on intrigue." Traxen clapped the male on the shoulder.

"Unlikely. I'm too damaged to appeal to a female. Besides, I haven't found my replacement yet."

"Never say never, my friend."

Traxen closed the hidden passage after the male left. **I will enjoy Ari Zunnax verbally riling the Court tonight. He frowned. If his instincts are correct, I will have to keep a closer eye on Rachel which won't be a hardship at all.**

Initiating a comm, Traxen squared his shoulders and put on his best royal face. A hologram of the Zuvgran emperor, Prigon n'Tuli, eventually appeared.

"Sovex. Why have you contacted me?" The older male growled impatiently. **His gray skin looks washed out, his brown eyes pale with age, and his fleshy countenance appears unhealthy. Even his horns appear yellowed. I'll have to check with my Spymaster about the potential succession if n' Tuli dies soon or is incapacitated.**

"I understand there is a virulent illness appearing on many worlds. We encountered it as well. I am sending you a file with information on the disease, along with the specifics for a vaccine and treatment plans."

"Why would you do that?" n'Tuli narrowed his eyes and glared.

"Despite what you did to my species, there are innocents on the worlds you control. We have no quarrel with them and see no need for them to suffer any more than they already do under your rule."

The Emperor snorted.

"You expect me to believe you haven't developed a biological weapon to destroy the Zuvgran?"

A slight sneer crossed Traxen's lips before he controlled it.

"You have numerous scientists who can verify the information or not. Your choice. My conscience remains clear by offering it to you. What you choose to do or not do for you subjects' health is entirely up to you."

"I hope you do not expect me to thank you if the information proves useful."

"Good day, n'Tuli." Traxen disconnected his comm and let his tail flick wildly for a few moments before he stilled it. **Crek. That was difficult, offering succor to our**

ungrateful enemy, but I will not stoop to biological warfare by withholding the means to stop the spread of the measles variant.

Traxen left his quarters after changing for evening meal. Hossix and Previv waited in the corridor for him.

"Sire. You may want to see this before you go downstairs."

"See what, Hossix?"

The guard tapped his comm and a holographic video played. Rachel appeared in form-fitting stretchy pants and a tight top that contained her full breasts and bared her abdomen. Sweat dotted her face and body. She sparred with one of his best guards in the royal training area.

"When was this?" Traxen's tail flicked rapidly as he watched her fall to the mat after a leg sweep by the male.

"A couple hours ago. She showed up with Lieutenant Tolvex, sparred with him, then offered to take on others when one of the guards insinuated Tolvex took it easy on her."

Rachel arched her back and bounced to her feet in a smooth motion before spinning and kicking the guard in the face then retreating. His head snapped to the side and a roar left his lips as he rushed her. She stood motionless until he closed on her position, then dropped and slid between his legs. Turning, she hit the male in the back with a straightened elbow and an open palm toppling him to the mat with a grunt. She wrapped her arms around his neck while sitting on his spine. Traxen growled when he saw the male's claws pierce her forearm. She held firm, choking the male until he tapped the mat. Immediately, she released him and stood holding her hand out to him. He rose without her help but gave her a warrior's clasp.

"I'm looking forward to sparring with her myself," Previv said.

Traxen's chest rumbled loudly. **I may kill one of my guards for drawing her blood.**

"She was hurt. That is unacceptable."

"Injuries happen when sparring. You know that, Sire." Hossix glanced at him sideways.

"She's a fragile female."

Both males laughed.

"Lady Rachel took on a half dozen guards after Tolvex. She won every match. This was the final one for today." Hossix grinned. "She is formidable. Her skills are unexpected, but she impressed all your guards."

"I will speak to her." Traxen continued walking, his tail flicking.

"I hope you compliment her skills," Hossix said quietly. "Lady Rachel strikes me as the sort of female to take exception to overbearing males."

"Did I ask your opinion?"

"No."

They walked in silence for a while, then Traxen sighed.

"I am pleased she can take care of herself. I am unhappy she was wounded."

"I can see why Commander Durek had her working on a training program for the **Invictus**. Some of the moves she makes I've never seen before," Previv offered.

"We believed you should be aware beforehand in case any of the Court heard of her time in the training area," Hossix said.

"I appreciate not being surprised by a member of the Court."

Traxen consciously stilled his tail and unclenched his fists. Fortunately, his claws remained retracted so he didn't drip blood in the pristine corridors.

Why am I so angry at her actions?

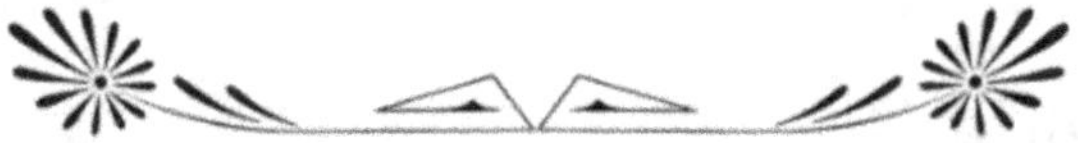

Traxen arrived in the main dining area before his off-world guests. Members of the Court milled around with drinks and small appetizers. As he made his way toward his seat at the head of the table, he nodded and greeted people by name, doing his best not to be ensnared into conversations he didn't want. The room fell silent as Canaan escorted Lady Ava while leading the others into the room.

Gasps and whispers broke out when Court members noticed the gold clan markings. Traxen bit the inside of his cheek when Vared growled loudly at a male who reached out toward Talia's clavicle as if to touch her. **I can always count on him to put someone in his place. I'm lucky he didn't punch the male.**

Ash'n and Lady Lin followed Lady Narilla, then Devik and Lady Emmy came next. A glass shattered when Ronan and Lady Natasha entered. The females wore an array of bright colors. Last came Rachel serenely holding onto Largon's forearm. Her dark gray silk gown flowed over her body, highlighting her curves and bringing out the blue in her eyes.

While her left shoulder was bare as per Svesti custom, a long sleeve covered her right arm. **Is that to hide her injury? No, the guard pierced her left forearm.**

Traxen looked closer and saw the faint redness indicating a healing wand was used. His shoulders relaxed, then his tail wrapped around his ankle when he noticed her bare thigh peeking through a long slit at the side of her gown. She turned and he sucked in a breath when he saw the opening in the back that revealed a long expanse of creamy skin and the dimples low on her spine. **Goddess, she's gorgeous.**

"Members of the Court, allow me to introduce our honored guests. Lady Ava Taylor. Lady Talia Sullivan Durek, fated mate of Commander Vared Durek. Lady Lin Chang Rivezt, fated mate of Healer Ash'n Rivezt. Lady Natasha Petrov d'Olorg, fated mate of Ronan d'Olorg. d'Olorg is the sole remaining issue of Saletta Yemez d'Olorg and cousin to the crown. Lady Rachel Llewellyn and Largon d'Ayen. The human females recently arrived from Earth. d'Ayen has spent over forty solars rescuing Zuvgran hybrids from captivity and relocating disaffected Zuvgran who disagree with their Emperor's policies and treatment of other species. He is also d'Olorg's adoptive father. I have offered asylum and sanctuary to d'Ayen and d'Olorg, as well as the younglings they rescued. I expect our guests to be treated with all the courtesy and graciousness this Court is known for." Traxen paused and looked around at the Court with a stern expression.

"As you can see, some of our guests from Earth have sparked fated mate bonds which we haven't seen in over a century. I take it as a sign that the Goddess approves of our reaching out to Earth and initiating a treaty. I have named Lady Talia and Commander Durek co-ambassadors to Earth. Sometime in the near future, they will undertake a mission to escort not only diplomats but also more human female volunteers to Costonia."

"Will there be Choosings for the unmated females?" Hil'n Glopiz asked.

"No. We will not force the females to enter birthing or troth contracts. Should they meet a male that interests them, and they wish to pursue such actions, we will allow it as we would for any other female."

Low grumbles sounded throughout the room. Traxen bit back a sigh.

"As human females can spark fated mate bonds, I believe it is best to allow potential relationships to progress naturally. As Svesti, we must learn to court human females not just with our own customs but theirs as well." He noticed the servers by the door. "Please take your seats and enjoy the meal."

He continued standing until everyone had found their assigned chairs. Rachel sat halfway down his table. Close enough that her unique scent tickled his senses but too far away for casual conversation. Winding his tail around a chair leg, he settled in for a long boring meal.

Chapter 6

Rachel would deny it if asked, but sparring with seven Svesti warriors back-to-back hurt a hell of a lot more than taking on seven human men. Thankfully, healing wands existed on Costonia, not to mention the huge bathtub in her quarters. **Fortunately, my muscles stopped cramping in time to prepare for this Court dinner. I shouldn't have let my need to get my anger out influence me quite so much. Live and learn. I only wish I could make a decision about telling the Svesti about my real occupation.**

She savored a bite of **clepella** before taking a sip of a light refreshing wine. Largon sat to her left with Lady Narilla on his other side, while a Svesti male named Wanon Reccix occupied the chair to her right. According to the file Xeliv sent, Reccix was seventy-two solars, although longer Svesti lifespans made him look younger. Fit and healthy-looking, his reddish bronze skin that looked like fur but wasn't, seemed to be a lighter shade than Karid's.

Casually, she glanced around the long tables and made silent observations about the interactions in the room, correlating them with the profiles she received. Whoever arranged the *seating* ensured the most vocal detractors to an Earth treaty were separated from the human women, Ronan, and Largon. **I guess I did receive some benefit from all those political dinners my parents made me attend.**

"Are you enjoying your meal, Lady Rachel?" Reccix asked.

"Very much. On Earth we have a similar dish called ratatouille."

"Did you enjoy your travel to Costonia?"

"Yes, the crew of the **Invictus** treated us well and accommodated our requests when we had them." Rachel allowed a genuine smile to lift her lips.

Reccix looked around at the other women.

"I admit I am surprised at the myriad of appearances of human females."

A soft laugh escaped Rachel and she tilted her glass in an encompassing circle.

"This is nothing. Women come in all shapes and sizes, not to mention skin, eye, and hair colors. Our personalities and interests vary, too."

His green eyes glinted as they grew wider.

"How fascinating." He leaned closer. "What do you think about the fated mate bonds? Are you hoping for one?"

"We don't have fated mates on Earth so for us it's a foreign concept, but seeing the results so far, I can't argue against them. All four couples are exceedingly happy."

"Do you know how the bonds triggered?"

She shook her head.

"No. All of them chose to commit because of deep, abiding love for each other. At some point, the bonds sparked. I do know it wasn't immediate." **No need to tell him about true mating. Let that come from the healers.**

His lips turned down, and in her peripheral vision, she saw his tail flick once.

"That's it? No special courting rituals?"

Shaking her head, she refrained from rolling her eyes.

"No. Each relationship progressed and developed at its own pace." She paused, then said softly, "You are aware that human women closer to your age would be infertile."

He sat back and his tail drooped.

"Yes. While that might be an issue for building our population, finding a compatible mate to share my remaining years…" His voice cracked and he cleared his throat. "The possibility of a fated mate…"

"Reccix, look at me," she said gently. **That combination of loneliness and hope in his eyes breaks my heart. How many of them feel the same way?**

"There is no magic formula. We have a saying on Earth—there is someone out there for everyone. Just be yourself when more women come to Costonia. It may take a while until you find each other, but keep your heart open to the possibility and don't push a woman before she's ready."

His expression cleared and he smiled.

"Wisdom and beauty. An intoxicating combination." He winked. "Too bad you're much too young for a male like me."

Laughing lightly, she said, "You, sir, are charming and much too nice for someone like me."

"I'm glad you are here, Lady Rachel. You grace our Court."

"Flatterer." She leaned toward him. "I take it you are not one of those purists I've heard about."

"Goddess, no. Even if I had been seriously considering such arguments, the fated mate bonds would convince me to revisit such a stance." He frowned. "You seem friendly with the Zuvgran. Many will judge you for the company you keep."

She pressed her lips together.

"Many ethnicities comprise Earth's population. The more enlightened of us judge an individual by their actions and heart, not their ancestry, gender, or orientation. Largon is an honorable warrior who I am proud to call a friend."

Reccix held up his hands in surrender.

"I just wanted to warn you, not upset you." He tipped his head toward Traxen. "If the king trusts him, d'Ayen obviously impressed him. King Sovex may be relatively young, but he consistently leads us with a clear head and honest motives. Much like his father before him."

The servers cleared their meals and brought out dessert. Rachel didn't recognize it, but the **leringa** sauce encouraged her to try the confection.

"Mmm, this is good. The base tastes similar to Earth's cheesecake."

"I hope to sample some human food."

"Lady Ava is a talented chef and recreates Earth recipes with Svesti ingredients. I imagine she will do the same here. Wait until you try her cookies. They were popular with the warriors on the **Invictus**."

She and Reccix chatted with those across from them. When Traxen stood, others left their seats to visit with others in the room. Checking with Largon to see how he fared, she smiled at his grumbling complaint.

"I feel as if I'm on display in a zoo. Svesti looked sideways at me as if I wouldn't notice, while others stared rudely."

"I don't know if you saw, but they did the same for us women. We're the new kids on the block. No one knows what to expect."

His forehead scrunched, and he huffed.

"New kids on the block? At least they weren't looking at you like you were going to unexpectedly rage during the meal."

"New neighbors? Unknown? I'm not sure the best way to explain the slang." Rachel shrugged.

His face cleared. "I understand now. Thank you."

She patted his muscular forearm in commiseration.

"We probably need to mingle and meet others." Her lips turned up at his growl, but he stood at her words.

Rachel fought to maintain a placid expression when speaking with the males who disrespected Largon. She mentally catalogued each name and face against the profiles she studied. Impressed with how well he verbally handled each situation, her respect for the Zuvgran increased. **His manners are impeccable. What is it with all these males taking my hand or touching my arm, though? I'm ready to break some fingers.**

Becoming separated from Largon, she searched the crowd for the others. Ava grabbed her elbow.

"Oh, stay with me, Rachel. They're driving me crazy with all the touching."

"Same here. I wonder what that's all about."

"They're hoping to spark fated mate bonds." The women turned to face the speaker, a male with lavender eyes and a scar near his ear.

Ava sighed heavily and held out her hand.

"Go ahead. Get it over with."

He raised his caramel bronze hands, and an exaggerated expression of horror crossed his face.

"Absolutely not. I have no desire to be tied to a single female for the rest of my life. I cannot, in good conscience, deprive females of all species of my attention." He waved his hand in front of his body.

Rachel said to Ava, "I guess he's a player."

"Thank goodness. Someone who won't touch me. Don't they know it doesn't work that way with humans?"

"Doubtful. Hopefully, the word will spread, and we won't have to deal with this too often."

"Our histories tell of bonds sparking from the first contact," the male said.

Both women shook their heads.

"Not with humans," Rachel said. "From what we can tell, both people need to make a real commitment to each other before the bonds trigger."

"Then I'm safe. I have an aversion to commitment." He lifted an eyebrow with a grin.

"You look familiar," said Rachel.

"I assure you I would remember if we had met, Lady Rachel."

The scent of oud, cherry, and almonds wafted toward Rachel.

"Ari Zunnax, are you harassing my guests?" Traxen stepped next to Rachel with crossed arms and an irritated expression.

"Hardly, Sire. We were discussing fated mate bonds and how I do not wish one for myself. I hadn't even had a chance to introduce myself."

"Ladies, may I present my very distant cousin, Ari Zunnax. His most honorable trait is his truthfulness about being dishonorable."

Rachel suppressed a grin at Ava's snort.

"You wound me, Cousin."

"I doubt that. You rarely attend Court functions. Why this evening?"

"Human females and Zuvgran at the palace. I will be able to dine on stories of this evening for months." Zunnax's shoulders rose and fell.

Traxen's thick braid slid across his shoulder as he shook his head. **Damn, he smells so good.**

"You never change."

"Only my clothes."

Ava laughed out loud. "Oh, thank you, Zunnax. This is the most fun I've had all evening."

Zunnax bowed.

"My pleasure, Lady Ava."

Despite Zunnax acting like a stereotypical rake, Ava's momentary happiness cheered Rachel. **She's been so upset about Karid. It's good to see a real smile on her face.**

"If I assure you I have no designs on your person, would you escort me for the rest of this event? I could use the comic relief." Ava's green eyes lit with mirth.

"I'm crushed you don't want me, but I am honored to keep you company." Zunnax offered his arm to Ava and led her away.

"Is she safe with him?" Rachel gazed upward at Traxen. Heat licked her spine when their eyes met.

"Despite his many faults, Ari would never hurt nor take advantage of any of my honored guests."

"Good to know."

"Are you enjoying yourself?"

Smirking, Rachel said, "I doubt anyone truly enjoys events like these unless they're social climbers. Moments, yes. The entire event, no."

Traxen chuckled low. He placed his large hand gently on her back and the heat in her spine became an inferno. Rachel concentrated on keeping herself relaxed and not moaning at his touch on her bare skin. **Shit. Do not get turned on by the king. Bad Rachel.**

"That is probably the best and most accurate assessment I've ever heard." He led her across the room toward Talia and Vared. "I understand you spent some time sparring today."

"Yes. Your royal guards are excellent. I arranged some space with the training master so I can continue self-defense lessons for the women. Most of the species we've encountered so far are much larger, and it's important they have some basic skills to protect themselves."

"They are lucky to be learning from you." He frowned. "How's your arm? I heard you got hurt."

"It's fine. Small punctures. A healing wand took care of the injury easily. I've had worse."

His tail flicked once before winding around his ankle.

"I dislike the idea of a female getting hurt."

She shrugged.

"It's all part of maintaining skill proficiency."

The discontented rumble of his chest echoed in her nether regions. Her thighs clenched. **That never happens when any other Svesti growls near me.**

His nostrils flared. **Shit. He can smell my arousal.**

"You did not have time to see our capital city today. I'd like to show you Trezoura. Unfortunately, my schedule for the next couple days is already full."

"That's not necessary. I'm sure Vared or one of the others will be happy to escort us."

"Perhaps."

Changing the subject, Rachel asked, "I like the paintings in this area. Are they all landscapes of Costonia?"

"Yes. Each depicts a well-known area in a House's domain. All twelve Houses are represented."

"No House favored more than another."

"Exactly. Ruling requires balance, even with decor in public areas."

"Have we made enough of an appearance? I'd like to leave now," Vared complained as they approached.

"Stop being rude." Rachel smiled at Talia shushing her mate.

Traxen grinned.

"He can't help himself, Talia. I must admit you are a good influence on him. This is the least disruptive Court dinner he's attended. Normally, blood is spilled."

"That was one time. Let it go, you **naroon**." Vared crossed his arms.

Rachel and Talia exchanged glances, then laughed.

"I think we should be good to leave any time," Rachel said. "It's been a long day, and I could use some rest."

"Me, too," Emmy said as she and Devik joined them. "We started much too early this morning."

"Go. I appreciate your patience." Traxen's hand dropped from Rachel's back, but the residual warmth stayed with her.

Rachel caught Largon's eye. He excused himself from a conversation and joined them.

"Are you ready to head to our quarters?" Rachel asked.

"Any time you'd like. I'm happy to escort you and leave this zoo." Largon's fangs shone brightly against his gray skin.

"Then let's go." **I need to get away from Traxen before I do something stupid.**

Chapter 7

Traxen willed his cock to soften as Rachel walked away with Largon and the others. Just before she left, he scented her arousal—**wimma**, **valli**, and leather--and it increased his own. His fingertips still tingled from their contact with her soft, warm flesh.

Attuned to her throughout the evening, he admired her ability to charm many of the Court and firmly put others in their places with a few carefully chosen words if they displeased her. All with a smile and humor. **Amazing how the males didn't realize she effectively called them naroons but instead believed she complimented them. She is a dangerous female—in more ways than one.**

"She's more observant than she appears. She knows she's seen me before but hasn't recalled where." His Spymaster spoke under his breath.

"Then you best avoid her in your other disguises," Traxen said quietly. "We'll meet tomorrow to discuss impressions."

"As you will."

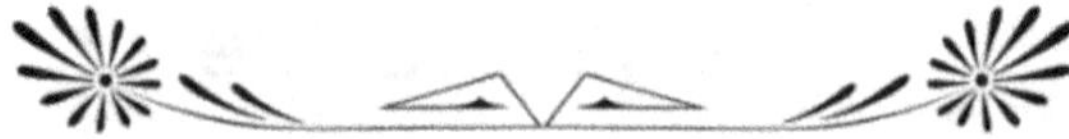

Disgusting.

Inwardly raging at the males fawning over the human females, the Svesti noble kept a pleasantly neutral expression on his face as he circulated around the room. While he spoke to each female, he carefully refrained from touching them. **They're small and weak. Unworthy of mating with Svesti. Who knows what diseases they carry?**

He didn't know how Sovex faked the fated mate bonds, but the clan markings must be unnatural. **Crekkin' Zuvgran still hasn't given me the virus that kills human fertility. All I need to do is infect one female.**

Watching the group leave, his tail flicked once before he controlled it. The perversity of a Svesti-Zuvgran hybrid repulsed him as much as the humans. He chatted amicably with other Court members awhile longer before claiming an early morning appointment and retreating to his flitter. All the while, his mother's words from their garden walks helped him maintain outward mastery of his emotions.

A king allows his subjects to see and hear only what he wishes them to know. You are not their friend. You are their leader. Their roles are to serve you and your greatness. Act accordingly now and keep your true thoughts and plans hidden. Your path to regain your destiny will be a lonely one, my son, but you shall be victorious and sit on Costonia's throne.

Later that evening, Traxen tossed his tablet onto the counter and grabbed a water pouch. His eyes burned from reading reports and his head ached. **Not enough hours in a day. We need to find the traitors.**

He stepped onto his balcony and filled his chest with the cool night air. Lacing his fingers behind his head, he looked at Dianthia overhead. The moon's light bathed the palace gardens with a shimmering glow. He glanced at the east wing while he stretched his sore muscles. The darkened windows probably meant everyone slept. **It's late. I should rest, too.**

Returning inside, he closed the balcony doors and stripped as he walked to the sanitary facility. After pulling his leather tie free, he used his claws to loosen his braid before turning on the shower. He groaned when the hot water hit his skin. Bowing his head directly under the stream, he felt his headache ease. He washed quickly, then stepped into the drying tube. Once he finished brushing his hair and teeth, he padded naked to his bedroom. He grabbed a pair of lounge pants and tossed them on the nightstand in case he needed to dress quickly.

Traxen slid between the sheets appreciating the silken material on his bare skin. Absently, he scratched his abdomen while he tried to empty his mind and fully relax. Thoughts of Rachel snuck in and his hand drifted lower. Fisting himself lightly, he thumbed his head nodes. **Crek. This isn't calming me.**

Frustrated, he released his stiff cock and rolled to his side. Plumping a pillow, he pushed it under his ear and wrapped his arm around it. **How many solars has it been since I pleasure mated? Four? Five? Before I was crowned, I know. Rachel is not for me. The fallout from the Court would be immense. I just need a visit to a pleasure planet.**

He fell asleep secure in his reasoning. His unconscious mind failed to get the message, and Rachel starred in his dreams.

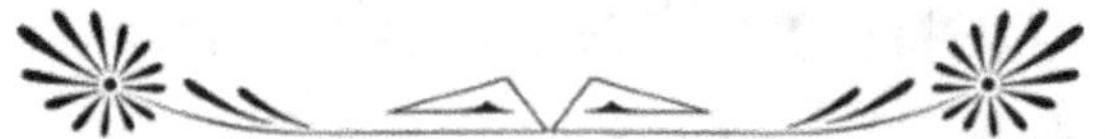

Over the next few days, Traxen's mood deteriorated. His Spymaster visited and transferred a file with his impressions from the Court event which, unfortunately, held no new information. Then the male disappeared to follow up on a rumor with no further word.

Xeliv attempted to keep his appointment calendar clear, but numerous Council members suddenly declared urgent business. Most brought a semblance of an issue to the appointments, but every one of them wanted to know more about the human females, fated mate bonds, and the Zuvgran.

If Xeliv hadn't scheduled midday and evening meal meetings with Vared and Talia or Largon, Ronan, and Lady Natasha, Traxen might not have eaten anything other than early morning meals alone. At least those meetings were productive. Largon and Ronan drew up a draft plan of how they envisioned Phoenix House. Traxen put them in touch with the architects and construction supervisors.

Using the requests received from Earth and Vared's experience as a warrior, Talia formulated what dignitaries they could accommodate on the **Invictus** and still have enough warriors for human protection as well as the ship's operations. She made recommendations for the humans limiting the number of support staff, checklists of required inoculations and approved items, and an initial learning program of Svesti customs and protocols. If attendees did not have the DNA strand requested by the Svesti, then the uploads to easily learn information that Talia and the other females received needed to be drastically reduced in capacity.

"Besides, if the information is in an official training program, they cannot claim ignorance," Talia smirked. "I'll keep working with the other women for what to include and get it to you for your approval. I'm thinking an initial data packet with the basics, then a more comprehensive in-person course when they're onboard the **Invictus**. Ash'n assures me the translators will work even without the DNA strand present, but there will be a longer adjustment period for those people. Something about a delay between the spoken word and the translation."

"I'm impressed with your organization and recommendations." Traxen sat back and wiped his mouth with a napkin. "I thank you both. The reduction in my workload just having you take care of the bulk of this is immense."

"You need to delegate more, Traxen. Even I can see it," said Vared. "That lesson was the toughest to learn as I moved up in the ranks. You need to surround yourself with those you trust to do the work well and within the proper boundaries."

Traxen barked out a laugh.

"It's funny to hear you speak about boundaries. You violate those on a regular basis."

"Asshole."

"Asshole?"

"An Earth insult my beautiful mate taught me." Vared's tail circled Talia's waist, pulled her closer, and he kissed her forehead.

Talia giggled.

"I call him that on a regular basis."

"Sometimes I even deserve it, **kirani**."

Traxen smiled at them. **They are good together.**

"I have good news which will affect your trip to Earth."

"What is it?" Vared asked.

"This is confidential information. A year ago, our technology scientists developed a way to increase the efficiency of our engines by redesigning our star drive reactors and adding another compound. They've tested on various sized ships successfully and the space cruiser chosen for six lunars of experiments just returned. They discovered a few necessary modifications for the larger the engine, but the upgrades will be ready to install on the **Invictus** in the next few weeks."

Vared leaned forward, excitement in his eyes.

"What sort of gains in efficiency?"

"For smaller spacecraft without anti-grav shielding, such as shuttles, double the speed. It could be more, but the stressors on life forms would be detrimental so we're limiting it. We might design new shuttles in the future to go faster. For a space cruiser, it's a little over double because of the enormous mass of the ship."

"Are you saying we'll be able to cut the time to Earth in half?" Talia asked.

"Yes. There'll be some training necessary for the command structure and engineering, but it shouldn't take more than a week."

"Gat'n Wrox will want to be present for any upgrade. No one touches his engines without his approval." Vared's fangs flashed. "Not even me."

"Arrange it. I'll comm you the contact information for the lead scientist."

"What is the timeline for upgrading the fleet?"

"Uncertain. We have to account for their current or projected position, time to return to Costonia, and time to train and install. We also must ensure their territory is covered during the upgrades. It's complicated."

Vared's lavender eyes became unfocused as he thought, his scar whitening on his cheek.

"What if you used the test ship?"

"Expound."

"If it can transport everything needed for upgrades, have it meet a space cruiser at its position. It's already faster than anything else. It reduces the round-trip travel time to a quarter by the one in position not travelling at all. Staff the test ship with enough warriors to protect the space cruiser's territory and the cruiser itself while it's being upgraded. If the test ship can carry the needed warriors and more than one set of upgrades, you'll save even more time overall."

Traxen grinned.

"Very logical. Good idea, Vared."

"I love how your mind works." Talia patted her mate's tail.

"This advancement is enormous, Traxen. Travel and response times cut in half. We live in interesting times."

"That we do, Cousin."

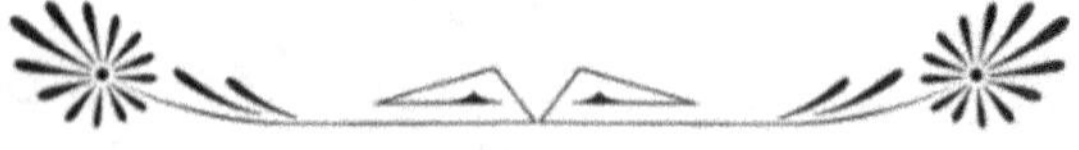

Traxen finally carved out some time to head to the royal guards' training area. He needed to work off his frustration and he didn't get down here as often as he would like. **Too much time being king and not enough time as a warrior.**

Several warriors practiced with various weapons in the outside area. He could hear blaster fire from the range further away. Wanting to spar and sweat, he headed inside the large building. Pairs of males sparred around the room, Vared and Ronan among them. The human females stood at the side near heavyweight bags while Rachel crouched behind a warrior. His tail flicked. *What is she doing?*

The head royal guard and Bavin's father, Lorriv Hossix, watched with Devik, Ash'n, and Ronan as Traxen approached.

"What's going on?"

"Rachel trains the human females in self-defense. I've never seen her do anything with the bags before. I'm sure it will be interesting. Her lessons usually are." Devik grinned.

"Why does she need the warriors?"

"Not sure. She asked for the shortest and tallest warriors here," Hossix said. "You should go assist. You're a little taller than Yanz."

Shrugging his shoulders and more curious than he was willing to admit, Traxen jogged to the females. **Crek. Rachel's ass in those stretchy pants gives me ideas.**

"I hear you need a tall warrior."

Rachel looked up at him from where she crouched behind the shorter male. She placed a piece of white tape on the bag. Traxen saw all the other bags had similar markings.

"Thank you, Yanz, but I think the king is taller than you."

"As you will, Lady Rachel. If you need any more assistance, just let me know."

Her smile lit the room.

"I will." She gestured to Traxen. "Stand with your back to the bag, please."

While he followed her instruction, his tail swayed.

"Be careful with that, Sire. I don't need a black eye." Humor laced her voice.

"My apologies." Her addictive scent filled his nostrils, and he concentrated on keeping his cock from standing at attention. He heard her tape more of the bag.

"Thanks. Could you move to the next bag?"

They continued until she marked all the bags. Her scent grew heavier, and he clenched his ass. Her soft gasp sounded loud in his ears. **Crek. Not in front of everyone.**

"That's all I need you for." Rachel rose fluidly. Pink flushed her cheeks, but her bright blue eyes met his. As she passed him, she whispered, "Damn fine glutes you have there, Sire."

He sucked in a breath and froze momentarily before jogging back to the other males watching.

"Do you observe them every day?"

Devik nodded.

"At least two of us. Initially it was for their protection, but then it became a learning experience for us. Just watch."

Rachel stood between the females and bags.

"All right, ladies, guess what? You're in space."

"Great way to state the obvious." Lady Emmy placed a hand on her hip.

"Every species we've encountered so far is bigger and stronger than us. So you need different skills."

"What are you teaching us today, Rachel?" Lady Natasha asked.

"How to disable a larger attacker long enough to escape." She gestured toward the bags. "I've marked each with your strike zones. We're going to be learning different kicks and using them from different positions. The zones represent where a knee might be. The good news is a solid kick to any area of the knee should do the trick. First up is going to be a roundhouse kick. Get in your stances."

Traxen's eyes narrowed as the females immediately spread their feet shoulder-width apart and bent their knees slightly with their backs straight.

Devik explained, "The first lesson she taught them was their center of gravity is lower than a male's. She had them get into their stances as quickly as possible when running, walking, or other activities to build muscle memory." Vared and Ronan joined them wiping their foreheads and chests with towels.

"Hmm." He listened as Rachel described how to execute the kick. The humans dropped their right legs back and kicked at the bags as instructed with Rachel correcting when necessary. Once she felt they understood the basics, she had them change legs. Then she taught them push, side, and back kicks using different parts of their feet.

"Now, let's change it up. Left roundhouse high." Whacks echoed in the room. "Right back low." Rachel called out legs, kicks, and knee positions at random until the females dropped to the mat exhausted. She tossed them water pouches and towels.

"One last question. You disabled your attacker. What do you do?"

"Run like hell," said Lin tiredly as she wiped her forehead.

"Excellent. Good job, ladies."

"I swear you are evil, Rachel. You enjoy this too much." Talia groaned as she got up, then bent and rested her hands on her knees. "I'm too old for this shit."

"Time for my favorite part," Ash'n said with a smile. "A hot bath and rubbing my mate's sore parts." He jogged and helped Lin to her feet. His tail rested on her back. He tucked her under his arm, and they left. The other mated males sprinted to their females. Largon and Hossix chuckled and shook their heads.

"Lady Rachel impresses me with her ability to teach effectively, especially smaller beings against larger opponents. I've been doing this a great many solars and it never would have occurred to me to set up visual strike zones for various body parts if it wasn't target practice with a weapon." Hossix's eyes gleamed. "I think I will extend her an invitation to train the guards." He walked toward Rachel.

"Do you want to spar?" Traxen looked at Largon.

"Let's do it."

Maybe the exercise will keep Rachel from my thoughts.

Chapter 8

Rachel's breath caught in her chest when Traxen removed his shirt. Golden bronze skin lovingly covered hard, powerful muscles that her hands itched to caress. Wide shoulders tapered to a narrow waist with the most gorgeous Adonis belt she'd ever seen. Her mouth watered with her desire to lick it. Earlier when he stood before her and his ass contracted under his tail, it took all her self-control to refrain from squeezing and testing the firmness of his glorious glutes.

While she talked briefly with Hossix, she watched Traxen and Largon spar. She narrowed her eyes when Traxen used his tail to pull Largon off balance. Largon reciprocated with an elbow to Traxen's upper thigh. **I haven't seen anyone else use their tail that way. They're well matched.**

Sweat beaded on the Svesti's flesh causing her pussy to clench. **Oh my. I better leave before Hossix realizes I have the hots for the king.**

Once outside, Rachel stretched before jogging around the building grounds a couple times to get some cardio and try to shake the memory of Traxen's body on display. She maintained a steady pace until she neared the palace entrance. Slowing to a walk, she nodded at the guards. **It didn't work. I think I need a cold shower.**

Maybe I should jump his bones and get him out of my system. A one and done. Problem is I'm not sure once would be enough.

"Hey, girl. We're heading into the city to check it out and do some shopping. The king is spotting us credits." Rachel turned from the breakfast buffet at Emmy's words. She smirked at her friend's top that said 'OCD—Obsessive Computer Disorder.' **How many T-shirts did she bring from Earth?**

"I'm in." Rachel joined everyone else at the table.

"I'm going to Phoenix House with Ronan." Largon bit into his *brellia*. He hummed around the meat pastry. "The temporary housing for the younglings is almost complete. We should be able to bring them down from the **Invictus** in the next couple days."

"How's the demolition going?" Talia spooned some fruit from her plate into her **pertiza**.

"The old building is down. Hopefully, the debris will be removed today. The architects should have plans for us to review tomorrow," Ronan said.

"Wow. When the Svesti decide to do something, they move fast. We only arrived a week ago." Lin smiled at Ash'n when he handed her some juice and mouthed her thanks.

Ava brought a platter of cinnamon rolls to the table. Hands flew quickly to grab one before they were gone.

"Lady Reena told me which shops would have the spices and supplies I want. Luckily, she already had what I needed for these."

"I really like the cinnamon rolls," Rachel mumbled around a bite of the soft pastry. **My mother would lose her shit if she saw me talking with my mouth full.**

Natasha said, "I need fabric to make more gowns for the Court functions. Xeliv told me they have them fairly frequently."

"You know you can synthesize them?" Emmy said.

"Not unless I have no choice. I enjoy sewing."

"Purist." Natasha ignored Emmy's smartass comment.

"If I give you some specifics for added features, could you do it for me?" Rachel asked.

"Like adornments?"

Rachel shook her head. "Hidden pockets in certain areas."

"Intriguing," said Devik.

Emmy slapped his shoulder.

"You're not allowed to think about what other women conceal under their clothes."

Everyone laughed at Devik's wounded expression.

"**Milara**, I only meant it may be helpful for you to have something similar."

"You'll never win this argument no matter how good your intentions, my friend," Vared said as he approached with his plate and sat next to Talia. "Admit defeat now and commence groveling." The laughter around the table grew louder. **I'm lucky I've made good friends out here in space, even if I haven't told them everything.**

"When are we leaving?"

"After everyone eats and Traxen finishes whatever he's doing," Vared said. **Traxen will be with us?**

"Do I have time to change my shoes?" **Maybe I should double up on underwear while I'm there.**

"Yes."

Rachel dumped her breakfast remains into the recycler.

"I'll be right back."

"Why don't we come by your quarters? I want to use the restroom before we go." Natasha looked at Vared. "Will that work?"

"We'll meet in the guest corridor when everyone is ready."

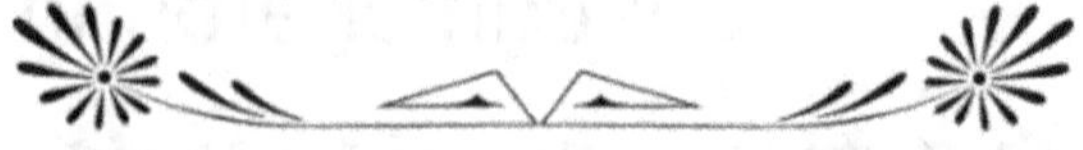

The Svesti noble answered his comm.

"The human females will be in Trezoura shortly."

"Alone?"

"All their mates are going except one. I thought I heard they waited for the king before leaving. I'm sure guards will accompany them."

"Good work."

"Always Svesti."

The noble disconnected and sat back, thinking. **I wish the Zuvgran had fulfilled our agreement and given me the virus.**

He checked the ships docked at the spaceport. Recognizing the name of one, he encrypted his comm before initiating contact. He spoke decisively and made the deal. The male on the other end of the transmission agreed once he received half the credits beforehand. Disconnecting, the noble smiled. **Excellent. It won't look like Svesti are**

involved at all. Maybe I'll get lucky and Sovex will die as well.

In her quarters, Rachel switched out her sneakers for comfortable ankle boots with a steel toe. She tucked an icepick into one, pulled her jeans leg over it, and double checked the daggers she strapped to her waist under her loose top. **After Theron, I won't be unarmed in public again. Not sure how the Svesti would take it if they knew I've been armed in some fashion most of the time in the palace. With the traitors still at large, I want to be able to protect the other women.**

She slipped out into the hallway to wait with the others for Devik and Emmy, as well as Traxen. The couple exited their quarters. Rachel smirked at Emmy's flushed face and wild hair. Emmy tried to smooth her curls before pulling them into a ponytail. With a satisfied grin, Devik adjusted his shirt. **Lucky Emmy. She got in a quickie.**

Smelling him before she heard him, Rachel turned to see Traxen arrive with the younger Hossix and Previv. The king wore a black short-sleeve shirt similar in cut to a T-shirt, but in a stretchy satiny material outlining his impressive muscles. A weapons harness wrapped around his torso.

Two other guards accompanied them to the rooftop. A large flitter with side windows awaited them. They clamored aboard and sat in the forward-facing seats.

"It's like a space-age short bus," Emmy exclaimed. "I didn't even realize you guys had vehicles like these." She started tapping on her tablet. "I want to see what other conveyances you have. Do you have anything like motorcycles?"

The women laughed at Emmy's excitement while the Svesti looked confused.

"Oh, look, a hover bike. Can you take me out on one of these?" Emmy peered up at her mate. An indulgent smile from Devik had her squealing and fist pumping, "Yes."

"Would you also like to ride on a hover bike?" Traxen spoke low and stirred the hair near her ear. Her skin tingled at his close proximity. Once again, he chose a seat next to her. **Bloody hell. I bet that gorgeous scruff on his face would feel amazing on my skin.**

"I'd like to learn how to operate one as well as flitters and motorboats, if you have them."

"I can arrange that."

"Thank you."

Rachel couldn't see the pilots, but she saw the guards boarded with them.

"Extra security?"

Traxen's braid slid over his shoulder as he dipped his head.

"Yes. The pilots will remain with the flitter, and the other four will come with us."

"It would be nice if we could walk around without protection."

His full lips turned down, and his tail wrapped around her ankle.

"Human females will be a curiosity for our citizens for a long time yet. And with me accompanying you, there will be even more eyes on all of you. For that, I apologize." He crossed his arms, biceps bulging. She wanted to lick them. "Then there's the other situation."

Drawn away from her musings about his body by his comment, she glanced up and met his lavender eyes. **Are they changing color? They look like amethysts.**

She whispered, "The traitors." He nodded.

Waving a hand at the window, she changed the subject.

"Tell me more about your capital city."

His chiseled face lit up and he pointed.

"Trezoura was established close to two thousand years ago. There have been many changes over the years as our population increased and technology improved, but we've always attempted to integrate with nature. We have a wide variety of plants and wildlife on Costonia. Maintaining a balance is important to us and keeps our planet healthy and beautiful."

"I'm still getting used to a periwinkle sky and blue grass and leaves. Earth's sky is blue and our greenery is well—green."

"If you look, you'll see the walkways simulate the pink stone that is abundant here."

"You don't use the actual stone?"

"Not for public thoroughfares. We used to, but now we use a facsimile that is permeable, slip-resistant, and comfortable to walk upon. It's easily recyclable and it is safer for our infirm and elderly citizens to navigate. We're over the main part of the city now."

"Wow. You can barely tell there's a city here. It looks like a bunch of people out walking in the countryside."

His pleased grin highlighted his strong chin.

"Exactly. Over there is our primary government building where the Council meets."

Rachel's brows drew together.

"I don't see any vehicles."

"None are allowed within the city center unless there is a private hangar on a building's rooftop. Instead we have large parking structures on the four corners of the area and we walk."

"Do you have a spaceport nearby for other species to visit and shop?"

"No. We have a trade spaceport further west, but we limit those ships to ones who have sustainable propulsion systems. If anyone wants to visit Trezoura, the beings must arrange transport via a Svesti flitter."

Rachel thought about his words for a moment.

"If I understand correctly, you, in essence, control the amount of harmful emissions that enter Costonia's atmosphere."

"Exactly."

"That's incredible. I admit there is so much of your world that impresses me." **Humans could learn a lot from the Svesti.**

"I have visited many planets, but Costonia remains my favorite and not just because it's home."

They disembarked when the flitter landed and began the walk to Trezoura's center where the majority of shops resided. Traxen's tail rested on her back. He frowned.

"Are you wearing something under your shirt?"

"That is a very personal question."

His tail dropped and his hand took its place, the warmth penetrating her thin shirt. His fingers lightly rubbed the outline of the strap and she sighed.

"I'm wearing my daggers underneath."

He stiffened before relaxing and bent to whisper in her ear.

"I find that incredibly arousing. The more I learn about you, the more attractive you are."

She inhaled sharply.

"I have to be honest. I find you sexy, but I'm not looking for a mate or contract."

He nodded curtly.

"I apologize. I should not be speaking to you in this manner. The nobles would lose their minds if I pursued anything with one of the first human females to visit Costonia."

"So we flirt but don't take it further?"

"That might be best."

Damn, there went my one and done.

Chapter 9

Traxen exhaled a silent sigh of relief when Rachel's addictive scent dissipated somewhat in the open air as they left the flitter. Glad he wore restrictive pants that hid his burgeoning cock, he still couldn't resist escorting her personally. He enjoyed introducing her to Trezoura. **If I were smart, I would spend my time with one of the couples to reduce temptation.**

When he looked into her dark blue eyes, ringed by black, tiny flecks of green and gold caught his attention. The smallest detail fascinated him. When she told him she wore hidden weapons, his cock surged. Her scent grew heavier and he envisioned undressing her slowly and disarming her—transitioning her from warrior to goddess.

Caught up in his momentary fantasy, he admitted his arousal before his brain engaged. That loss of control concerned him, but her easy acknowledgment of why he shouldn't follow up just increased his attraction. **No pushing for more because of my title or a desire to influence or manipulate me.**

Part of the group entered a shop with cooking supplies with Lady Ava saying they would meet up with the rest at the weapons shop before looking at fabrics. Rachel's eyes lit up when she saw the displays of daggers and knives. Reverently, she picked up a dagger with a polished bone handle and tested its weight and balance in her small capable hand.

"It looks like nacre, mother of pearl, from Earth." When he raised an eyebrow, she added, "It's the inside coating of a mollusk shell."

"It is **pyrix** bone from Ladorta. Highly prized," said a Svesti male.

"It's beautiful and the entire item is well made." Rachel tilted her head at the male. "Do you make the daggers yourself?"

"Yes. I use quality materials for all my handmade items."

"Wonderful craftsmanship. I love how the carved design flows with the iridescence of the bone. Amazing."

The male's wrinkled face lit up.

"Thank you. I am Rostrox Dresiv, the owner."

"Rachel Llewellyn."

He gestured at the dagger.

"There is another if you would like a set. I can offer a discount if you purchase both."

"Let me see what else you have first before I decide."

She reluctantly replaced the dagger on the shelf. When she turned away, Traxen held up two fingers to Hossix and motioned at the weapon. Hossix searched the area for the matching dagger.

"Do you have any garrotes?

Traxen's head jerked back to Rachel and Dresiv.

"Over here."

"I want something lightweight, unobtrusive, and rolls flat."

"Something like this? It's made from extruded *valadium*." Dresiv held up a flat coil of wire with each end hardened into small rods.

"That's perfect. Do you have another?"

"Here. Anything else?"

"Specialized jewelry."

He grinned, his fangs yellowed with age.

"Come. Let me show you."

Traxen hid his smile as Rachel picked out a ring, necklace, and hair combs—all with reservoirs for poison. **The female is deadly.**

"I do not sell the poison. However, King Sovex may know who carries it."

"Do you plan to assassinate me, **belgella**?" Traxen murmured.

"No. However, I will protect you and the women, if necessary." Rachel's voice, though quiet, affected him as if she breathed directly into his ear. Heat licked his spine.

"It is my duty to protect you."

"How about we protect each other?"

"Stubborn." Traxen chuckled at her crossed arms lifting her perfect breasts while her foot tapped.

"Hossix."

The guard placed the two daggers with Rachel's other items. Dresiv smiled and reached under the counter and pulled out various sheaths and straps. Rachel fingered the straps.

"What is this material?"

"Something of my own design combining an arachnid silk from Ladorta and fine plastoy fibers."

"Plastoy?"

"An alloy of plastic and metal. The material breathes, but the tensile strength rivals pure metal. I include these for free. All I ask is you return to tell me if the design irritates human skin or if you have ideas for improvement."

Rachel's eyes brightened.

"You have a deal."

Traxen paid Dresiv and arranged delivery of their purchases to the palace. Then their group meandered to the fabric shop. Lady Natasha peered in the window.

"I'm not sure all of us will fit in there. How should we do this?"

Hossix jerked his head at two guards. Each rounded the building on opposite sides. Traxen knew it was to check for additional entrances. After Hossix received the report a rear door existed, he instructed them to cover that exit.

"Sire, we can remain outside if you like."

"We don't need anyone inside but the women," Lady Lin said.

"Well, we need one to pay." Lady Emmy raised her eyebrows.

"Ash'n, you accompany the females. We'll assist the guards." Vared kissed Talia and whispered in her ear. Pink suffused her face.

"Lady Natasha, will you assist my mate in choosing materials for new gowns?"

Lady Emmy pouted.

"Do you not trust me to do it myself?"

"**Milara**, you will not get enough. Lady Natasha has a good eye and great taste."

"Are you insinuating I don't have good taste? I chose you, didn't I?"

The males chuckled. Vared tilted his head toward Traxen.

"He's determined to grovel today."

"Nah, he just likes makeup sex." Lady Emmy stomped into the shop with Ash'n and the other females close behind her, laughing. Traxen admired the sway and shape of Rachel's ass in her jeans.

"She's correct. I do." A huge grin spread across Devik's face.

"As do I," said Vared.

Amused, Traxen chose a spot where he could keep the females in sight as they shopped. He alternated his attention between them and scanning his surroundings.

About a half hour later, he watched a half dozen Durelians sit down at an outdoor restaurant, while four Frezzians stopped at the window of Dresiv's establishment. Another four Durelians stood a few doors away talking and pointing as they viewed a holographic map with their black, bulbous eyes.

"Are you seeing this?" Traxen murmured as he shifted his stance to easily access his weapons.

"Devik, to the rear, just in case," Vared ordered quietly. Devik sauntered away.

"Their numbers imply interest in the females rather than you, Sire," Previv said as Hossix communicated with the other guards via his earpiece.

Vared comm'd Ash'n. From the corner of his eye, Traxen saw the healer gather the females and speak to the owner.

"Another five near the back entrance. I've comm'd for more warriors." Hossix appeared relaxed, but Traxen noted the hard expression in his eyes. "They're still five minutes out."

"I could use a good fight," Traxen said, stretching his neck.

"I would prefer you join the females, Sire."

"Are we going to have the same old argument, Hossix?" Traxen rolled his eyes, then his shoulders.

The male, who had guarded him his entire life, sighed heavily.

"If you die on my watch, I will have to kill you myself."

"That is acceptable."

The Frezzians and the Durelians on the street walked toward their group from opposite directions. A glance at the aliens at the restaurant indicated they watched but were not moving to engage yet. **Must be backup.**

The Durelians with their orange skin and three eyes were close in height and weight to the average Svesti. The Frezzians stood a half head shorter with grayish-green skin, oval heads on thin necks with elongated slits for eyes, and spindly limbs.

Traxen's nose twitched as the unpleasant odor of the males registered when they grew closer. Frezzians smelled moldy with an acidic undertone, while a Durelian's scent always reminded him of untreated sewage. Both species struck him as uglier than other humanoids. **Maybe it's because most are dishonorable beings who see nothing wrong with trading in flesh.**

The Frezzians bumped into the Durelians and an argument ensued in front of Traxen, Vared, and the two guards. Traxen consciously kept his body loose as he waited for them to give up on their deliberate distraction. His arm blocked a Durelian's knife when the male unsheathed it suddenly and spun toward him. With his other hand, he pressed his thumb on a pressure point on the attacker's hand, squeezed, then raised the arm while turning simultaneously before bringing it down onto his bent knee. He used his blocking arm to push hard against his opponent's upper bicep. The Durelian screamed as his elbow snapped and the knife fell to the ground. He kneed the male in the face before letting him drop.

Spinning, he faced a Frezzian with a blaster.

"I don't think so, Your Majesty. Drop your weapons."

Traxen sighed as he took his time removing one item at a time. He raised an eyebrow.

"Are you sure you want to do this, Frezzian? I had planned on keeping one of you alive to interrogate, but now I'll have to kill you." In his peripheral vision, he saw three more Durelians join the fray just as the other attackers fell. **Must be some from the restaurant.**

The Frezzian's small lips pinched, and he jerked his weapon at Traxen as he stepped closer.

"I'm the one with the blaster."

"True, but you forgot one thing."

"What's that?"

"I'm the one with a tail." Traxen's tail flicked sharply upward and knocked the male's arm sideways while unsheathing his claws. The blaster left the male's hand in a high trajectory. He slashed the Frezzian's neck and stepped sideways to avoid the worst of the black blood spurting. Looking down at the male squeezing his neck in the vain hope of surviving, he said, "I warned you."

Female screams pierced Traxen's ears, and he spun towards the shop. Six Durelians aimed blasters at the females while a seventh fought Ash'n and another one fought the owner. **Where the crek did they come from?**

Traxen tried to fight his way to the door to reach the females. Rachel stepped toward one Durelian, hunched slightly with her arms wrapped around her torso. When the male yelled at her, she shook her head as if in fright. He took a step toward her. Her arms flung upwards, knives glinting in her hands. Slicing the wrist holding the blaster, her back leg rose in a high kick knocking the Durelian into two of his companions. The three fell to the floor.

Another raced toward her as if to tackle her. She stepped into him, grasped his arm, turned, and sent his body crashing through the display window. Shattered glass tinkled to the ground. Traxen crouched, clawed the male before he could get up, then jumped through the new opening into the shop. His tail whipped at a Durelian's ear from behind causing the attacker to stagger toward Rachel. She pushed the palm of her hand into his falling face and kicked at his knee. Screaming, the Durelian sank to the floor.

Traxen turned to the remaining attackers. Ash'n stepped over the still bodies of the mercenaries he and the owner had overcome. He nodded at Traxen as they approached the fallen ones trying to get their associate's limp body off them—a puddle of green blood under his sliced wrist. Ash'n grabbed a Durelian's head and twisted until his neck snapped. Traxen wound his tail around another's neck and squeezed until the male suffocated.

The remaining Svesti from their group ran into the shop from the front and rear entrances. Other royal guards held the perimeter.

"How did they get in here?" Vared demanded.

Lady Emmy pointed toward the ceiling where a hole had been cut out.

"**Crek.**" Traxen looked at Hossix. "They were prepared."

"Ladies, if you would come with me to the transport, we will return you to the palace. You, too, Sire." Set in hard lines, Previv's face showed he intended to forcibly make Traxen leave.

"Just a moment, Previv." Traxen turned to the shop owner. "Sir, I apologize for the destruction of your shop and merchandise."

The male's claws dripped green blood from the Durelian he'd killed. He bowed to Traxen.

"Your Majesty, you are not at fault. These dishonorable degenerates caused this."

"Regardless, I will send someone from the palace to assist in your assessment of damaged goods, arrange repairs, and pay for it all."

"Thank you, Sire. Did you wish to take the females' purchases with you?"

"Please give them to my representative when he arrives and he will take care of it."

The male nodded and turned to the human females.

"Ladies, I hope to see all of you again. I enjoyed your visit immensely before the attack."

"As did we," Lady Natasha said with a smile. "If I have questions about any of the fabric, may I comm you?"

"Please do."

"Sire, it's time to go." Hossix growled.

Traxen nodded and followed the females out of the shop into the transport with guards surrounding them. His tension ratcheted down a notch when his tail circled Rachel's ankle after they were seated, but part of him worried she hid an injury. **I need to get her alone and find out.**

Chapter 10

Adrenaline coursed through Rachel's body after the attack. Perusing the other women, she saw they all seemed to be doing well, especially with all their mates fussing over them. Previv spoke with Ava somehow making her laugh.

Rachel shook her head when Ash'n approached her with a healing wand. She watched as he used it on the males addressing their minor cuts and bruises. **We were lucky no one was seriously injured.**

Traxen sat silently next to her. The pressure of his tail on her ankle soothed her, but his heat and scent so close to her as she rode the adrenaline high unbearably aroused her. Inhaling measured breaths through her mouth, she tried to calm herself.

The short trip to the palace and walk to the east wing seemed endless. Traxen accompanied them and everyone peeled off to go to their own rooms. At Rachel's door, she turned to thank him, but he crowded close.

"I need to talk to you," he rasped.

Locking her gaze on his darkened eyes, she backed into her quarters with him keeping pace. When the door closed, he reached for her and restlessly ran his hot hands over her arms.

"Were you injured?"

She shook her head.

"No, you?"

His fingers rose to burrow into her hair, his callused palms gentle, but unyielding on her cheeks. His amethyst eyes searched her face, then his lips crashed onto hers. Need raced in her veins as she returned his voracious kiss. Warm hands drifted down to cup her ass and squeeze. Bending his knees and turning, he lifted and pinned her to the wall with his body. She wrapped her legs around his trim waist while her fingers traced his nape and shoulders. Writhing, she tried to relieve the pressure in her core against his trapped erection. **Holy fuck. He's a great kisser and his cock feels huge.**

His mouth left hers and kissed a path to her ear. She shuddered when he bit her lobe and her clit throbbed. Her head fell back, and she gasped for breath.

"I thought you said we couldn't do this."

"When you were in danger and fighting, protecting you was my focus. I needed to know you were safe." His breath stirred the hair on her neck and she shivered as the scruff on his face brushed her skin.

"I can take care of myself."

"Yes, and it's sexy, but it doesn't negate my desire to keep you from harm."

"So, what's this?" She wriggled against him. He froze and sucked in a breath.

"I shouldn't have done this. My apologies." He stepped back after she slid down his body to rest on shaky legs.

"I don't understand, Traxen."

Rumbling low in his chest, he shook his head. **That growl sounds primal and makes me want to jump back on him.**

"I don't either, Rachel." His jaw flexed. "My guards are waiting."

After the door closed behind him, she sank to floor, resting her forearms on her knees. **What the fuck just happened?**

Tilting her head back, she breathed heavily. Her breasts and pussy felt swollen. Her fingers touched her lips. **Hell. They're swollen, too.**

Slowly standing, she pushed off the wall and made her way to the shower. She stripped and stepped into the warm stream of water. Her soapy hands caressed her oversensitive skin. Cupping her breasts and plucking her nipples, she moaned softly while imagining Traxen's large hands kneading her flesh. Her fingers smoothed down her stomach to circle her clit with increasingly firm pressure. She gasped as her orgasm built to overtake and stiffen her body before she shuddered with pleasure.

Her hand thudded against the shower enclosure to keep her on her feet. She bowed her head under the spray and licked the water from her lips. Her breathing slowed to an even rhythm, and her lips twisted. **Maybe I should just avoid him for now and save myself the grief of figuring out what his contradictory behavior means. I'm not sure I completely trust my instincts after the shitshow of Jonathan. My focus should be on identifying the traitors.**

Turning off the shower and stepping into the drying tube, she squared her shoulders as the warm air whisked the droplets from her body. **How hard can it be to avoid one high-profile man?**

Rachel and Natasha left Largon and Ronan talking with the demolition crew at Phoenix House. Unfamiliar bird calls sounded in the background, sunshine in a periwinkle sky above warmed them, and recently mowed blue grass cushioned their feet as the women meandered closer to the flitter.

"Any word about Karid?"

Natasha shook her head and frowned.

"According to Ash'n, the guys try to comm him every day, but Karid refuses all contact with them."

"Ava's cooking up a storm in the kitchen and avoiding all of us. She's hurting, too."

"If this continues, we'll need to intervene for both their sakes."

"I agree. Let's give them more time, though. We've only been here a week."

"What's he doing here?" Natasha stopped and crossed her arms.

Rachel laughed and waved at Klero Rovex as he jogged toward them.

"I've been training him."

"Are you nuts? He's the one who scares Lin." Natasha's lips thinned.

"I honestly don't think he means to." Rachel's shoulders lifted and fell. "After I put him on his ass that day, he came to me and asked for my help to improve his skills. All the females in his immediate family died of the virus and his father raised him. He has potential, but he still has a long way to go. When he's not with his friends, he's a different person."

"Well, his friend Nerid Mantoor almost killed Vared. And Sproid is just creepy."

"True, but Mantoor was brainwashed."

"Who's to say Rovex didn't do it?"

"His shock seemed genuine."

"Ladies, good day to you both." Rovex dipped his chin. His brown eyes warmed as he greeted them.

"Rovex, how are you?"

"I am well, Lady Rachel. I appreciate you taking the time to give me a lesson today." He turned to her companion. "Lady Natasha, I hope you are enjoying Costonia."

"I am." Natasha's eyes narrowed. "I'm curious as to why you asked Rachel to train you."

"I wish to transfer to a position with more room for advancement. Working in supply is comfortable but doesn't allow me to hone my skills. Lady Rachel is formidable, and if I ever hope to find a female for a troth or breeding contract, I need to learn more about human females. I do not want to scare them as I did you in my ignorance."

"Hmm." Natasha leaned back on the flitter and fluttered her fingers. "You two do your thing. I'll just watch from here."

Rachel and Rovex moved away from the flitter and sparred. Every time Rovex attempted a move, Rachel blocked him. After ten minutes, he stepped back and growled.

"How is you know what I'm going to do before I do it?" He blew out a harsh breath.

"I've told you—you telegraph your moves. It makes it much easier for an opponent to use it against you."

"I don't understand what you mean." Rovex stomped his foot.

Largon and Ronan rushed toward them.

"Is this male bothering you?" Largon's biceps bulged. Ronan checked over Natasha to ensure she was unharmed.

"No. I'm training him. Largon, Ronan, this is Rovex."

The males nodded at each other.

"Perhaps you should spar with Largon. Maybe his insights would help."

"If he is willing, I would appreciate it."

Rachel stepped back and let the two go at it. Largon countered every move before Rovex made it. Rovex finally stepped back.

"Your eyes and your muscles give you away, warrior," Largon said. "I know what you're planning to do as you think it."

"Exactly what I've been telling him," Rachel said.

"How do I change it?" Rovex ran a hand over his head. "I don't even know I'm doing it."

Largon spoke quietly for a bit before gesturing to Rovex to continue. They sparred again and this time, several of Rovex's moves made it through Largon's defenses.

"Good improvement," Largon said when they were finished. "Keep working on it."

Rovex grinned.

"Thank you both. I feel I've learned something today."

"Remember, Rovex, your strength is important, but don't rely on it. Your brain is your best asset." Rachel slapped his bicep.

Rovex ducked his head.

"My father told me to rely on my strength since I'm not smart."

Rachel heard Natasha suck in a breath.

"I think relying on brute strength is stupid. A smart male uses all the tools available to him. If you truly believed as your father does, you never would have asked me for help," said Rachel. "The fact that you know and want to improve shows your intelligence."

"Lady Rachel is correct. Training your brain is no different than training any other muscle," Largon added with a smile. "I'll be happy to work with you when I can."

Rovex's smile brightened against his bronze skin. He said his goodbyes and left.

"Okay, maybe you were right. He's not so bad." Natasha elbowed Rachel.

"Like I said, he's got potential."

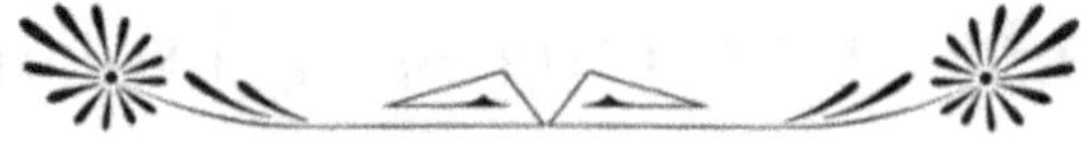

Several days later, Rachel huffed in frustration. No matter how hard she tried, she somehow kept ending up in the same place as Traxen. She expected to see him at the elaborate Court dinners which tended to be every four days but avoided spending time with him alone by mingling. However, when she accompanied Largon and Ronan to the Phoenix House location, the king showed up with the architects or the construction crew. While training the women on self-defense, she would look up to find him watching. She started changing the times she arrived in the training area for her own exercise and sparring.

Yet here he was again as she and the senior Hossix ended their bout. Sweat dripped from her forehead and she gratefully accepted a towel and water pouch from one of the watching warriors. Sucking down the cool liquid, she wiped her face and shoulders. Hossix matched her movements.

"Thank you, Lady Rachel, for the match."

"You made me work for it." She grinned at the older male.

"Good day," Traxen said as he approached them. Her face tightened.

"Good day, Sire. Do you require a sparring partner?" Lorriv Hossix tossed his used towel into the refresher. "I'm available."

"I was hoping Lady Rachel might spar with me today."

"I'm not sure that's a good idea." Rachel frowned. **Damn, he smells good.**

"Hmm. It would be useful for him to learn to counter your techniques, Lady Rachel." Hossix tilted his head. "He is a seasoned warrior but could always improve."

Traxen lightly slapped Hossix's shoulder. "Perhaps I should spar with you and teach you a lesson."

"You could try, Your Highness." Hossix's fangs flashed brightly.

Traxen gestured with an open palm towards the mat.

"I would be honored if you would spar with me, Rachel."

Sighing, she threw her water pouch into the recycler and towel into the refresher.

"As you wish." She stepped onto the mat and faced off against him.

They spent the first few minutes testing each other's reflexes and searching for weaknesses. Remembering the fight in Trezoura, Rachel kept track of his tail. Trying to ignore his wonderful scent and the bunching of his beautiful muscles, she instead concentrated on what his movements told her. She feinted to the left, and when he blocked with his forearm, she drove her right fist into his abdomen. A small smile graced her lips at his involuntary grunt and narrowed eyes.

He countered with a leg sweep which she hopped over. Landing lightly, she pivoted, dropped her shoulder, and used her body weight to impact hard into where a human kidney would be located. He spun and punched at her stomach.

She twisted to avoid his fist so it only grazed her and kicked out at his shin. He whirled out of the way and snapped his tail at her legs. **He's fast for such a big guy.**

They continued with neither gaining a significant advantage. Rachel noted that he stopped pulling his punches to keep from hurting her the longer they sparred. **Good. He's taking me seriously.**

Each suffering blows from the other, both began to breathe heavily from the sustained exertion. When she observed his tail stiffening, she dove forward and wrapped one hand around the base and the other further down to handstand briefly before rotating her body. Her legs dropped onto his shoulders from behind and she locked her ankles together using her core muscles to pull up while releasing his tail. Her movements caused Traxen to overbalance and she felt the whoosh of air as they fell backward towards the mat. **This is going to hurt.**

Chapter 11

The shock of Rachel's hand squeezing the base of his tail stunned Traxen. Electrifying pleasure spiked his spine at the intimate touch. When they fell backwards, a number of things happened simultaneously. Rachel's aroused scent from her hot core behind his neck struck him hard, and he sucked in a breath. Having her legs wrapped around his head made him wish he was facing toward her. One of his hands reached up and behind her to cradle her neck and head while his other arm and tail attempted to support her spine as they toppled. He twisted them slightly so he landed on his side and not directly on her body or his tail.

Air whooshed from his lungs when they hit the mat. Her legs loosened slightly and he turned his face into her warm thigh.

Nudging her flesh with his nose, he inhaled deeply and willed his cock to ignore the stimuli unsuccessfully.

"Are you hurt?" he mumbled into her leg. **I want to taste her.**

She laughed breathlessly and wiggled.

"I'm fine. You?"

"Surprisingly well, considering." He couldn't resist nipping her thigh. He smiled when she shivered. Her legs released him, and she scrambled out from under him. He rolled over to hide his erection and composed his expression. **A king pouting is not a good look.**

Traxen looked up at her as he rose to his knees resting his hands on the mat. Her heaving chest and flushed face brought a smile to his face.

"Shall we consider this a draw?"

She placed a hand on her hip and tilted her head. Her blue eyes sparkled.

"Oh, I think that match went to me."

His braid smacked his shoulders as he shook his head.

"I don't think so."

"You just don't like losing."

"True, but I didn't this time." He grinned as he stood.

"You're delusional."

"I think you argue just to argue."

She stuck out a pink tongue.

He licked his lips and took pleasure in how her eyes darkened. **I shouldn't want her, but I can't help myself.**

"Will you be attending evening meal with the Court tonight?"

"I'll be there." She patted his forearm, then strode from the training area. Her firm, rounded ass swayed in her tight pants. He shifted his stance attempting to ease the discomfort in his groin as she walked away. Absently, he took the water and towel from the head royal guard.

"She's a formidable female," the older male said.

"I agree." Traxen sipped his water.

"Attractive and intelligent, too."

"Hmm."

"The type of female that inspires the loyalty of those around her. All admirable traits for a king's consort."

Traxen stiffened and stared at Hossix.

"The Council would argue a king abused his position if he actively pursued one of the first females from Earth."

"One might also suggest the king leads by example." Hossix's expression turned serious. "Ruling is a lonely occupation, and not many are truly suited for it. If the opportunity arises to find someone to share the burdens who also brings you happiness, you should make the effort to see where it goes."

"My father expected me to put Costonia first."

"Your father would never have wanted you to forego the chance at a truly compatible mate. He, more than anyone, understood that a happy, contented ruler makes better decisions for his people. He loved your mother dearly and nothing would have made him happier than for his only son to experience the same joy."

Traxen grunted. His tail flicked.

"I have to consider the consequences, Hossix. My position demands it."

"True. Just don't forget to weigh the benefits as well. It's quite obvious to anyone with a nose that Lady Rachel finds you appealing, not your rank."

Traxen mulled over Hossix's words as he headed back to his quarters to shower with Previv and the younger Hossix following. **Was Lorriv correct? What would the former king advise if he were still alive?**

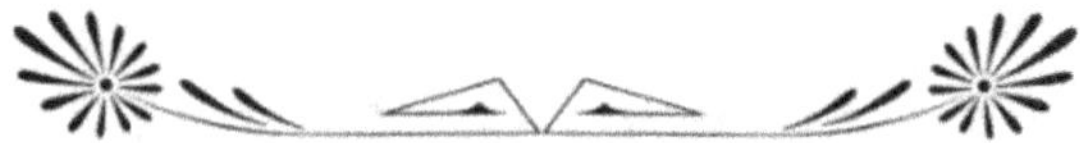

Traxen glanced up from his desk as his Spymaster, dressed in servant garb, entered from the hidden passage.

"What news?"

The Spymaster took a water pouch from the cooling unit before sitting.

"The Wing Raiders secured an invitation to Rumaska, but it isn't for another three weeks. There is a planetary celebration taking place that prohibits outsiders until then. They continue to gather intel beforehand on the various trading opportunities and potential contacts to focus their efforts while there.”

“Disappointing, but unavoidable.”

“Rumors are n’Tuli is dying.”

Traxen sat back in his chair and stroked his chin.

“He did not look well when I contacted him about the vaccine.”

“My sources tell me he has not authorized production of the vaccine. However, doses have been appearing at the underground clinics where slaves are receiving them, even if their masters are not.”

Satisfaction filled Traxen and he knew it showed on his face.

“Largon and Ronan.” The Spymaster nodded and looked smug.

“Yes. They disseminated the information to their contacts and the protection is spreading to the most vulnerable first.”

"Excellent news. Who is n'Tuli's heir? What do we know about the line of succession?"

"He hasn't named one. He has no acknowledged young. Even if he chooses someone before he dies, the Zuvgran will have internal issues for some time. There are too many factions and all will try to seize power. Many are military."

"Hmm." Traxen drummed his fingers on his desk.

"We may have the opportunity to sow dissent or provide aid to a contender that suits our needs."

"I'm not sure I wish to get too involved in the governance of our enemy."

"I'll send a report on potential scenarios so you have as much information as I do."

"I assume you will include your recommendations."

"Of course, Sire. As well as issues that may arise from any particular course of action."

Traxen pursed his lips, then sighed.

"Very well. I look forward to it."

The Spymaster chuckled as he walked to the bookcase.

"No, you don't."

A reluctant grin crossed Traxen's face.

"You are correct, my friend. But, unfortunately, it's my job."

Pausing before he stepped into the passage, the older male dipped his chin and bowed.

"You do it well, Sire. Costonia is lucky you learned what your father taught you."

As the bookcase slid back into place, Traxen murmured, "It doesn't make it easier." He rolled his shoulders and went back to work.

65 years earlier
October 15, 1972 (Earth calendar)
Resthaven (mind healing facility on Costonia)

"It's good to see you, my son." Estra Trahiz rose from the garden bench and extended her hands. He squeezed them gently and kissed her cheek. Small wrinkles lined her eyes hinting at her advancing age, yet her gaze remained bright. When she retook her seat, he sat beside her in the shade of an old **trulet** tree.

"You're looking well, Mother. It's a beautiful day to spend outside." He looked up at a flock of birds crossing the periwinkle sky.

"How is your sister?"

"Grissa is settling into matehood well. She appears happy caring for their home." He fought back a grimace.

Estra's tinkling laugh made him smile.

"I know you don't like him, but if she is content, let her enjoy it. She's not like us."

He tilted his head.

"How do you mean?"

"Her ambitions are small. She cares little for our lineage and what should be ours."

He cast his gaze around ensuring they were alone.

"You've never explained why you believe our status should be different, Mother. Don't you think it's time?"

She patted his hand and a wily look crossed her face.

"How much do you know about the history of the throne?"

"House Davelk has held the throne since all can remember."

Shaking her head, she let out a low growl.

"That's what they want you to believe. Nine centuries ago, House Nuxar sat on the throne. In fact, it was one of our ancestors, Verrat Trahiz who ruled. You are a direct descendant of our ill-remembered monarch."

"How I did I not know this?"

"Prior to Verrat, the Durek family was the ruling family. The last direct descendant, a female, bore Verrat. When the king died unexpectedly, Verrat was crowned."

He stiffened and leaned toward her.

"What happened?"

"Verrat ruled for almost forty solars when a male of the Sovex line appeared. His mother was a Durek cousin and hid his existence from all. According to the stories, she wanted him to live as a commoner, not a royal, so that he would understand the needs of his subjects."

"So he just took the throne? Was there any proof of his claims?"

"He had the lavender eyes that only that line has borne. The people were unhappy with Verrat's laws and policies. Rumors of him assassinating rivals before and after his reign began worked against him. The Council took harder stances against him and subsequently replaced him with the Sovex male. Verrat died in prison but left two young sons. Our line's history passes down each generation quietly. No one has had the courage to challenge the Sovex rule in all these solars."

"Until me."

Her fangs gleamed in the sunlight.

"Until you, my son. Abide cautiously and choose your supporters wisely. Learn all you can. You'll know when the opportunity arises to make your move. Our patience will be rewarded. I look forward to the day when you lead our planet."

"So your father relegated you to Resthaven even though he knows the truth?"

Estra scoffed.

"My father is weak and afraid. He does not have our strength."

"You've given me much to think about, Mother."

She gently caressed his cheek.

"I know you will not disappoint me, my son. You will be the one to retake our rightful place on Costonia."

"Yes, Mother."

Chapter 12

Rachel reviewed the catalog of contents Xeliv sent her of the main palace library as she walked the wide hallway. They were no closer to identifying the traitor and without Karid's assistance and input, the investigation crawled. The upload she and the other women received about Svesti politics while on the **Invictus** seemed minimal at best. She hoped she could find something in their political history that might give her a direction.

She paused outside the library door when she heard a voice within say "humans." Glancing both directions, she saw no one in the hall. She stepped closer to the door and eavesdropped. Garbled male voices frustrated her and she looked down to see there was an old-fashioned doorknob. **I'm lucky the door didn't open automatically.**

Fortunately, the only doors in the palace with that type of technology seem to be the sanitary facilities.

Carefully she opened the door slightly and the voice became clearer.

"Mating with humans will irrevocably change our species. That cannot be what the Goddess wants." **The voice sounds familiar. Who is it?**

"The problem is we have no other viable alternatives. I'm afraid it's them or the Svesti die out." **That sounds like Yistax Minnet.**

"The humans will weaken our bloodlines. There are many others who believe as I do. Change is coming, but not the way Sovex believes." **Glopiz. Hil'n Glopiz. That's who it is.**

"What do you mean?"

Glopiz spoke in a sly tone.

"I have it on good authority that there will be no treaty with Earth."

"I can't believe the majority of the Council will vote against it, especially with the fated mate bonds."

Glopiz scoffed.

"Faked."

"No. How?" Incredulity laced Minnet's voice.

"I don't know, but they have to be counterfeit. There is no way the Goddess approves."

"Unless you have proof the markings are false, I have to believe the Goddess wants us to breed with humans. Despite I how I personally feel about the change, I must go with the evidence of my eyes."

"Then you are a fool and your faith is fragile." Rachel heard the thump of a tail hitting the floor.

"Attacking my faith in the Goddess is not the way to secure my support." Minnet huffed. "Enough of your nonsense. I need to go prepare for my meeting with the king."

Shit. Rachel hustled to the end of the hall, turned the corner, and pressed her back to the wall. Listening intently, she heard the males leave the library and walk the other direction. Her body loosened, and she closed her eyes in relief. Her eyes popped open when a warm hand squeezed her shoulder and Traxen's scent hit her nose.

"Is all well, Rachel?"

She stared into his concerned face. His guards stood a few paces behind him.

"Uh, yes. I'm fine. Just trying to avoid a couple males." **At least it's the truth.**

His jaw flexed and his fingers tightened momentarily.

"Was someone bothering you?"

She shook her head and stepped away from his touch.

"No. I wanted to ensure there wouldn't be an issue." **Like having them know I was eavesdropping.**

Traxen tilted his head and gestured for her to join him.

"We can escort you to wherever you were headed."

"I wanted to go the library." She walked beside him, and he opened the door for her.

"Were you looking for something specific? I can help you find it."

"Don't you have a meeting?"

"How do you know that?" **Bloody hell. I'm not supposed to know that, am I?**

"You're the king. Don't you always have meetings?" She laughed. "I wanted to delve into Costonia's political histories."

He tipped his head, and his full lips lifted.

"So, some light reading."

Her grin matched his.

"Something like that." She followed him to a set of bookcases with doors tucked deep within the room.

"Many of our history and genealogy books are in climate-controlled cabinets to preserve them. I ask that you use caution handling them."

She stared at the volumes revealed when the doors opened after he pressed his hand to a control panel.

"Should I wear gloves or anything like that?"

"Yes. There are some over there." He gestured to a large round wooden table. "I'll set the timer on the cabinets for you to have access for four hours. If you haven't finished by then, please let me know. The controls only recognize my DNA." He pointed to the bookcases nearby with covered glass doors. "Those have the newer volumes and are available to anyone."

"Knowing it requires DNA access makes sense as why such irreplaceable books are kept in a semi-public area." She opened a box on the table and pulled on a set of white gloves that shrunk to fit her hands perfectly before returning to peruse the available titles. She chose one and carried it carefully to the table.

"I'll leave you to it. Enjoy." Traxen caressed her shoulder lightly before nodding and leaving with his guards.

Rachel savored the last hints of his scent and touch even as she wished she wasn't so attracted to Traxen. It just complicated things. Exhaling heavily, she turned her attention to the heavy book in front of her and sighed. **Earliest Records of Costonian Governance. This is going to take awhile.**

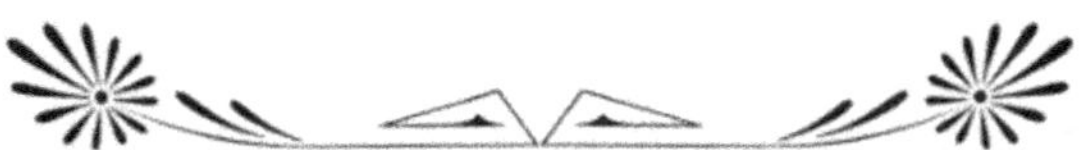

At the formal Court function, Rachel found herself seated between Reccix and Minnet.

"Once you have settled in, if you and the other human females would like to visit my estate, I would be happy to host all of you," Reccix said as he sipped his wine. "In fact, we have one section devoted to growing the fruit for this wine."

"Why would they wish to visit farms, Reccix? There's nothing to see or buy," Minnet leaned forward to speak.

Reccix smiled good-naturedly.

"The land that provides the food for our people is part of the Goddess' bounty. It has a beauty all its own. House Midnar works hard and eats well."

"I could take them to tour my shops and warehouses. There are many pretty trinkets to catch their eyes."

Rachel refrained from rolling her eyes. **Does Minnet think we're brainless twits?**

"I'm not sure the king wants us taking long trips just yet."

Minnet whispered, "He's not keeping you prisoner, is he?"

Her brow wrinkled as she looked at the older male.

"Of course not. However, we are few and not all are happy we're here. He's concerned for our safety."

"House Troliv would keep you safe." Minnet's eyes narrowed. "Assuming you trust us to."

Rachel widened her eyes.

"I would never insinuate the males of this world could not keep us defenseless women safe."

An arrogant expression settled on Minnet's face.

"Some Houses are more suited to guarding treasures and females. House Troliv is experienced at guarding valuables."

Reccix coughed into his napkin. His eyes twinkled.

"Lady Rachel, did you train today?" **Oh, you rascal.**

"Why, yes, Reccix. Lorriv Hossix and the king both graciously sparred with me."

Minnet sputtered.

"You sparred?"

"Of course." Rachel dusted her forearm with her fingertips. "I regularly train with the Royal Guards. It's good exercise."

"But you are a female."

"I have been since birth. I'm not sure I see your point."

"You could be hurt."

"How sweet of you to worry about that, Minnet. A few bumps and bruises are of little concern." She deliberately gave him a vacuous smile.

"The Goddess would not like that. Her teachings say females are to be protected."

She frowned.

"Tell me more about your Goddess. All of you invoke her name, but I've seen no churches or religious texts."

"It is considered blasphemous to write her teachings down. Her words have been passed down orally for generations," Minnet said.

"How convenient."

"What do you mean?" Reccix tilted his head.

"There's no written proof of her teachings which makes them even more subject to the interpretation of the living."

"You dare suggest we would dishonor her by changing her words." Minnet growled low and his tail flicked hard.

"Not intentionally. We have this game on Earth called 'Telephone' where someone whispers a sentence or phrase in someone's ear, who whispers it to someone else, and so on. By the time the last person hears it and says it aloud, it rarely matches in words or intent of the original." Rachel shrugged. "Honestly, it's usually played as a party game, but it illustrates that people don't always hear what you say."

"Interesting." Reccix's tail swayed.

"Truthfully, even though religious texts are written on Earth, they are still subject to interpretation by those who read them. There have been too many wars and conflicts on our planet by factions who differ in their beliefs of what the words mean. I'm not sure mere mortals are meant to know what a God or Goddess intends."

She finished her dessert and dabbed at her lips with her napkin.

"If you'll excuse me, I wish to mingle. Reccix, Minnet, thank you for the conversation and I will let you know if we would like to schedule a visit to your respective Houses."

Reccix rose and bowed over her hand.

"Lady Rachel, as always, your company was delightful."
What a charmer.

She lowered her eyes.

"Thank you, kind sir."

As she walked away, she noted Minnet remained seated and watched her through narrowed eyes. **Not sure about that one. Although given what I overheard earlier, he's less fanatical than Glopiz.**

She smoothed her gown before approaching a group of males with Glopiz at the center. Pluvi Frulix and Marek Tolvex stood along the fringes. Everyone stopped speaking when she arrived.

"Oh, don't mind me. I don't think I've met all of you yet," Rachel said.

The males introduced themselves while Rachel mentally catalogued each in her mind.

"Dinner was wonderful, wasn't it? I believe Lady Ava taught Lady Reena one of her bread recipes. The rolls reminded me of home." Rachel smiled engagingly.

Tolvex grunted and crossed his arms.

"It was acceptable. I did not see my son here this evening."

"I'm not sure where he and Lady Emmy are. I haven't seen them all day."

"I cannot believe he mated a human."

Rachel worked hard to keep her voice level and a pleasant smile on her face.

"They make a wonderful couple. They're fortunate to have a fated mate bond."

"Tell us the truth, Lady Rachel. How did the females manage the gold clan markings?" Glopiz said.

"They just appeared. Humans don't have experience with fated mate pairings, so we were surprised when it was explained to us. Your Goddess seems to know what she's doing. Each couple is perfect for one other."

"I doubt it is the work of the Goddess. She can't mean for us to mate with such an inferior species." Some of the males inhaled sharply at Glopiz's words and began backing away.

"You are entitled to your opinion, of course, regardless of how wrong it is." Rachel beamed. "What matters is how happy the couples are, not whether the Goddess approves or disapproves."

"I disagree," said Frulix. "The Goddess guides us, and we all endeavor to live up to her teachings."

"Well, then, she must believe this inferior species has something meaningful to offer the Svesti." Rachel spine tingled when she felt Traxen's hand at the small of her back.

"Is all well here?" **I love how his voice rumbles in his chest.**

"Yes. We were discussing the Goddess and her favor of the Svesti and more recently, humans."

Several males coughed.

"May I steal you away for a moment, Lady Rachel?"

"Of course, Your Highness." She nodded at the group. "Thank you for the cordial conversation." **Chew on that, Glopiz.**

Traxen led her away toward the doors leading to the gardens.

"Would you like to get some fresh air?"

"That would be lovely."

Dianthia shone brightly in the night sky. Rachel looked up at the multitude of unfamiliar stars. **So far from home.**

Traxen's golden bronze skin glowed in the moonlight as he led her to a secluded bench. They sat, thighs touching, his warmth emanating at her side keeping the cool night air at bay.

"Did you enjoy your time in the library?"

"Enjoy might be too strong a word." Rachel grimaced. "The verbosity and handwritten nature of the older texts makes them tough to read and comprehend quickly."

"You would think they would have shortened their sentences if they were writing them all manually." Humor lit Traxen's lavender eyes.

"Exactly. There is a middle ground between boring facts and overblown prose."

"The group I rescued you from seemed tense."

She waved a careless hand.

"Oh, Glopiz shared his belief that the fated mate bonds were falsified since the Goddess could not mean for the Svesti to mate with an inferior species like humans."

Traxen's tail slapped on the ground.

"**Crek**. He insulted you."

"And you. I overheard him earlier talking to Minnet stating he believed you instigated the supposed ruse."

He released a breath on a long exhale. He took her hand in his.

"Do you think he is the traitor?"

"I think he should be high on the list to be investigated. I'm just not sure the traitor would be as vocal around me."

"My Spymaster is looking into him, as well as several others."

"Spymaster, huh? I wondered if you had a separate department for such activities." Rachel cast a teasing glance at him. "Have I met your Spymaster? I haven't heard him or her mentioned at all." **Maybe I can work with the Spymaster and stay on Costonia.**

"The position requires the utmost discretion, and his identity is kept secret—only known to a few."

"Please tell me he has others working with him. It's too much to do alone."

"Yes. He has a network spanning multiple planets."

She nodded sharply.

"Good."

He squeezed her hand gently.

"You seem to be fairly knowledgeable about how much work the job entails. Why is that?"

"Because I am, well, I was a spy. That's why my country sent me."

Chapter 13

Traxen froze at Rachel's admission. Letting out a long exhale, he relaxed his body.

"Why are you telling me?"

She glanced at him before looking back at the stars.

"My government lied to me about the agreement. Then when I called them on it, they threatened my family and tried to gaslight me saying it didn't matter because of my oath to my country." Hard blue eyes met his. "I've done many things in service to my country, some I'm not so proud of, but I always had all the available facts to decide what I was willing to do. They didn't even give me the courtesy of telling me the truth.

Loyalty means something to me, but it works both ways. I am more than a pawn to be manipulated."

She's beautiful when she's angry.

"Is your family safe?"

A wicked grin crossed her face highlighting her symmetrical features. **Crek. She's beautiful all the time.**

"I threatened them and told them I would publicly release classified material if any harm came to my family. The recovery from that type of fallout would keep them busy for years." She appeared sheepish. "Uh, I may have suggested you would help me with a planetwide transmission."

"Good for you." His tail surrounded her ankle. "What do you plan now? Will you return to Earth with Vared and Talia?" **Please stay here longer.**

"I committed to living with aliens for eighteen months. I hadn't even considered returning earlier." Her full lips puckered. "That surprises me because I usually look at all options. Until I know we've caught the traitors and the women are safe, I wouldn't feel right about leaving."

He reached out and clasped her small hand relishing in the pleasure of her fingers resting with his. His eyes traced her face.

"Perhaps Costonia and its inhabitants holds some appeal as well?" **What am I? A youngling?**

"Hmm." She tilted her head and tapped her chin with a finger from her opposite hand. "It is beautiful here, and I would miss the food." Humor brightened her eyes. "Oh, and I would miss Reccix. That male is charming. A bit like Hunnek, but not as grumpy."

His chest rumbled despite knowing she teased him.

"Both males are too old for you, **belgella**."

"They are both entertaining company, though." Her laugh floated in the night, making Traxen smile.

"That is true." He glanced away, then back. "I've noticed you comport yourself well at these functions. Well, everywhere, but you know what I mean. Is that from your training?"

"Some. But mostly from my parents. My father is a member of the House of Lords, which is part of our legislative body in my country. He taught me that two people can say the exact same sentence, but unless you understand each person and their motives, those words could have completely opposite meanings and intent."

"Your father sounds wise."

"Or just experienced in politics and human nature. My mother, on the other hand, taught me how to walk, talk, and smile even when you want to rip the hair from someone's head."

A surprised laugh exploded from him.

"Did she really say that?"

"No. I added the last bit myself." Her eyes danced with delight.

A comfortable silence fell between them. His thumb stroked her hand. Her scent grew stronger and overrode the garden flowers' sweet odor.

"May I ask a question? You don't have to answer."

"Of course. I'll tell you if I feel you've crossed a boundary." She paused and looked thoughtful. "I do want to tell you that with the exception of saying my occupation is security and not specifying it was national security, I have never outright lied to you or anyone else since beginning this trip."

"I appreciate knowing that. I wonder what your leaders wanted you to discover."

Rachel waved her free hand.

"The usual. Military weapons, resources, tactics, and so on. When I spoke to my former boss last week, he wanted to know more about intergalactic politics. I'm assuming they want to determine if there's another option they would rather pursue. Must be something in the proposed treaty they don't like. I think it's the fact that you're offering medical and financial resources, not weapons."

"What did you tell them?"

"Pretty much any species who has the ability to travel between populated worlds outguns Earth in a significant way, and I think the Svesti is our best option for an ally."

He leaned back and looked up at Dianthia.

"Do you think we should offer weapons to Earth?"

She shook her head so hard her dangling earrings slapped her cheeks.

"Absolutely not. An influx of high-tech weapons, especially ones they don't necessarily understand would be too dangerous. Things like that end up in the wrong hands. I can't even count how many cases I worked that involved arms dealers who then sold the weapons to terrorists. Although…never mind."

"No, please finish your thought."

"If you were to offer some sort of shielding technology, not the most recent tech, but an older design that could be built with resources Earth already has, that might be a compromise they'll accept. Something that could protect legislative buildings, vehicles, or individuals. If you were honest about limitations upfront and let our own scientists try to improve it, I believe it would be safer for all."

He turned to her and traced his forefinger along her cheek, softly rubbing where her earring hit. Her eyes drifted shut.

"Just when I think you can't impress me further, you prove me wrong…again. You are a fascinating female, **belgella**."

She spoke softly.

"That sounds much more serious than flirting, Traxen."

"I know." His finger lightly outlined her lower lip. "But I want more with you, Rachel."

Her eyes flew open.

"I'm still not looking for a mate or contract. It's not you. I have serious trust issues from a previous relationship. I don't know if I have it in me to pursue something long term with anyone. And no offense, but something serious with you comes with its own set of complications. Hell, I don't even have a job anymore."

"I don't know what this is or where it's going. I only know I want you. More than any other female I've ever met." Slowly, he drew her closer and nuzzled her cheek with his nose.

"Your scent entices me."

He raised their entwined hands and kissed them.

"Every part of your capable body is perfection."

His free hand gently brushed her hair from her forehead.

"Your lively brain delights and awes me."

His tail left her ankle and rose to gently tap between her breasts.

"And your heart is caring, giving, and loyal to those you deem worthy. I've seen you with the other females, the younglings, and how you assess each individual you meet."

Her hand cupped his cheek and her face softened.

"Don't put me on a pedestal, Traxen. I don't deserve it, and you'll be disappointed when I fall off."

He scoffed. "You're not perfect. But you are an amazing female who I want to know better."

Her hands fell away, and she drew back. Her chest rose when she drew in a deep breath.

"I need to think about this."

His tail flicked in short, fast motions.

"Have I offended you, **belgella**? That was never my intent."

"No, not at all. I'll be honest, if you were just looking for hot, sexy times, it would be easier for me to say yes. But the problem is I'm drawn to you, too, and it makes me cautious." Her forehead wrinkled. "I don't want to hurt you."

"So the issue is you want me too much?" He raised an eyebrow. "I think I can work with that."

The tension eased from her face when she laughed.

"Maybe move slower until I decide what I want and need?"

"As you wish. Does moving slower mean I can still kiss you?"

"If we don't let it go too far."

Traxen slowly dipped his head closer.

"If you want a job, I'm sure we can find something that suits you. I can't do anything about the complications of my being king, but I have no doubt you can handle whatever you choose. As for trust…" He hesitated a hair's breadth from her lips and whispered, "I think you already trust me a little. Otherwise you wouldn't have told me you're a spy."

She stared at him, her eyes darkening. Her hand reached up to his nape sending his nerve endings wild.

"Kiss me." Rachel pulled him the last, short—and longest—distance to her lips.

Their tongues danced and explored. His cock pressed against his pants seeking her warmth. Their breathing quickened. He moved his hands to her waist and rubbed small circles over her gown. Her arousal scent filled his nostrils. Her fingers tangled in his beard as she pressed her torso closer to him.

Minutes, or maybe hours later—Traxen didn't know—he reluctantly shortened their kisses to lingering pecks, then drew back. His heart thumped erratically when he saw the haze of desire when her eyelids lifted lazily.

"Spend the day with me tomorrow."

"What do you have planned?"

"I'm not sure yet, but I think maybe teaching you to operate a hover bike might be involved."

"You do know how to make an impression." She lightly tapped his nose with her finger. "Let's do it."

"Meet me in my quarters for morning meal. We can dine before we leave."

"Okay." She looked around and sighed. "I guess we should go back."

"Unfortunately, yes. I think this qualifies as one of those complications you mentioned."

He stood then offered her his hand. She clasped it and rose before smoothing her gown.

"Good thing I didn't wear lipstick."

Traxen chuckled.

"But you did wear the ring and daggers we bought." At her quizzical look, he said, "I felt the sheaths at your waist. Did you obtain any poison?"

"Not yet. I wanted to start wearing the jewelry so it wouldn't seem unusual to see me with it." She sent him a coy glance. "Don't worry, I have no intention of using any of it on you."

"I admit that would be a terrible way to utilize the gifts." His hand rested on the small of her back as they walked through the garden.

"I agree. Very tacky. My mother would be horrified if I acted in such a crass manner."

"I would be disappointed as well." They shared a smirk.

They rounded a corner and met Vared and Talia, both appearing slightly disheveled. Traxen suppressed his laughter. He didn't mind embarrassing his cousin, but he didn't want to upset Talia. Rachel didn't seem to share his reservations.

"Really? You have a beautiful room upstairs," she joked with an indulgent smile.

"I have an irresistible mate." Vared sued his tail around Talia's waist to pull her closer.

"Stop long enough for me to fix myself," Talia playfully slapped Vared's bicep.

"They will smell you, **kirani**. They will have no doubt that you're mine."

"This is one of those marking your territory things again, isn't it?" Talia sighed heavily. "We've spoken about this."

Vared widened his eyes like a youngling.

"I don't know what you're talking about."

Rachel said, "I'll walk in with, Talia. Maybe the absence of your mate will confuse the males long enough for us to get to our rooms."

Talia kissed Vared on the cheek.

"I'll see you upstairs."

Traxen and his cousin watched the women walk away.

"She's partially right. Marking her scent was a nice bonus to the actual activity."

"No wonder she calls you 'asshole' as much as she does," Traxen said with a chuckle as he slapped Vared's shoulder. "Let's go. I've had enough of the Court tonight."

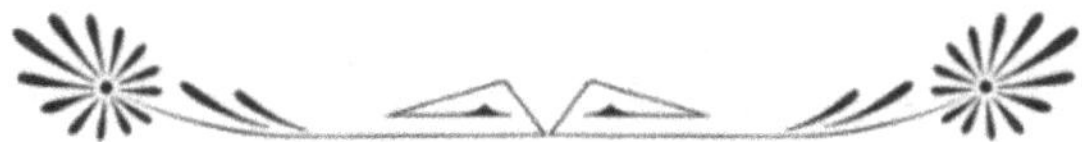

The next morning, Traxen sent a comm to arrange for the day's activities, then tossed his tablet onto the table. **I think Rachel will like what I have planned.**

He readied himself for the day by outfitting himself in a similar manner as when they visited Trezoura. Dressed and armed as a warrior for the second time in a week, he savored the familiarity of old routines. He missed them. The years of low-level frustration and stress of his royal duties cleared from his mind and body. It wasn't until it was gone that he realized how much it constantly weighed on him. Even with the attack on the females, the traitor still unidentified, and the future of his species undetermined, he felt energized and more like himself than ever. **Is it because of Rachel? Or because I have the opportunity to utilize my hard-won, but neglected, warrior skills?**

While he waited for Rachel and their food to arrive, he pondered the matter. **As king, I protect my people and our world daily, but I can admit to myself my soul sometimes feels like it's withering. I miss my**

brotherhood of warriors, because I've let myself be kept outside it. Helping to personally protect six alien females with males I trust cracked the door open to the part of myself I pushed aside for the greater good.

He frowned. **Do I want to be a king?** Snorting, he shook his head. **Too late. I already am. It wouldn't have been my choice to hold the throne this early in my life, but I think I do a good job keeping peace and prosperity for my people a priority. But if I continue to ignore the warrior within, I worry it will affect my decisions and attitude eventually. A better balance is necessary for my own sake.**

When the door chimed, he ceased his internal musings and instructed the staff to set up morning meal. He thanked and dismissed them before informing his guards of the plans for the day. Several minutes passed before Rachel arrived. As she walked toward him, he inspected her choice of garments. Her pants were made of a sturdier material he learned was called denim. Boots with a low heel and a short-sleeve shirt in a breathable material completed her outfit. **She looks comfortable and sexy.**

"Just in time, **belgella**. Morning meal just arrived." He pushed in her chair when she sat before taking his place at the table.

"It looks wonderful."

They filled their plates. He picked up something he didn't recognize and held it up.

"What's this?"

"Toast. Made with bread. Crunchy on the outside and softer in the middle. For breakfast, sometimes people spread things on it. Butter, nut spread, jellies, jams—things like that. You can also use it to sop up sauces and gravies."

"So, a multi-purpose food."

Her blue eyes danced as she cracked a smile.

"I guess you could say that." She took a slice of toast and slathered butter and **tempika** jam on it before taking a bite. "So what's the plan for today, Your Highness?"

He pretended to glare at her.

"First, no more titles—just call me Traxen."

She hummed her agreement around another bite of her toast.

"Second, after we eat, you need to pack a small bag with swimwear and an outfit for hot weather."

"Oh, beach time?"

"Something like that. What you currently wear will be good for our earlier activities, although you may want a light jacket, just in case."

"You have a lot of instructions, but your elucidation of the specifics is lacking."

He chuckled when she pointed her toast at him and squinted.

"By design. I want to surprise you." He chewed for a moment and swallowed. "How many weapons are you wearing?"

"That's a very personal question to ask a lady. Hardly polite of you." Her playful smile caused his heart to skip a beat.

"Then a lady of mystery accompanies me today."

"Don't you forget it."

Belgella, everything about you is memorable.

Chapter 14

Rachel eyed the royal flitter with excitement when she and Traxen arrived on the palace rooftop. Much smaller than the transport shuttle she was used to, but definitely large enough to hold an entourage, its sleek surfaces gleamed brightly in the warm morning sunlight. As per usual, Previv and Hossix trailed behind them with two additional guards—Wexan Yanz and Jespan Kragen.

They hadn't even left yet and already the day seemed magical to her. During breakfast, the lighthearted banter with Traxen, his unique aroma filling her nostrils, and the simmering heat of their attraction all conspired to center her attention on him. He acted as if a burden had been lifted—like he'd changed into soft, comfortable sweats after wearing an itchy sweater. Whatever it was, it ratcheted up her interest and intrigued her.

Despite the risk that she could end up in deeper emotional waters than she would like, after their talk the night before, Rachel knew she had no choice but to see where their relationship went. Being with him was like riding a rollercoaster…safe, steady, and calm interspersed with periods of intense, thrilling exhilaration. It appealed to every part of her.

Traxen carried their small bags and gestured to her to precede him into the flitter.

"Come let me give you a brief tour." Traxen set their bags in a small compartment.

Instead of the metal surfaces of the transport shuttle, a cushioned floor met her boots and cream walls topped with carved **trulet** molding surrounded them. Comfortable seating and tables lined the outside walls. **Definitely traveling in style.**

"This is the main area. As you can see, it seats eight with work surfaces available." He gestured to the front of the flitter. "The cockpit and a small kitchen area are that way, while to the rear there are two sanitary facilities, weapons storage on both sides, and a separate sleeping area with its own sanitary facility."

Yanz and Kragen headed to the rear to check the other areas of the flitter for threats while Previv and Hossix guarded the ramp until it closed.

"It's beautiful." She went to take a seat.

"No, there's more." He took her hand and led her toward the cockpit.

Two familiar faces greeted her in the large cockpit. They sat at the front near the center of the space. Unfilled chairs were located behind them, one on each side the flitter so all the seating formed an upside-down U.

"Sire. Lady Rachel. Good morning."

"Tesix. Westov. What are you doing here? Aren't you supposed to be on leave?" Rachel smiled in genuine delight to see them. Krivez Tesix and Slaiv'n Westov served on one of Devik's security teams on the **Invictus**.

The males returned her grin while Traxen nodded at the males.

"Lieutenant Tolvex asked for volunteers to provide extra security for you females while the **Invictus** is here. We told him when we were available and he pulled us from the on-call roster for your trip today," Tesix explained.

"In addition to the Royal Guards?" She lifted an eyebrow at Traxen.

"It has the benefit of trusted warriors you females already know protecting you while introducing unknowns to a security detail that increases difficulty for outsiders to predict."

"Smart." She pursed her lips. "Why didn't I see any last week when we went shopping?"

"Trezoura is close enough to have the bulk of the royal guards available. Besides, we had three from the **Invictus**—Vared, Devik, and Ash'n."

"Makes sense. It's good to see you both. I guess we'll let you get to it." She turned to leave, but Traxen's tail blocked her.

"No, **belgella**. Our outing starts now."

Westov stood and moved to one of the other chairs. Traxen motioned for her to take the seat Westov vacated. Traxen leaned over her shoulder and spoke close to her ear. Goosebumps rose on her arms.

"You said you wanted to learn how to fly a flitter. This is your first lesson." He straightened and crossed his arms. "I wanted to take a smaller one and teach you myself, but considering the rest of our itinerary for today, this option prevailed as the best."

"Really?" **Oh my god. I just squealed like a teenage girl at a concert.**

A soft, indulgent look from Traxen eliminated her momentary embarrassment.

"Really. Put on your safety restraints. Tesix will conduct the majority of your lesson." Traxen sat in the remaining empty chair and strapped in. Rachel followed his instructions and eagerly looked at Tesix.

"The computer controls are the same on both sides of the cockpit with the most used ones closest to where your hands rest. The remainder circle outward from the center based on how often you may need them in comparison to the others. There are also manual controls located underneath the console you can pull up if needed." Tesix explained each function and showed her how to release and replace the manual controls with Rachel occasionally asking for clarification.

Tesix walked Rachel through preflight checks saying he would show her how to do the outside of the flitter later. Then after having her input their coordinates and altitude, he told her, step by step, how to start and takeoff. Rachel followed his instructions exactly. She whooped and pumped her fist when they were airborne.

"Yeah, baby! I did it."

The males laughed at her joy.

"Your lesson isn't over yet, Rachel. Don't get overconfident." Traxen winked at her.

"Bring it on." She turned to Tesix. "So the coordinates I put in, where do they lead?"

"The Southern continent. Specifically, the Warrior Academy." Tesix looked confused. "Didn't you know where we were going?"

"Sneaky, **belgella**." Although Traxen's eyes narrowed menacingly, his tail swayed contentedly.

"Never try to keep secrets from me. I always find out." They shared a meaningful look.

"I have no doubt. But allow me to surprise you once in a while."

"Honestly, this is a great start to the day. Thank you." She grinned, then looked curious. "What do the controls do where you're sitting?"

"These are the weapons controls. This flitter is armed against airborne attacks."

"Oh, I definitely want to learn more about those, too." She licked her lips.

"Patience. Wouldn't you rather learn more about evasive flying?"

She whipped her head toward Tesix.

"Evasive flying?"

"Do you want to start with the regular controls or the manual ones?"

"Which do you think is easiest to master first?"

Westov said, "Regular." But Traxen and Tesix said, "Manual."

She turned to Westov with her eyebrow raised.

"I'm more comfortable with computers," he said. "To me, they make sense."

"I imagine Tesix would agree, but I think the manual controls allow you to intuitively feel what to do, although it may take you longer to learn to be as precise in your movements," Traxen said. Tesix nodded.

"No offense, Westov, but I do better with physical rather than tech." Rachel released the manual controls while Tesix did the same.

As she learned more about the manual controls, she privately agreed with Traxen and Tesix. The rolling balls, sliders, and buttons reminded her of playing video games when she was younger and after a short adjustment period, her hands and fingers carried out her commands without thinking about it. Westov made an announcement to the other guards about newbie flight training and strapping in, just in case. Rachel turned and stuck her tongue out at him.

Her face felt flushed as Tesix had her climb higher. Conducting turns, dives, and rolls, she relished the feeling of flying something so responsive. Her heart raced with adrenaline when Traxen suggested they snake through a long ravine before they reached the ocean. Tesix agreed.

When they reached the end of the ravine with Tesix intervening only once, she was ecstatic. **That was bloody amazing!**

"You ran that ravine at a higher speed than I would have recommended for a beginner, but I have to admit, I'm impressed with how quickly you've taken to flying," Tesix said with a pleased smile once they returned to cruising altitude and were on course over the ocean. "I'll send some material to your comm for you to study with more basic flight information that is useful no matter what craft you're operating. I will be happy to continue training you if you like when I'm available. We have nothing but water for the next hour or so. Why don't you take a break? If you want to learn landing sequences today, I'll call for you when it's time."

"No sense learning how to fly if you can't land afterwards." Rachel released her restraints and let Westov take her place. In the more open area, she placed her hands in the back pockets of her jeans and stretched backwards. "Wow. I didn't realize how much I tensed up."

"That's normal." Traxen rubbed her lower back. "Once you garner more experience, it won't happen very often."

She bit back the moan that rose at his touch.

"Thank you for the lesson, Tesix. I had fun."

"You're welcome, Lady Rachel." His fangs flashed. "This is much less stress on my body than you tossing me on a mat." Everyone laughed.

As soon as she and Traxen left the cockpit, she stopped and hugged him hard. His arms wrapped around her, and his tail wrapped around her ankle.

"Thank you, Traxen. I'm not sure your other surprises can top this one." Her fingers rested lightly on his face, and she tilted her head back.

"You are an exceedingly capable female. Making you happy pleases me." He brushed the hair from her eyes with a gentle finger.

"Lean down so I can kiss you."

"As you command, **belgella**."

Their kiss began much like the one the night before—slow and exploratory, but after long moments heated up. Her nipples pebbled and her lower body pushed closer to him.

His fingers clenched on her waist, and he lifted his head to rest his forehead on hers.

"We must stop. As much as I'd like to take you to the bedroom area and let you have your way with me, now is not the time."

She pouted and stepped back.

"You're right. You're just so…you." She sighed in frustration.

He chuckled and released her.

"I completely understand how you feel. Shall we get a drink and relax?"

"I'd like that."

Letting out a relieved breath, Rachel sat back after her first time landing a flitter and shutting it down. Tesix guided her flight path verbally, informing her that they avoided the training areas of the Academy for everyone's safety. The landing itself was easier than she expected it to be since she didn't need a runway to slow down.

"Good job. We get to walk away from this one." Tesix held his hand up for a high five, something he learned from the humans. Rachel slapped his palm with her own.

"I've heard many pilots on Earth say landings are just controlled crashes."

All three males chuckled.

"That's accurate," said Traxen. "Shall we?"

All six warriors accompanied them off the shuttle. A single older male with reddish bronze skin and brown eyes awaited them.

"Your Majesty. Welcome."

"Lady Rachel, allow me to introduce Commander Oriba Lunex of House Binova, Headmaster of the Warrior Academy. Commander, this is Lady Rachel Llewellyn of Earth." Traxen's tail circled her ankle and his hand rested on her lower spine.

"Well met, Lady Rachel."

"Commander Lunex, it's a pleasure to meet you. How long have you been here at the Academy?"

"Almost fifty solars, although I was the Assistant Headmaster prior to being promoted to my current position fifteen solars ago."

Rachel smiled. "Then I have had the pleasure of meeting many warriors you've trained. Their skills are impressive."

Lunex's fangs flashed.

"I'm just smart enough to recognize talented instructors and place them correctly."

Laughing, Rachel said, "You're too modest. You should be proud of your success."

"Thank you. Lorriv Hossix tells me you have had warrior training on your own planet. On a day when the king does not have plans for you, I would be interested in learning more." Lunex smiled pleasantly.

"I would be honored, Commander."

"Sire, everything you asked for is in readiness for you."

"Then, let's proceed, Lunex. I think Lady Rachel will enjoy what we have planned."

Rachel snorted.

"I finally get to know?"

"One portion at a time, **belgella**. I wouldn't want to overwhelm you all at once."

Rachel elbowed him and he grunted. The Commander led them to a smaller flitter with no roof. **Futuristic golf cart?**

Rachel felt the urge to giggle. Everyone took a seat, and the driver took off.

"We won't be conducting a full tour at this time, Lady Rachel, due to the time constraints of your activities, but our first stop is just ahead." The flitter landed and they disembarked.

She followed him through a building but couldn't determine what it was used for. Then they came out the back side of what looked like a motocross training area. She saw cylindrical posts spread out at staggering intervals, ramps, dips, paved and unpaved surfaces, twists, turns, straightaways, muddy areas, and more.

Traxen led her to a series of hover bikes lined up.

"Hover bike training?" she asked hopefully.

"Of course. Hop on." He watched her straddle the machine and fit her heels over the foot supports before he began explaining the controls. When he felt she understood, he stepped back. "Watch Yanz complete the course before you begin."

So engrossed in learning to operate the hover bike, she'd missed Yanz take one and proceed to the starting point. He took off at a moderate speed and ran the course.

"No helmets?" Rachel wasn't sure about that.

"Automatic shielding engages once the hover bike is in motion. You can manually override it if you need to, but the most important thing to remember is that with the shielding on, you cannot take turns so steep or fast as you might otherwise. The shielding might cause you to bounce off the surface and go the opposite direction."

"That's handy information to have." She watched as Yanz approached and turned off his hover bike.

"It's a complex course, Lady Rachel. I suggest for your first time you take it slower like I did," Yanz said with a smile.

"If I want to try it with a helmet, is that possible?"

Lunex nodded to his driver who immediately left.

"Learn with the shielding first, then depending on your progress, I will allow it."

The aide returned with several helmets. Rachel nodded. **Watch this, boys.**

She started the hover bike and took off toward a straight paved section at similar speed to what Yanz used. Testing the controls and the feel of the machine, she grinned when she leaned sideways far enough to bounce. **Okay, now I know where the limit is.**

She turned back to the cylindrical posts and used them as she would traffic cones on Earth—making S-turns through them, incrementally giving the vehicle more power. Once she felt comfortable with that, she made her way to the starting point and increased her speed, whooping loudly as she proceeded through the course. **I want one of these babies. They're more fun than motorcycles.**

Even with the shielding, she bounced hard after the first ramp, but the airborne rush was incredible. She pushed harder through the course before stopping so hard the rear end tipped up before settling. Her eyes met Traxen's. He grinned widely and looked proud.

"A bit too tame for you, **belgella**? How about a race?"

"With the shielding off?" she prompted eagerly.

"Of course." Traxen took two helmets from the aide and handed her one.

"Sire, I must protest, you should not be operating a hover bike without shielding." Lunex's tail flicked in short bursts.

"Your objection is noted and overruled, Commander." Traxen donned his helmet and threw his leg over the seat of another hover bike.

"Anyone else want to compete?" Rachel asked as she put on her helmet. It shrunk to fit comfortably on her head and there seemed to be airflow. The inside lightened and it was as if she could see with no obstructions to her peripheral vision. A smallish window appeared at the top which showed behind her. **Oh, seriously cool. I want one of these, too.**

Hossix said, "Previv and I could use some time on hover bikes, but we'll just follow at a more reasonable pace."

Westov shook his head and stepped back with his hands raised.

"You, Lady Rachel, are much too competitive. After watching you go through the course the first time, I believe you might even be insane."

Everyone laughed.

"Let's do this." She moved her hover bike to the starting line. Traxen pulled up beside her.

She startled when Hossix's voice came through her helmet.

"On three. One, two, three."

"Eat my dust, boys," she yelled as she and Traxen took off at high speed. She could feel the air through the helmet and bent forward to reduce the drag. **What a fucking rush!**

Chapter 15

She is crekkin' magnificent.

Traxen leaned forward on his hover bike and kept pace with Rachel. Just like earlier, she pushed the vehicle and herself hard through the course. Watching her eagerly learn to fly and now racing, like the hounds of Ladorta chased them, thrilled him. Her exclamations of joy and smart talk, as well as Hossix's "Dear Goddess, she's as crazy as the king" and Previv's laughter, overrode the rushing of air through his helmet. He smirked. **Obviously, Hossix still remembers my antics when I was just a prince.**

He dropped back slightly before the first ramp to eliminate the risk of tangling with her vehicle if something went wrong. When he saw her ass tightly outlined in her jeans, only years of training kept him from losing control of the hover bike. His already hard cock burgeoned even more against his pants. A warrior's shout left his lips as he went airborne. **Goddess, I forgot how much I enjoy things like this.**

Depending on which part of the course they were on, he alternately held back or stayed level with her. When they reached the straightaway, they both raced neck and neck to the finish. They tied with no clear-cut winner. She spun in circles before shutting down her hover bike and taking off her helmet. He halted near her and did the same. She tossed the helmet onto the seat and jumped into his arms, her legs wrapping around his waist and arms circling his neck. Surprised, he caught her with his hands under her ass and his tail supporting her back.

"That was incredible!" Her pink-flushed face and sparkling eyes radiating happiness caused his heart to stutter. **I've never seen her look more beautiful.**

She leaned forward and enthusiastically smacked their lips together, then leaned her forehead on his.

"Thank you, Traxen. We have to do this again sometime. This was fantastic." She pulled back and unhooked her legs.

He let her slide down his body to stand on her own. He cupped her face in his palm.

"**Belgella**, seeing your joy is all the thanks I require."

"You're such a sweet talker. I think we're more alike than I originally thought. Did you let me win?"

"Of course not. It was a tie."

"Nuh, uh. I clearly crossed the finish line first." Her blue eyes twinkled.

He tapped her forehead with his forefinger.

"Maybe Westov is correct, and you do need a mind healer." He smiled when she giggled.

Hossix and Previv walked up to them after they finished the course.

"I thought the days of my heart stopping because of your death-defying stunts were over when you were crowned king. I'm getting too old to watch you try to kill yourself," the older guard said with an indulgent shake of his head.

"At least now we know your heart still works, Hossix."

Everyone else approached.

Lunex rubbed the back of his neck.

"I thought I'd seen everything in my time here, but obviously I was wrong. Reckless, both of you."

Traxen might have been concerned about the Commander's statement, but the male's tail swayed slowly.

A small drone landed in the palm of Westov's hand. He tapped on his comm for a few moments, then everyone's comm chimed.

"Video proof of your insanity," Westov said with a grin. "Honestly, the skills you both showed impressed me."

"I'll watch it later," Rachel said. "Thanks."

"Would you like to try the advanced obstacle course?" Tesix asked. "You might be at a disadvantage with your shorter legs, though."

"Can I?" She looked at Traxen in askance.

"Commander?"

"We can head over there now. I think there's a class just wrapping up." Lunex gestured for everyone to follow him.

When they reached their destination, warriors began standing at attention and thumping their chests when they realized the king was in their midst. Then their eyes widened when they saw Rachel. Lunex quietly spoke to the instructor, then addressed the class.

"As you can see, King Sovex is here with Lady Rachel Llewellyn, one of Costonia's human guests. As a warrior on her home planet, she has expressed interest in our training methods. I request four volunteers to demonstrate our advanced obstacle course."

Amid low whispers, multiple warriors stepped forward and the instructor selected four who then completed the course. When they were finished, Traxen arched an eyebrow at Rachel.

"Ready to lose this one, **belgella**?"

"You are delusional if you think you'll win." She winked.

"After you." Traxen nodded at Yanz and Kragen. "Would you like to join us?"

"Why do I feel we're going to look like newbies?" Yanz rolled his shoulders and stretched.

"We can only hope the king's advanced age will allow us to make a good showing in front of the students." Kragen's fangs flashed.

"Let's see if your young muscles can keep up," joked Traxen as they walked to the starting line.

"Your Highness, with your permission, I'd like to have my two best warriors join your contingent. Competing against royal guards will be good for them," the instructor said.

"Of course."

The instructor called out two names and the males took positions at either end of their group next to the guards, leaving Traxen and Rachel in the center positions. They took off, with Rachel trailing with her shorter legs as they ran. However, when they reached the **trulet** logs situated above a muddy pit, she quickly made up the time with her lighter frame and surefootedness. At the first climbing wall, she pulled ahead of all the males. **She's as fast as an arachnid pulling herself up. And her ass and thighs are amazing.**

When Traxen reached the swinging vines, he tugged on his and it broke off in his hand. He growled in frustration. Rachel looked back after completing her swing and saw his predicament. She swung her vine back to him, yelling, "Catch." Then she ran forward again. Her help kept him from falling behind the others.

He caught up to her at the stone pillars sitting flush against a high wall. There were no handholds in sight. The way to complete the obstacle required placing her back against one pillar and her feet against the other as if she were sitting and creep upwards. Although she was tall for her species, the interval between the pillars was built for Svesti and was just a little too wide for her to make much headway. When he reached her, he said, "Let me help."

He scooted under her so she could sit on his shoulders. His hands gripped her feet and pushed up. His height, combined with hers, allowed her to reach the top of the wall and pull herself up. She swung her legs over and balanced on her stomach and said, "Come on." Her arm and hand extended to offer him assistance.

His braid whipped side to side as he shook his head.

"No, I've got this. Go."

She grimaced, then nodded before she disappeared from his sight. Rapidly, he made it over the wall and saw the next obstacle. A number of thick wires a little over knee height were strung across the area. The males were stepping over the wires, rotating their bodies back and forth to maximize their speed. Rachel threw herself to the ground and military-crawled underneath and passed them all.

Several more obstacles had Traxen passing all the males except Kragen and catching up to Rachel. The next challenge involved thick ropes at head height strung between posts over another muddy pit. Kragen threw himself forward, catching the rope and swung hand over hand. Rachel, however, jumped up, caught her rope, pulled herself up to balance upright on her feet. Her arms outstretched, she slid her feet along the rope and rapidly made her way across. His breath caught in his chest at the dangerous sight and he kept her in his peripheral vision as he crossed in a similar manner as the other Svesti. He passed Kragen and trailed Rachel.

Sweat ran freely off his body and the blood coursed hot in his veins. His breaths came faster as they approached the last few obstacles. **It feels great to push myself this way.**

A wide swath of flowing water was next. Rachel hopped from exposed slippery boulder to boulder. **I hope her boots have good treads.** They made it across with Kragen falling behind slightly.

Running up a steep incline, they stopped briefly to clip harnesses to themselves and attach them to the ropes strung from columns and fell to the lower ground below. She turned to him, her face red with exertion, hair plastered to her head, and said, "I'll be waiting for you at the finish line." She leaned and stepped forward, belaying herself at a perpendicular angle to the surface, before jumping to rappel face-first with a wild yell. Traxen laughed boisterously as he did the same. They took large bouncing steps off the vertical surface, belaying themselves mere feet from the bottom.

Again, they found themselves neck and neck at the end of the course, students cheering them on. Crossing the finish line together, they both bent forward with their hands on their respective knees. With the exception of sucking in huge, gasping breaths, both were silent. A water pouch appeared in front of Traxen's face. He took it, straightened, and gulped the cool liquid.

"Thanks, Hossix." Traxen looked to see Previv had done the same for Rachel. When Rachel finished her water, she used her hands to dust off the dirt from her arms and clothing.

The remainder of the males finished, with Kragen and Yanz finishing close together, then the students less than a minute later.

"You do understand that most rappel in the normal fashion," the instructor said with a grin. "Now I'll have to ensure we have more healing wands available as word gets around that the king and a human female rappelled face-first."

"Happy to help," quipped Rachel as she wiped her forehead on her arm. "I enjoyed that workout."

The instructor turned to his class and raised his voice.

"You just observed our king, a human female, and two royal guards complete the course ahead of the best of your class without preparation. King Sovex and Lady Rachel tied for first place easily ahead of the others. What I want you to realize is they also did so by working together as a team when needed. I think we can all agree that both are highly competitive and pushed to win. But by their actions, I can see that while they were trained on different worlds, the mindset each gained is similar--no warrior left behind. King Traxen assisted Lady Rachel when the stone pillars did not allow for a quick completion of the obstacle. Lady Rachel sent her vine back to the king when his broke. Had they not aided each other, neither would have finished as quickly. If you learn nothing else from today's lesson, learn this. Your skills add value to your team. It is your responsibility and duty to use those skills to help your team perform at peak efficiency. Each of you have different strengths. Use those to shore up those who need it and do not be too proud to accept another's aid. Dismissed."

The instructor extended his arm to Rachel. Rachel gripped it in a warrior's clasp.

"It has been an honor, Lady Rachel, to watch you give my students something to aspire to."

Rachel laughed.

"That wasn't my objective, but if it works for you…"

Traxen accepted the male's warrior clasp.

"Thank you for allowing us to interrupt your class today."

All their comms chimed. Traxen's group all turned, saying, "Westov."

Westov opened his arms with his palms facing forward and elbows tucked to his waist with an innocent look on his face.

"What? After that speech, I thought he could use the video for training purposes."

Traxen chuckled. "Let's go have lunch."

After an entertaining lunch in the cafeteria with the Commander and several instructors, Traxen leaned toward Rachel. His tail shifted from where it was resting on her back to circle her ankle.

"Are you enjoying the day so far?"

"Absolutely. What's next?"

"When we're done here, the Commander has asked we speak to an assembly answering questions about the potential treaty and human females. After that, we change our clothes and I have another surprise for you."

"All these surprises might spoil me." She laid her hand on his thigh.

"You're worth spoiling, **belgella**."

Traxen nodded to Hossix, who then gestured to the other guards. Everyone but Hossix and Previv left.

"It's strange," Rachel said looking over the crowd of students.

"What is?"

"I thought Talia told me Vared and the others attended the Warrior Academy in their late teens. Yet, every student here is much older."

His jaw flexed, and he sighed.

"You are correct. While we do cycle some of our warriors through the Academy for additional training during their careers, those who attend for the first time now are adults who have decided to pursue warrior training after doing other things. This last decade has seen the smallest cohorts in our history."

"Will you open the Academy to females if they want to pursue a career in the military?"

"It hasn't been discussed yet, but I think your performance today makes a good argument for allowing it."

"Good. It will be almost two decades before any new Svesti-human hybrids will be old enough to attend."

"That's an excellent point. If any human females bring younglings with them, some of those may wish to pursue it as well."

She rested her chin on her hand, elbow on the table.

"There are so many moving parts to consider merging two species from different worlds. The more I think about, the more I'm impressed with the draft treaty Talia and Vared came up with, especially in such a relatively short period of time."

"As am I. They offered ideas I hadn't even considered. They make a good team."

They rose when the Commander indicated it was time to proceed to the assembly. The attendees peppered them with questions about fated mate bonds, humans and their courtship rituals, and expected timelines. Lively discussion ensued. Traxen made it clear that as more human females arrived, they were to be treated with courtesy and respect.

When they were done, Previv handed their bags to them. In an unoccupied office, Traxen changed into loose shorts that would dry quickly, as well as beach shoes. Rachel exited the attached sanitary facility, and his eyes drifted over her outfit. Underneath a white shirt that slid off one shoulder, her breasts were supported in what appeared to be the top of a blue swimsuit. Black shorts exposed her long, toned legs to his admiring gaze. White strappy sandals replaced her boots. **Beautiful.**

The commander's aide accompanied them in a small flitter to a stretch of beach on the far side of the Academy's grounds, mentioning areas of interest as they passed. They disembarked to find Westov standing on a dock.

"We use this area for ocean survival training." He pointed to a land mass in the distance. "That island is also utilized." He looked at Traxen. "Is there anything else you require, Your Highness?"

"No. Thank you for your assistance in accommodating all my requests."

"Please extend our gratitude to the Commander for allowing us to disrupt the Academy's routine," said Rachel.

The aide grinned widely.

"It was a pleasure. There will be talk of your visit for many lunars."

Traxen led her across the pure white sand to the boat tied to the dock. He hopped in, then held his arms out to lift her into the watercraft. Tugging her hand, Traxen began explaining the capabilities of the twelve-seater boat as they walked to the front. They reached the controls, and he showed her how to start the engine. Westov untied the rope and jumped in to join them.

Traxen talked her through the operation of the boat, and she beamed as she moved them into open water.

"We're headed to the island, but you can maneuver as you like for a little while before we go there." Traxen's tail snuck around her waist.

Face upturned and eyes sparkling just as brightly as the sunlight on the water, she said, "Let's see how fast this thing can go." Then she shouted, "Westov, hold on."

Traxen's braid streamed behind him as she increased the speed, and the wind caused his eyes to water. Rachel's short hair whipped around her head, and she laughed with delight. **Goddess, so much joy is a wonder to behold.**

Eventually, she steered them to the island, and he gave her tips for docking safely. Yanz caught the line Westov tossed and tied the craft to the dock.

"The island is secure, Sire," Hossix said. "Tesix is monitoring air traffic from the flitter, while Kragen and Previv are already in position to provide ground security at strategic points. Yanz and Westov will take their positions. I will remain nearby." He handed Traxen a pack. "Here are the items you requested."

Traxen shifted the pack to his shoulder and used his other hand to catch Rachel's.

"Come, **belgella**, let's walk."

Chapter 16

The white beach sand quickly made its way into Rachel's sandals. Traxen led them a short distance, closer to where the waves met the shore, and opened the pack. He snapped a blanket and it floated to the ground. They sat and removed their shoes. With her legs extended straight, she leaned back on her palms and dropped her head back to look at the periwinkle sky before closing her eyes. **I might have a pink nose and cheeks at the end of the day, but a sunburn is worth all the fun I've had today.**

The rhythmic sounds of the water crashing as it hit the shore before rolling back down the wet sand filled her ears. Traxen's scent mixed with the tang of the salt water on the gentle breeze. The air tasted fresh and untouched. The sunlight bathed them in its warm glow. **What a perfect moment.**

"Happy, **belgella**?"

"Mmm." Without opening her eyes, she lazily smiled. "This feels great."

His hand covered hers and squeezed.

"I'm glad you like it."

She leaned into his arm, bumping him gently.

"This has been a wonderful day."

"It's not over yet. If you'd like, we can go swimming. I also have snacks if you're hungry." His voice rumbled low.

"No competition?"

"Just relaxation. We've earned it."

She turned her face and softly kissed his bicep. Opening her eyes, she saw him gazing down at her affectionately.

"Thank you, Traxen. As first dates go, this one tops them all." She tightened her fingers around his. "You seem a little different today."

"In a good way?"

"The best."

He turned to stare out over the water. Strands of his hair that escaped from his braid danced in the wind. **What a handsome profile.**

"I feel more like me than I have in a long time."

"How so?"

"After my father died, I focused on Costonia and adjusted to being a monarch. I expected to rule, but in the distant future. And even then, I thought my father's guidance would still be available to me. It's not been easy."

"I'm sure it's been a lot. You must miss him."

He nodded.

"He was a good male and king. All of Costonia misses him."

"I meant you must miss your father, not the king."

"I do. I always will."

"So what's different today?"

"I realized that I've been neglecting my personal needs. First and foremost, I am a warrior. I miss activities like pushing myself physically in different situations and the sense of everyone working toward the same objective."

She tilted her head and pursed her lips.

"I understand what you mean. A great deal of what I did on Earth involved undercover work where I might only have myself or maybe one other to rely on in any given situation. It's lonely. I liked today much better." She pulled off her white top and stood. "We're being too serious for such a beautiful day. Let's go play in the water." She shimmied out of her shorts and placed a hand on her hip. Arching an eyebrow, she said, "Well? Why aren't you moving?"

His chest rumbled, and his tail swayed. Darkened amethyst eyes trailed over her body.

"The view of you undressing stunned me."

Her nipples beaded and she licked her lips. Flashing a grin, she ran toward the water calling over her shoulder, "Watch it from the back, then, slowpoke."

She heard his laughter from behind her as she lifted her knees high to navigate the water closest to shore. Waves buffeted her as she went deeper. They calmed when she was far enough out. She turned to look for Traxen but didn't see him. She scanned the beach and noted guards to her far left and right and Hossix at the tree line directly behind the blanket. Not seeing Traxen in the water, she frowned. **Where did he go?**

Hot hands grabbed her legs and pulled her under. When her head broke the surface, she sputtered. **Oh, it's going to be like that, is it?**

His boyish grin fell, and his eyes narrowed when she splashed his face. They tussled and wrestled in the ocean like kids. Their laughter rose around them, until he caught her and pulled her slippery body against his, then it trailed off as they stared at each other. Breathless, she shifted against the evidence of his desire. **The cold doesn't seem to be affecting that part of his body at all. Lucky me.**

"Rachel, I would like to kiss you." His voice rumbled low and the echoes of it resonated throughout her body centering on her clit.

"I'm not stopping you." Her eyes lowered to his full lips and watched them draw closer until they met hers.

His arms surrounded her, palms and fingers smoothing along her back eliciting a moan from her. His tail caressed her calf and shivers followed its path. His beard softly abraded her skin raising goosebumps along her arms. Their tongues tasted each other and dueled for supremacy before an unspoken truce of equality guided their movements.

She broke the lip lock to lick along his neck and ear. He grunted when she bit his earlobe.

"You are playing with fire, **belgella**."

"I like to live dangerously."

Chuckling, he brushed her wet hair from her eyes.

"I've noticed that about you. You're very subtle about it."

Playfully, she slapped his shoulder.

"Nice use of sarcasm, Your Majesty."

"Traxen." He nipped her lower lip with his fangs. "I want to hear you breathe my name, chant it in passion, and scream it to the Goddess in ecstasy."

She moaned. **Bloody hell, he's good at dirty talk.**

"The guards are watching…Traxen."

"They can't see below the water, and we're far enough out they'll only hear you if I reach my goal." His tail slipped under her bikini bottom and played with her clit.

Her fingers dug into his shoulders, and her head fell back.

"Oh my God. I didn't know you had that level of control of your tail." Her breathing quickened and her channel flooded.

Dark and thick as molasses, his voice throbbed in her veins when he said, "Oh, there is so much more I can do with it, Rachel."

She gently raked her fingernails down his pecs to his abdomen. Her fingers separated and snuck under his waistband to close over his thick hardness.

"Maybe you can scream my name."

His tail loved her clit with a steady pressure while his hips thrust into her fist. Their mouths met and their breathing quickened as they pleasured each other. Heat centered on her nub while she wriggled her upper body and rubbed her erect nipples on his chest. One of his hands clenched on her ass cheek.

"So close, Traxen." She broke off their kiss and shouted into his shoulder.

"Come for me, **belgella**," he grunted. His claws pricked her ass. That hint of danger had her stiffening, then quivering uncontrollably as she screamed his name. Moments later, he grunted and shouted hers.

Rachel had no idea how much time passed before their bodies gentled. Her head rested on his shoulder, and she licked the salt of his sweat and ocean from his neck while her hands roamed his back. He shuddered at her caress. When her head stopped spinning, she tilted it back to smirk at him.

"I'm now officially a fan of your tail. I'm looking forward to finding out what else you can do with it."

"So am I," he growled. Her breasts tingled. **Damn, I'm ready for another round.**

His comm chimed. His forehead furrowed, but he raised his arm and answered it.

"Sire, I apologize for interrupting you, but you are needed back at the palace."

"What is it that can't wait until morning, Xeliv?"

"Emperor n'Tuli died."

"**Crek**. I'll be there as soon as we can."

"Thank you, Sire."

"Emperor n'Tuli?" Rachel asked.

"The Zuvgran emperor. As far as we know, he didn't name a successor."

"So mayhem and chaos as factions fight for control."

"Exactly."

"Well, let's go, then."

He kissed her forehead.

"I'm sorry we have to shorten our outing. I've enjoyed every moment with you."

"Me, too. It's not your fault, Traxen. Let's swim back."

He shook his head, droplets spraying her, and tapped his comm.

"Hossix, we need to return to the palace immediately. Please have Tesix pick us up."

"As you will, Sire."

Rachel's jaw dropped. At the shoreline, she saw Hossix run to the blanket while speaking on his comm. He gathered their items, stuffed them in their pack, and threw the pack over his shoulder. Yanz and Westov ran to meet him, sand spraying beneath their boots. The flitter came into sight from the west, lines dangling with Previv and Kragen climbing them. The flitter hovered over the guards on the beach, and they grabbed the lines and began climbing them. Previv and Kragen reached the ramp door and turned to extend their hands to help the others. Tesix piloted the craft to hover over Traxen and her.

"You ready to climb, **belgella**?"

She shook her head in disbelief.

"Efficient. You do this for all your dates?"

"Only the special ones." His fangs flashed. "Females first."

She caught a dangling line and twisted the rope between the soles of her feet while pulling up with her arms.

"You just want to look at my ass on the way up," she shouted behind her.

"Of course."

Grimacing at the male laughter above and below her, she climbed while the guards hauled the line up to hasten the process. She slapped her hand into Previv's when she was close enough.

"Men, you're all the same," she grumbled. "Where's a healing wand? I think I have rope burns."

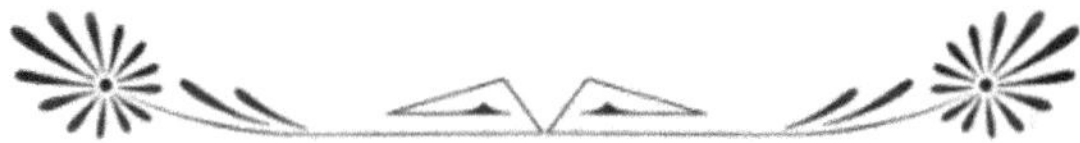

Since their day at the beach, she and Traxen began eating morning meal together in his quarters every day, before each headed off to their separate activities. Much of their together time involved discussing the Zuvgran and how much or how little Costonia should insert itself into their internal affairs.

No successor had been named, and the Zuvgran empire currently operated under military rule led by a male called Commander Rufen d'Urfan. If Rachel understood correctly, the Commander rank for the Zuvgran was the equivalent to the British rank of General or Field Marshal—if it were still more than an honorary title. Other commanders vied to take the top spot, but so far, d'Urfan had held his own. She learned that the n' prefix of a Zuvgran last name indicated noble blood, while any other prefix indicated what they considered commoner ancestry. In essence, the nobles, with their belief in their superiority, wanted one of their own in charge. **It seems the universe is the same no matter where you go. Guess the term human nature isn't broad enough. Being nature? Sentient nature?**

Frustration at the lack of verifiable intel usually colored Traxen's words when he spoke on the subject. In the meantime, some Council members hounded him to start a war, believing the lack of clear leadership indicated Zuvgran weakness. But the fact that d'Urfan seemed to hold control easily, at least from their removed standpoint, urged Traxen toward caution. Rachel listened, offered suggestions, and sometimes just held his hand in silence while he thought. In public, he behaved as the strong leader he was, but in private, she watched as the carefree Traxen of the beach started to bend under the weight of his position and the situation. It surprised her to discover how much she hated how it affected him. **Somehow, he's making me want to trust again.**

Traxen ticked all her boxes. Urbane, yet rough and ready. Sexy beyond belief and a dirty talker. Physically and mentally strong, yet gentle and generous. A good heart and an unshakable moral center guided his decisions and actions. Rather than becoming threatened by her strength and intelligence, he encouraged her to improve her skills even further and found it one of her sexier traits. She kept searching for signs of treachery or self-serving motives, but for all her poking and prodding, neither seemed to be part of his personality. **That bastard Jonathan really did a number on my ability to trust. I can't find anything to indicate Traxen is anything but who he is. I'm glad. I don't think I can resist him. He's the total package, and that terrifies me. I don't know if I'll recover if I'm wrong about him. I won't be able to trust my instincts…ever.**

Chapter 17

"Sir, our informants tell us King Sovex is becoming quite fond of Lady Rachel and spends as much time with her as he can. It is believed they may take their close friendship further soon."

The Svesti noble's tail flicked sharply, then stilled. His guard faced him impassively awaiting a response. **Crekkin' Sovex cannot be allowed to beget an heir. This situation is becoming untenable.**

"Can you put someone in place for the next Court function in two days?"

"Yes, sir."

"Someone we can trust to hold their tongue if caught?"

"Several. However, if you wish someone expendable who knows nothing that traces back to you, I can arrange that as well."

The noble smiled. **That's even better.**

"The second option. He may target Sovex or Lady Rachel, whichever is easier in the moment. Either eliminated will work for now."

"Just to be clear, sir, you wish termination, not incapacitation?"

"You understand me correctly."

"As you will."

After his guard left, the noble sat back in his chair. **Soon, Mother, your faith in me will be realized.**

Thud.

Traxen punched the hanging bag in his private training area adjacent to his living quarters. Satisfaction at the reverberation of the hit throughout his knuckles and arm helped relieve some of his frustration. Between being no closer to the identification of the traitor, navigating the Zuvgran government upheaval, planning to upgrade the military fleet engines while waiting for word from the Wing Raiders to obtain the bremmite need, and calming the ramped-up Council about both the proposed treaty as well as the talks of war, he needed a release to keep his temper under control.

Thud. Thwack. Thud. Thwack. Thwack. Thud. Thud.

Unconsciously, he settled into a rhythm, punching and kicking the bag while his mind churned.

Dealing with all this also reduces the amount of time I can spend with Rachel. Although, eating morning meal alone with her every morning starts my day on a

positive note. It's just not enough. Ever since she admitted she was a spy, her defenses are lower, but there's still something holding her back. Something that makes it difficult for her to trust a male completely. I can admit I hold back some information, too. It's still early in our relationship and while I don't believe she is, she could still be spying for her government.

She understood his cutting their day short at the Warrior Academy. Most females would resent his duties, but she supported him. When he shared his thoughts about any of what he dealt with, she listened and offered meaningful input. Her intelligence and experience on Earth gave her a unique perspective, and he found her suggestions practical and often addressed the problems from multiple angles. Her general comprehension of politics, even without knowing all the various people involved, revealed a keen sense of potential undercurrents. **I can easily see her as my queen, ruling by my side, if only we can get beyond the remaining trust issues.**

Thud. Thud. Thwack. Thwack. Thud. Thud. Thwack.

The stretch and burn of his muscles drew sweat from him. Droplets on his forehead and chest flew from his body arcing into the air before falling to the floor when he changed positions rapidly. His chest began to heave with his exertions.

Memories of their time in the water fueled more than a few orgasms for him in the days since. Watching her come apart felt like a gift and her hands on his body a reward he didn't deserve. Most mornings, they spent a short time kissing and exploring each other. When he thought of the weight of her perfect breasts filling his hands, his cock rose. Her body spoke to his on a cellular level, and a beautiful unspoken honesty flowed between them during their most passionate moments. **Our bodies can't lie to each other.**

Her sense of humor and attitude matched his well. And her beauty and passion in how she approached life appealed to him greatly. A protector like him, she cared deeply for the human females and appointed herself in charge of their safety. He enjoyed listening to her describe what she learned from the old Svesti texts and clarifying information for her. She asked incisive questions.

Ending his workout session, he toweled off and hydrated on the way to the shower. Anticipation built as he cleaned himself and dressed for the day. **She'll be here for morning meal soon.**

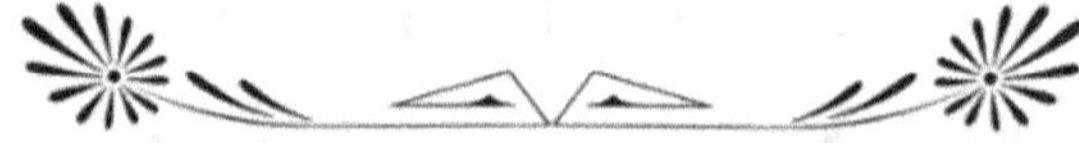

"What is this?" Traxen pointed to the fluffy circular items on his plate.

"Looks like pancakes and some breakfast meat. Either Ava cooked the meal or she taught Reena the recipe." Rachel slathered some whipped butter on each of her pancakes and poured some **tempika** berry syrup on it. "Try it. I think you'll like it."

He copied her actions, then took a bite.

"Mmm, this is good. Lady Ava has introduced so many new things to our palates in the past few weeks."

"Earth food, when done right, is exceptional. We have so many different cultures worldwide and the different types of food can be found almost anywhere." She tilted her head. "You know, it just occurred to me that some of Earth's early recipes aren't only based on what was available locally at a given location but was also affected by poverty levels."

"How do you mean?"

"Well, if you're poor, you can only afford the cheapest crops or meat. Most of us like our taste buds to experience diversity. I can't even tell you how many ways there are to cook potatoes or chicken. That's why talented chefs like Ava are popular—they can find new ways to use not only new foods and spices, but to mix up the tried and true."

"Interesting theory." **Her mind is always looking for patterns and reasons.**

"I have a question. One of the books I'm reading says that the royal line originated with the Dureks. Thank you, by the way, for giving me unlimited access to the oldest volumes. Some of it is fascinating to read." Rachel gifted him with a bright smile.

"You're welcome. And the book is correct. Eventually the Sovex line took the throne when the last female Durek mated with a Sovex about a thousand years ago."

"The tome mentioned another line ruled briefly." Her forehead wrinkled. "It was unclear what happened."

Finished with his meal, Traxen sat back and relaxed.

"I'd forgotten about that. I think his name was Verrat Trahiz or something similar. It was a very short blip in our history, maybe forty or fifty solars."

"What happened?"

"If I remember correctly from my tutors, he assassinated the grandfather of the first Sovex to take the throne. The daughter had left the public eye before my ancestor was born to raise him as a commoner, and he was still a youngling when his grandfather died. Trahiz took the throne and made some very unpopular decisions, as well as assassinated those who disagreed with him. When my ancestor was old enough, he overthrew the male with the support of the Council. It was believed Trahiz suffered from a mental illness. I think my father once told me that at least one member of their line required extensive mind healer care each generation ever since." He frowned. "It's sad that we haven't discovered yet what causes such breaks from reality."

"Neither have humans." She sipped her juice.

"There is another Court function in two days. Will you be attending?"

"Of course."

"Devik's brothers will be here to meet Lady Emmy."

"Oh, you need her for a command performance? She hates big social affairs." Rachel smirked.

"I know Marek can be difficult, but Devik's brothers are good, interesting males. She should meet his family. Lady Ava has been absent as well."

"She has some personal issues she's dealing with, but I can ensure both are there."

"I would appreciate it. I believe it would be best to divert the Court's attention from the Zuvgran succession to the proposed treaty with Earth." He paused. "Are you finished or would you like more?"

"I'm done." Rachel placed her napkin on the table.

He stood and offered his hand to her, then led her to a couch. He sat and pulled her onto his lap.

"I must leave soon, **belgella**. Let me hold you before I go."

She leaned into his kiss and her tongue met his. Her fingers tunneled into his beard and cupped his jaw. His hands smoothed along her back while his tail snaked between them to tease her nipples.

"I really enjoy beginning my day like this." Her words floated quietly in the air.

"I hope soon we can end our days like this as well." His fangs elongated and he swallowed hard. "Whenever you're ready, Rachel. Not before."

"It's difficult to trust myself, Traxen, but please don't doubt I want you."

"Will you tell me why a smart, capable female like yourself has doubts?" **Will she finally open up to me?**

Traxen kept his caresses calming and non-sexual while his tail moved to rest along the outside of her thigh. He waited patiently for her to answer. Finally, she let out a long breath.

"I guess it's time. I've never shared the full story with anyone."

"Your secrets are safe with me, **belgella**."

She smiled sadly.

"As you know, I worked as a spy and did a lot of undercover work. Six years ago, they assigned me a partner, Jonathan Barlow. Jonathan and I closed a number of cases, once stopping a planned terrorist attack on the main transport system in our capital city. We worked well together, and I liked him a lot. At some point, we began to have a sexual relationship. I thought I knew everything about the man and believed he was the one I would spend the rest of my life with. I didn't have to keep secrets from him in the interests of national security because he was my partner. I could just be me whenever I wasn't undercover for a case."

"Go on." Traxen consciously controlled his reaction to hearing about another male touching her.

"Three years ago, my boss called me into his office. They said Jonathan was a traitor and he was selling illegal weapons to our enemies, as well as sharing top secret intel. At first, I didn't believe them."

"Did you tell him?"

"No. I requested to review the evidence against him first." Her eyes slid away to stare out the window. Her fingers kneaded his chest. **I don't think she's even aware of what's she doing.**

"The evidence was definitely pointing at him. I pushed to lead the investigation. I believed I could find the true culprit setting him up."

"Was he innocent?"

"No." She looked back at him. "I followed him and discovered him making an illegal arms deal. I called for backup, then confronted him. The asshole pointed a gun at me and laughed, saying I was just a means to an end. He'd requested to be my partner because I had higher clearance than him and the agency bumped up his so he could work on my cases. He said he didn't need me anymore, and he couldn't have me hunting him."

"What happened?"

"I moved suddenly just before he pulled the trigger. The bullet grazed me, but I threw one of my daggers at him and severed his wrist tendons. When he went to flee, I shot him in the ass."

Traxen laughed, the rage he felt at hearing she had been shot by a former lover diminishing.

"In the ass?"

She shrugged. "It seemed like a good idea at the time. I figured his immediate future involved a lot of sitting, so I should make it painful. My backup arrived in the middle of all this and arrested the men buying the weapons. I placed the handcuffs on Jonathan myself."

He brushed her hair from her face and tucked some short strands behind her shell-like ear.

"It sounds like you did everything right. Why have you doubted yourself?"

"I worked, lived, and slept with the man. I was a spy. And I never saw the betrayal. I never suspected anything." Her eyes flashed and her teeth clenched.

His fingers gently traced her jawline attempting to soothe her.

"You had no reason to believe he was anything but what he portrayed himself to be. He is the one who betrayed your trust and that of your government. Not you."

"My superiors would disagree with you."

"What do you mean?"

"They felt I should have known. Even though I was the one who arrested Jonathan, they gave me less important cases after that. It was one reason I was surprised when I received the assignment to Costonia. I thought they were beginning to trust me again, but instead they lied to me about the truth."

"Their failure, Rachel. Not yours." He rested his forehead on yours. "You gave your trust to those who didn't deserve the gift—one a male who should have thanked the Goddess for your attention and your own government that should have recognized the loyalty of one of their best agents."

"That's why I'm not sure I can trust my instincts anymore. Do you or Costonia deserve my loyalty?"

Kissing her forehead lightly, he said, "I thank the Goddess multiple times a day for your presence in my life. As for Costonian government, I hope you can at least trust me, if not some of the Council." He pulled away. "I now understand your hesitation. All I can do is continue to be me and let you decide how far we progress."

"If you're everything you seem to be, Traxen, maybe I'm the one who doesn't deserve you," she whispered.

"Maybe we deserve each other. I'd like to think I could deserve someone as wonderful as you."

Chapter 18

Rachel tugged at Emmy's curly brown hair.

"For crying out loud, will you please sit still? You're like a little kid with ants in their pants."

"Why do I have to go to this Court dinner?" Emmy whined. "And dress up. You know how I feel about this kind of stuff." Her knee bounced under the midnight blue gown she wore. The satiny fabric caught the light with her movements. One shoulder was bare revealing her gold clan marking indicating her fated mate bond.

"Your normal snappy T-shirts are not suitable attire. You're representing Earth tonight. There's been a lot of unrest since the Zuvgran emperor died. I think the king is trying to give the Council members something else to think about." Rachel frowned as she brushed Emmy's hair. "I think I hate you. You made me sound like my mother." She twisted her friend's unruly mane into a high chignon and pinned it ruthlessly, teasing small portions out to draw attention to Emmy's high cheekbones and neck. "Besides, it's been almost three weeks since we arrived on Costonia and this is only the second one you've been to. This makes six or seven for me. I've lost count."

Emmy snorted.

"I didn't ask you to help me."

"Well, someone had to. Natasha's helping Ava. You're meeting Devik's father and brothers tonight." Rachel picked up some shimmery brown eyeshadow and aimed the applicator at Emmy's face. "Close your eyes." She gently swooped the makeup along Emmy's eyelids. "Open."

Rachel cocked her head and studied Emmy's face.

"Well, are you done?"

"Geez, you're an impatient bitch. You need a little mascara and some lipstick."

"I hate wearing makeup."

"Make sure you get some cheese to go with that whine. You'll like it when Devik sees you."

"You said Ava's going tonight? She hasn't been to one since the first either."

"We're staging an intervention. Natasha's going to kick her in the ass and push her to do something about Karid. We're worried about both of them. Karid won't talk to anybody, and Ava's been hiding in the kitchens licking her wounds."

Sadness filled Emmy's eyes.

"Karid won't answer any of Devik's comms. Devik is really concerned and upset."

"We all are. I don't know what happened to Karid while he was in captivity on Millus, but it's not good for him to withdraw from everyone. He needs help, and we think Ava's the only one who might be able to reach him."

Emmy nodded in agreement.

"Did you know they were seeing each other on the **Invictus**?"

"No. I don't know how I missed that. I worked with Karid almost every day trying to trap the traitor into making a mistake." Rachel frowned. "Now that I think about it, with the exception of Talia, all of you were pretty tight-lipped about your relationships."

Emmy's expression turned dreamy.

"Some things are so good you just want to keep it to yourself as your own private secret."

Laughing, Rachel said, "Hold still again." She applied the rest of the makeup, then opened a drawer. "Are these the only earrings you have?"

"Yes.

Rachel sighed heavily.

"Good thing I brought these then." She held up a pair of gold dangling earrings studded with dark blue stones. "These will pop against your gorgeous skin and look great with that dress. Natasha did a fantastic job making our gowns for this evening. If she ever wants to give up medicine, she could probably make a living as a clothing designer."

Emmy took the jewelry from Rachel and put it on.

"They are pretty. Thank you."

"Here's the matching necklace." Rachel fastened the fine chain around Emmy's neck. The matching pendant rested above Emmy's cleavage. Rachel rested her hands on

Emmy's shoulders. "You look beautiful and ready to meet the in-laws."

Emmy's eyes widened as she saw herself in the mirror.

"Wow. I look…wow."

"I had Natasha synthesize some low chunky heels for you so you feel more comfortable." Rachel smiled. "If you start feeling nervous, remember you look fabulous, and Devik loves you. And ignore Marek if you can."

"Devik's told me about his dad."

"Well, then you know—don't take anything he says personally. You are Devik's fated mate. It's one of the most enviable statuses to be had among the Svesti."

Emmy slid on the shoes, then stood.

"These are comfy." Emmy hugged Rachel hard. "I know I've been bitchy, but I really do appreciate your help." Her teeth gnawed at her lower lip. "I'm really nervous about meeting Devik's family."

"You'll be fine. And stop biting your lip. You don't want lipstick on your teeth."

Emmy glared at her, then they both laughed. They turned when Devik entered the room. He sucked in a breath, and his teal eyes darkened.

"**Milara**, you look absolutely stunning." His normally deep voice dropped another register.

Emmy twisted her fingers together.

"You think so?"

"You are a goddess amongst females." He pulled her hands apart and tugged her close to him.

"And that's my cue to leave," Rachel said. "Don't mess up your hair and makeup until after evening meal."

Emmy's giggle followed Rachel out the door.

Unobtrusively checking her hidden weapons one last time, Rachel entered the dining area alone, smiling and greeting various Court members. At each Court meal since n'Tuli died, Rachel's assigned seat somehow ended up next to Traxen. This was the third one, and she heard the whispers growing about their relationship. She didn't care. Her presence seemed to strengthen Traxen's ability to maintain calm. While they flirted, kissed, and pushed sexual boundaries when alone, they had yet to have full-blown sex, and she was more than ready. **Tonight, I'm going to have my way with him, even if I have to tie him down to do it.**

Her pussy pulsed at the thought of having Traxen at her mercy.

"What are you thinking, **belgella**? The look in your eyes and your scent are intoxicating. I'm not sure I want other males to be around you when you're like this." Traxen's breath heated her ear with his quiet words and his hand smoothed along her back to rest at the bottom of her spine. Only sheer force of will kept her knees from buckling.

"I'll tell you later when we're alone. I might even demonstrate." She turned so their faces almost touched. A small smile rose on her lips as she saw his eyes darken to amethyst. **Damn, I love seeing how his eye color changes when he's aroused.**

"I would like that. May I escort you to your chair?" He licked his lips before raising his head and straightening his shoulders.

"Please."

They slowly made their way to the table, occasionally stopping to chat with someone. She noted his cousin, Ari Zunnax, across the room. She met and held his lavender eyes for a moment before her gaze drifted over his scar. A small smile tipped the male's lips before he turned away to attend to his duties. **He still looks familiar. Why can't I place him?**

Once she took her seat, she saw Ava sitting between Reccix and Largon in a cream-colored gown with brown lace accents. **Natasha must have made the gown. It looks great on her. She should be fine where she is.**

Emmy sat between Devik and his brother Solen. Rachel met him earlier and found him to be a lot like Karid—a gregarious sense of humor and respectful of females. Devik's father sat across from her flanked by his other sons, Pex and Rassix. **Good, she'll have support as she deals with Marek. That dour male needs an attitude adjustment.**

Situated closer to the area where the kitchen staff entered and exited, Talia and Vared sat with Canaan and Lady Narilla. Ash'n and Lin sat near Zunnax at the same end of the long table, while Ronan and Natasha were grouped closer to Ava in the center of the table.

A reddish bronze arm appeared in her peripheral vision and poured some wine into her glass. She glanced up at their usual server and thanked him quietly. He returned her smile and moved on to fill Traxen's glass. She turned her attention back to the conversation around her. Unfortunately, Frulix and Glopiz were close enough that she could hear their offensive purist rhetoric. **Keep a pleasant smile on your face, Rachel, even if you want to stab them.**

As the meal progressed, Traxen barely touched his wine. **Probably wants to keep his head clear as he deals with keeping the peace and redirecting topics during the meal. Can't blame him.**

While Glopiz expounded on what he believed the Goddess wanted for the Svesti—for the eighth time no less—while they ate, Rachel saw a caramel bronze hand replace Traxen's mostly full wineglass entirely. It took her a moment to realize what she'd seen, but when Traxen wrapped his hand around the glass and began to lift it, she instinctively slapped it from him. The liquid spilled and then began to sizzle holes in the tablecloth. Shouts sounded up and down the table. Both of them jumped up and back knocking over their chairs. Her eyes searched for the male who had set the glass down. She saw someone hurrying toward the kitchen area.

"Stop him." She yelled and pointed at the male who began running. Zunnax held out his arm and clotheslined the perpetrator. He fell to the floor and Vared punched him once before restraining the male with a nod to Zunnax for his assistance. Zunnax's eyes were concerned when he looked back at Traxen. Royal guards took the male away.

"Are you okay?" Rachel scanned Traxen's clothes to make sure nothing burned. **Shit. That was too close.**

"I'm fine. You?" Traxen's jaw tightened. "You could've been hurt."

"Me? You were the one who almost drank whatever that is." She waved at the remnants of the fluid.

Hossix said loudly, "Everyone please remain at your seats, but refrain from eating or drinking anything." The room quieted as the implications of what just occurred settled on the crowd.

Some males rushed in and took samples of the liquid, packed away the wineglass and cloth separately, carefully identifying it all. At a nod from Hossix, Devik directed the males to collect all the wineglasses and mark them with who had been seated at the places. **Looks like Devik might be in charge of the forensic portion of the investigation. Good.**

Frulix spoke into the silence.

"Obviously, Sire, there is someone who disagrees with your leadership."

Traxen's tail flicked once before winding around her ankle hidden from view under her gown. Rachel's fists clenched briefly, then she consciously loosened them.

"Your keen sense of the obvious amazes me, Frulix. There are many who take issue at my leadership at one time or another, including yourself." Traxen said nonchalantly. His tail tightened and released on her ankle.

Rachel saw the flash of hatred briefly in Frulix's dark eyes before he donned a placid expression. **That's interesting.**

"Or perhaps the Zuvgran hired someone to do their dirty work." He tilted his head toward Largon. "Or the humans don't want a treaty. We really don't know anything about them. Sire." His tone bordered on disrespect as he glared at Rachel. **Oh, no, he didn't. The fucking asshole.**

"A thorough investigation is already underway, Frulix, and the Council will be given a copy of the final report. Making baseless accusations without any proof should be beneath you." Disdain laced Traxen's voice.

"Hossix, are my guests required for anything else?" Traxen asked calmly.

"Each will be questioned about their observations before they may leave, Sire." Hossix paused. "However, those who are staying within the palace may return to their quarters with an escort. By doing so, we will require less of your other guests' time. With your permission, may I secure Lieutenant Tolvex's assistance in taking their statements?"

"That is acceptable." Traxen leaned to whisper in her ear. "Meet me in my quarters later? I'm not sure how long I will be."

She dipped her chin almost imperceptibly without looking at him. When Vared and the others began to gather, she walked with their group to her quarters.

"Where do you want me to meet you for my statement?" she asked Devik before she went into her room.

"Vared's quarters."

"I'll be there shortly."

The door closed behind her and she quickly changed into workout clothes and packed a small overnight bag. Taking a few moments to remove her makeup and jewelry, she washed her face and stared at her reflection—pissed and ready to find out who dared to try to assassinate Traxen. **I don't know who you are yet, but I'm coming for you.**

Later, after Devik interviewed the women and they waited for word, Vared's comm chimed. His tail flicked in short bursts, and he growled when he looked at her.

"What is it?" asked Talia.

"The would-be assassin stated his instructions were to target Rachel or Traxen, whichever was easier."

"Why would anyone target Rachel?" Emmy said. Devik rubbed her thigh, and her knee slowed its bouncing. Tears ran down Lin's cheeks and Ash'n pulled her onto his lap.

"To weaken Traxen. Make him vulnerable." Rachel bit out. "It's not a secret that we've been getting closer. If something were to happen to me, it might affect Traxen's decisions."

"The fact that the order included both of you suggests sabotage of the king's rule or the proposed Earth treaties," said Devik.

"Why not target Vared or me?" Talia rubbed Vared's tail where it sat around her waist. "We're the ones negotiating the agreements."

"Traxen is a strong leader. Without him, chaos will ensue even as his successor takes over. It provides opportunities for others to press for their own agendas even more quickly," said Largon. "Similar to what's happening with the Zuvgran."

"Exactly." Rachel paced. "Everyone needs to be even more careful than they have been. Right now, it's me in the crosshairs, but these traitors have been unpredictable."

"So the purists are trying to ensure the Svesti don't mate with humans?" Natasha held Ronan's hand.

"That's the problem. We don't know what their end game is. Is it racial purity or is that an excuse for something else?

Money? Power? Revenge?" Rachel pushed a hand through her short hair. "Too much is still unknown."

"Rachel is correct." Vared's scar whitened along his cheek when his face hardened. His eyes narrowed at her. "I know you are capable, but for now, go nowhere alone. Take no chances."

"I don't like it," Rachel huffed. "But I won't take any unnecessary risks." She glanced around the room. "Traxen wanted me to meet him in his quarters. Should I call the guards or would one of you like to escort me?"

"I'll take you." Devik stood. "**Milara**, please wait here for me." Emmy nodded.

As they left the room, Devik said, "Thank you for being reasonable and not arguing about increasing security."

Rachel shrugged. "I'll agree until I don't anymore."

Devik chuckled and shook his head. His braids brushed his shoulders.

"I would expect nothing less…or more."

Chapter 19

Under normal circumstances, Traxen attempted to keep his tail under control in public, but tonight it snapped behind him as he strode to his quarters with double the usual guards. Hossix stopped him with a hand on his shoulder and a shake of his head. Traxen gritted his teeth, his fangs scraping the inside of his mouth. Previv entered first.

"Bloody hell! I could've killed you, Previv. Warn a girl next time." Rachel's welcome voice, even when angry, slowed his tail's movements.

"Lady Rachel, I apologize. I did not know you were here." Previv paused. "I will check the rest of the quarters."

"Go ahead. I already did a sweep, but I understand."

Short moments later, his guard returned unharmed.

"All clear, Sire."

"Thank you, Previv."

Traxen tugged Rachel into his arms as soon as the door closed behind him. Feeling her safe against him, he finally let his emotions calm. Tucking his nose where her neck met her shoulder, he inhaled deeply her leather, **wimma**, and **valli** scent. His tail circled to rest below her ass cheeks. She hugged him back just as fiercely.

"I missed you," he breathed against her skin. "I can't stand that you were targeted."

She drew back slightly and raised her chin. "You were targeted, too. That poison was meant for you."

"What made you realize something was wrong?"

"A different colored arm replacing a mostly full glass. We usually have the same server during the meals. I almost didn't realize in time." Her hands restlessly ran over his biceps and chest. Her fingers unfastened the magnetic catch of his shirt and opened it to press her palms on his bare skin. He groaned, and his shaft twitched.

"Did you have enough to eat before the meal ended? I can get something for you," he said in a low voice.

"I'm only hungry for you, Traxen. I want all of you. Naked." His cock hardened at her impatient words. **How can I resist?**

She fell to her knees to open his pants. She licked her lips and gazed up at him with darkened eyes.

With her hands on his thighs, she leaned forward to tongue the head of his cock. He shuddered when she traced his head nodes. She licked his pre-cum and hummed happily.

Wrestling out of his shirt, he tossed it somewhere. Although his pants were around his ankles, his boots prevented him from removing them. Her fingernails dug into his flesh as she tasted his engorged shaft with languid strokes of her pink tongue. Her left hand moved to gently roll his balls. Opening her mouth wide, she slid down on his cock as far as she could flattening her tongue along the underside. **Sweet Goddess, that feels incredible.**

Tenderly, he stroked her cheek, the sight of her pleasuring him a visual delight. Her right hand wrapped around the base of his shaft. She moved it in time with the bobs of her head.

"You look so beautiful, **belgella**, with that sassy mouth sucking my cock. I can smell your arousal growing." She widened her knees, and his tail snuck between her thighs to rub against her clit. With her clothing in the way, he increased the pressure, and she moaned around him. He slid both hands into her hair and gently held around her ears and laced his fingers around the back of her head.

"Can you take more of me?"

Her blue eyes twinkled when she tilted her head further back and slowed her movements. She opened wider and relaxed. He thrust gently into the warm wet cavern of her mouth touching the back of her throat. Watching closely for any signs of discomfort, he held her steady and thrust deeper before pulling back. Her hand on his balls remained gentle.

"The way you look submitting to me humbles me, Rachel. Faster?"

Her eyes grew hazy as he sped up, occasionally bumping the back of her throat. Her eyes watered as she took him deep. She swallowed around him, and he almost came. He pulled out of her mouth, his cock wet with her saliva.

"My turn." He reached down to lift her to her feet. Kissing her deeply, he undressed her from the waist up. He smiled when he found her knives sheathed to her side. Carefully, he removed them and set them aside. **My warrior goddess.**

Alternating between wet, openmouthed kisses and sharp, tiny nips to her flesh, he worshipped her skin along his path to her breasts. Cupping her soft, firm globes in his hands, his thumbs drew lazy circles on her skin and her pink areolas, avoiding her burgeoning nipples.

Dropping to his knees, he licked a nipple while using a hand to unfasten his boots. Opening wide, he sucked as much of her breast into his mouth as he could, using his tongue to tease the bud, and smiled at her gasp. He contorted his body to kick off his pants never losing contact with her flesh. He reduced the pressure on her skin and slowly drew back closing his lips around her nipple until it released with a pop. Pride filled him at the sight of her reddened flesh and he gave her other breast similar attention.

He pulled down her stretchy pants, and her scent deepened around him. His tail stroked her ass cheeks, and she wriggled. She toed off her shoes and lifted one leg at a time so he could remove the remainder of her clothing. He moved downward from her breast and licked and nipped his way to her cunt. Inhaling deeply, he nuzzled her between her thighs mixing their scents together. He wouldn't be surprised if his cock was hard enough to bore a hole through concrete, but he wanted to put it somewhere much softer and wetter. Giving her a kiss above her clit, he rose and lifted her into his arms.

She swayed slightly before her hands clasped behind his neck. He carried her to his bedroom and tossed her onto the bed. She bounced and laughed. He grasped her ankles firmly and pulled her to the edge of the mattress. Kneeling again, he pressed his shoulders under her thighs and lapped at her wetness with long, slow strokes. Her fingers tunneled into his hair and her nails bit at his scalp. He welcomed the small bite of pain.

Taking his time, he discovered where and what she liked best. Her gasps and moans as well as her verbal feedback were music in his ears. Suddenly her thighs squeezed his head hard and she bucked up against his mouth.

"Oh my god. Right there. Don't stop," she cried out.

Far from a stupid male, he continued licking along the bottom of her clit in side to side motions never changing his speed. He inserted one finger, then a second into her wet channel, pumping slowly. A low wail left her lips and grew louder until she screamed his name when she came against his face. His tail across her stomach, he held her down when she convulsed with pleasure. As her movements slowed, he stopped licking and pressed his tongue flat along her slit when he withdrew his fingers. He spread her wetness on his cock while enjoying her unique taste. Softly, he began tonguing around her entrance with a barely there touch.

"Oh, that's so good," she sighed between ragged breaths. "Just right."

I could stay here between her thighs forever.

"I want you inside me." She tugged on his hair.

He lifted his face and met her passion-glazed eyes, feeling her wetness on his face and beard.

"As you wish, **belgella**."

Traxen rose to his feet, tucked his hands under her knees, and lined up his cock with her entrance. Slowly, he pushed his girth into her watching her greedy cunt swallow him.

"I wish you could see this. Your gorgeous cunt sucking in my cock. So hot and tight and wet. You'll be the death of me." He bottomed out and his balls rested on her ass. Her insides squeezed his shaft, and he clenched his teeth at the intense pleasure.

"But what a way to go," she smiled lasciviously. "Come closer. I want to touch you."

He lifted her legs to lay flat along his torso and her ankles rested on his shoulders. Leaning forward with her flexible body folded almost in half beneath him, the change in angle made her moan. Her hands caressed every part of him she could reach.

"Fuck me, Traxen. Fuck me hard."

He withdrew almost all the way and slammed home again jarring both their bodies with the impact.

"Yes," she shouted. "More."

Grunting with exertion, he flexed his hips and attempted to burrow deep into her body. She lifted to meet his every thrust. Their combined aroma lay heavy in the air, their moans and groans counterpoints to the sound of their slapping flesh. Sweat beaded on her forehead and trickled down his spine. In mild shock, he felt his fangs elongate. Their bodies slickened and slid against each other.

Her cunt rippled and squeezed his cock hard when she orgasmed around him, once again screaming his name. Unable to hold back, he grunted her name from behind gritted teeth and filled her with his come. Flashes of light filled his vision as his pleasure erupted into her.

Gasping, he let her thighs drop and rested his weight on his elbows so as not to crush her. Languidly, he kissed her and nuzzled her ear.

"You were magnificent, **belgella**."

"Not so bad yourself, big guy."

Hugging her to him, he rolled over and scooted them into a more comfortable position. Hands explored and caressed in lazy motions.

"Is this what you were thinking about earlier?"

Laughing low, she said, "Actually, my thought was that I was going to have my way with you tonight even if I had to tie you down to do it."

He chuckled. "That might be interesting." He arched a brow. "But only if I can reciprocate."

"Deal." She kissed his pec. "I'm glad the assassin didn't succeed, Traxen."

"Me, too."

"Don't leave me alone in a room with him or I'll gut him."

He smiled at her fierce look.

"Understood. Stay?"

"Yes."

Traxen awoke later to her kissing and licking his chest and caressing him. Moonlight shimmered on her body as she knelt above him and rode his cock slowly, dragging out their mutual pleasure. His hips rose and fell to the pace she set while his hands squeezed and traced her soft flesh. When they came together, her head fell back, and he thought he'd never seen anything more beautiful than the taut lines of her body quivering in sensual joy. **I'm a lucky male.**

Traxen looked up when Xeliv announced his next appointment.

He stood and smiled. "Lady Ava, please come in and have a seat."

"Thank you for agreeing to see me, Your Majesty." The female seemed a little nervous as she moved to the chair in front of his desk.

"I'm curious why you requested a private audience." He sat after she settled.

She laced her fingers together in her lap. Drawing in a deep breath, she said, "What is the status of Lieutenant Wurvez? It's been over a month since his rescue, and there has been no word on how he's doing."

"He's recuperating from his ordeal."

"No, he's not." She stared at him.

"What makes you say that?"

"You are aware I spend a great deal of my time in the palace kitchens when I'm not at Phoenix House?"

"Yes. Many are enjoying your meals."

"I hear the whispers, Your Majesty. Karid is not eating; food is going bad. But he's going through alcohol at record levels. I've heard he's lost even more weight and looks sickly."

"The staff should not be gossiping," he grumbled.

"That's like asking the sun not to shine." She grinned. "It's not going to happen."

"True. What is your interest in Lieutenant Wurvez, Lady Ava?"

"We were friendly on the **Invictus**. I believe I know some of what he is experiencing and I can help."

"I doubt you know what he's going through."

Her eyes narrowed. "Did Rivezt ever show you my medical records?"

"No. As far as I know, there was no reason to."

"May we comm him now? I think it's relevant to our conversation."

Tapping his tablet, he initiated the connection with Rivezt.

"King Sovex. What can I do for you?"

"Lady Ava asked that we speak. I'm not sure why."

Lady Ave rose and moved behind him.

"Rivezt, when you treated me the first day we met, did you take scans of my body?"

Rivezt nodded. "Of course."

"Did you keep notes about your speculations on what you found?"

Cautiously, Rivezt said, "Yes. I healed what I could. I never discussed it with you since it had no bearing on any future treatment." **What are they talking about?**

"I appreciate your past and continued discretion, Rivezt. However, I need you to share those scans and notes with King Sovex. I think he needs to see them to have a better understanding of why I believe I can help Lieutenant Wurvez."

Rivezt's blue eyes widened. "Oh." His face turned hopeful. "It hadn't occurred to me, but Karid may need to hear what you have to say." He tapped some buttons. "I just sent it to King Sovex."

"Thank you, Rivezt." She smiled sadly. "Obviously, this stays between us."

"Of course, Lady Ava. Anything you can do to help Karid would be welcome. He's one of my best friends."

Traxen disconnected the comm and read the file while she returned to her chair. He clenched his teeth as he read Rivezt's report about the number of broken bones, internal fractures, and scars. **Sweet Goddess, what did she suffer through?**

"It says that these injuries would have taken place when you were a youngling."

She nodded, her own jaw hardening. "I don't wish to discuss the causes of the injuries, but if you consider where I am now versus where I was then, you should see that maybe I do have something to offer toward Karid's healing, Your Majesty."

"Call me Traxen." Traxen sighed.

"Then please call me Ava."

He leaned forward. "Karid suffered greatly while in captivity, Ava. I can't reveal what he endured. I'm not even sure he's told us everything because he won't speak to anyone. But you are correct. He isn't getting better. He refuses to meet with a mind healer and chases away all that care for him. He probably won't talk to you, and he may get violent." **What they did to his body was the work of psychopathic animals.**

"I understand that, Traxen. But I'm not so easy to chase away." She squared her shoulders. "I also don't believe Karid would ever knowingly harm me or any other female."

"What do you need from me?" **These human females are brave despite their small stature.**

"Is there an extra bedroom where he's staying?"

"Yes, he's in one of the cabins in the King's Forest."

"Then I need your permission to stay with him. Food deliveries per a list that I'll provide weekly and no more alcohol unless I order it. No visitors without my approval."

Traxen inhaled deeply, his tail swaying. "Do you think you can bring him back?" **I hope so. The male does not deserve to be alone in his pain.**

Ava shrugged. "I doubt I'll make him any worse than he is." Her face tightened. "You do realize he may never return to the way he was, right? He can't help but be different."

"Yes, I know." Quietly, he said, "I don't care if he ever returns to his warrior status. I just want him to find enjoyment in living again. Right now, he's barely existing."

She reached out and squeezed his hand. "I don't know how long it will take or how much help I will be, but I have to try."

Traxen squeezed back. "When do you want to leave?"

"As soon as we can coordinate it. I have the first grocery list ready and two bags packed in my room."

"Then let's get you an escort to take you." He stood and offered his arm. "Please update me regularly and let me know if you need anything more."

She placed her hand on his forearm. "You've got a deal, Traxen."

Chapter 20

What a week.

Rachel sat in Talia's quarters with all the other women except Ava, who convinced Traxen to let her go to Karid. The mates and Largon went to Phoenix House to check on the construction, while Traxen dealt with his kingly duties. Despite being interrogated multiple times a day, the assassin insisted he didn't know the name of the leader of the purist movement or specifics of any future plans. Everyone believed he told the truth. **The damn traitor is still one step ahead of us. It's bloody frustrating.**

"Has anyone heard from Ava?" Lounging on a couch with her feet tucked under her, Natasha sipped her wine.

Emmy shook her head, her brown curls bouncing.

"No. And Devik made me promise not to track her."

"Vared hasn't said anything. He just growls and looks like he wants to punch something whenever Karid won't answer his comms." Talia bit into a cheese cube on a green cracker. "He's worried."

"Ash'n said he thought Ava might be the only one who Karid might let help." Lin chewed on her lower lip. "He won't tell me why he believes that, though."

"Traxen seems hopeful that Ava is making progress with Karid. He said she requested some supplies to build a firepit and outdoor grill, as well as some items for Karid's sculpting hobby." Rachel swirled the wine in her glass. "He showed me a statuette Karid made for him of the former king. He's very talented."

"Karid is an artist?" Talia leaned forward. "I'll have to ask Vared if he has any of his work." She looked thoughtful. "I've never written about a character who was an artist. I wonder if Karid will let me watch him work and pick his brain when he's feeling better."

Rachel tipped her head and viewed Talia with fond amusement. **I wonder what she'll come up with if she decides to immerse herself in sculpting in order to research a character.**

 Lin frowned as she picked up a cracker.

"We're out of chocolate. When we go back to Earth, we'll have to get more."

"The stashes we brought didn't last long, did they?" Talia sighed. "We've had more than our fair share of stress eating the past few months." All the women nodded in agreement.

"Maybe I'll ask if the king will allow us to bring back cacao trees to plant on Costonia," Lin looked pensive. "Maybe some wheat and corn seeds, too."

"I miss strawberries, apples, and cherries." Natasha looked at Talia. "When does the **Invictus** head back?"

"In about a month." Talia shrugged. "I'm looking forward to seeing Joshua, Krista, and the girls. I hope they'll be ready to travel back with us."

"That would be nice." Lin smiled. "I think I'm going to try to see if my parents can meet us when we get there. I'd like to introduce Ash'n to them."

"I'll probably stay here with Ronan and Phoenix House. I'll miss you when you go." Natasha gazed into her wineglass.

"We'll be back before you know it," said Talia. "Maybe I'll bring back some sewing supplies for you."

Natasha's face lit up.

"I can give you a list of stuff I'd love to have."

"I'd be happy to get you what you want." Talia turned her attention to the former hacker. "Emmy, can you write a program for us? Something that will tell us the date and time on Earth and the Svesti equivalent. Sometimes I think my brain will break trying to do the conversions when I'm trying to set up a call with my son or sister."

"Don't forget to factor in Earth time zones," Natasha reminded. "They don't have those on Costonia."

"Sure." Emmy pursed her lips. "I might be able to combine an Earth program or two with a Svesti one to make it easier and faster to develop. Let me talk to Devik and see what might be a standard one here to start with."

"Can you make it so we can input a date/time in the future for one of the other planets?" Rachel liked the idea of the proposed program. **It would be like those clocks at work showing the time in different cities around the world.**

"Once I've got the main portion done, adding that would be easy," Emmy said.

"Thanks."

"So…Rachel. You and the king, huh?" Emmy leaned forward and smirked. "Do tell."

Natasha playfully slapped Emmy's upper arm.

"Everyone else had time to enjoy the beginning of their relationships without the rest of us in her face. Give Rachel the same courtesy." Natasha turned and winked at Rachel. "Unless, of course, you want to talk about it. Then we're all ears."

"Smooth, Natasha." Lin giggled.

"We're taking it day by day. There's just so much going on with the traitor, assassination attempt, and the Zuvgran. Our focus is divided." Rachel shrugged. "Besides I have my own trust issues I need to work through."

"Been there, done that," said Emmy with a sympathetic smile. "You guys helped me through it. Can we help you?"

Rachel smiled at the younger woman affectionately. **She's grown so much emotionally on this trip.**

"I appreciate the offer, but I know what my issue is. I think it will just take time for me to decide if Traxen is worth the effort to work through it."

"If you're waiting for the perfect time or things to quiet down, it will never happen. I had to work through my shit while infected with a virus that could kill off both our races." Talia shuddered.

"And I was kidnapped and trying to figure out how to halt the spread of a measles variant across worlds," added Natasha.

"I like the king. He treats everyone with respect." Lin's cheeks turned pink. "He looks at you the way Ash'n looks at me."

"She's right." Natasha's brown eyes sparkled. "You look at him like he's sex on a stick."

Rachel fanned herself.

"Well, he is."

"So he knows how to use what he has?" Emmy smirked.

"Oh, yeah. Absolutely no complaints in that area." The women laughed when Rachel mock leered.

"You do realize technically you're the king's consort," Talia teased.

"If you mated, you would be the queen." Emmy dramatically put a hand over her heart and bowed low, almost falling off her chair. "Your Majesty." Everyone laughed.

Rachel wrinkled her nose.

"You're making the case to run far and fast from Traxen, you know."

"You'd make a great ruler," Natasha said seriously. "You seem at home with the Court functions, and you're much smarter than most of them realize."

"And you're a badass." Lin grabbed the wine bottle and refilled her glass.

"Thanks. I think." Rachel shrugged. "I grew up on political dinners. My father is a member of Parliament.

"I didn't know that." Natasha picked up a piece of fruit and popped it into her mouth. Everyone else looked at Rachel in surprise.

"When I was a kid, I hated it. I always felt on display and couldn't just be me, especially with my mother always harping on appearances. Now, it doesn't really bother me. I wouldn't go out of my way to go to one if I had another choice, but I usually attend without wanting to punch somebody."

"Could you teach Vared that?" Talia grinned. "I've been working on it, but his default is go bloody or go home."

All the women laughed, while Rachel just rolled her eyes.

"I'm not a miracle worker."

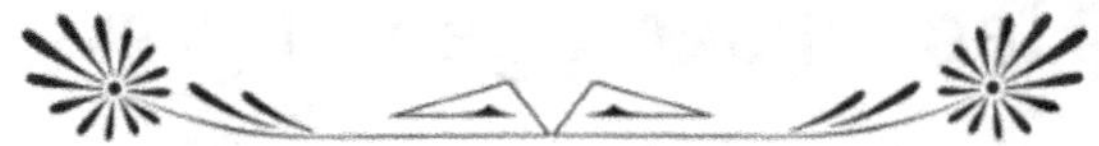

Rachel picked up her bag with overnight clothes and glanced around her quarters. **I haven't been spending much time in here lately. Every night I stay with Traxen.**

She missed spending free time with the other women. Lately, Court meals, self-defense training, or visiting and planning things for Phoenix House all took priority. It seemed like forever since they just sat, drank, and gossiped. **Hopefully, Ava will be back in the fold soon. It sounds like she's making progress with Karid. Even though we only met less than four months ago, they've become my best friends. I had a lot of acquaintances back on Earth, but true friends were a rarity with my job.**

As she left her rooms, she nodded at Yanz and Kragen. They followed her to Traxen's quarters. **I'm not pleased to have guards assigned to me. I'm used to being the one who protects. Now I understand how Traxen feels.**

After Yanz cleared Traxen's rooms, she left the males in the hall and unpacked her bag in the bedroom. After placing a short silk robe and a midnight blue thong teddy on the bed, she put the rest of her things in a drawer. **I can't believe how much of my stuff is already here.**

She toed off her sneakers and sat in an oversized chair. Tucking her feet under her, she snuggled into the luxuriously comfortable upholstery. She admired the fact that the space was not overwhelmingly masculine. **Trulet** wainscoting stained a dark purplish hue traveled halfway up the walls and topped by creamy walls with an organic design in shades of amethyst and gold surrounded the bedroom space. Hand-carved crown molding with the same design in miniature drew the eye with its intricacy. Small tables in the same wood flanked the bed on both sides as well as the chair she occupied. Bookcases lined the majority of two walls. A darker gold dotted with uneven flecks of purple made the comforter pop against the darker wood. **I really like this room.**

Turning her face into the chair, she caught a faint whiff of Traxen's oud, cherry, and almond scent. She rubbed her cheek against the fabric and mentally rolled her eyes at herself. **I'm like a bloody teenager with a crush.**

Blowing out a breath, Rachel uncurled her body. She padded to the kitchen area to get a water pouch. Then she made her way to the sanitary facility after picking up the lingerie and robe. **I think I'll take a bath while I wait for him. But no more alcohol for me right now. I overindulged a little with the girls.**

As she waited for the bathing pool to fill, she undressed, tossed her clothes in the refresher, and placed her weapons on the counter except for one dagger she hid on the ledge of the pool behind some soap. Steam rose in the air. Naked, she stepped in and sank down onto a submerged bench until the water covered her shoulders. A deep groan echoed in the room when the heat infused her muscles. Leaning her head back, she closed her eyes and let her mind drift.

This past week she split her time between training the women, helping the younglings choose their beds for Phoenix House, reading the old Svesti texts, and spending each night with Traxen. A generous and inventive lover, he also had incredible stamina and always ensured she had multiple orgasms. **He was also hung like a horse. And those nodes. I can't decide which is the best—the base node that hits my clit or the head nodes which feel great inside when he pounds me.**

The bathwater rippled as she shifted her legs. The first night she'd awoken in the dark and he wasn't there in bed with her. At the time, she didn't think too much about it, because information about the assassination attempt would have been enough for his staff to awaken him. But it also happened two other nights that she knew of. His side of the bed would be cool and there would be no sign of his presence in the quarters. But he was always there in the morning when she awoke a second time at a normal hour.

Three nights ago, she opened the door to the hall looking for him and found his guards stationed there as usual. When they looked at her quizzically, she just asked them if they had heard an unusual noise. They answered in the negative, so she simply nodded and closed the door. The whole thing told her that Traxen never left through the main door. **That means a secret entrance. He shouldn't be going off on his own, especially with someone trying to kill him. I don't know if I should ask him about it or try to follow him.**

She pondered the situation while she washed herself. **He's hiding something and I need to know what it is. After the mess with Jonathan, I don't trust myself enough to be secure in my faith that Traxen isn't hiding anything harmful.**

 Hearing a noise in the bedroom, she moved her hand onto the ledge and rested it on her dagger. Traxen's scent arrived moments before he entered, and she drew her hand away from the weapon. Peering up at him, she noted the fine lines bracketing his eyes.

"Join me?" She waved her hand at the water. His lavender eyes darkened to amethyst and his tail swayed. Watching him strip, she licked her lips as more of his sculpted flesh revealed itself to her ravenous eyes. Trim waist topped by an eight-pack of abs, toned pecs and arms, and an Adonis belt that bunched and flexed as he bent to pick up his clothes and put them in the refresher. She wanted to nip at his taut ass. Watching his enormous cock sway with his movements sent a flood of wetness to her core. **I still can't believe that monster fits inside me, but I'm so glad it does.**

The water level rose as Traxen lowered himself into the bath next to her. He turned his face, cupped her cheek, and languidly kissed her. With her head tilted back on his hard bicep, she savored the contact and reached up to untie the leather that bound his thick braid. Gently, she threaded her fingers through his hair loosening it to fall around them. Her hand drifted lower and kneaded his nape. Ending the kiss with a soft peck, he laid his forehead on hers.

"That feels wonderful, **belgella**. My day just improved significantly." His callused hands lightly rubbed her arms and down her torso. Delightful shivers tickled her body. **I love how his body temp is just a little higher than mine.**

"You need to relax." Her fingertips feathered and smoothed the stress lines on his face. She twisted and threw her leg over his lap to face him. His fingers kneaded her ass, and his tail stroked her back. His cock twitched against her stomach, its length sliding against her clit causing her to shiver. **Down, girl, this is about him, not you.**

She reached behind her and found the soap. Lathering her hands, she rubbed behind his ears and caressed the slight point atop each one with a fingertip. After she washed his nape, he tilted his head back to give her access to his neck. A quiet groan left his lips as she walked her fingers into his short beard and used her thumbs to massage his cheeks and jaw. Silently appreciating the sweep of his dark lashes as his eyes closed, she traced the length of his nose before her hands moved to his shoulders.

Alternately soaping, washing, and kneading, she lavished attention to his arms and fingers. Her hands slid in broad sweeping strokes over his pecs and abdomen. She smiled as she watched the tension leave his body a little at a time. **Good.**

She lightly propelled herself backwards from his lap and crouched as she smoothed along his thighs and calves. His toes wriggled as she washed his feet. **Hmm, is he ticklish?**

"Turn," she said huskily.

Silently, he obeyed her instruction, and she caressed his shoulders and back. Finding muscles knotted, she pressed hard in small circles. He groaned louder. When she came to his ass, she squeezed his glutes, then rubbed. **Such a fine ass.**

She paid special attention to his tail, loving the sounds of his pleasure when she squeezed its base. Suppressing her own moan, she played with the end of his appendage briefly closing her eyes when she thought of how talented his tail could be, in battle and during sex. After lathering her hands again, she plastered her breasts to his back and reached for his cock. She wriggled against him as she stroked his engorged length in a slow, firm grasp.

"Rachel, I should take care of you." He grunted when she squeezed him hard and twisted her wrist over his head nodes.

"Later, Traxen. Let me do this for you."

"Your hands are miraculous. I feel a thousand times better than when I walked in."

"If you can still talk, I'm not doing this right." She lightly bit his nape loving how his hips bucked into her hand. His low chuckle reverberated against her nipples. **Oh, shit, that feels so good.**

She yelped when he suddenly growled and spun to clasp her waist and lift her onto his lap again. Water sloshed over the edges of the pool. His tail grabbed the soap and dropped it into his waiting hand before supporting her back. His hooded eyes gazed at her while he soaped his large hands.

"Your turn, **belgella**." Her nipples beaded as his palms stroked her. A mischievous look crossed his face before he extended a claw and traced the hard buds. She shuddered at the caress. **Oh, fuck, that feels fucking amazing.**

Chapter 21

Grateful for Rachel's tender care, Traxen let the day's stressors fall away and concentrated on remaining in the moment with her. Her breasts swelled as he teased them with a claw and his fingers. Unable to help himself, he bent her backward to lick and suck on her. The contrast between her soft squeezable flesh and hard nipples always fascinated him. Her moans as he feasted on her filled his ears. **I love how vocal she is.**

Trapped between their bodies, his cock sought even greater contact with her. **Not yet. I need to make her come first.**

He thumbed her clit while inserting two fingers into her molten core. The slick heat coated him as he coaxed more from her. Moaning his name, she writhed on his lap. Her skin flushed with excitement and her head fell back. He added a finger and curled it to find that spot within that made her crazed. Water spilled around the sunken tub when he stroked that small patch. His tail gripped her shoulders to keep her from hitting her head as she frantically shook. Her channel squeezed his fingers hard enough to stop his blood flow. **Sweet Goddess, you gifted humans with the most amazing cunts in the universe. Wet, hot, and so tight. I need to be inside her.**

Drawing his fingers from her, he wrapped his arms around her and stood in the pool. He laid her on the floor at the edge of the bath and spread her thighs. Eyes hazy with desire gazed up at him.

"You look like a sea god rising from the water. So fuckin' hot." She licked her lips.

Traxen lined up his cock and teased her opening. Slowly, he pushed into her feeling her cunt quiver around his shaft. Her legs wound around him and her heels pulled him toward her.

He tightened his ass to control the speed of his thrust. She narrowed her eyes.

"You think you've got me where you want me?"

"I believe I'm exactly where **you** want me, Rachel." He chuckled darkly. His tail brushed the wet hair from her face.

"Not yet. I want you deeper and harder."

Leaning forward, he kissed her, his hair dripping around them. His fangs elongated and he moved to scrape her neck with them. Her head fell back. She shivered and her cunt clenched his cock. **She likes that.**

He pulled back, grasped her wrists, and pinned them over her head with his tail.

"You'll take what I give you, **belgella**."

"You'll give me what I take, Traxen." Her smile grew wicked when her heels kicked his ass.

He withdrew slightly, placed his hands over her shoulders, then thrust forward hard while tugging her body toward him. They both groaned when he bottomed out inside her.

"That's what I'm talking about," she said breathlessly. "More."

Relishing the feel of his head nodes dragging along her inner flesh, he began a leisurely rhythm to enhance the pleasure for both of them.

"Faster," she demanded, kicking him again.

"So impatient." He grinned as they fought an erotic battle for control of the pace. He hissed when she squeezed his cock with her cunt. "You don't play fair."

"You're just figuring that out?" she gasped. Sweat formed on her flesh and he bent over her to lick a drop falling toward her ear, the salty taste mingling with the tang of her leather, **wimma**, and **valli** scent. He smiled against her skin when she shivered. Her breasts crushed against his chest, he swiveled his hips and she moaned.

"You are a wondrous and delicious female, Rachel. I'm going to take your pleasure and multiply it until we can't walk," he growled low in her ear. His tail released her wrists. Immediately her hands moved to touch him. Her fingertips squeezed his back and her blunt claws dug in hard.

"Yes, mark me, **belgella**. I want every male to know you are mine." He picked up the pace, her slickness sucked at him, and the pool formed waves that splattered over the edge of the tub.

"Every female will know to stay away from you," she snarled. **Yes, be possessive. I love it.**

"No other female could draw my attention." She moved her hands to his chest and raked her nails down to his abdomen.

"Fuck me hard, Traxen. Make me feel it for days." She stared into his eyes.

"I can only deny you for so long." He pumped faster. His balls slapped her ass repeatedly. The humidity of the room grew heavier with their combined scents and exertions. Her hand slid between them, and his tongue licked his lips as he watched her push her pleasure higher. Her knuckles brushed against his cock sending a lick of fire to his spine. His tail snuck underneath her and pushed at her rosebud.

"Oh my god." She wriggled, and his tail slid in further. Her cunt began to ripple and squeeze his cock harder. Her hands tightened around his biceps and her body stiffened before quaking uncontrollably.

"That's it, **belgella**. Take what I give you," he growled.

"Traxen," she screamed, her back arching. **So crekkin' beautiful.**

"Milk me, Rachel. Take my seed from me." Her cunt clutched his cock even harder, and he roared as his release exploded. His movements became jerky, then slowed. Breathing heavily, he rested his forehead on hers, savoring the small, intermittent spasming around him as her orgasm tapered off and her legs fell from around his waist.

Long moments passed as they regained their breath and caressed each other.

"I think we need to rinse off again," she said.

Laughing, he grasped her ass and wound his tail under her back to lift her toward him. They sank into the water still connected.

Laying her head on his shoulder, she said, "Now you finally look relaxed."

His chest rumbled with amusement, and he hugged her closer contentedly.

"Thanks to you, sweet one."

Eventually they made it to the bed and explored each other more. After the third round, Traxen returned to the sanitary facility to wet a cloth with warm water. Tenderly, he cleaned the sticky mess of their activities from Rachel. Sleepily, she murmured her thanks. He tossed the cloth on the bedside table and wrapped himself around her with her back to his chest. She snuggled closer, and her breathing evened out. He tucked his nose into her hair and drifted off with a smile.

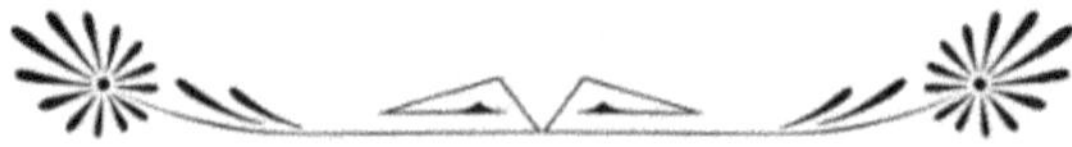

Traxen suppressed a groan when his comm silently alarmed in the middle of the night. Gingerly, he disentangled himself from Rachel's limbs and strode quietly to the sanitary facility. Taking care of his personal needs, he washed his hands and splashed water on his face before quickly tying back his hair. Reaching into the refresher, he found his cleaned clothing from earlier and dressed. Once back in the bedroom, he put on some soft-soled shoes and checked on Rachel, barely refraining from brushing her hair from her face. **She's still sleeping. Good.**

Noiselessly, he moved to one of the bookcases and pressed the control to open the hidden passageway. Traveling the dimly lit, narrow corridor, he unlocked and locked doors behind him before reaching the main tunnel taking him to his destination. Once, he thought he heard something behind him, but when he looked, he did not see or scent anything unusual. **All I can smell is Rachel's scent on me.**

At the center of the tunnel, another door requiring his DNA awaited him. He gained access and found his Spymaster arrived ahead of him. **I'll be glad when we can go back to a normal schedule of meetings during the day. I hate leaving Rachel alone in my quarters. What if she wakes up and I'm not there?**

"What do you have for me?" Traxen took a seat in a comfortable chair, shaking his head when his Spymaster offered him a drink.

"The assassin is a true believer. No credit transfers to follow."

"Of course not. Why should it be easy for us?" Traxen grumbled.

They chatted for several minutes discussing various leads and theories. Traxen rose to get a water pouch. **I'll have to remember to restock the cooling unit. Probably need more liquor, too.**

"You should consider another Court function. One to show you're unafraid and two, the traitors may try something again."

"I dislike the idea of knowingly putting the females in danger." Traxen's tail flicked.

"They don't have to attend."

"You think Rachel would stay safe in quarters if I asked?"

"You are the king. You could order her to stay in her rooms." The male smirked.

Traxen snorted. "You aren't a very good judge of character if you think she'd listen to me."

They both stiffened and drew weapons when they heard a noise.

"What do you mean we can't get to any of them?" The Svesti noble growled, and his tail smacked the floor.

"Enhanced security, sir. It's too difficult to insert one of our people inside the palace."

"We have people already inside, don't we?" The older male drummed his extended claws on his desk.

"Yes, but if they act, we will lose our advantage for intel." The guard stood impassively. **Crekkin' male is correct.**

"Find a way." **Maybe that nephew of mine can make himself useful for a change.**

After the guard left, the noble's temper exploded and his mind churned with black and red chaotic images. When he became aware again, his chest heaved as he looked at the room's state of disarray caused by his rampage. Furniture destroyed, fabric ripped, loose items thrown and broken littered the space. He squeezed his head and tried to slow his breathing. **Crek. This is the worst yet.**

"What?" he roared when there was a knock at the door.

"The healer is here."

"I didn't call for a healer."

"I took the liberty, sir." The guard opened the door and scanned the room, expressionless.

The healer, a male older than the noble, followed the guard into room, his eyes widening when he saw the destruction.

"It appears you are building an immunity to the current treatment, sir. I will change the medication."

"Maybe it's time to discontinue altogether," the noble growled.

"That would be inadvisable. Episodes like this would increase and worsen."

The healer injected him. The noble felt the sharp edges in his mind smooth out. **Yes, I can think again.**

"I want you to wear a monitor so I can track your medical stats. I may have to adjust the frequency or amount of the dosage."

"That's fine."

"Sir, may I suggest you relocate to another location so you will not be disturbed while this room is…redecorated?" the guard said.

"Excellent idea. Sir, when we reach the new room, I would like to administer a sleep aid to hasten your recovery."

The noble stood and straightened his clothing.

"That is acceptable."

Once the trio reached the new quarters, the noble changed into his sleep pants and gave permission for the sleep aid. He noted the healer leaving and the world receded as the med took hold. He never saw the guard approach and switch out an upload in his implant. Nor did he hear the guard comm someone saying, "It's done. Transfer my credits." He definitely didn't recognize the change in the repeating subliminal audio changing from "You will be king" to "Take action soon."

Chapter 22

The sheets rustled over Rachel's bare skin as Traxen slipped from the bed. Peering through her lashes, she watched him pad to the bathroom and waited to see if he was returning to bed or going off on one of his mysterious nighttime escapades. When she saw him exit dressed, she knew. Regulating her breaths to feign sleep, she kept her muscles loose when he approached the bed. The heat from his hand emanated near her scalp briefly before it moved away without him touching her.

She observed his actions closely and saw how he opened a space behind a bookcase. As soon as the bookcase closed, she sprang out of bed and dressed hurriedly. Strapping on her daggers as she walked, she searched with her fingers for the control for the hidden doorway. **Yes.**

Moving stealthily, she only traversed about twenty feet on a downward slope before she faced a metal door. She unlocked it and continued before finding herself in front of another door with three locks. **Damn. One of these looks to be coded to DNA.**

She rushed back to the bedroom casting her gaze about for something with Traxen's DNA that might work. When she saw the cloth on the nightstand, she grinned wickedly. Stuffing the cloth in her waistband, she rushed back and took care of the first two locks before lifting the cloth to the scanner. A barely audible click met her ears and she mentally fist pumped. Then she frowned when she entered a larger, dimly lit tunnel. **Which way? Right or left?**

She closed her eyes and attempted to visualize when she was in relation to the palace layout. **Left goes outside the palace, while right stays underneath.**

She hesitated briefly, then turned right. Her gut told her he wouldn't leave the palace without someone knowing his movements. **I hope I'm correct, or I'm going to have to backtrack again.**

As she came to other doors spaced at intervals, she opened each and checked them out. Most were empty or held what appeared to be antiques. Eventually she found one with a DNA lock. **Duh, Rachel. You could've saved yourself some time if you'd considered he'd be going somewhere safe.**

Tugging the cloth from her waistband, she straightened her shoulders before unlocking the door and pushing the fabric back into its hiding place. **He's probably going to be pissed.**

Rachel stood motionless so the tips of the two daggers pointed at her didn't graze her.

"**Crek**, Rachel. We could've hurt you." Traxen lowered his dagger and stepped back. "You may as well come in."

The older male took a pace back, still holding his dagger at the ready. **He's the servant I've been noticing.**

She squinted and tilted her head.

"Ari Zunnax?"

The male lowered his weapon and tucked it away.

"The eye color is different and no scar, but you are Zunnax," she insisted. The male glanced at Traxen who sighed.

"Rachel, I'd like you to meet my Spymaster, who goes by many names. Ari Zunnax is one of them." Traxen's tail swayed, and he tugged her toward him. Once his arm and tail circled her waist and ankle respectively, he continued, "How did you bypass the locks?"

She lifted her shirt to show the dirty cloth. Inhaling, the Spymaster choked back a laugh when he realized what it was and Traxen just shook his head.

"Creative. She definitely uses whatever is at hand," the older male said with a twinkle in his brown eyes. "I like her."

"I'm so glad for you," Traxen drawled.

Rachel grinned and stroked his arm.

"So this is where you run off to in the middle of the night."

"I didn't realize you were aware of my leaving."

"I'm a spy, Traxen. I notice lots of things."

The Spymaster poured himself another drink. He gestured to Rachel, and she nodded. He handed her a glass and she drank.

"Mmm. Estalan liquor. I've already developed a fondness for it." She licked her lips and Traxen's chest rumbled. He sat back in his chair, pulling her to land sideways on his lap. "So what did I interrupt?"

"Brazen female." Traxen's hand stroked her back. He took her glass and sipped before handing it back to her.

"We should ask her what she thinks." The Spymaster tilted his head to the side.

"Ask me what?" Rachel wrinkled her nose when she heard the suggestion. "I'm not keen on exposing you so soon after an assassination attempt. However, it might open up an opportunity to gather more clues." She sighed heavily. "And it's normal on Earth to show terrorists they can't intimidate leadership."

"If I do this, I would request the human females do not attend." Traxen's tail circled her ankle.

"All except me, correct?" She tipped her glass at him.

"I prefer you not be exposed to more danger." His jaw flexed.

The Spymaster's eyes bounced between the two of them. The corners of his lips turned up slightly. Rachel pinned him with a glare.

"You're enjoying this, aren't you?"

"It's not often someone stands up to the king," the male said, brown eyes twinkling.

"**Belgella**..." Traxen's voice trailed off when she turned her glare on him.

"Traxen, if you go, I go."

His lavender eyes darkened, then he exhaled heavily.

"I don't like it, but I'll allow it."

"You say that like you have a choice." She kissed him on the cheek. His soft beard tickled her chin. "Is there more you need to discuss tonight, or can we head back and get some sleep?"

Traxen looked at the older male who shrugged.

"Our contacts for Rumaska are still waiting approval to land on the planet, Sire."

"Then we're done for now." They all stood and Traxen leaned to whisper in her ear. "I'm not sure sleeping is what we'll be doing."

She winked at him. "I hope not."

The next day, Rachel left the guards' training area with Yanz and Kragen following. She stretched and flashed them a grin.

"Hope you brought your running shoes, boys. I'm in the mood for some cardio." She took off at a steady pace along the pink path that circled the shooting ranges. She heard the guards behind her. White puffy clouds in the periwinkle sky crossed the sun briefly as they passed the tree line. The aroma of growing plants surrounded her as the forest enclosed them in its midst. **I love this planet. No smog. No**

traffic noises. Just fresh, clean air and nature prominent—not tech.

Deep on the forest path fifteen minutes later, she heard two thuds behind her. She turned to see Yanz and Kragen on the ground. Scanning the area, she ducked low and rushed back to them. She felt a sting on her shoulder and numbness overtook her body. She fell forward onto Kragen's chest and her arm scraped a root drawing blood. **Bloody hell. I can't move. Hope I didn't break Kragen. At least he's breathing.**

Scuffling noises approached from multiple angles. A familiar voice said, "Hide the guards and put the human on the maglev. I'll crate her."

"Do we kill them?"

"No, **naroon**, not if we don't want every Royal Guard out for our blood. It's not time yet."

Hands lifted her none too gently onto a maglev. A face from the **Invictus** grew larger in her vision. **Lerix Sproid. Creepy bastard.**

"I know you usually have weapons on you, female. Where are they?" **I'm glad I can't feel his paws on me.**

He searched and found the daggers Traxen bought her strapped to her waist, but missed the small icepick she placed in a hidden horizontal pocket on her sneaker. "Oh, good. These look recognizable. It should distract Sovex when you disappear." Taking her knives, he put them into two empty sheaths on his chest. He tapped his comm and whispered urgently.

"Rovex. I saw some males take one of the human females. I'm following them now. Can you meet me and help recover them?"

"Where are you? I'll comm the Royal Guards to help."

"No. If we retrieve her without their help, the Commander will have to reconsider our transfer to security."

"I don't like this, Lerix. We should call for assistance." **Good for Rovex. He's learned caution.**

"We'll have better chances to meet females if we're on the security teams, Klero. A future." Sproid grimaced at her as he talked on the comm.

Rovex reluctantly agreed, and Sproid told him to meet him near the edge of the forest closest to the north side of the palace grounds. After Sproid disconnected from the comm, he laid out narrow rods around Rachel. He pressed a button and they expanded to create a cage around her. **If I weren't stuck in here, I'd think that was interesting tech. I wonder if it has a force field, too.**

Rachel couldn't believe a weasel like Sproid got the drop on her and her guards. Out of the corner of her eye, she saw the drag marks where the other males hauled Yanz and Kragen off the path. **I hope they're all right. They're going

to be as pissed as I am. Damn, how long will it be before I can move again?

Sproid pushed the maglev through the trees and met his conspirators at the edge of the forest. She heard them murmur low, then Rovex burst into the tree line. His brows drew together when he saw Sproid talking with two males and Rachel in a cage.

"What in the Goddess' name is going on here?"

"We saved her, Klero. The males who kidnapped her ran off. We're just not sure how to release her," Sproid lied. **No, Rovex, don't trust him.**

Rovex moved closer and peered into the cage.

"Don't worry, Lady Rachel, we'll get you out of there." She tried to signal him with her eyes about the betrayal.

When Rovex turned around, Sproid stabbed him near his heart with one of Rachel's daggers. Rovex toppled to the ground onto his back, bumping the maglev.

"Why?" he mumbled.

"I've always hated you, Klero Rovex, and I need someone for the king to blame for the human's disappearance. Killing you with her weapon should keep the suspicion from me." Sproid looked at the other males. "Cover her up and take her to the flitter. Sell her at Gladdeus as a pit prize. I'm sure the fighters will appreciate her." He glowered at her. "You think you're special, but when those animals are finished with you, you'll realize you are nothing. You're worth nothing more than that hole between your legs, and it's not good enough for the Svesti race."

"Can we take our satisfaction from her before we sell her? Most brothels won't take our money," one of the males asked hopefully. **The Svesti have incels, too? Just my bloody luck.**

Sproid grimaced.

"Give her doses every six hours. Do what you want but leave no marks on her. The money you receive when you sell goes to the cause, not your pockets." Addressing Rachel, he said, "If you're fortunate, the paralytic won't wear off before you're used up. It shouldn't take long." **When I get free, I'm coming back for you, and I will gut you like a fish, Sproid. I'm going to take my time ensuring you suffer, you fuckin' cocksucker.**

"Always Svesti." The males intoned before tossing a tarp over her cage and carting her away.

Rachel listened intently and kept trying to move parts of her body. Her fingers twitched. **Yes. Maybe I can get enough feeling back to take them down before my next dose.**

Her mind raced while cataloging everything she heard, even the misogynist drivel from her captors' mouths. **Traxen is going to flip out when he realizes I've been kidnapped. I hope he doesn't do anything stupid. How did we miss Sproid as a suspect?**

Chapter 23

When Traxen answered his comm, Lorriv Hossix's set face and angry eyes practically burned a hole in the hologram.

"Sire, Lady Rachel has been kidnapped."

"What happened?" Traxen's tail flicked in short bursts and adrenaline shot through his veins. He stood abruptly. "Where are you? I'm coming to you."

"I'm on my way to Yanz and Kragen. While on a run with Lady Rachel, they were drugged and can barely move. They're near one of the forest paths."

"Which one?"

Hearing the location, Traxen burst from his office and shouted, "To the lower garage." Previv and Bavin Hossix raced after him.

Once there, they each grabbed a hover bike and sped toward where Rachel was last seen. They arrived before any other guards to Rovex bleeding out on the ground. **I recognize that knife. I'll kill the male myself.**

"Where is she?" Traxen wrapped his hand around the wounded male's throat.

"Sproid. Traitor. Taking to Gladdeus. Pit prize. Save Lady Rachel." Rovex coughed up blood and his erratic breaths gurgled. Traxen loosened his grip.

"Did she do this?"

"No. Caged. Sproid comm'd." Cough. "Said save female." Gurgle. Cough. "Arrived. He stabbed." Rovex tried to spit through his choppy words, pain glazing his irate eyes. "Lady my friend."

Previv said, "Healers are on the way, Sire."

Traxen glanced up to see other guards running toward them.

"Make sure he receives the best care and is interviewed as soon as practical. Stop all traffic attempting to leave Costonia. Make it sound like a tech problem on our end." He pointed at two other guards. "You're with us. We're going after her."

The other guards hopped on the hover bikes behind Previv and Hossix. Traxen led the way to the closest parking structure. Before they reached it, they came aside two males pushing a maglev with a covered crate. The shock in their eyes as they saw Traxen caused him to spin back toward them, kicking up dirt and stone. Stopping in front of them, he dismounted and grabbed one by the throat while striking the other in the neck with his tail.

The other guards pulled up next to him and took the gasping males into custody, restraining them. Traxen ripped the tarp off the maglev and roared when he saw Rachel immobile. **They put her in a crekkin' cage.**

Her eyes met his, and his thundering heart calmed as he realized she was conscious and aware.

"Let's get you out of there."

"Traxen." Her mouth strained to form his name.

"Save your strength, **belgella**. You can tell me all about it once the healers check you over." Previv's hand appeared in front of him with the controller for the cage. Traxen pressed the button and the metal contracted to several small rods.

As Previv gathered them, he said, "A medical flitter is en route, Sire."

"Thank you, Previv." Traxen laid gentle hands on Rachel's arms. "Are you hurt anywhere? Any pain?"

She blinked once.

"One is no?"

She blinked twice. Then her lip twitched on one side.

"I just realized that I could still misunderstand you. One is no, and two is yes."

She blinked twice.

"Oh, thank the Goddess." He lifted her into his arms, cradling her to his chest. Burying his nose in her short, silky hair, he spoke low. "They're fortunate I haven't killed them, **belgella**, for taking you." The weight of her soothed him and his tail slowed its furious movement. **Thank you, Goddess, for allowing me to reach her before she was seriously harmed.**

Whispery words barely moved his hair. "Help Rovex."

He drew back to look into her eyes.

"We found him. He's being treated now. I won't lie. He was in a bad way."

Her blue eyes saddened, and her head shook slightly.

"They'll do everything they can for him."

"Sproid. Traitor."

"We know. Now stop straining yourself." His chest rumbled at the glare she gave him. "I will have to rethink how many guards you have."

She squeezed her eyes together once. Hard.

"You don't like that."

Blink.

His shaky fingers stroked her hair and his tail rubbed against her ankle.

"I might win an argument with you like this," he teased.

Blink.

"How can you make me laugh when you can't speak or move?"

He hugged her closer as a flitter landed near them. Healers rushed over and attempted to take her from his arms.

"Cease. I'll carry her." He strode toward the flitter. Hossix and Previv followed him.

"The other guards will return the hover bikes. They'll set up one to auto follow," Hossix said.

"Thank you. Let's ensure Lady Rachel suffers no ill effects from whatever they gave her."

"Of course, Sire."

Traxen carried Rachel out of the palace med bay.

"I can walk."

"The healers said you need to take it easy for a few days. Just because they administered an antidote to the paralytic does not mean your body is healed completely." His tail rubbed her thigh.

"I feel foolish being carried in the palace," she grumbled.

"You are not weak, **belgella**. No one sees you that way." He kissed her forehead.

"The traitors do. I still can't believe they were able to take down all three of us."

From behind them, Hossix said, "All of you were attacked from behind, Lady Rachel. None of you could see the dishonorable males."

"That really doesn't make me feel better, Hossix. I'm glad I saw Yanz and Kragen in the med bay and that they're doing well." She pinched Traxen's forearm. "No one's carrying them place to place."

Traxen heard his guards snort at her comment.

"If they need assistance, the healers will use hover lift chairs."

"This is embarrassing." She crossed her arms, and he grinned down at her.

"You are grumpy when you don't get your way."

"Don't you forget it, Sire." She stuck her tongue out at him. He bent to press his mouth to hers. Pleased to better occupy her mouth, he nonetheless kept one eye open to watch where he walked. **She may be in a bad mood, but she's not rejecting my affection. I'm relieved she will be fine.**

In his bedroom, he sat in his favorite chair holding her in his lap. Alone with her and safe, he tenderly stroked every part of her he could easily reach.

She rested her head on his chest.

"I know I gave you a hard time, Traxen, and I'm sorry. I'm glad you found me before we left Costonia."

A contented growl rumbled in his chest. **She's safe and warm in my embrace. All is well.**

"Can you tell me what you remember?" he asked quietly.

As she relayed all that happened, especially what the males said, his ire rose, and he concentrated on keeping his claws from extending, his tail from flicking, and his throat from roaring.

"I'm sorry you went through all of it, **belgella**."

"I'm fine, Traxen. More angry than anything. You found me before the worst occurred." Her fingertips traced his jaw and rubbed his beard. "Although, I will admit I fantasized on how I was going to pay back Sproid when I freed myself."

"I expect nothing less from you. Perhaps a bath and we can share our favorite ways to torture the male?" He raised an eyebrow.

"I like that idea. You might have better ideas than me." She yelped when he stood. "I can still walk."

He held her close and touched their foreheads together.

"Please let me pamper you, Rachel. I need to. This incident scared me more than the others because I wasn't with you. I had no way to protect you."

Traxen met her searching gaze knowing she would see his residual fear and his overwhelming relief at her safety.

"It's still early in the day. Don't you have appointments?"

"I comm'd Xeliv earlier and instructed him to reschedule everything for the rest of the day." **I wouldn't be able to focus on work at all.**

"Let the pampering commence." She waved her hand in an exaggerated, but graceful, motion and laughed huskily.

"You may be joking, **belgella**, but I have every intention of treating you as royalty."

She returned his kiss and murmured, "I like the way you think."

Traxen immediately answered his comm when he saw the caller's name.

"Karid. It's good to see you. How are you?" Traxen perused the male's face. **He looks healthy and sober.**

"I'm doing much better. I still have some more healing to do, but I feel better overall."

"That's wonderful news. We've been concerned about you."

"I know. I have a request."

"Name it, my friend."

"I would like to invite you, Vared, Devik, and Ash'n to a late evening meal here at the cabin sometime in the next couple days, if possible. I think I might be ready to talk, but I don't think I can tell the story multiple times just yet."

Traxen sat back and steepled his fingers.

"Did Ava give her approval?"

When Karid questioned him, Traxen explained Ava's conditions. Unfortunately, Traxen was unavailable that evening, but he would coordinate with the others. They would let Karid know what night they could be together. He then comm'd his cousin.

"Vared. Good news. Karid is asking to see us, along with Devik and Ash'n. He suggested an evening meal in the next several days. I can't do tonight, but whatever else works for the three of you, I will do."

Lavender eyes so much like his own lit up with happiness.

"Truth, Traxen? He really wants to see us?"

He smiled. "Yes, he says he might be ready to talk about what happened."

"I'll find out what night is good and let you know."

"Thanks."

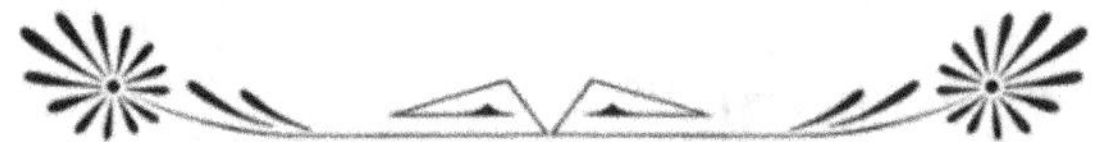

Two evenings later, Traxen leaned back in his chair, stuffed full of the wonderful meal Ava served them. She inquired about the progress at Phoenix House. When Devik told her it was close to completion, her face lit up and she made him promise to take the cookies she had baked back for the younglings.

Vared shared how his father accepted Ronan and Largon into the family and House after a recent visit to the Durek estate. All present agreed that Karid would like both males when he met them.

Ash'n said his grandmother wanted to throw a party in celebration of his and Lin's fated mate bond, but Lin asked her to wait until Karid and Ava could attend. Ava seemed touched by Lin's request.

"Why don't you males go start a fire in the pit while I clean up," said Ava. They stood and went outside. "Karid, hold on, I've got something for you to bring out."

The cool evening air filled Traxen's lungs as he watched Ash'n gather some firewood and kindling from a pile. He handed it to Vared who began arranging it in the firepit.

"He looks and sounds good," said Vared.

"Much better than he was," Traxen agreed as he took a seat.

"I hope tonight doesn't set him back." Ash'n sighed with worry.

"I've missed him," Devik said quietly.

Karid joined them with two bottles of Estalan liquor.

"Is Ava joining us?" asked Ash'n.

"No, just us."

Vared lit the kindling.

"Traxen said you built this."

"Yes. Also the grill." Karid handed the bottles to Devik as he sat in the chair next to him.

"You did a good job. They look solid." The growing fire cast an orange glow and flickering shadows on everyone's faces. Vared rose and took his seat.

"Glasses or straight from the bottle?" Devik asked.

"I never want to drink straight from a bottle again." Karid shuddered.

Traxen hid his grimace. **I'm surprised you didn't poison yourself with how much you were drinking.**

"Glasses, it is." Devik poured and handed out the drinks.

"I like this. It's relaxing to sit out by a fire," said Traxen. Everyone nodded.

Ash'n took a sip, then asked quietly, "Do you need more time?"

Karid shook his head before he stared into the flames. Initially, Traxen felt as if he were receiving an after-action report, except Karid refused to look at them. When Karid began relaying the torture he'd endured at the hands of the Zuvgran, the depravity of it all shocked him. Listening to Karid's words about his captivity, his time alone before Ava moved into the cabin, and his distress clutched at Traxen's heart, and his jaw tightened. Traxen wrapped his tail around the leg of his chair when it wanted to flick in anger. **It's unfathomable to me that he's endured so much and is still standing. Karid truly is a male to respect.**

After Karid stopped talking, the male closed his eyes. The silence remained unbroken except for the fire crackling, Karid's harsh breaths, and the usual forest noises. **The air is heavy with emotion. I need to lighten the mood a little. That's usually Karid's function.**

"So you're the one I need to bill for repairs to the walls. Good to know," Traxen said. The other males chuckled.

Karid still wouldn't open his eyes. Vared jerked his head at all of them and knelt before Karid. Traxen joined Devik and Ash'n to complete a half-circle around the brave, but hurting, male.

"Look at us, Karid," Vared said.

Vared clasped the back of Karid's neck, rested their foreheads together, and told Karid, in his unique way, that they would always be there for him. Vared released him with a clap to the shoulder and Devik took his place.

"You survived something horrific. I'm beyond grateful to the Goddess you are choosing to live again." Devik's deep voice cracked. He gave Karid a bone-crushing hug. "We've missed you."

Ash'n spoke words of understanding, but he also informed Karid how hurt they were he refused their aid for so long. When the healer also spoke words of forgiveness, Karid broke down. Traxen waited until Karid composed himself before he rested his forehead against Karid's.

"I know I haven't shared the same depth of friendship with you as the others. As your friend, fellow warrior, and your king, I have to tell you how proud I am of you. You are an honorable warrior. You stumbled and fell into a deep dark existence because you temporarily forgot to lean on your brothers. The measure of a male's character is who he becomes after a heartbreaking, soul-crushing experience. You could have given up, but you didn't."

Karid whispered, "If Ava hadn't shown up, I might have never crawled out of the despair and shame."

"We know. She has a special place in our hearts for reminding you of who you really are and returning you to us," said Ash'n.

Everyone went back to their chairs and Karid shared that he wished to ask Ava to true mate, but his concerns about what had been done to him still held him back. Each of them encouraged him to move beyond his fears and trust that Ava would remain honest with him. **I hope we convinced Karid. She's a miracle worker, and he deserves happiness.**

They spoke a bit about Karid's father's unauthorized visit recently and Ava's reaction. Then Traxen remembered something from Karid's retelling of the mission.

"You said you ordered Jevax back to the ship. Why?"

Karid frowned. "Didn't he tell you?"

His friends glanced at each other.

"What do I not know?" Karid said.

"Jevax is still missing. We found the debris from the *Tenacity* in the asteroid field, but no evidence of biological matter. We were hoping you knew what happened."

Karid fell back in his chair, stunned.

"**Crekkin'** Zuvgran was telling the truth when he said they'd destroyed a ship." He sucked in a breath. "I ordered Jevax to get word to either of you…" He nodded at Vared and Traxen. "About the Svesti noble who met with the Zuvgran, then return for me."

Traxen and the others leaned forward eagerly.

"You know who the noble is?" Traxen said.

"Pluvi Frulix." They all growled when Karid said the name. Tails flicked and snapped. **My Spymaster needs to know this, and we must focus our efforts on Frulix.**

"He's the one who clawed my jaw. He said he was going to be king."

"Over my dead body," Traxen bit out. **Just give me proof that he was behind the poisoning or Rachel's kidnapping, and he'll rot forever on a prison planet—if Rachel doesn't kill him first.**

"I think that's probably his plan," Karid said with a straight face.

There was a moment of shocked silence before they all laughed.

Devik said, "It's good to have you back, you **naroon**."

Karid grinned. Then his face fell.

"Are we still scanning for Jevax's tracker?"

Everyone nodded.

 "He's a dedicated warrior," Karid said. "If he's alive, he'll be trying to complete the mission." He paused. "Did you ever receive our transmissions about the labs? There were solar flares in the Lestanus system, and we didn't know if they went through."

"No."

"I'll try to recall everything and send it to you tomorrow. The coordinates may not be entirely correct." .

"We'll expect it."

They sat quietly enjoying the fire and being together, the shock of Karid's revelations and the intense emotions settling. **I miss this camaraderie—much more than I realized.**

"Sire, there's an emergency." Traxen looked up at Xeliv's words.

"What is it?"

"The kitchen delivery males just reported there is evidence of struggle at the cabin where Lieutenant Wurvez and Lady Ava are residing. Neither is there."

"Get Vared now."

"Yes, Sire." Xeliv tapped his comm.

Things moved quickly after Vared answered. Vared brought Devik into the conversation and Devik began searching for Ava's tracker. Vared arranged a search party to go after their missing friends.

Traxen couldn't concentrate on his work while he awaited word. They found the pair unconscious in a crashed transport with three dead Svesti. Traxen ordered them to the palace med bay, but it was still hours before they arrived. Traxen watched as the healers treated Karid and Ava. Vared and Devik waited with him.

Ava woke first and panicked until Ash'n and Natasha reassured her that Karid was fine and unconscious in a med bed next to her. **Karid, my friend, you definitely need to ask her to true mate. Her love for you is obvious.**

"Can I get something for this headache?" Ava asked.

Ash'n injected her with something, and when she was ready, she told them what had happened. Tails flicked and growls rumbled in the air, his among them.

"There were three of them. I know Karid killed one when he took the ship. The last I knew, the other two were only unconscious," she said.

Devik spoke for the first time. "None of them survived the crash."

"Do you know where they were taking you or why?" Vared asked.

"No. But they wanted Karid. One of them said they thought he was supposed to be alone and drunk. I was a complication. I think the plan was to use me to coerce Karid in some fashion."

"Is there anything else? If not, I'd like to give her something stronger for the pain so she can rest comfortably," said Natasha.

"Ava, I apologize that this happened while you were under our protection," Traxen said. **Goddess, haven't they been through enough?**

She waved a hand half-heartedly. "Not your fault, Traxen." She looked at Ash'n. "How bad are Karid's injuries? How long before he'll wake up?"

"He had some broken bones and deep lacerations, but he'll be fine in a day or so. Like you, he needs some uninterrupted healing rest."

Traxen smiled to himself when she insisted the healers move her closer to Karid and she rested her hand next to his before falling asleep. **Would Rachel be as adamant to be near me as Ava if we were in a similar situation? I believe so. I would.**

"Investigate and report to me," Traxen ordered Vared and Devik. "Coordinate with Hossix for any resources you need." He lowered his voice. "See if this traces back to Frulix. First Rachel, now Karid. I've had enough."

"As you will, Sire." Both males thumped their chests and left the med bay. **I'm glad I have people I can trust. Now, time to update my Spymaster and Rachel.**

Chapter 24

Nine days since Sproid attempted to kidnap Rachel. Six since he was caught hiding and imprisoned while further the investigation continued. Three days ago, Karid told Traxen that Pluvi Frulix gave him to the Zuvgran to torture. Yesterday, she discovered the Frulix/Sproid link to the Trahiz family in the genealogies. **So simple, yet so complicated.**

Rachel's trust in Traxen and herself had only grown since the day of her attack. His pampering included washing the scent and touch of the males from her body, alternating between tender care to growly protectiveness—all of which soothed her. Then he massaged her head to toe with those huge, callused hands of his until her body became relaxed and pliant. By the time he made love to her, she couldn't count the number of orgasms she received.

She and the Spymaster advocated for another Court function to which Traxen eventually agreed. Reluctantly, he stopped arguing with them about her attendance. Four days ago, that evening meal went off without a hitch before they knew about Frulix.

Then there was the incident in his office a few days ago. Interrupted by an urgent comm from the Spymaster, they ceased their kissing and heavy petting. She squatted to pick up items that had fallen from his desk during their passion. He answered the comm about new information about the acting Zuvgran emperor, Commander d'Urfan. Feeling naughty, she knelt and squeezed herself between Traxen's legs under the desk. Her fingers made quick work releasing the magnetic fastening of his pants. Her hands snuck inside the fabric to pull out his cock. She licked, sucked, and thoroughly enjoyed trying to ruin his composure during the comm. Then she darted away, giggling, when the comm ended. Later in his quarters, he paid her back in the most delicious ways.

They spent every night together and grew closer, sharing stories from their childhoods and more recently. She found herself planning for her time with Traxen. Whether she arranged special food delivered to him or a meal while he worked, prepared a seduction, or remembered something interesting to share with him from the books she perused, he occupied her thoughts more and more. She grew impatient at times, wanting to smell his unique scent or feel his warmth next to her. Always independent and capable, her comfort at routinely sitting on Traxen's thighs surprised her with how she associated the position with her femininity and his care.

Rachel began seriously considering what she could do full-time on Costonia. Spying like she did on Earth wouldn't work—she was too recognizable, both as a human and a woman. **Maybe something in security for the humans that emigrate later or helping Largon and Ronan with their efforts to free other hybrids might be a good fit.**

Of course, now he has to go and piss me off.

She overheard Kragen and Previv talking about a mission taking place soon to investigate the location where the traitors planned to take Karid and Ava. She wanted in on any operation that could lead to apprehending anyone involved with the kidnapping of her friends. However, Traxen never mentioned it to her. **Damn male probably thinks he's shielding me. He's going to need protection if I don't go on this mission.**

Rachel's guards blinked when she left her quarters dressed in black with daggers strapped to her thighs.

"Armory. Now," she grunted. Yanz and Kragen shrugged and followed her.

Light-footed, they approached the last corner before the armory. Voices became louder as they drew closer. She heard the four friends—Vared, Devik, Ash'n, and Karid, as well as Tesix and Westov.

"It's best you don't go, Sire." **That definitely sounds like Xeliv.**

"I should be gearing up with them." **So should I, Traxen. I don't like the double standard.**

"I know you want blood, Cousin, but your place is here." Vared clapped Traxen on the shoulder just as Rachel rounded the corner.

"I'm going." Everyone turned to her.

"You are not," Traxen said.

"I am tired of these traitors messing with us. I have a right to go."

"Female, cease this nonsense." Traxen's tail slapped the floor.

Rachel narrowed her blue eyes and glared at her lover.

"I think she should go," Karid said quietly. Everyone turned to him. "She's correct, she has a right to go, but more importantly Rachel is a warrior that those that don't know her would underestimate. I've sparred with her many times and I can attest to her skills." A steady, unhappy rumble emanated from Traxen's chest.

Karid looked at Rachel. "You do realize we do not expect to find anyone at the location? They must know by now their warriors are not arriving and have gone to ground."

Rachel nodded. "I understand. No offense meant, but I have different training than all of you, and I might see something you miss."

"None taken," Devik said as he glanced at Traxen. "My experience is the human females are well aware of their own capabilities. If she believes she will be an asset, I am prone to believe her."

"I forbid it." **Oh, no, you did not just say that.**

Rachel stalked up to Traxen and poked his chest with a single finger. "Never try to tell me what to do, Your Majesty."

"Rachel, if you go, you must promise to follow my orders," Vared said. **Oh, I didn't expect his support.**

"So long as those orders don't include me babysitting the shuttle, I'm fine with that."

"Does anyone on the team believe Lady Rachel will hinder our efforts or put any of us in peril?"

All the males shook their heads.

"I don't like it," Traxen said. His lavender eyes darkened to amethyst.

Rachel started to speak, but hesitated when Vared shook his head at her.

"My hand-picked warriors, Traxen, feel confident in Rachel's skills. I am also certain that my team will not put anyone in unnecessary danger, especially a female. Rachel will follow orders that will not include babysitting the shuttle. She goes." Vared dipped his chin at her as he uttered his last statements.

"Watching the shuttle is my job," said Tesix with little expression, but his eyes twinkled.

Traxen stared at his cousin before nodding curtly. "Very well. I'll hold you responsible, Commander."

"Everyone finish gearing up. We leave in ten minutes," Vared told the group.

Rachel began taking items from the armory that wouldn't hinder her flexibility. Traxen stepped closer and spoke in a low tone.

"**Belgella**, be careful."

"I'm always careful, Your Majesty." **My mother would be proud of the disapproving clip in my voice. Bloody hell. He's making me act like my mother. That's just wrong on so many levels.**

"Rachel…"

"Do you like how it feels when the Royal Guards hold you back when you know you are more than capable?" she hissed.

"You know I don't." His tail flicked.

"Then why do you keep making me feel the same way?" She bent to tighten her shoelace when her eyes watered. She blinked rapidly. **I won't let him see me cry over this.**

His tail stilled, and he sighed heavily.

"That is not my intention. I just want to protect you."

"That's all they're doing, too. It doesn't change the feelings." She straightened.

"You're important to me."

She whirled and slapped his chest with an open palm. His scent invaded her nostrils. He wrapped his hand around her forearm to hold her against him.

"You're important to me, too. But you're not important enough to lose who I am, Traxen. I can't allow that."

Turmoil swirled in his lavender eyes.

"I don't want you to be anyone other than who you are, **belgella**."

"Your actions don't always support your words." Frustrated, she blew out a breath. "We'll talk when I return."

He nodded, released her, and stepped back.

"Let's get you to the others."

On the shuttle, Tesix and Westov headed to the cockpit while Rachel and the others sat in the back. Her lips tilted up when the usual banter began. She leaned back with her legs stretched out and rested her head on the hull.

"I'm glad you decided to join us," Devik said as he shoulder-bumped Karid.

"You couldn't keep me away. I want the ones who put Ava in danger," Karid growled. "I need a better insult than **naroons**. The word doesn't convey my anger enough." His tail slapped the metal floor.

"Emmy has been teaching me more Earth slang. Assholes, shitheads, and dickheads are a few that might work for you." Devik grinned.

"I've heard Lin say bitch and prick," Ash'n offered.

"Talia uses asshole a lot," Vared said with a smile.

"Is that her pet name for you?" Karid teased.

Vared faked a slap to the back of Karid's head. "No respect. We need a sparring match so I can remind you who is in command."

"I personally prefer bastards, fuckers, motherfuckers, and cocksuckers. Adding a goddamn in front of any of them provides more emphasis," Rachel said.

Westov's voice came over the speaker. "I'm taking notes. This is good stuff. Did you notice almost all of them use body parts?"

They heard a slap and grunt. Then Tesix said, "Apologies, Commander. We had you on speaker in case you discussed the plan."

Karid belly laughed. "Instead you are receiving a mini-lesson on Earth insults." Everyone shared his amusement. **It's so good to see him acting like himself again.**

"What is the plan?" asked Rachel. "What do we know about where we're headed?"

Vared nodded at Devik who tapped his tablet. A holographic image of a long, rectangular building with small, high windows in a huge clearing appeared.

"No cover to approach." Rachel frowned.

"We've been monitoring the location via satellite since we discovered it. There's been no activity," said Devik.

"Where is it located?" asked Karid.

"Between Nuxar and Srotix territories," Vared said.

"The two Houses that believe in racial purity. Not surprising." Karid's shoulders bunched.

"What was the building's original purpose? It looks to be too large to have been a home," Ash'n asked.

"Interestingly, we have found no record of this building being erected." Devik's tail flicked a couple times before it stilled.

"So we have no idea of its interior layout." Rachel's eyes narrowed.

"Correct." Vared nodded his approval at her observation. "We will arrive after dusk. Tesix will hover over the roof while cloaked. Instead of using the ramp, we'll use that hatch and rope down." He pointed, then looked at her. "Will that be an issue?"

"Not a problem for me."

"Good. Rachel and Westov will position themselves at the center of the long sides, while the rest of us will take a corner. We'll rappel down from our positions and attempt a look in the windows. On the ground, we'll quietly take out any guards we might find. We enter simultaneously on my command. Any questions?"

"I'm assuming we'll have comms and grappling hooks." Rachel said.

"Yes. We'll don the rappelling gear and each take our own equipment."

"What's the objective once inside?" asked Westov from the cockpit.

"We take out any opposition, preferably without killing them and look for information to identify more traitors. Depending on how many, if any, we find, we may need to call in for more help to transport. If I know Traxen, he's got a team following us, just in case."

The joking continued after the briefing. When Tesix informed them they were fifteen minutes from their target, Rachel pulled out a jar of cream and rubbed it on her face darkening her pale skin. She donned a black cap and tucked her blond hair inside, then encased her hand in black leather gloves.

Devik handed out the comms, and Karid showed Rachel how they worked. After testing them, Westov joined them, and they all began gearing up for the insertion.

Vared tested the rope secured to the floor of the shuttle and opened the hatch that was just large enough for a Svesti male to fit his shoulders through. When they were over the structure, he tossed the rope down. Westov was first, then it was her turn.

Rachel enjoyed the cool night air with a light breeze against her skin and used her feet to control her descent. Lightly, she landed and ran for her middle section. She attached her grappling hook and waited for Vared's command to continue.

Once she began lowering herself, she peered into one of the high windows. **Looks like it's an open space, not offices or bedrooms.**

Her constant scan found nothing of importance. Over the ear comm, Devik said he thought he saw an office. Reaching the ground, she stealthily ran to enter the building behind Ash'n who picked the lock and breached at Vared's command. She kept one hand on a dagger as she stalked behind the healer.

The more building they traversed, the more confused Rachel became. No security cameras. Some carpets and stacked chairs. Nothing else until they reached the large corner room Devik mentioned.

When the group entered, the males growled when they saw half the room was actually a cell. Dried blood stained the floor and the cot in the empty space. Westov rushed to a workstation across the room. He began typing and downloading information, then he smiled.

"I don't know what's here, but I will get everything copied."

Rachel pursed her lips.

"This building doesn't make sense." She walked back to the main open area and down the center of the room with Vared and Karid trailing.

"What are you thinking?" asked Vared.

"One cell in this huge space. No quarters for guards. Not even a food synthesizer. Just chairs and rugs." She kicked the edge of one of the carpets. "They're not even dusty. Why aren't they rolled up and stored like the chairs?"

Karid crouched, lifted a rug, and grinned widely.

"Probably to hide something like this." He pointed to a hatch in the floor.

Vared comm'd for the others to help. They found twelve hatches. Surrounding one with weapons drawn, Vared nodded for Karid to open it. Devik illuminated the darkness with a portable light which showed a ladder. Vared gestured for Devik and Ash'n to go down. She waited with the others until the pair returned safely.

"It appears to be a tunnel leading north," said Devik quietly. "Evidence of recent activity. No security cameras in the section we traveled."

Karid closed the hatch. Vared motioned for them to move to another. They discovered the four center hatches held supplies, including weapons. The outermost hatches were tunnels leading in eight different directions. After they investigated the last floor opening, Vared ordered them to replace the carpets and ensure there was no evidence they had been there.

"Get your grappling gear and meet in the clearing to the south. Tesix, land there and pick us up in five minutes," Vared said.

Rachel hustled silently to follow his commands. On the shuttle, Westov handed the data disk he copied to Vared before they stripped out of their gear.

"Devik, ensure we continue to monitor this building. I will brief the king in person. I will strongly suggest multiple teams to simultaneously explore the tunnels and see where they lead." Vared speared each of them with a hard glance. "No one speaks of what we discovered."

I'm glad I came on this mission.

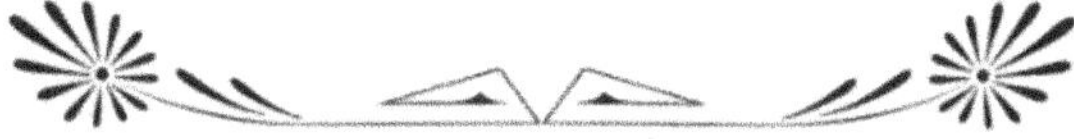

"Where is he?" Frulix's tail flicked sideways in furious motions.

"We just found his location, and a plan is in motion to retrieve him.

"Has he held up under interrogation?"

"Our source informs us he hasn't said a word."

"Good. It's the least he can do after botching the mission." The noble paused. "Have him brought to me when we have him."

"As you will, Sir." The guard left the room.

The noble paced, his thoughts relentlessly tumbling in his skull. His instincts told him it was time to take action, but his mother's voice warned him to be patient. His inner war grew until his breathing grew short and he crouched in a corner clutching his head. He rocked and moaned.

He barely registered when the healer entered and injected him with another dose. His muscles grew lax, and he slid to the floor as the voices grew dimmer. **Finally, some quiet.**

Chapter 25

After the shuttle left, Traxen went back to work for the remainder of the day. Too many times he found himself gazing out the window instead of reading reports. **I know she can take care of herself. I know the males with her will protect her. But I want, no, I need to be the one keeping her safe. I unintentionally upset her. How do we reconcile her needs and mine?**

Finding no satisfactory answer by the time he finally gave up the pretense of accomplishing anything useful, it was long past evening meal. He sighed and realized he hadn't eaten since morning meal. Striding to the empty kitchen, he rummaged in the large cooling unit and grabbed two **maxiem** sandwiches, two water pouches, and a piece of pie. Taking a bite, his tail swayed happily. **I do like the Earth**

sandwiches. They're convenient, tasty, and there seems to be a nice variety of choices.

He was just digging into his pie when Ava came in. She briefly hesitated when she saw him.

"Ava, would you like to join me?"

"Sure. Let me grab something for myself." She went to the large cooling unit and retrieved a similar meal to his, but in a lesser quantity, and sat across from him. "So why are you sitting by yourself?"

"I needed some time alone to think." **Not that it's helping much.**

"Oh, I can just pack up and leave you to it."

"No. Please don't. Until you showed up, I didn't realize that I wanted company I could relax with."

"Are you sure?"

"Absolutely."

Ava unwrapped the plasfilm from her sandwich and took a bite. After she swallowed it down with some water, she asked, "Do you want to talk about it?"

"About what?"

"About whatever is bothering you."

"Not particularly."

"Okay." She ate a few more bites. "Did Rachel go on the mission?"

"Yes." His tail began to flick.

"You're worried about her. She can take care of herself."

"I know she's competent, but I can't help feeling it was wrong to let her go."

Ava pointed a forefinger at him. **These Earth females do like to poke with their fingers.**

"I'm surprised you haven't learned yet that telling a human woman what she can or cannot do is a one-way ticket to pissing her off." She shook her head and teased, "And I thought you were an intelligent male."

A reluctant laugh left his chest. "It's ingrained in our DNA to protect females."

"There's a difference between protecting and controlling. It can be a fine line, Traxen. Sometimes trusting we know our limitations and just being there if we stumble is the best course of action."

"You're very wise for someone so young." His tail slowed. **She makes a good argument. I know Rachel has trust issues. If I don't trust her training and knowledge of her own abilities, how can I expect her to trust me?**

"Yeah, well, life's kicked me in the teeth more than once."

"I did not mean to bring up unhappy memories."

She waved her hand. "No worries, Traxen. I don't need to be treated with kid gloves."

His brows knit as he struggled to understand her words.

"Kid gloves?"

"The phrase is slang for fragile or prone to break at the slightest stress."

"Your language can be confusing."

Her lips turned up. "For us, too."

"Do you believe Karid was ready for this mission?"

She sighed. "I hope so. If he hadn't spoken with all of you, I'd be extremely concerned. The fact that they're looking for clues as to who kidnapped us will probably keep him focused."

"You don't mind if he continues as a warrior? He could sculpt full-time here on Costonia and provide well for you. He wouldn't be putting himself in danger." **I can't see Rachel**

giving up all her training just because I would worry less.

She shook her head. "I want him to be happy. If he chooses to leave the military because he wants to, that's fine with me. If he chooses to leave because he doesn't trust himself, I'm against it. Besides, are you telling me you would not allow me to travel with him wherever and cook for the warriors?"

"You're not a warrior."

"Nope." She emphasized the p. "I wouldn't be going on missions unless they were humanitarian ones like Talonka Six."

"So you're staying with Karid?"

"We plan to true mate. He even gave me a ring today when he asked." She held up her hand to show him.

"Congratulations. I can think of no one better suited to be his mate." **They both deserve happiness.**

"Thanks."

"Will you miss your life on Earth?"

"I'll miss my dad and grandmother, but between trips to Earth and comms, it won't be as bad."

"What does your father do?"

"He's a detective." When Traxen looked at her in askance, she explained, "Law officer who investigates crimes."

"Something similar to our peacekeepers, then." **I wonder if her family would like to move to Costonia.**

"Probably." Finishing her sandwich, she pulled her pie closer and cut into it. "So how long have you been king?"

"Three solars. My father died unexpectedly."

"I'm sorry for your loss."

"Thank you." He glanced away, then back. "I'm constantly surrounded by people, but few understand the complexities of ruling."

"Alone in a crowd," she murmured.

"Exactly. That's why I sent my guards away, although knowing them, they're not far. But then you came in and I wanted company. Strange, isn't it?"

"Perhaps you need to spend more time with people who want to interact with Traxen, not those who want the king's ear."

Barking out a laugh, he smiled. "I think you may be correct." **That's one of the reasons I enjoy Rachel's company. I'm a male first, not the title.**

"Of course I am." She arched a brow. "How could you doubt me?"

He shook his head, his thick braid moving slowly across his shoulder. "Yes, Karid chose well. You even share his sense of humor."

Ava became serious. "I just heard about his father being ill. Do you know the prognosis?"

"Not good. The healers can slow the progression, but not cure it. One moment, he is lucid and reasonable, then switches to aggressive and violent. He will get worse over time."

"I'm not sure how Karid will react when we tell him."

"It doesn't seem fair, does it? He has so much to contend with all at once."

She pointed her fork at him. "That's why he has us."

They chatted for an hour about myriad subjects. While Traxen enjoyed the conversation with the chef, he knew they were both trying to distract themselves from worrying. **I wish**

their shuttle already had the new star drive engine. They might be back already.

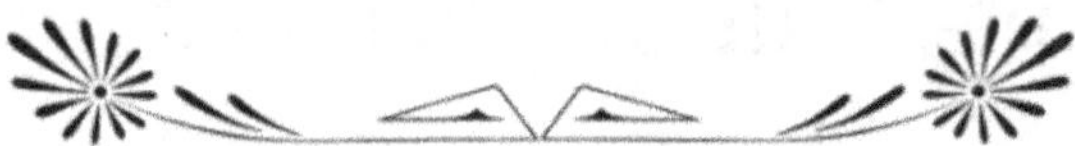

Later that night, Traxen rose from his favorite chair when Rachel and Vared returned. He sniffed and relief coursed through him when her scent only had notes of excitement and no blood or distress. He and his cousin clasped each other's forearms in the standard warrior greeting.

"Sit and report." Traxen's tail circled Rachel's waist and he drew her onto his lap when he returned to his seat. He hid his amusement at her huff. **You may be mad at me, but you can be angry where I can hold you after worrying about you all day.**

Vared told him what they found.

"Rachel was the one who questioned why the building was left the way we found it. Without her observations, we may not have discovered the tunnels."

"I have no doubt you guys would have figured it out…eventually," she said with a grin.

"Accept the compliment, **belgella**. You were correct. You needed to be on this mission." Traxen kissed the top of her head. "I apologize that I didn't recognize that before you left."

Her eyes grew wide, and her mouth formed an adorable oval.

"We're not going to fight about it?"

"No."

They turned at Vared's chuckle.

"Already groveling, Cousin? You've always been a fast learner."

Traxen met Rachel's eyes.

"I want Rachel to introduce me to the human tradition you males mentioned."

Her nose wrinkled.

"Which one?"

"Makeup sex." Traxen winked. He barely noticed as Vared mumbled his goodbye and left. Her devilish expression captivated him.

"I think this session needs to be hard and fast." Her fingernails dug into his chest.

His cock stood at attention under his sleep pants.

"Let's get naked, **belgella**, and show me what you want."

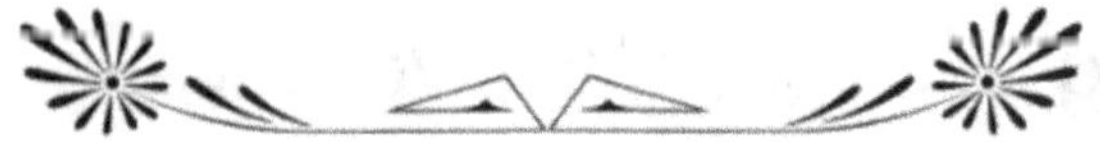

Traxen ground his teeth when he registered his Spymaster's words. His tail slapped the floor.

"Find out how deep these traitors have infiltrated and ensure they're caught."

"Agreed, Sire."

"Anything else?"

"The Wing Raiders request to give their report to whomever you will be sending to Rumaska. According to them, it must be a female and at least one male, but they want there to be no misunderstanding about what may be required." The Spymaster frowned. "Captain Makai said your representatives would have better chances if they were sexually compatible but refused to expound on his statement."

Traxen raised an eyebrow.

"Who do you suggest we send?"

"None of my trusted female contacts would be suitable. Most don't have the experience to interact at a planetary negotiation level. Perhaps one of the mated couples?"

"I'm not sure Vared can be expected to keep his temper under control. Karid requires time before a mission without backup. Ronan is too recognizable. Lady Lin, while intelligent and pleasant, doesn't exude tough negotiator and Lady Emmy is too forthright."

"Lady Rachel would be perfect. She can easily work around unexpected issues. I've seen her verbally eviscerate individuals while keeping a smile on her face, and she's more than capable of physically taking care of herself. But who goes with her?"

"Let's hear what the Wing Raiders have to say. Perhaps we can send her with some of your female contacts as security." **I will never agree to another male touching her intimately, not even for Costonia.**

"I arranged with Xeliv to open your schedule in two hours to speak with them."

"How have you interacted with them?"

"As Zunnax."

"Be here as Ari to obtain the report with Rachel. I'll remain, but not in view."

"As you will, Sire." The Spymaster left Traxen's office through the hidden passageway while Traxen comm'd Rachel.

She arrived ten minutes later, and he embraced her while dropping into his chair with her on his lap. Her scent filled him as he inhaled deeply.

"I have a mission for you, if you are willing, **belgella**."

"Tell me." She straightened, and her face lost some of its softness.

Traxen explained about the Svesti's need for bremmite to power their faster engines, Rumaskans refusing to negotiate with males, and the upcoming report from the Wing Raiders.

"Of course I'll do it. Just give me the parameters of what I can offer." Her eyes shadowed. "I'm not entirely comfortable in acting in a sexual manner with another male. All my previous ops where it might have been an issue, I was partnered with Jonathan or it only involved showing affection with hugs or kisses."

His chest hurt from the growl that escaped him.

"No other male, **belgella**. We're hoping to send you with a female security force."

Her expression lightened.

"I'd prefer that."

His hand cupped her breast, its weight soft and solid in his palm. He thumbed the erect nipple. He leaned down and nipped her earlobe.

"We have some time before the comm." He licked the shell of her ear.

"Oh, did you have any ideas on what we can do while we wait?" Her blue eyes glittered.

"I was thinking I would bend you over my desk and **crek** you hard." His hand drifted lower to play between her legs. His middle finger lightly parted her and dipped into her growing arousal and pumped. Her breath caught and she widened her thighs.

"What if I'd rather ride you in your chair?" Her skin flushed and her eyelids drooped while her fingernails dug into his forearm. When she shifted on his lap, her ass brushed his rigid cock.

"If we rush, we can do both." Smiling, he kissed her neck as he added another finger and increased his tempo. **Goddess, she's dripping with desire.**

"No rushing. We'll do it your way this time." Her sultry laugh stuttered as her cunt squeezed his fingers.

"That's it, Rachel, let me watch you. You're glorious when you come." Traxen's tail hit a hidden button which locked all the entrances and erected a sound shield around his office. "No one can hear you but me."

Her breathing grew erratic and blood rushed to her face. Her body began to quiver and shake. He pressed his thumb to her clit and made small circles. When she bowed her back and screamed his name, pre-cum dampened the front of his pants. He slowed his movements and waited until she came back to herself.

"Yes," he growled. "Strip."

She grabbed the hem of her shirt and pulled it over her head, then removed her bra. Sliding from his lap, she stood shakily and toed off her shoes before pushing her panties and leggings down and kicking them off. He hastily undressed and ran his hands over her exposed flesh. He pinched her nipples as he devoured her mouth. His tail dipped into her core, and she threw her head back.

Spinning her, he swept his arm over his desk sending his tablet to the floor. Lightly pushing on her shoulder blades and pressing his leg between her knees, he spread her open. He kneaded her firm ass, his thumbs dipping between her crease, and she moaned. Her arms gripped the edges of the desk.

"Are you ready for me, **belgella**?"

She nodded frantically.

"Take me, Traxen. I want you to never look at this desk the same way again."

He withdrew his tail and slowly fed his cock into her wetness, hissing as her tightness surrounded him.

"Your cunt sucks my cock beautifully—like it wants more."

"It does. It wants all of it. Fill me and fuck me."

His shaft grew even harder at her words and her heavy arousal scent. His hands gripped her hips, and he bottomed out. They both groaned. His wet tail snuck between her body and desk and teased her nipples. She attempted to push back, but he held her in position.

"Stop being greedy. I want to savor this. Goddess, this beautiful ass just beckons me to slap against it."

She groaned.

"Slap it with your body, your hands, your tail, just move, dammit."

A dark chuckle left his lips.

"Always so impatient. Hold on." He withdrew until his swollen head almost left her, paused, then thrust forward hard, the front of his thighs smacking her ass and his balls impacting her clit as they swung. Her arm muscles strained to keep her in place.

"Yes. More."

Over and over, he repeated his actions, keeping her writhing on the edge waiting for him to fill her again. His tail moved down to her clit and circled it. As she gasped, he picked up his pace and slammed into her faster. Sweat covered both their bodies causing his hands to slip slightly.

She chanted. "Yes. Yes. Just like that."

He bent over her and nipped at where her shoulder met her neck.

"Come for me now, Rachel."

She keened when her orgasm exploded. Her insides rippled and squeezed his cock setting off his own fireworks. Light dimmed around the edges of his vision as his seed rocketed into her. Her uncontrollable spasming almost bucked him off her and he wrapped his arms around her lifting her backwards to rest against his chest. He stumbled to his chair. When he abruptly sat, his cock pushed deeper into her, and they both groaned.

His hands smoothed over her feeling her skin shiver and twitch. Her head fell back on his chest, and he dropped small kisses and licks on whatever flesh his mouth could reach. He filled his nostrils with her scent, and her body relaxed against his. **Each time with her is better than the last.**

As their heavy breathing slowed, he murmured endearments in Svesti, not even sure what he was saying. She turned her head and met his mouth with hers, their tongues slowly intermingling in a tender moment.

"I think your way works really well, Traxen." She smirked. She groaned when his chuckle set off another round of spasming within her.

"Our ways work well together, **belgella**."

Chapter 26

Tingles resonated throughout Rachel's body while she recovered from the hard pounding against Traxen's desk. A self-satisfied smile crossed her lips as his warm hands traversed her skin and his kisses rained affection on her body. **Damn, I love how he doesn't just roll over, so to speak, and ignore me. I really like how he is after sex.**

Eventually, they roused themselves enough to use the sanitary facility attached to his office. They quickly shared a shower and dressed. She refrained from pouting as he covered up his handsome body. Fluffing her short hair with her fingers, she decided she was presentable enough for the comm with the Wing Raiders. She squeezed Traxen's butt cheek as he turned to go back to the office and grinned when he arched an eyebrow at her playfulness. **Even in the**

middle of serious business, we have fun. I feel freer than I have in years.

She and Traxen spoke at length about potential trading options for the bremmite, from credits to other goods Costonia could provide. She received a mini-lesson on the measurement of the ore, as well as the quality standards. Traxen comm'd Ash'n asking him to prepare an upload for her on the various ores available and testing procedures. He gave the healer the name of a geologist who could provide accurate information.

A short time later, the Spymaster entered in his Ari Zunnax persona. He sniffed and shook his head indulgently. **Svesti noses give them an unfair advantage.**

"I suggest Lady Rachel and I sit here." He gestured to the chairs across from Traxen's desk. "And you, Sire, can remain in your normal seat. I can set up the comm on your desk."

Traxen nodded but moved his chair to a better vantage point on her side of the desk. They checked to ensure he would remain out of sight to the Wing Raiders before Traxen soundproofed the room again and Zunnax initiated the encrypted comm.

Rachel eyed the large blue male on the hologram. He had multiple dark braids, but two white ones on his left side. Green eyes met hers before moving to the older Svesti.

"Zunnax."

"Captain Makai. Allow me to introduce Lady Rachel."

Makai dipped his chin and smiled. **Yes, he has fangs, too.**

"Lady Rachel, well met. I'm assuming you know Lady Talia and Commander Durek."

"Pleasure to meet you, Captain. And yes, I consider both to be friends."

"Please extend my greetings to them when next you see them. Knowing we have humans on our crew, the Svesti ensured we received vaccines. I assume Lady Talia is healthy?" His green eyes looked concerned.

"Yes, she's fine. She and Durek are fated mates."

"That doesn't surprise me." Makai chuckled. "During our dealings, he exhibited a pronounced urge to protect her."

Rachel smiled.

"That hasn't changed in the least."

"Allow me to introduce Kara and Crax."

A pink-haired human woman with blue eyes appeared and pushed at Makai who sighed and stepped back out of view.

"Hi," she squealed, bouncing excitedly. "I love your accent. So British."

Rachel bit her tongue to keep from laughing.

"You must be Kara."

"And this is Crax." She tugged into view a tall, fit, blue male with part of his head shaved with the remainder of his hair in braids. He grunted.

"Don't mind him. Let us tell you about Rumaska." Kara ran her hand through her shoulder-length tresses. "Talk about a fucked-up place."

"How so?"

"It's a female-dominated world, and when I say dominated, think BDSM club on serious estrogen. They call their males 'body servants,' but in most cases, they're slaves—at least in the higher echelons of their society." Kara frowned.

"But not in all cases?" Zunnax prompted.

"Further outside the city, males are still subjugated, but have a greater amount of freedom—as in allowed to cover their dicks in public."

"Excuse me?" Rachel's eyes stared at Kara.

Crax's deep, raspy voice joined in.

"In the city, most body servants wear pain collars, no shirts, and pants cut out at the crotch to show their assets. A body servant's cock must be caged or alternatively, displayed erect. The females are called 'Mistress' and many of their public functions involve body servants 'honoring' the mistresses with sexual contact."

Rachel swallowed hard.

"Sexual contact?"

"Sucking of nipples, cunnilingus, things like that." Kara waved her hand distractedly before tapping on her tablet. "No penetration of females in public, but more than once we saw males being pegged."

"Are you serious?"

"Absolutely. I'm sending you some video of one dinner we attended. It's a freaky-ass place."

Watching the video, Rachel took note of the clothes. Many of the females wore outfits with cutouts over their breasts and genitals. Some wore demi-cup corsets that exposed portions of their nipples, while others wore panties that barely covered their pussies under translucent gowns. Attired as Crax stated, the skin of many of the males appeared oiled and she saw more than one female leading a male around by his stiff cock, while others used a leash.

Humanoid with two arms and legs, the Rumaskan skin tones ranged from a light blush pink to dark magenta. All of them had two gray eyes with pale yellow pupils that were widely set with orbital sockets that seemed to be deeper than human ones. Male penises looked thinner and longer than human or Svesti ones with a triangular glans. They appeared to have cat-like ears that swiveled independently. **Probably have sensitive hearing.**

She saw one group with the females talking while their body servants sucked on their breasts and another group seated with thighs spread on queening chairs having a conversation while their males licked their pussies. Some of the males served appetizers and when one female became upset about something, she pointed a controller of some sort at a male and he dropped to the floor writhing in agony. **I've seen some wild things, but this is out there.**

From the corner of her eye, she saw Traxen's tail flicking and his claws extending, but heard no growl. **At least he's holding it together so far.**

"The one who punished the male is Mistress Pitman, who owns the largest bremmite mine on Rumaska. This video was taken at one of her parties." Kara paused the video to show Pitman's face. "She's also one of the cruelest females on the planet." She fast forwarded the video to show two other females. "Mistress Overly on the right and Mistress Thespa on the left both own bremmite mines as well. Of the three, Mistress Thespa has the smallest operation but treats her body servants better."

"We were able to visit the towns nearest the mines," Crax added. "The males at Pitman's mines are sent there to work until they die. Overly uses hers as a punishment, but if she believes the males have learned their lesson, she eventually brings them back into service at one of her homes as a 'lower'—a body servant who receives no sexual favors. Thespa, on the other hand, hires mated males and pays them a small living wage."

"Mated males?" Zunnax asked, arms crossed.

"In the rural areas, many of the females who find compatible males will mate them. The males are still subservient to the females, but overall, it seems more of a lifestyle or cultural choice, rather than slavery. Those males usually wear special collars to show they have the favor of a mistress— not a pain collar." Kara bit her lip. "In upper society, males are not raised with their mothers or fathers, only females. In the rural areas, the children are raised in family households or in the orphanages where society's male children are sent."

Rachel leaned back and blew out a breath.

"If I show up with a female security team and no male, what do you think will happen?"

Crax braids brushed his shoulders as he shook his head.

"They won't even allow you on the planet, let alone negotiate with you."

"He's right. If you can't show that you can control a larger male, then you have no chance of earning their respect or attention." Kara looked at Zunnax. "No offense, you're an attractive male, but Rachel will require someone younger and harder-looking to impress the Mistresses. The more dangerous he appears, the better. Body servants not only serve the females sexually but also provide protection." She patted Crax's arm. "Physically, Crax is a good example of the rough and ready look the mistresses prefer."

"Are you able to secure introductions to the bremmite mine owners for Lady Rachel?" Zunnax asked.

Kara nodded. "We put out the word that there were buyers from Costonia looking for new suppliers. We mentioned fabrics, ores, and food delicacies as potential items you might be interested in."

"Excellent." Zunnax's eyes turned thoughtful.

Kara tapped her tablet.

"I'm transmitting some things for you. Clothing patterns that meet current fashion on Rumaska for a synthesizer. Also, some patterns to make either cock cages or cock rings, depending on which way you go in the disguise."

Crax rumbled.

"You'll need accurate measurements. I adjusted the designs for maximum comfort and for the cock rings, I added timed releases of pressure to avoid damage to a male's genitals. The Rumaskan dinners and parties last forever."

"Oh, one other thing." Kara looked at Rachel. "Some of the mistresses like to share their body servants with others and might expect you to do the same. You should have a good cover story as to why you won't. At least I'm assuming you won't."

"They pimp them out, too?" Rachel's teeth clenched.

"In a manner of speaking, yes. They do it to incur favor with another mistress." Kara's blue eyes hardened. "Rumaskan customs are as skewed as human traffickers on Earth."

"I'm curious. How many humans do you have in the Wing Raiders?" Rachel tilted her head slightly.

"Four." Kara smiled. "We're pretty happy here."

"Sometime in the future, I'd like to arrange a visit to meet all of you. I know the other women here would like that, too." Rachel returned Kara's grin.

"We'll figure something out." Kara nodded. "It's nice to see women who are here by choice."

"Thank you for your report. If we have any further questions, we'll contact you." Zunnax disconnected the comm.

Traxen's arms circled her from the back, and he pulled her close.

"You are not going to Rumaska."

She slapped his forearm.

"Of course I am. You need me to."

A loud angry growl rumbled against her spine.

"No male will be touching you like that."

"Well, if you weren't so recognizable, you could go with me."

"Changing his looks isn't the problem," Zunnax said. "It's him disappearing from Costonia for the time needed to complete the mission that's the issue."

Rachel pinned the Spymaster with a glare.

"Wait. We can disguise him well enough for him to go?"

"Of course."

"What about his clan marking?"

Zunnax's tail swayed.

"We have technology that can mimic Svesti skin and alternate clan markings. It's only good for about a lunar, but it works well for shorter lengths of time."

"If you insist on going, I will go with you." Traxen's tail wound around her ankle and he rested his chin on the top of her head.

"But can you act like a body servant and take orders from me?" she smirked.

"If it will keep you safe, yes."

"Sire, I'm not sure this is a good idea." The Spymaster's eyes narrowed.

"This is how it's happening. Now let's figure out how to have me out of the public eye on Costonia for this mission."

They brainstormed well into the evening, before the Spymaster left and Traxen called in Lorriv Hossix, Canaan and Vared Durek, as well as their trusted guards. Rachel suggested they see if Tesix and Westov would be willing to go and watch over their transport. When she and Traxen finally retired to Traxen's quarters, he programmed the synthesizer for the clothing and accoutrements they required. Arms around each other, they fell asleep exhausted. **This is going to be an interesting mission.**

The next day, Traxen and Rachel dressed normally. Tesix and Westov picked up their bags as well as the items Traxen synthesized for them and disappeared.

Xeliv and Canaan awaited them at Traxen's office.

"Vared and Talia boarded the royal flitter in the middle of the night," Xeliv informed them. "You and your guards will go there shortly so you can show Lady Rachel more of Costonia."

"The official stance is you are taking a short vacation leaving me in charge temporarily," Canaan added. "You better come back before I get buried in paperwork."

Traxen clapped his uncle's shoulder.

"I appreciate this."

"You do deserve some time off after this mission. You haven't taken any since you became king."

"From your mouth to the Goddess' ears, Uncle."

"The first location you will visit is the **Star Devil**. Once there, you'll meet with Zunnax for the king's disguise, then board the **Nova**. The **Nova** is large enough to carry the **Firebrand**, the **Star Devil's** commander's shuttle, where Tesix and Westov await. Yanz and Kragen will pilot the king's flitter with

Vared and Talia around Costonia for the next week, keeping onlookers busy guessing your whereabouts. Once the **Nova** is just outside of Rumaska's scanning range, you and Lady Rachel will take the **Firebrand** to the planet with Tesix and Westov. Hossix and Previv will remain cloaked on the **Nova** in case you require more backup." Xeliv took a breath. "If I may, Sire, are you sure this is a good idea?"

"I understand your concern, Xeliv, but given the intel we received about Rumaska, it is imperative I accompany Lady Rachel in disguise for the negotiations."

"As you will, Sire."

"No discussion of my true location outside of a sound barrier and encrypted comms only with Lady Rachel or the guards," Traxen ordered. **Damn, he's hot when he's in charge.**

"Anything else?"

"Did Lady Rachel receive her upload?" Canaan asked.

"Yes, Ash'n gave it to me last night." She rubbed behind her ear. "Fortunately, it wasn't a very large one."

"Trackers?"

"He implanted mine as well," Traxen thumbed a spot on his upper arm. "We confirmed Rachel's tracker is still active. The guards have the frequencies."

"Then let's get you on the king's flitter so you can return faster and save me from this job." Canaan grinned.

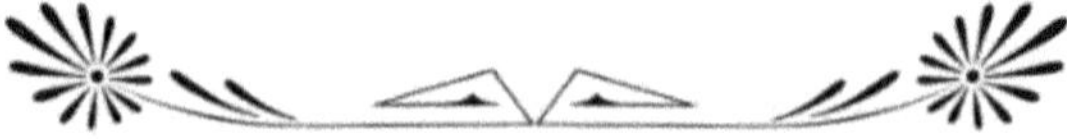

Rachel disembarked from the flitter in the mostly empty hangar bay on the **Star Devil**. Already parked, the **Nova** took up a good portion of the space. Yanz and Kragen stood by the ramp.

"Everyone else is onboard." Kragen dipped his chin.

"Thank you. Rachel, please go and wait for me. I'll be back as soon as my disguise is in place." Traxen gestured to the **Nova**.

"Who are you taking with you?"

"Hossix. Previv will remain with you."

"Well, you should be safe on a space cruiser."

His fangs flashed bright against his caramel bronze skin.

"I'm only going to that ship over there." Traxen pointed to a flitter on the opposite side of the bay.

"Okay. Don't get into any trouble." She rose up on her toes, kissed him on the cheek, and walked onto the large transport.

"This way, Lady Rachel." Previv waved a hand to the rear of the **Nova**. They entered a much smaller hangar where the **Firebrand** waited.

She laughed.

"I feel like I'm in a set of nesting dolls."

"I don't understand."

She tapped on her tablet and pulled up the Earth's internet and showed him a picture as they boarded the **Firebrand**.

"Your reference makes sense now. Thank you." Previv smiled. **He looks so much like his brother Talen.**

Tesix and Westov stood when they entered. Wearing the pants Traxen synthesized for them, they also added rectangular pieces of black leather hanging from their waists front and back covering their genital areas.

"Didn't like the style?" she teased.

"I have no desire to have my parts sticking to the seat," Tesix grumbled.

"These pants are definitely airy," Westov quipped.

"If it becomes necessary, we can remove the extras, but we thought the king might appreciate us being covered with a female onboard." Tesix grinned. "I like my head on my shoulders."

"Good call." She grimaced. "I'm not looking forward to any of my outfits. They are nothing I would choose to wear in public." **Maybe in private with Traxen, but not for everyone else to see.**

"We'll avert our eyes," Westov promised.

"Thank you for agreeing to this mission and taking extra time from your shore leave to come along," Rachel said. "It helps to have people I trust at our backs."

Both males thumped their chests with their fists.

"It is our honor to protect you and the king," Tesix said.

Westov nodded and handed her a necklace with a small carving of Dianthia on it.

"I made this for you, Lady Rachel. If you press hard on the carving, it will send us a distress signal."

"A panic button? Good idea." She put on the necklace. "I can't accidentally set it off?"

"It's remotely possible, but highly unlikely."

"Okay. Thanks."

"Are you giving Lady Rachel gifts, Westov?" Traxen growled.

She turned and gasped at Traxen. His lavender eyes were now brown and his hair almost black. Shirtless, his clan marking now showed him from House Nuxar and a mother from House Binova. Still wearing his normal pants, his face surprised her the most. Three long scars traversed from over his left eyebrow down to his cheek. **Wow. The Spymaster even made the eyelid appear puckered. I'm seriously impressed and he's still devastatingly handsome.**

"Do the scars need to be reapplied regularly?" She extended her forefinger to trace one as he bent toward her.

"No. They'll last for a lunar unless removed with a special solvent. Same with the clan marking."

"Does it affect your vision at all?"

"No. It just feels strange when it pulls my skin." He turned and showed her his back. A matching set of scars ran from his right shoulder blade diagonally across his back. "Dangerous enough?" He grinned.

"Oh, I've got an idea." She tapped on her tablet and found something. "I'll be right back." She pushed past Previv and ran off. A few minutes later, she returned with a piece of black cloth. "Sit so I can reach. Let me see how you look with this."

She wrapped it over him so it covered his scalp and the top half of his head. Ensuring he could see through the two eyeholes, she tied it over his braid. **Oh, he looks like a fucking hot pirate, like the one in that movie from that twentieth century movie. Richards? Roberts?**

While facing him, she placed her fists on her hips and tilted her head left and right.

"Even better as a disguise. Everyone will be focused on your eyes and the hints of scarring."

"I agree," said Hossix. "Is the pattern still in the synthesizer? I'll make a few more for your visit."

She nodded and the guard left. When he returned, he handed another four to Traxen. He lifted his hand to his ear.

"The **Nova** is ready to depart. We'll head away from Rumaska at normal speed until we're out of tracking range, then cloak and go on course. We should be there tomorrow morning."

"Who's flying the **Nova**?"

"My father and Zunnax."

"Your father?" Rachel heard the surprise in her voice.

"He arranged for someone to take over for him at the palace. He said if the king was on a mission, he was going, too."

Hossix chuckled. "I tried to talk him out of it, but he's stubborn."

Traxen crossed his arms, and his tail flicked.

"And he waited until it was too late for me to stop him. You could've mentioned this sooner, Hossix."

"My father threatened to replace me as your guard." Hossix shrugged. "Besides, you know neither of us would win the argument with him. The fact that he didn't attempt to dissuade you from going on the mission should have been a clue."

"**Crek.** You're right. He never protested." Traxen's tail slowed.

"Well, we're off." Tesix rose from his seat. "We'll return to the **Firebrand** when we're about an hour from leaving the **Nova**. But for now, we'll let you have your privacy."

"Really? No guards for the rest of the day?"

"The **Nova** was cleared before your arrival, guarded, and we know everyone onboard," Hossix explained. "One of us will remain in the hangar, just in case, but unless you leave the **Firebrand**, you won't see us. Fresh food is in the kitchen area if you get hungry."

The four males left with Westov making some comment under his breath and Tesix slapping the back of his head. Rachel suppressed a laugh at their antics. When the ramp closed, Traxen's tail pulled her close to him.

"Let's be dangerous together, **belgella**." His tongue licked the shell of her ear. "Maybe you can model some of your outfits for me and I can practice honoring you."

She giggled and took off running toward the bedroom.

"Only if you can catch me, body servant."

His growls followed her, and he caught her at the door. He lifted her and devoured her mouth before tossing her to the mattress. After her body stopped bouncing, she offered her hand to him. He took it and knelt on one knee next to her.

"Time to please me." Her lips pursed. "What should I call you on Rumaska? I'm not going to call you servant or slave. We can't use your name."

"You'll figure something out, Mistress."

She tugged on his braid.

"Get to work, pet."

He grinned.

"Whatever my mistress wants."

They both laughed before they filled the room with moans.

Chapter 27

Traxen grumbled under his breath as he stuffed his flaccid cock into the metal cage. With a self-locking design, the click seemed ominous. **Better this than having my cock on display for everyone. The things I do for my planet.**

Rachel keyed the digital locks for every device to her thumbprint but also added his pinky finger, just in case. After donning the rest of his Rumaskan attire in addition to the head covering Rachel suggested, he looked in the mirror. Critically, he studied his image and bared his fangs. **I don't believe anyone will recognize me. Crek. I don't even recognize myself.**

Although he wasn't happy about the situation or the disguise, the fact that he would be Rachel's personal protector for the mission reassured him. **No other male will touch her. We'll be relying on each other—no guards trailing us. It's exciting. I just hope I can act subservient enough to fool the Rumaskans.**

"Honestly, why don't they just go naked if they wear shit like this?" Rachel complained.

He turned and inhaled sharply. Like him, her clothes were black. A corset woven with a shiny silver ribbon pushed her breasts together leaving her shoulders exposed, and barely covering her nipples. Her tight pants opened at the crotch. Tiny black panties cut low to just above her slit drew attention to her soft, pale skin. Black studs dusted with glittery gem fragments pierced her earlobes. The panic button necklace adorned her neck and one of the hair combs she purchased in Trezoura pulled her hair up on one side. He smiled when he realized she wore her usual boots with hidden weapons.

"**Belgella**, you are a vision."

She perused him and whistled.

"That is a different look for you, too." She frowned. "Other women will be seeing you like this."

He placed his hands on her upper arms.

"Other males will see you in that outfit, and I'll have to pretend it doesn't bother me. But we'll be together."

She sighed.

"I know it's necessary, but I don't have to like it."

Leaning down, he kissed her gently.

"I like that you are jealous, Rachel. But no other female can compare to you."

Her hand rested on his chest.

"You need one more thing to complete the look."

His lips twisted and his tail flicked.

"I know. The pain collar."

She shook her head.

"No. I won't put that on you, even if it is disabled." Leaving his arms, she retrieved something from her bag. "I made this for you. Bend down, please." She attached it to his neck.

Looking in the mirror, a wide strip of black lay across his skin. Rather than a true collar, the soft leather lay flat along the perimeter of his neck and formed a deep vee in the center. He narrowed his eyes and peered closer at the pattern etched in thin silver strands in the leather. A highly ornate "R" in an Earth alphabet sat at the point of the vee while the remainder of the collar had a repeating loop that spelled Costonia in an ancient Svesti script.

"Kara said favored males wore other collars, so I decided to do the same for you." Pink tinged her cheeks. "What do you think?"

"I think it's perfect. The symbolism of the pattern does not escape me and it's entirely accurate. You and Costonia own my heart."

Her skin reddened further, and her eyes were bright.

"I saw it more as you are the protector of both, rather than being owned by either."

"Even better, **belgella**." He kissed her. "I will wear it with pride. Thank you."

She sniffed.

"Bloody hell. I have to go out in front of Tesix and Westov this way."

"I have an idea." Traxen opened a compartment in the wall and pulled out some fabric. He wrapped it over her shoulders and fastened it at the neck.

"A cloak?" She tugged the edges closer together in the front. "This will work."

"You can wear it on the ship and keep it on until necessary while on Rumaska."

Tesix's voice came over a speaker.

"We'll be in range of the planet in ten minutes."

"I guess that's our cue," Rachel said.

"After you. Mistress."

When they entered the cockpit, Tesix glanced up briefly before turning back to the console. Traxen saw they were wearing less ornate versions of his leather necklace rather than pain collars.

"We will be in hailing distance soon."

"Excellent. From here on out, Lady Rachel is Mistress Rachel, and we are her body servants. Do not use my name or title, even within this ship." Traxen's tail rested on her spine, and he took a step backwards so Rachel was in front of him. He rested his hands at the small of his back.

"As you will."

"Should we take off the extra clothing?" Westov asked without looking behind him.

"No. Unless there's a chance of someone seeing you standing, you may remain as you are," said Rachel.

"Yes, Mistress," Tesix and Westov said in unison. Traxen saw Westov smirk and almost slapped him on the back of the head like Tesix was wont to do. Rachel's fingers twitched as if she wanted to do the same.

"Transmission from the planet, Mistress. Should I answer it?" Tesix's hand hovered over the console.

"Yes." Rachel straightened and her face hardened.

A hologram of a sour-faced Rumaskan female appeared in front of them.

"Who are you and what is your business on Rumaska?"

"Mistress Rachel from Costonia. I am seeking trade opportunities on your planet."

The pink female's feline-looking ears twitched.

"What sorts of trade opportunities?"

"To whom am I speaking?"

"Why does it matter?"

"I like to know who I am dealing with." Rachel's firm voice remained pleasant.

"You don't need to know my name. And you don't look Svesti."

"Do put on someone with real power, would you, dear? I hate to waste my time on underlings. Insult me further and my credits will go to another planet."

"How dare you?"

"Pets, disconnect the comm and set course for Ladorta. It's quite obvious Rumaska doesn't want my credits."

All the Svesti said, "Yes, Mistress." Tesix disconnected the comm.

"Did you really want me to set course for Ladorta?"

"Start heading that direction slowly but remain within hailing distance of the planet."

A minute later, Westov said, "Rumaska is requesting to talk to you."

"Open the comm."

A different Rumaskan female appeared, darker in color and younger than the first. Rachel spoke first and in a bored tone.

"What is it? I've already told the first lackey that I am no longer interested in spending my credits on your rude planet."

"Mistress Rachel, I am Mistress Relim, the supervisor of the day. Please allow me to offer my sincerest apologies for Mistress Akka's behavior. She will be reprimanded for offending a mistress of your standing." Her thin face frowned. "How may I help you?"

"I have Costonian buyers who are interested in regular trade with Rumaska. For now, fabrics, food stuffs, ores, and whatever else Rumaska may have that might provide profit for my clients." Rachel's voice firmed. "I am authorized to sign hefty contracts if I find items of worth. However, if I am treated with disrespect, the credits will go to a more deserving planet."

"A reasonable stance, Mistress Rachel. Any female who controls three large protective males without pain collars should be respected." Mistress Relim's eyes traveled over the Svesti in a covetous manner. Her gaze stopped on Traxen and his unusual headgear.

"My pets need no pain collars. They are devoted to me."

"On Rumaska, we call our males body servants."

Rachel tilted her head.

"My males are my treasured pets. They serve me in all ways, not just my body." She waved her hand absently. "However, that seems to be a cultural difference not worth quibbling about."

"It is rare we see humans here."

"At last, an enlightened mistress." Rachel smiled. "Mistress Akka had no idea of my species."

"We recently had a human mistress visit."

"Mistress Kara? She was the one who brought Rumaska to my attention."

Mistress Relim's longer incisors touched her bottom lip when she smiled.

"Mistress Kara delighted many in our capital city. Her body servant also made an impression." She shuddered delicately. "Quite a dangerous Jalaxian, but he honored her well and often. I would personally love to hear about human training techniques."

Traxen bit the inside of his cheek to keep his laughter restrained. **Honored her well and often? I wonder if that means what I think it means.**

"Perhaps we can discuss it some time, Mistress Relim. Am I cleared to land on your planet?"

"Of course, Mistress Rachel. I am sending coordinates to you now. Have you arranged lodging yet?"

"No. I intended to remain onboard the **Firebrand** with my pets."

The Rumaskan appeared horrified.

"Please allow us to extend our hospitality to you, Mistress. My cousin, Mistress Hower, owns the best hotel in our capital city with beds large enough for you and all your males if you like."

After a pause, Rachel said, "I would like to experience your planet. However, two of my pets will stay with my ship for security. I will only bring one with me for protection and to show my faith in your hospitality."

Westov made a sound that could have been choked laughter. Rachel squeezed his shoulder.

"I will reward you generously when I return from my business dealings, my pets."

"Yes, Mistress," Tesix and Westov said.

Mistress Relim sighed.

"So well behaved. You trust them without guidance?"

Rachel's voice firmed.

"My pets would never disobey me unless they felt I was in imminent danger."

"No offense intended, Mistress Rachel. If you would allow me, I will personally escort you to my cousin's hotel."

"That would be acceptable, Mistress Relim. I look forward to meeting you in person."

Tesix disconnected the comm.

Traxen leaned forward. His breath stirred Rachel's hair when he said, "Well played, Mistress."

Rachel slapped his chest with the back of her hand.

"Behave or I will punish you by withholding my favor, pet."

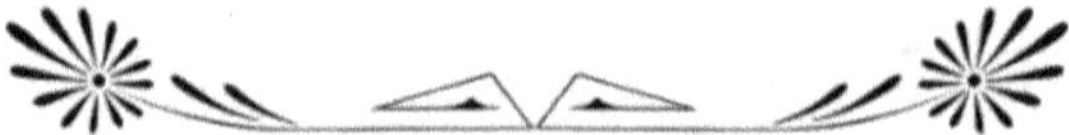

Goddess, this female can talk.

Their bags slung over his shoulder, Traxen followed slightly behind Rachel and the verbose Mistress Relim. Tall modern skyscrapers lined the capital city center and a greenish sky overlooked the planet. Heat shimmered on the sidewalks and beings rushed about—either walking briskly or in flitters.

Most of the Rumaskan females were shorter than Rachel, while many of the males were slightly taller than her. Very few reached his own height.

As they entered the Hower Hotel, he inhaled air no longer laden with humidity. Large windows gleamed throughout the large structure. Kiosks lined the walls of the lobby, while comfortable seating groups and plants filled the space. The majority of the females he saw were Rumaskan, while the males came from a huge variety of species. **I've never seen this many cocks on display. Crek. That male there has three. How in the Goddess' name does that work?**

The Rumaskan led them to a female staff member at the far end of the space.

"Mistress Relim, welcome," the young female chittered.

"Good day. Is Mistress Hower available?"

"She's on her way. I comm'd her when I saw you arrive."

Mistress Relim smiled indulgently.

"I do like initiative. Thank you."

"It is my pleasure."

An older magenta female approached with a smile.

"My cousin, what a nice surprise."

"Mistress Hower, it is always wonderful to see you. I would like to introduce you to Mistress Rachel. She's here on business from Costonia, and I recommended your establishment to her. Please tell me you have a suitable room for her."

"Mistress Rachel, welcome to the Hower Hotel. Unfortunately, I do not have a room, but I can offer you a suite."

"It is a pleasure to meet you, Mistress Hower. A suite will be fine."

"Excellent." She waved at the staff member who tapped on a tablet. "If you are comfortable telling me about your business, I may be able to effect introductions to the proper mistresses."

"I am interested in trade opportunities. While I have potential buyers for fabrics, foods, and ores, if I come across other items that I believe I can secure sales for, I would be willing to hear proposals for those options as well."

"Hmm. Mistress Pitman is holding a party this evening. Many of the most influential mistresses in the city will be present. I may be able to have you added to the invitation list."

Rachel smiled.

"I am pleased Mistress Relim recommended your hotel to me. The service so far is impressive."

Both Rumaskans enthusiastically shared information about the various females who would be in attendance and what their businesses entailed. The staff member approached and handed something to Mistress Hower.

"Oh, good, your suite is ready. Here are your digital keys." Mistress Hower dropped them into Rachel's hand.

Traxen took the one Rachel gave him and tucked it into one of his tight pockets.

"You give your body servant his own key?" Mistress Hower's eyebrows raised.

"How else can he fetch me things I need?"

"Most mistresses only give them to their body servants when they actually want something."

"Well, my pet is trustworthy." Rachel caressed his chest. **Hmm, maybe now is the time to act more in character.**

Traxen stared at her in adoration and his tail swayed.

"Thank you, Mistress. I live to serve you."

He swallowed his gasp when she tweaked his nipple. **Mischievous imp. She'll pay for that later.**

"I would like to settle into my suite now. You'll comm me with details for this evening if you are successful?"

"Of course, Mistress Rachel. If you would like to see more of our city, please let our concierge know. She'll provide recommendations and assistance."

"Thank you, Mistress Hower. I look forward to my stay."

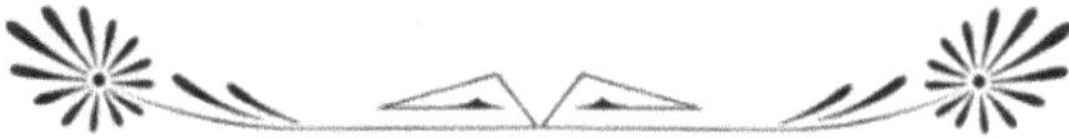

When they entered their lavish suite, Rachel said, "Pet, do be a love and perform a security sweep. You know how some of these planets like to learn more than they should about me."

Traxen pulled out a device from his bag and walked slowly around the rooms. He pointed when he found listening devices in the bedroom and living area. One camera hidden high in a light fixture over the bed caused his chest to rumble. Fortunately, the sanitary facility had none.

"Mistress, perhaps we should return to the **Firebrand**. You will be safer there."

"No, pet. It's a nice enough suite, though it's a bit too high tech for my tastes. Now come help me bathe. You should be rewarded for your diligent attention to my safety."

"As you wish, Mistress." He followed her to the sanitary facility.

He began running a bath, and she leaned forward to whisper in his ear. His spine tingled. His cock tried to stiffen but the cage blocked it. **What an odd sensation.**

"We'll leave the bugs in place and feed them misinformation if necessary."

"Of course. There is a camera over the bed."

"I guess we'll have more water play this trip, then." She gripped one of his ass cheeks. "Have I mentioned how sexy your glutes look in these pants?"

Turning, he extended a claw and pulled down the top of her corset, exposing her breasts. Her scent grew stronger.

"While I like this top on you, I believe you look better without it." He retracted his claw and untied the ribbon. She shimmied and it fell down over her hips to the floor. He dropped to his knees and unfastened her pants. Tugging them downward, taking her panties with them, he bared her to his voracious gaze.

"How may I serve you, Mistress?" he growled low.

"Join me in a bath, pet." A lascivious grin met his hungry eyes.

He gathered her in his arms and stood. He bowed his head when her comm chimed.

"Crek."

She answered her comm on voice only.

"Mistress Rachel."

"This is Mistress Hower. Several mistresses you might like to meet just arrived for a meal in our restaurant. I can make the introductions if you come down."

"I'll be there shortly." Rachel sighed after she disconnected the comm. "Put me down so I can get dressed."

Hugging her closer, his tongue slipped between her lips. They eventually broke off their kiss, breathing heavily. He dropped his forehead on hers and let her legs drop.

"The sacrifices I make for the good of Costonia."

Laughing, she pulled on her clothes. Once they were in the bedroom, she comm'd the **Firebrand**.

"Pets. I'm sending you a list of names. I require you to do some research on them. Public records only. A couple have been helpful to me, and I'd like to find appropriate gifts."

"As you wish, Mistress," Tesix said. Westov began typing on the console.

"Is all well on the **Firebrand**?"

"Yes, Mistress."

"Thank you, pet. I'll reward you when my business is concluded."

"We await you willingly, Mistress," Westov said with a smirk.

Rachel shook her head as she terminated the comm.

"Let's go meet some mistresses."

Chapter 28

Rachel met Mistress Hower in the lobby. Scanning continuously, Traxen silently followed a step behind her. The hotel owner led them to the restaurant where large spaces separated the tables and translucent half walls surrounded each grouping of seated females. Some of the females had males standing behind them. As they passed the first one, she realized force fields, not walls, encircled the tables.

Mistress Hower noticed her peering closer at the technology.

"The fields provide some privacy from other diners. They also keep each party's sound from others in the room. When a mistress chooses to reward or punish a body servant, the noise does not bother anyone. We see many business meetings taking place during meals here."

"Interesting," Rachel murmured. Louder, she said, "Who exactly am I meeting?" **Glad I remembered to say I and not we. I really don't like this planet's customs.**

"Mistresses Pitman, Thespa, and Summi. Mistress Summi owns a lovely fabric factory you might be interested in, while the other two own bremmite mines."

"Isn't Mistress Pitman the one you said was hosting a party tonight?"

"Yes. Hopefully, she'll invite you after you meet."

"I appreciate your assistance, Mistress Hower. Tell me, do you receive a finder's fee for facilitating new opportunities?"

A cunning expression crossed the female's face.

"Some mistresses choose to gift me with credits or gifts. However, the social status I enjoy and loyal customers to my establishment mean more to me."

"I'll keep that in mind."

Rachel recognized Pitman and Thespa from the Wing Raiders' video. Pitman's body servant knelt at her feet with his head bowed, while the other males stood behind their mistresses. **The older fuchsia female with a high hairdo must be Mistress Summi. Her deep orbital sockets make her appear even more elderly and gaunt.**

As Mistress Summi disengaged the force field, the youngest Rumaskan said firmly, "I have told you numerous times, Mistress Pitman, my land and mines are not for sale."

"You hardly make a profit on your mines. I can do it better."

"My profits are none of your concern." Mistress Thespa turned at their approach and her set face softened. "Mistress Hower, good day to you."

"Felicitations. May I introduce Mistress Rachel from Costonia?" Mistress Hower made the introductions. "She is hoping to secure trade opportunities between our two planets."

"Mistress Summi, our hostess tells me you own a fabric factory. What types of cloth do you manufacture?" Rachel focused her attention on the elderly female.

"All types, although my production tends toward the more luxurious fabrics for clothing and home decoration."

"Would it be too forward of me to request a tour?"

"I would love to show you. Are you free later today?"

"Absolutely. I appreciate you fitting me into your schedule so quickly."

Mistress Pitman interrupted. An unnatural smile appeared on her salmon-colored skin. She wore her lime green hair in a severe ornate bun. **She takes resting bitch face to a whole new level.**

"I own the largest bremmite mine operation on Rumaska."

"How lovely. And you, Mistress Thespa?" Rachel turned to the blush pink female who tucked a strand of her long, green hair behind her pointy ear. **I think I'm finally getting used to their eyes.**

"I also mine bremmite."

"Are there many uses for bremmite?"

As Mistress Pitman expounded on the ore, Mistress Summi gestured for Rachel to sit with them. Traxen held her chair for her, pushed her closer to the table, then stepped back. Mistress Hower left.

"Interesting," Rachel said when the Rumaskan finally took a breath. "Do you have any suggestions on how I might spend my free time while on your planet?"

"If you like animals, we have a wonderful zoo outside the city with many examples of our native wildlife," Mistress Thespa said.

"She obviously requires higher culture than the zoo." Mistress Pitman raised her nose and sniffed. "I'm hosting a party this evening. Anyone who is worth knowing will be there." She glared at the younger female. "Even some who aren't worth knowing will be there as well." **Wow. Catty much?**

"Mistress Pitman, our guest is probably too busy to attend your little gathering on such short notice." Mistress Summi took a bite of her meal.

Rachel widened her eyes.

"Was that an invitation, Mistress Pitman? If so, I would be happy to attend. Just send me the details."

A meal arrived for Rachel compliments of the hotel owner. While she ate, she committed the Rumaskans' words to memory as they shared information about who else would be attending the party. She made mental notes to seek out several to shore up her alias while on Rumaska. **I'll have to ask Traxen if there was anything else Costonia might be interested in.**

The more the females talked, the less she liked Mistress Pitman. Self-important, nasty, and taking pleasure in the debasement of the male at her side, the Rumaskan obviously had an inflated view of her own importance.

"Pet."

Traxen stepped forward and leaned down.

"Yes, Mistress."

Rachel speared a bite of the meat on her plate and held it up to his mouth.

"Eat."

Traxen's eyes darkened as he stared into her eyes and opened his lips. He chewed quietly. She fed him several more bites before leaning back.

"Thank you, Mistress."

She caressed his face smoothing the flesh near his fake scars peeking out from his head covering.

"Were the tastes to your liking?"

"Anything you feed me from your own hand has a wonderful flavor, Mistress."

From the corner of her eyes, she saw Mistress Thespa hide a smile, while Mistress Pitman pinched her lips together.

"How did you manage to secure Svesti as body servants? They are exceedingly difficult to catch in the wild," the disagreeable female said. "I heard you have three of them and not one of them in a pain collar."

"In the wild?" Rachel motioned for Traxen to step back and turned her attention to Mistress Pitman.

"Our body servant market finds unsecured males on other planets and brings them here to sell so we have a steady supply."

Rachel frowned. "That sounds like slavery to me."

"Oh, males aren't intelligent enough to know how to take care of females unless they are properly trained. We are doing them a favor." She turned to her body servant. "Don't you agree?"

The poor male's face tightened momentarily before he replied, "Yes, Mistress Pitman."

The Rumaskan pressed a button on a controller and the male fell forward writhing in pain on the floor at her feet.

"You hesitated in your response."

When she released the button, the male gasped for breath and pushed himself to his knees.

"Thank you for correcting me, Mistress."

Mistress Summi made a moue of distress.

"Mistress Pitman, you know I dislike when body servants are punished publicly."

Mistress Pitman snorted at the older female, then turned to Rachel and smiled victoriously.

"That is how you properly train a male."

Rachel clenched her fists in her lap to keep from choking the cruel female. Taking a measured breath, she relaxed her shoulders.

"We will have to agree to disagree. I find your methods appalling and unnecessary."

"You mean to say you have never punished your body servants? I find that unlikely. You would be unable to control them."

"My males do not serve me out of fear. I find males who crave what I give them. Any discipline simply means withholding my affections for a time."

"Affections?" Mistress Pitman scoffed. "Their duty is to serve our needs."

Rachel shook her head.

"In my opinion, a good mistress truly cares about her males." She crooked a finger at Traxen. Grateful she once worked a case that involved a BDSM club, Rachel used what she learned from a dominatrix about male chastity and orgasm denial to her advantage.

"Pet, please answer honestly for the other mistresses. If I told you I was going to keep that lovely cock of yours caged indefinitely, not allow you to touch me, and I would limit my affections, what would your reaction be?"

"Mistress, have I upset you? Please tell me what I need to do better. I know you own my pleasure." He closed his eyes and bowed his head close to hers. "Feeling your touch and being allowed to honor you is all I require to be a happy male." **Wow. He played the part perfectly.**

Rachel tugged on his braid and pulled him close enough to kiss but stopped. He opened his eyes at her. She smiled and against his lips said, "No." Then she released him. He groaned and stepped back, his tail stiff.

She swiveled to face the other females. Mistress Summi's eyes were wide, while Mistress Thespa appeared amused. Mistress Pitman's eyes blazed in anger.

"As you can see, a firm but gentle interaction is all that is required. There are ways to increase his desire to serve me, but I don't think you're ready to hear those."

"I would like to hear more about your training philosophy," the eldest female said. "Perhaps I can take you on a tour of my facilities now and we can discuss them."

Rachel dabbed her lips with her napkin.

"That is an excellent idea."

After taking her leave of the mine owners, Rachel, with Traxen silently opening doors or trailing behind her, spent the next several hours with Mistress Summi and arranged for samples to be delivered to the **Firebrand**. **The quality**

fabrics might be needed when more humans emigrated to Costonia.

Returning to their suite, Rachel stripped her clothes off.

"Come, pet, let's finish that bath that was interrupted earlier."

With the water running, Traxen took off his pants and head covering. He crowded her into the sink. She inhaled his unique scent and her breasts felt full against his chest.

"You deliberately tried to arouse me all afternoon, **belgella**. Your hands drifting on my skin, fingers pulling on my nipples, and your fingernails digging into my ass. This **crekkin'** cage keeps my cock from becoming erect. It is most uncomfortable," he growled low. His callused hands cupped her ass and lifted her.

A teasing smile lifted her lips.

"I had to keep you looking like a needy male desperate to do anything for me for our cover."

"I need you. Now release me so you can ride me."

She laughed.

"I'm enjoying this. Keep the cage on so you're in character for the party tonight."

"I'm going to be humping your leg if this keeps up much longer." Frustration laced his voice.

"Come on. Let's wash up while we talk about today. Then we can figure out what we need to wear tonight."

Pluvi Frulix glared at his nephew, Lerix Sproid. The younger male appeared disheveled and exhausted.

"You failed."

"I had her. The two transporting the human lost her. I even arranged for it to look like someone else."

"You failed and made me look incompetent." Rage filled Frulix and his vision dimmed. **Take action now** chanted in his head.

"Uncle, you need to calm yourself. I can fix it."

"Do not tell me to calm myself, you useless **naroon**." Frulix's claws extended as he yelled.

Fear crossed Sproid's face.

"Uncle, I apologize for my missteps. What can I do to make it up to you?"

A disjointed smile crossed Frulix's face.

"You can die." Sproid's shock at the claws opening his throat was the last thing Frulix saw.

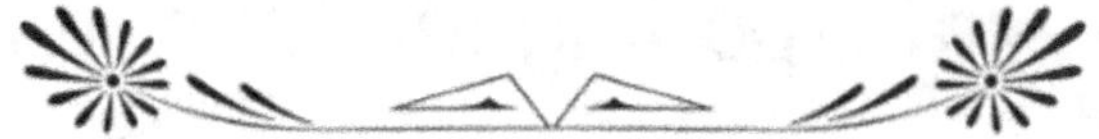

Miffed at the revealing outfit she wore, Rachel strove to keep her discomfort from her face as they arrived at Mistress Pitman's estate. After asking her name, a body servant with a small bell hung from his erect cock directed them to the gardens. Her mood improved as she heard the tiny tinkle of the bell when he moved to greet the next attendees. As per his role, Traxen followed her when they stopped in a line.

"What's going on?" Rachel asked the female in front of her whose clothing was even more outrageous than what Rachel had on.

"We wait to be announced and allow our body servants to honor us in front of the crowd." The small female looked at her with her eyebrows raised. "First time on Rumaska?"

"Yes."

"I hope you enjoy your visit." The female looked Traxen over. "You have a fine specimen. I hope he honors you well."

"He always has."

Mistress Pitman approached.

"Oh, good, you're here." She looked at Traxen's genitals and frowned. "I had hoped you would have displayed your body servant's cock for our pleasure."

"His cock is for my pleasure, Mistress Pitman."

The arrogant female reached out to Traxen's cock. Rachel's hand immediately grasped the Rumaskan's wrist and squeezed, stopping her from touching him.

"No one touches my pets but me."

"We can arrange a swap of body servants for the evening." Mistress Pitman waved a large Jalaxian closer to her. "Manx here will give you much pleasure."

Rachel's lips thinned.

"No. I do not share." The other females waiting in line avidly listened to their discussion.

Mistress Pitman laughed uncomfortably as she tugged on her arm. Rachel refused to let go.

"Come now. We all do it."

"Pet, kneel." Traxen knelt in front of her. "Take off your head covering." He slowly untied the fabric and pulled it. When he exposed his face, loud gasps sounded from the crowd around them.

"Those scars, as well as the ones on his back, occurred the one time I allowed another female an evening with him. The mistress involved knew he was to be treated with care, yet she marred his perfection." Rachel's voice hardened. "I. Do. Not. Share."

Mistress Pitman's eyes widened, and she shuddered.

"His face is hideous."

Rachel's hand gently caressed his face and leaned to kiss his scars.

"His face is a testament to his loyalty to me. He did not hurt the mistress, just restrained her long enough to comm me for instructions."

The small female in front of them asked quietly, "What happened to the mistress?"

Rachel allowed an evil smile to cross her face.

"She bears double the number of scars she inflicted on my pet. I enjoyed punishing her as I will any other female who touches or harms what is mine." She stepped back and released Mistress Pitman. "Pet, please don your head covering."

"Thank you, Mistress."

"You may stand." He nodded and fluidly rose to his feet.

Mistress Pitman narrowed her eyes.

"I think you care too much for your males. They aren't worth the effort." A cunning expression lit her face.

"Again, Mistress Pitman, we will have to agree to disagree. While my pets love to safeguard me, I protect them equally for their faithful service." Rachel turned to Traxen.

"Pet, while we are on Rumaska, if any mistress attempts to touch or harm you when I am not present, you have my permission to defend yourself."

Traxen's full lips tipped up at the corners and he nodded once.

"As you wish, Mistress."

"How dare you give such an order?" Mistress Pitman snarled. "That is dangerous. He could hurt any one of us without provocation."

"He would use the least amount of force necessary to carry out my instructions if any mistress is foolish enough to disrespect **my** boundaries."

Mistress Pitman stomped off, her skinny ass cheeks visible under her transparent pink gown.

"It appears our hostess is upset." The small female grinned. "I like you already."

Rachel smiled back at her.

"It's been an interesting day."

Chapter 29

Traxen's cock wanted to bust out of its cage when Rachel put Mistress Pitman in her place. The intense pressure made him want to squirm. Her explanation of his fake scars gave her a perfect reason to keep from sharing him. And her public order to keep other females from touching him gladdened him. **She really is my warrior goddess.**

The line moved forward and over the shorter Rumaskans, he could see the front. He bit the inside of his cheek when he saw the next female announced. She stepped forward onto a lighted platform and her male knelt in front of her. The male kissed her cunt and the female spread her legs wider. Her head fell back, and she gripped his head to her. Eventually, she pushed him away, her pink face flushed. **Crek. I'm not sure what we should do. While I'll take any**

opportunity I can get to be between Rachel's thighs, I really don't want others to see her pleasure.

When Rachel's shoulders tensed, he knew she saw the next female being pleasured on the platform. She waved him closer, and he bent toward her.

"Are you okay with this? I can arrange an emergency for us to leave," she breathed in his ear.

Shivers ran down his spine. He looked out at the party and saw that many people ignored the introductions, although with Rachel being new to the planet, he expected more to pay attention when she was announced. The males didn't look at the activity on the platform at all, either serving their own mistresses or scanning for threats. Making the decision, he nodded once to her.

"I'm fine, Mistress. Thank you for asking." He straightened.

"Mistress Rachel of Costonia."

Rachel's back straightened and she strode confidently to the platform. The blue gown she wore shimmered in the moonlight, then turned translucent when the bright light on the stage hit it. Her lithe form showed clearly. The bustier barely covered her nipples, while her panties cut downward in a low vee above her cunt. He lowered himself to his knees and gazed up at her. **Goddess, she's gorgeous.**

She met his eyes as he slowly pressed his lips to her panties and placed an open-mouthed kiss there. Inhaling her arousal scent, he growled low against her and her hips jerked forward. He wanted to pull her to him, but all the other males he saw only touched their mistresses with their mouths. He clenched his fists on his thighs to keep from reaching for her.

His tongue slipped below the vee of her panties and licked her clit. Her hands rested on his shoulders and her eyes never left his. He smiled against her flesh when her fingernails pressed into his skin.

Tonguing her gently, he let the crowd fade away and concentrated solely on her. Using a rhythm and pressure he knew she liked, he took his time building her pleasure. Her eyelids drooped as she relaxed, but she continued to stare at him with a fond smile. Her fingers kneaded his skin, and her scent grew heavy in the air around them. Watching her delicate skin flush as her body reacted to his ministrations brought all his protective instincts forward. **Mine. All mine.**

Her limbs stiffened, and she shuddered when her orgasm overtook her. Desperately, he tried to force his tongue lower to taste her where her wetness flowed. **Crekkin' panties.**

She came back to herself and placed her hands on his cheeks and tugged his head backwards. She leaned down and placed a warm kiss on his forehead.

"Good pet. You honor me well."

His cock surged against his cage. **Crek. I adore this female. I never would have guessed I would enjoy acting submissive for any female.**

"Thank you, Mistress." He stood and escorted her from the platform.

The small Rumaskan who had been before them in line tittered as they descended the platform.

"Your body servant brings you great status, Mistress. Congratulations."

Rachel nodded.

"Thank you. I'm Mistress Rachel."

"Mistress Linoro. I hear you are searching for business opportunities."

Rachel tilted her head.

"Have you any suggestions?"

"I have an estate by the sea with a fishery. I raise **wutta**, a flaky fish that is considered a delicacy on many planets. In fact, Mistress Pitman may be serving some this evening."

"I might have buyers interested in something like that. Could you send me the appropriate information? I may also wish to tour your fishery."

"I'd be happy to." Mistress Linoro leaned closer and lowered her voice. "Anyone who stands up to Mistress Pitman is someone I would like to know. Just be careful. She doesn't like to be upstaged."

"Thank you for your warning."

Traxen took a closer look at the female's body servant. An unmarred, healthy body with a pleasant expression on his face, the Rumaskan male gave the appearance of being well treated. He wore a jeweled collar indicating status as a favorite. **I hope Rachel agrees with me that we should only deal with mistresses who aren't deliberately cruel to their males. We can't change their culture and we need the bremmite, but we can spend our credits with the females who are kinder.**

He followed Rachel as she mingled at the party, fetching her food and drink when she requested it. The soft lighting under the bright moon highlighted her features and he found himself struck anew at her beauty. Listening as she arranged tours of Mistress Linoro's fishery and Mistress Thespa's mine for the next day, he surreptitiously licked his lips to capture more of her essence leftover from their arrival in the gardens. He breathed in her scent still heavy on his face. His cock continued to strain in its cage. Need built within him. **I want to bury my cock in her. The cage seems like it's making my desire even greater.**

While his mind never completely stopped pondering the information Rachel gathered, he found it more relaxed as she made the decisions and directed his actions. **I wouldn't like being submissive all the time, but focusing completely on her needs has its own alluring quality.**

As interesting as the personal revelations were to him, he kept an eye on Mistress Pitman. He didn't trust her and believed she would retaliate against Rachel at some point.

He also watched Manx. **How did she get a Jalaxian for a body servant? The male's face remains impassive no matter what she says or does. Even his short tail doesn't reveal any emotions.**

The longer Traxen observed the blue male, the more he realized that Manx did no more or less than ordered. Like him, the males with Mistresses, Summi, Thespa, and Linoro took small anticipatory actions to increase their comfort without being asked. Not Manx.

The way the females dressed reminded him of visiting pleasure planets, with the exception of the males not enjoying the experience. Inwardly he winced when a collar shocked a male and he grunted in pain. One poor male, one of Mistress Pitman's, screamed while her eyes eagerly absorbed his agony. Manx's eye twitched and his fists clenched before he relaxed them, almost a mirror of Traxen's reaction. **That female is an abomination, and Manx is not as stoic as I thought.**

Not long afterward, Rachel made her excuses and they returned to the hotel. Her face set in tense lines, she waved him to the sanitary facility.

"Someone needs to stop that female," she hissed as she ran the water in the shower.

She undressed quickly and he followed suit. Reaching down, she released his cock from its cage with a gentle tug. Her small hands massaged his shaft, and his erection sprang to life. She pulled him under the water and pressed against him, firmly stroking his cock. When she suddenly dropped to her knees and her hot mouth encased its tip, he slapped his hand on the wall to keep on his feet. **Crek. That feels even more intense than usual.**

Traxen groaned loudly as she licked and sucked his engorged flesh using her hands to reach everywhere her mouth couldn't. Heavy lidded eyes watched her pretty mouth engulf as much as him as she could manage. She swallowed and the suction sent licks of fire up his spine. **I need to be inside her.**

His tail wrapped around her upper arm and pulled. Her mouth reluctantly left him with an audible pop. He squatted, lifted her, and pinned her to the wall. Devouring her mouth, he tasted his pre-cum mixed with her own addictive flavor. Spearing her with his fingers, he found the overwhelming evidence of her desire. **Thank the Goddess.**

Withdrawing his fingers, he lined up against her entrance and slipped into her warm, wet cavern in a single thrust. They both moaned.

She wound her legs around him and broke off the kiss long enough to demand, "Fuck me. Hard."

"As you wish," he grunted. Maneuvering his hips, he pummeled in and out of her. His tail teased her hardened nipples, and she slid up the wall each time he bottomed out inside her. His base node slammed into her clit repeatedly.

"Yes. Yes. Yes. More," she chanted, her hands desperately skimming and squeezing his flesh.

Traxen gazed down at her, loving the rising color under her thin skin. Her rippling cunt squeezed his head nodes each time he rammed into her. Primal heat and joy filled him.

"Come for me. Now." His raspy words stirred her wet hair.

Rachel screamed as her orgasm overtook her. She convulsed hard around his cock as it fought its way into her before it erupted spreading his heat into hers. They held onto each other tightly as they gasped for breath.

He supported her with his arms and tail when her legs dropped to stand shakily. Dropping a tender kiss on her lips, he savored her languid softness against him.

"You're mine, Mistress."

A tired grin lifted her lips.

"And you're mine, pet."

While she leaned on him, he took his time washing her hair and body before quickly taking care of himself. He dried her with a plush towel and carried her to the bed. Throwing an arm and leg over him, she snuggled close while he combed her hair with his claws.

"We should discuss today," she murmured low.

"Rest now. Talk in the morning." His tail stroked her calf and his hand rested on the small of her back.

"You sure?"

Louder, he said, "Rest, Mistress. It was a long day."

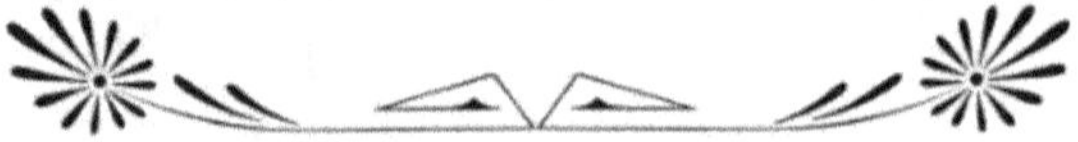

The next morning while they were getting ready in the sanitary facility, they compared impressions of all that occurred. His cock wasn't happy about its relegation to the cage again. But pleased that they were in agreement about which mistresses were worth pursuing, Traxen checked his prosthetic scars, eyes, and clan marking. All seemed to be well. After donning his head covering, he looked at himself from different angles and decided he enjoyed the rakish look. Chuckling to himself, he followed Rachel into the bedroom. **Time to talk for the listening devices.**

"Are you ready for morning meal, Mistress?"

"That's a good idea, pet."

"Do you wish to eat in or go to the restaurant?"

"Order us something, please. You know what I like."

Traxen contacted the concierge for food to be delivered. He helped Rachel into her chosen outfit—one similar to the day they arrived.

When their meal showed up, he laid it out on the table and served her before taking his seat.

"What are your plans today, Mistress?"

She hummed around her bite of crispy meat.

"We shall return to the **Firebrand** and visit Mistress Linoro's fishery. Then this afternoon, we will tour Mistress Thespa's mines."

"Will you need to file a flight plan with the Rumaskans?"

"Thank you for the reminder, pet. I'll comm Mistress Relim and check on that."

"Happy to assist, Mistress."

"We'll head to the **Firebrand** early so I can give some attention to my other pets before we need to leave. I know they don't like to go long without my presence." She smirked at him.

He glared at her teasing.

"As you wish, Mistress." **Fortunately, the camera doesn't face this direction or our watchers would know my face doesn't match my pleasant words.**

Laughing sultrily, she said, "You know you're my favorite." A coy expression filled her eyes as she sipped her drink.

"Yes, Mistress." **You'll pay for that later, belgella.**

They briefed Tesix and Westov before Rachel informed Mistress Relim on their intentions. Tesix piloted them to the fishery while Westov reported the results of their research.

"The planet is beautiful, especially outside of the cities," Traxen said as they flew over lush forests and mountains with yellow foliage and colorful flowers.

"If only their culture matched," Rachel grumbled.

"There is a huge disparity of treatment of their males."

"Anyone who believes a pain collar is necessary and enjoys using it is a despot." Rachel frowned. "That Pitman woman is cruel. Not a dime of Costonia's money should line her pockets."

"We need bremmite, but I agree. She should not profit from us."

They approached a pink ocean lined with black sand, and Tesix landed them near the fishery.

Mistress Linoro met them as Traxen and Rachel disembarked leaving Tesix and Westov to guard their ship. The female was dressed much more conservatively in pants similar to Rachel's but of a rougher material. Her breasts were lifted by a demi-bra. She wore an unbuttoned short-sleeved blouse over it tied at her waist and comfortable shoes.

"I'm so happy you made it." She looked at Rachel's outfit. "We dress more casually in the rural areas and usually allow our males to cover their cocks unless there's a function to attend. It can be dangerous for them otherwise while they're working."

"Pet, cover up."

"Yes, Mistress." Traxen pulled out the fabric Tesix had fashioned for him similar to what he and Westov used to shield their cocks from Rachel. He arranged it and hid his satisfaction at removing his shaft and ass from public view.

Traxen found the tour interesting. Mistress Linoro's knowledge of each step of the process impressed him, as did the good humor of those who worked in the fishery. The Rumaskan males jested and laughed as they toiled, and one group sang as they conducted their duties. While females supervised, they did not abuse the males but instead treated them as peers.

"I see you don't use pain collars."

Traxen perked up at Rachel's statement. **She's right. None of them wore the atrocities.**

Mistress Linoro pursed her lips.

"Many of us don't. Those collars started being used several generations back when Rumaskan elite mistresses decided they wanted offworlder males for body servants and began purchasing slaves to train. Their behavior leeched into more of our society. It's much worse for males in the cities. Out here, our males are raised to revere females, while females are taught to care for their males and not take their service for granted. That's why I sought you out after your disagreement with Mistress Pitman. Your treatment of your body servant aligns with my beliefs."

Traxen silently approved of Rachel's subsequent arrangement to purchase several stasis cases of **wutta** to take with them. The females talked about quantities, pricing, and potential delivery schedules. **I can think of several Svesti that may want to add wutta to their import list.**

Rachel comm'd Tesix to open the **Firebrand** to load the fish while assuring him he didn't need to change his apparel. Mistress Linoro grinned when she saw the other Svesti.

"You have good taste, Mistress Rachel."

Rachel shrugged.

"Thank you for everything, Mistress Linoro. I'll contact you after my buyers have the opportunity to sample the **wutta**. I'm certain we will be doing business in the future."

Pluvi Frulix stared at the scene in front of him in shock. His nephew lay dead on the floor eviscerated by multiple claw wounds. The poor male's eyes bulged and bloody handprints ringed his neck.

His healer suffered a similar fate. An injector rested beside his lifeless hand. Blood spray and spatter coated the walls and surfaces. Frulix looked down at himself and began to shake when he realized his hands and clothes were soaked in the males' blood. **What have I done? Grissa will never forgive me.**

Frozen, he stood there as the blood dried on his skin. When the door opened, palace guards in armor pointed blasters at him. He heard someone say, "**Crek.**" Another male gagged.

As a guard pulled his arms behind him to restrain him, he didn't resist. His shoulders and tail drooped.

"Did you do this?"

Bewildered, Frulix shook his head.

"I don't know."

Chapter 30

Rachel loaded up a tray with sandwiches and water pouches from the cooling unit to take to the cockpit. The Svesti thanked her and ate while the **Firebrand** flew toward Mistress Thespa's bremmite mine. On the far side of Rumaska, it would take another two hours before they would reach their destination.

While the males talked, she reviewed everything they'd learned about Rumaska so far. **What a weird place.**

She hoped her impressions of Mistress Thespa were correct. **I'll be disappointed if she fails to give her workers dignity and respect. The Wing Raiders said she had the smallest mine on the planet. Is she capable of handling the amounts Traxen needs for the new**

engines? If not, maybe the rest can come from Mistress Overly.

"**Belgella**, are you all right? You seem distracted." Traxen brushed her hair from her face.

"Just thinking about our next stop and whether we'll be successful." She turned her head into his hand and kissed his palm.

A low rumble reached her ears, and she inhaled his woody aroma. **Damn, he's hot—in more ways than one.**

"We'll be fine. You've played your part perfectly." He winked at her. "You make a wonderful mistress."

"And you an exemplary pet."

"What about us?" Westov chimed in.

"Oh, you're good pets, too." She threw the plasfilm from her sandwich at him. "You just need a lot more positive reinforcement than others."

"I'm wounded, Mistress." Westov clutched his chest in an exaggerated movement.

Tesix slapped Westov on the back of the head.

"You can't help yourself, can you?"

"Would you stop hitting me? Mistress, he keeps smacking me. Make him stop," Westov whined with a grin.

Everyone laughed at Westov's antics. Traxen's relaxed demeanor pleased her. **Even with the discomfort of acting like a slave, he needed this time away from Costonia. With all his responsibilities, I think he forgets to take time to be himself.**

"Come. Let's go wash the fish smell off us before we reach the mine. It feels like the odor has taken up permanent residence in my nostrils." Traxen offered her his hand.

"I wasn't going to mention it, but yes, you do stink," Westov said. He ducked when Tesix's hand reached toward him. "I'm serious. Stop hitting me."

Rachel shook her head in exasperation as she allowed Traxen to help her up.

"Play nice, pets. We'll be back."

As they landed, Rachel asked, "Are you sure this is the mine?" The ship sat in front of a beautiful mountain with dark green grass. Black-barked trees covered the rising landscape.

"I can see the entrance there." Tesix pointed.

When Mistress Thespa approached the ship, she wore pants that looked like denim and a tight-fitting shirt that covered her breasts. Rachel and Traxen disembarked from the **Firebrand** and greeted the Rumaskan.

"Welcome." Mistress Thespa greeted them. "We're looking forward to having you tour the mine."

Rachel saw numerous men loading up the ore and transporting it to another location.

"Where are they taking it?"

"To be processed. The raw ore itself is filled with impurities."

They watched as another group of males came out of the entrance and swapped positions with the ones loading the ore.

"Why are they doing that?" asked Rachel.

"Because the ore can be dangerous in enclosed spaces, I have the males rotate out every hour and change duties. I automate as much as I can to minimize the risk to my workers. Everyone is also checked every lunar by a healer for any potential health issues."

"That's very progressive of you." Rachel nodded.

"I wouldn't want my profits to come at the expense of others' health."

Rachel smiled and talked about tonnage and delivery needs. Mistress Thespa's face started to fall.

"What seems to be the problem?"

"At this time, I can't handle that large of a contract."

"I'm sorry to hear that. Is it a supply problem? Or do you not have enough resources?"

"It's a bit of both. While this mine is small, a recent geological survey shows a large deposit elsewhere on my property. I don't have the funds to develop it properly at this time." She frowned. "Also, six weeks ago, one hundred of my workers went missing."

"Missing?"

"They were our single males, not specifically attached to a female. They were in their barracks at the end of one day and missing the next. There were signs of a struggle, but as of yet, no one knows exactly what happened. I contacted our ruling commission for assistance and they say they are investigating, but I haven't heard anything yet." The Rumaskan's fingers whitened as she gripped her hands. "I hate thinking they are in danger but not being able to help them."

"Is this type of disappearance common?" Rachel's eyes scanned the area.

"Over the last several years, we've seen more of them. At first, mistresses reported the loss of one or two males and everyone assumed they chose to escape. But then greater numbers started disappearing. It's disheartening. Even with the extra security I put in place, it still occurred."

"I'm sorry to hear about your males." Rachel thought about the new ore deposit. "What would it take to mine the other location?"

"Machinery and staff. Unfortunately, I don't have enough of either. Most of my credits go to support those on my estate."

"Do you expect to operate the new mine in a similar manner as you do here?" Rachel took the Rumaskan equivalent of a human hard hat offered by Mistress Thespa.

"If I could, I would automate even more to further reduce risk to the workers." The Rumaskan led them into the well-lit entrance. Fortunately, Traxen didn't have to stoop to fit inside.

They entered a lift and descended into the bowels of the earth. Mistress Thespa handed them masks.

"Please wear these to filter the dust."

When they exited, Rachel scanned the large tunnel. Bright lights illuminated their way. They approached a half dozen males using a machine to extract the purple ore.

"In its raw state, bremmite is brittle and requires careful handling. As you can see, they stack it in containers and seal them when full. Then the containers are transported to the refinery. Once the ore is processed, it changes to a silver color. On average, each container yields about half its size in purified bremmite."

"Fascinating. What do you do with the waste?"

Mistress Thespa grinned.

"We liquefy it and sell it as dyes or paints. In some cases, we add various elements to create other colors. After bremmite goes through the purification process, the excess no longer poses a health risk." **I like that nothing is wasted or tossed into the environment.**

"Impressive."

As they toured the mine and the refinery, Rachel noted everyone worked hard, but overall, they were cheerful. Rumaskan females showed up at break times with snacks and beverages and shared genuine affection with their males.

Several times, various males approached with a tablet for Mistress Thespa to approve some data or action. Courteous and pleasant, she interacted with all as she would females. **I believe our best option is Mistress Thespa. I wonder if she's willing to negotiate differently.**

"Have you drawn up a business plan for the new mine?"

"Yes, in the hopes of securing a loan. However, the terms were not to my liking."

"If you are willing to share that and the geological survey, I may be able to help."

Mistress Thespa's lips pressed together.

"I'm not willing to give up any percentage of the mine's ownership."

"I wouldn't suggest it. If my buyers believe your plan is financially sound, I may be able to convince them to purchase the equipment in return for a guaranteed minimum amount of refined bremmite for a set number of years. A total amount would be the overall goal, which you could supply sooner, if you wished. Once you've supplied them with the total, the contract could have a provision for their cost of any additional bremmite for the life of the contract."

The Rumaskan narrowed her eyes.

"Would they expect all the bremmite we mine during the contract?"

"Doubtful. Since it wouldn't be prudent to leave you without profits to reinvest on your own, I imagine the cost of the equipment, refining costs, your projected estimates of how much you can safely mine in the time period, as well as the size of the deposit would all be considerations in what percentage of the mined ore would need to be factored in by all parties." Rachel grinned. "Of course, my buyers would expect a better rate per tonnage than the rest of your customers as they would have to wait to see a return on their credits versus paying upon delivery."

"What if something happens and I can't deliver?"

"They would retrieve their equipment and bill you the difference. We could have the contract specify how much bremmite is required for each piece of equipment or batch of supplies, so there can be no doubt how much of it you own outright after providing any of the refined ore."

Hope shone in Mistress Thespa's eyes.

"Do you really believe you can convince them?"

"I think obtaining a steady supply from someone who treats her workers well will make them seriously consider making you an offer. Whether or not all of you can agree on specific terms, I cannot foresee."

Mistress Thespa tapped her tablet.

"I've just sent you the geological survey. I will work up a proposal based on my business plan for the rest and send it to you within a week."

"Excellent. I believe this is the best option for all parties."

Traxen's tail tugged at her waistband as she moved to follow the mine owner back to the **Firebrand**.

"Excellent job, **belgella**," he said quietly. "A solution I'm not sure I would have considered."

Rachel flushed with pride. **I'm glad he supports the idea. It helps her and helps Costonia. I guess all those years observing my father taught me something.**

Chapter 31

Traxen strode down the hotel hallway. They received a call from the concierge, stating there was a delivery for Rachel. He was looking forward to spending the evening with her as he entered the lift. Three other males joined him. Not recognizing them, he just nodded and moved to the corner.

The lift stopped unexpectedly between floors. One of the males moved closer and injected Traxen. His vision began to blur and his claws extracted. The other two males restrained him.

One said, "It's time for you to come with us."

Traxen's knees were weak, and he could barely walk. The males wrapped his arms over their shoulders and restarted the lift moving. As they got into a transport, he heard one of them say, "Maybe now she'll leave us alone for a while."

"That's unlikely. Don't you think?"

Traxen heard no more as he passed out.

When he regained consciousness, he was manacled to a wall with his arms and legs spread. The space around him appeared to be a bedroom decorated in gaudy, overblown textures and colors. As he tried to clear the fog from his mind, he heard footsteps approaching and a door open. Mistress Pitman entered the room with Manx in trail.

"Now I have you where I want you."

"Mistress Rachel will not be happy," Traxen growled.

"Mistress Rachel will never find you. I have done this before, and I'll do it again." A look of self-satisfaction crossed her narrow face.

"What does that mean?"

"It means I take what I want, and I want you."

"I will defend myself."

"That would be something to see." With an evil smile, she pressed the button on a controller and electric shocks sent lightning throughout his body. **Crek. I didn't notice I had on a pain collar.**

Trying to hold in his howl from the pain coursing through him, he gritted his teeth and grunted. His knees buckled, his shoulders strained from the weight of his body, and the restraints chafed his skin. When she released the button, the excruciating pain subsided, although the effects still shook his body. He glared at her. **I've never harmed a female before, but now I'm willing to change that.**

Mistress Pitman approached and took off his head covering.

"You do look dangerous. I like taming dangerous men."

"You will never tame me."

"Don't be so sure about that."

She reached down and grasped his caged member. Traxen grimaced at the feel of her cold hand on his body. His nostrils flared at her rancid scent so close to him.

"I'll have to get someone in here to take this off you."

"It's coded to my mistress."

"That's okay. We have ways around that. Manx, check him for a tracker." **Crek.**

The Jalaxian pulled out a scanner and made some adjustments. He ran it over Traxen's body keeping the screen tilted away from the female. Traxen dropped his eyelids and remained impassive when the screen turned blue indicating the tracker in his arm. Manx turned off the scanner.

"Nothing, Mistress."

Traxen kept the surprise from his face. **Interesting. Do I have an ally?**

"Mistress Rachel isn't as smart as she thinks she is if she didn't chip you. Unfortunately, I have an important function I need to attend tonight. I'll play with you tomorrow." The Rumaskan left the room.

Manx stepped forward and silently offered Traxen water before following the female. When Traxen started to speak, the Jalaxian's lips thinned, and his eyes darted to the side. Traxen subtly dipped his chin and let the male know that he understood there were surveillance devices.

Alone, Traxen breathed through the pain. When he regained control of his limbs, he slowly stood. He rolled his head trying to relieve the residual tension in his neck and shoulders. **Time to examine my options. Valadium restraints—that's a problem.**

Three doors. The one the Rumaskan and Manx used should be an exit. One was probably the sanitary facility. The third might lead to another room or possibly a closet. Floor-length curtains obscured what appeared to be two large windows. **I have no idea what floor I'm on. I'm obviously no longer in the hotel.**

His lips twisted in disgust as he looked for potential weapons. **This room is exceedingly ugly. Mistress Hower has much better taste.**

Somehow I need to get the control for the pain collar from her so I can escape.

Traxen tried to find a comfortable position while he bided his time. **At least my torture won't truly start until the morning. I hope Rachel finds me before then.**

Traxen woke when he heard a sound. He had no idea what time it was and couldn't see anything in the dark. **Sleeping

standing up hurts. I'm glad I relieved myself before I left our suite or I'd be even more uncomfortable.

He concentrated intently trying to determine what interrupted his fitful rest. A large hand covered his mouth.

"Not a word. Nod if you understand." The barely audible words were spoken near his ear. Recognizing Manx's scent, Traxen indicated his compliance.

Manx silently released the restraints, catching the chains and gently straightening so they didn't clink. With his back to Traxen, he placed one of Traxen's hands on his shoulder. Traxen followed him matching step for step as they left the room.

They had to stop and hide several times to avoid discovery. Eventually Manx led him outside where the sun barely lit the sky as dawn approached. Traxen took in their surroundings as they ran through a garden and a thick stand of trees. On the other side, a mountain faced them. Unlike the one on

Mistress Thespa's estate, the land had been stripped leaving ugly scars on the landscape.

Once inside a storage shed near the mine entrance, Manx relaxed.

"I don't have time to explain everything to you right now. I have to get back to her before she notices my absence. She will be able to track you via your collar. You need to be found in this area."

Traxen's tail flicked, and he growled.

"I need to escape and contact my people."

"Mistress Rachel and others will be here within the hour, but this will only work if Mistress Pitman is near the mine when they arrive. Much depends on it." Manx's face hardened. "I know you have no reason to trust me, yet I am asking anyway."

Traxen studied the male. **If he's telling the truth, then Rachel and our security will be here soon to even the odds.**

"If you are lying to me, I will hunt you down."

Manx grinned.

"I expect nothing less." The Jalaxian slid out the door. Traxen followed a few moments later to relieve his bladder before returning.

He glanced around the shed. Gathering some jumpsuits, he rolled them into a makeshift pillow. He sat in a dark corner and rested his head on the lumpy fabric. **Might as well make myself comfortable.**

Some time later, voices aroused him from his rest.

"He's here somewhere. Find him and bring him to me," Mistress Pitman screeched.

Traxen unfolded his body and stood. A ferocious smile broke out on his face. **Time to fight. I'm going to enjoy this.**

The same three males who kidnapped him entered the building. Traxen punched the first one before pivoting and kicking the second in the stomach. The smallest male hung back behind the other two.

The first one grunted when his head snapped back from the force of Traxen's attack. He roared and attempted to tackle Traxen around the waist. Traxen pushed the second male, who bent over gasping, into the first. Extracting his claws, he dug into a shoulder of each of them and tightened his grip. They both screamed in pain and dropped to their knees, hands frantically trying to dislodge the Svesti. Traxen's tail whipped across their faces with a loud snap.

He turned to the third male when he saw movement in his peripheral vision. Retracting his claws, he let the first two go to block the stun stick the last male wielded. A jolt ran down his arm. Ignoring the pain, he twisted to grab the barrel and wrenched it away from his opponent and touched his torso with it. Eyes rolling back in his head, the smaller male fell to the floor right before Traxen stunned the other two.

Crouched and ready, he stilled to see if anyone else would enter. The building shook. A minute later he heard Rachel's livid voice.

"Where is my pet?"

Traxen opened the door and took in the scene. Rachel, Tesix, and Westov stood at the bottom of the **Firebrand**'s ramp. Rachel pointed a blaster at Mistress Pitman's head with Manx several steps away.

"Manx, protect me."

"I don't think so."

Mistress Pitman saw Traxen and tapped on her tablet. He fell forward catching his weight on his quaking hands and knees. Head bowed, he tried to ride out the electricity squeezing his body, but his vision dimmed, and he collapsed.

Chapter 32

Rachel fell asleep while waiting for Traxen to return from picking up a package. Disoriented when she awoke, she stumbled in the dark to the bathroom and splashed cold water on her face.

Stepping into the bedroom, she realized Traxen wasn't there. She padded silently to the living area and found it empty as well. Growing concerned, she checked the time. **Damn. It's been almost three hours. Where the hell is he?**

She rushed down to the concierge, only to discover there never was a package and no one had seen Traxen. She demanded to see Mistress Hower.

The Rumaskan frowned when she heard Rachel's pet was missing.

"He wasn't wearing a pain collar. Are you certain he isn't trying to escape?" Mistress Hower asked delicately.

"I'm positive. I need to review your video footage." Rachel followed the scurrying female to the hotel security office.

Rachel informed the security officer of where and when to begin looking. It wasn't long into the video before she saw three unknown males practically carrying Traxen from the lift. His limbs were limp, and his head drooped as if it were too heavy for his neck. **What in the bloody hell did they do to him?**

"Please arrange a ride to my ship. I wish to check on my other pets in person." Rachel drummed her fingers on the counter but refrained from tapping her foot.

Mistress Hower jerked her head at one of the security personnel in the room.

"Take her." She turned to Rachel. "I hope you find him."

On the **Firebrand**, she ordered, "Find his tracker now. He's been taken."

With hard faces, Tesix and Westov began tapping on the console immediately. Low growls and snaps of flicking tails broke the silence of the cockpit as Rachel waited impatiently.

"Got him," Westov crowed.

"Where is he?"

"Mistress Pitman's house near her mine." Tesix's tail smacked the floor.

"Get me Relim."

The hologram of the Rumaskan popped up a minute later.

"Good evening, Mistress Rachel. How may I help you?"

"My pet is late returning from an errand. I wish to retrieve him."

Mistress Relim frowned, and her ears twitched.

"Unfortunately, I cannot approve your request at this time. Less than an hour ago, the Rumaskan Ruling Commission put a hold on all air travel planetwide. Anyone discovered disobeying the directive will be shot down."

"Why?" **I wish I had a tail to snap.**

"They only stated security issues. The hold is in effect until one hour before sunrise. I can approve your request then."

"How do I obtain special dispensation to leave now?" **Keep calm, Rachel. Don't take your anger out on her.**

"Only the Ruling Commission can make an exception."

"How do I contact them?"

The female's ears twitched faster and she grimaced.

"I'm passing along your request to speak now. I cannot guarantee someone will grant you an audience." Mistress Relim disconnected the comm abruptly.

"**Crek.** Should we take off anyway?" Westov ran his hand through his hair.

"What are their planetary defenses?"

"They could easily target us remotely," Tesix said.

"Let's see if the Ruling Commission deigns to speak with me first."

"We should inform the **Nova** of the situation." Westov cringed.

Rachel crossed her arms.

"What do you think their reaction would be?"

"They'd come in cloaked, attempt to rescue him, and most likely create an interplanetary incident." Tesix's shoulders stiffened. "I'm not sure we're desperate enough for that yet."

"Besides, I want to take care of Mistress Pitman personally." Rachel's jaw hurt from how hard she clenched her teeth. **That bitch needs to learn a lesson.**

"Encrypted comm request," Tesix said.

"Open it."

A hologram of the oldest Rumaskan Rachel had seen so far appeared. The bubblegum pink female with faded green hair in a simple chignon exemplified classic beauty regardless of species.

"Mistress Rachel, thank you for your patience. Allow me to introduce myself. I am Mistress Lyet, the senior member of the Rumaskan Ruling Commission." Her stately demeanor suggested she wielded power effortlessly.

"Mistress Lyet, I wish we were meeting under happier circumstances. I must retrieve my pet, and I'm told I require your approval."

"I cannot give it to you until the planetary hold is lifted."

"My body servant was stolen."

"I am aware, Mistress Rachel. He is currently safe and will remain that way until morning."

"He is in the hands of a sadistic mistress." Rachel's hands fisted.

"Mistress Pitman is not at home. She will be unable to reach her estate until shortly before sunrise traveling by land, as she cannot travel by air either." Mistress Lyet pinned Rachel with a solid stare. "There is more at stake than a single body servant, Mistress Rachel. A number of moving parts must be in place at the proper time for events to proceed for maximum effect."

Rachel narrowed her eyes.

"Where is Mistress Pitman now?"

Mistress Lyet nodded to someone offscreen. The hologram split into two with the female on the left and a scene from a party on the right. Mistress Pitman was speaking with another mistress with a sour expression on her face.

"Is this live?"

"Yes."

"What is her current location?"

Rachel dipped her chin at Tesix when the Rumaskan read off the coordinates. Tesix pulled up a map with the female's location as well as Traxen's.

"I am asking for your patience, Mistress Rachel. All will be clear when you reach the Pitman mine in the morning. I suggest you leave as soon as the ban is lifted. Please accept my sincerest apologies for not explaining further at this time. It is for security reasons." The older female frowned. "In the interests of being as transparent as possible and alleviating some of your concerns, my sources tell me your body servant received a high dose of a sedative during his kidnapping which kept him unconscious long enough to avoid most of Mistress Pitman's attentions, although she did shock him with a pain collar before she left for the function she is attending now. Your male will not be waiting where she left him when you arrive. That is all I can say.”

Rachel narrowed her eyes and perused the Rumaskan's face for any micro expressions that might indicate a lie. **Do aliens even have the same micro expressions as humans?**

Her gut told her the female told the truth.

“I want to go on record that I do not like this. If my male is harmed by this delay, I will rain hellfire down on this planet.”

“I understand you are very protective of your body servants. There is no need for threats. All will be well. I am certain events will unfold to your satisfaction.” Her lips turned up slightly. “I look forward to meeting you in person, Mistress Rachel.” The hologram disappeared.

“Goddamn mother fucking assholes.” Rachel turned and let loose. The seat she punched vibrated rapidly from the force of her blow.

"I'm thinking you can spar with her, Tesix. I like my head on my shoulders."

"I think Mistress Lyet told the truth," Tesix said cautiously.

"So do I. That's what sucks. I hate waiting and leaving him there."

"As do we." Tesix sighed. "Do you need to spar?"

Rachel glanced at the Svesti's forlorn face and laughed.

"No need to look like that, guys. I'll go hit a bag for a while to work off the frustration. I don't need to beat on live targets."

Westov grinned and spoke in a sing-song voice.

"Oh, thank you, Mistress. We are so happy you don't require our assistance."

Rachel smacked him with an open palm on the back of the head.

"Tesix can't have all the fun, smartass."

The night passed slowly, and Rachel's ire turned ice cold. As soon as the travel ban lifted, they departed for Mistress Pitman's estate. She had the Svesti arm themselves, and she strapped on a blaster along with her normal clothes and hidden weapons. The sun was lightening the sky when they landed.

Mistress Pitman stood with the Jalaxian several steps away.

"Where is my pet?"

Rachel pointed her blaster at the female's head.

"Manx, protect me," Mistress Pitman ordered.

"I don't think so."

The Rumaskan tapped on her tablet. Rachel held back her gasp as Traxen fell to the ground shaking before he passed out in front of a shed.

"Stop now or I'll kill you."

"If you kill me, he will eventually die as the collar constricts without another command," Mistress Pitman gloated.

Two huge ships landed next to the **Firebrand**. Mistress Thespa stepped out of one with several males, while Mistress Lyet and eight other Rumaskan females disembarked from the other.

"Cease this now, Mistress Pitman, by order of the Ruling Commission," Mistress Lyet said.

The younger female pouted but tapped her tablet.

"Manx, if you will," the older Rumaskan said.

The Jalaxian swiped the tablet from Mistress Pitman while using his tail to restrain her hands. As she struggled, she screamed at him. He tapped on the tablet, then pressed her finger to it.

"I have control of the pain collars," he said.

"Send a signal for all the males to report here," Mistress Lyet ordered.

Manx tapped.

"Done."

"Remove his pain collar. Now," Rachel bit out. She turned to Tesix and Westov. "Guard her." From the corner of her eye she saw Tesix pull out valadium restraints. She approached Traxen and felt for the collar release. The offending item fell into her hands. She checked him over. **Good. Strong and steady pulse. Breathing a little ragged, but with the shock to his body, I'm not surprised. Time for the bitch's comeuppance.**

She kissed Traxen's forehead and gently stroked his chest before standing. Stalking toward the Rumaskan, she asked through clenched teeth, "Does anyone need her alive?"

"Unfortunately, yes." Mistress Lyet's eyes were hard.

"Good." Rachel placed the collar around Mistress Pitman's neck, and it snapped together with an audible click and gently buzzed. "Hand me that tablet, Manx."

He glanced at the other mistresses, and they nodded. Gently placing the device into Rachel's hands, he briefly instructed her on its usage. Traxen's image still showed on the screen.

She heard low voices and looked up. Hundreds of emaciated males in ragged clothing were leaving the mine in groups, some supporting others. Pale, dirty, and dusty, they looked like they'd been in a war zone starving. Squinting in the morning light, many of them took deep breaths of fresh air before hacking uncontrollably. Many of the females hissed in surprise. The hardier males strutted with stun sticks hanging from their waists.

Mistress Thespa cried out.

"You stole my workers." One of her body servants held her back to keep her from attacking Mistress Pitman. Tears of anger and grief rolled down her face.

Rachel smiled coldly, jerked her head at the Svesti and Manx to step back, then pressed the tablet. Mistress Pitman screamed, clawing at the collar and falling to her knees while she convulsed. Rachel handed the tablet to Manx and walked back to Traxen who was regaining consciousness. She knelt next to him as he sat up and blearily scanned the area.

"How are you feeling?" She rubbed her hand on his back soaking in his warmth and his scent. **I'm so glad he's okay.**

"I've been better, but I'll survive." He tipped his head at the female writhing on the ground. "Your work?"

"You know it. No one messes with the people I care about."

"My **belgella**. I'm honored." He shook his head. "Help me stand, please."

Mistress Lyet said, "Enough of that for now." Manx turned off the female Rumaskan's pain collar. Mistress Pitman lay twitching on the ground, drooling, with tears streaming from her eyes.

"Mistress Thespa, are your stolen males here?"

"Yes, Mistress."

"Do you need assistance transporting them to your estate?"

"No, although I would like to request healers to assist. They will require much medical attention."

Mistress Lyet nodded to one of the females with her, who began comm'ing.

Manx spoke loudly to the males.

"Any males who belong with Mistress Thespa, please make your way to her ship. You'll be returning home."

A round of quiet cheers sounded as males broke away to hobble toward the appropriate ship. Numerous males and females from Mistress Thespa's ship hurried to help them.

"Can you remove their collars? I don't want them wearing them any longer than necessary," Mistress Thespa spat out. Manx tapped the tablet.

Quietly, he said, "All the collars controlled by this tablet are disabled except Mistress Pitman's and the males wearing stun sticks." He raised his voice.

"Who here was a free male before being abducted and brought to Rumaska?"

About sixty males raised their hands tiredly.

"Come stand by me, please." Manx pointed to an open area.

"Manx," Mistress Lyet began.

"No, Mistress. The agreement between the Rumaskan Ruling Commission and the Interplanetary League was that I would go undercover to investigate the males being stolen and any males I found during my investigation of slave trading who were previously free would come with me.”

“Interplanetary League?” Rachel murmured quietly.

“I’ll explain later,” Traxen said. Tesix and Westov approached and nodded as they took places on either side of them.

Another ship landed. **Damn, it was getting crowded around here.**

Armed males of different species disembarked. One nodded at Manx and began ordering the others to help the newly freed males to their ship. Several detoured to the shed and obtained three other males who looked like Traxen had fought with. Manx removed his collar and snapped it in half.

Appearing confused, the remaining body servants stood or sat awaiting instructions. The females from Mistress Lyet’s ship spoke quietly with one another before they all nodded and stepped back.

Mistress Lyet projected her voice.

"Rumaskan law is clear. If a mistress steals a body servant from another female, the harmed female can request up to three males from the offending mistress. Since Mistress Pitman stole one hundred males from Mistress Thespa, Mistress Thespa has the legal right to request up to three hundred others here."

Mistress Thespa looked shocked.

"What will happen to them if I don't take them?"

"We will attempt to find homes for all of them." The older female looked concerned. "However, many of them are in bad shape. I'm not sure we'll be able to find mistresses for all."

Mistress Thespa squared her shoulders.

"Those of you who are willing to work on my estate, you are welcome. You will be treated with courtesy and dignity, so long as you treat others the same way."

One Rumaskan male slowly approached with his eyes downcast.

"Are you Mistress Thespa?"

"Yes, and you are?"

"I am called Ryost, mistress."

"You may look upon me, Ryost," Mistress Thespa said gently.

"Is it true what I've heard others say? Your workers receive a wage and are not forced to stay in the mines breathing bremmite dust very long?" His hands shook.

"Yes, Ryost. I also have everyone checked by a healer on a regular basis. I want my workers healthy and happy. I will not tolerate cruelty, either by male or female on my estate."

"May I offer my service, then? I'm not sure I will be able to work in the mines again, though."

"We'll find something for you, Ryost." She appeared thoughtful. "Have you been here long?"

"Too long, Mistress."

"Are there any males who don't belong on my estate?"

His entire body trembled, and he whispered, "All of them with the stun sticks and the three from the shed. They enjoyed hurting us."

"Thank you, Ryost. Please board my ship." Mistress Thespa gestured in that direction.

The males Ryost mentioned with the exception of the three in Interplanetary League custody swaggered toward her.

"We were supervisors in the mine, Mistress, and would like to serve you," one said with an arrogant grin.

"I see. You'll have to disarm. No one is allowed on my ship with weapons."

"You will provide us others when we arrive so we can ensure your orders are carried out?" The males dropped their stun sticks.

Mistress Thespa shook her head.

"No. You will not be going with me to my estate. I do not believe your temperaments are a good fit. Perhaps the Interplanetary League can find you new homes."

One raised a hand to strike her. Manx and Tesix both grabbed the male. Manx called out to some of his colleagues, and they restrained the males before force marching them onto their ship.

Some of the workers approached saying they belonged to other mistresses and wanted to return to them if the females were willing. Mistress Lyet's contingent worked with them contacting the mistresses. **This has got to be a logistical nightmare.**

"Ah, Mistress Pitman, are you back with us?" Mistress Lyet's eyes narrowed.

"Where are you taking my males?" Spittle flew from the disheveled female's mouth as she rose shakily to her knees.

"You mean the males you stole from other mistresses or were illegally made slaves? They are going back to where they belong. The others will be given to the affected mistresses in accordance with Rumaskan law."

"You can't do that. You'll bankrupt me." Her face turned beet red.

"Speaking of that, your assets will be sold to reimburse the mistresses for the lost labor of their males. I expect you will not be able to afford it all. However, you won't have much need for credits on the prison planet." Mistress Lyet's voice changed from saccharine sweet to tempered steel. "You are an embarrassment to our planet, our gender, and your family line. Take her away."

Rachel wanted to grin, gut the struggling Mistress Pitman, hug Mistress Lyet, and do a happy dance all at the same time. Instead, she linked hands with Traxen and stroked his tail when it circled her waist. **I can't stop touching him.**

"We'd like to leave now and return to Costonia."

"I ask that you make yourself available for questioning if we need more information."

"Of course, Mistress Lyet. Contact the palace admin. He will forward your requests."

Manx stepped forward and exchanged a warrior's clasp with Traxen.

"I'm sorry I couldn't explain everything earlier, but risking the case was not an option."

"Understood." Traxen dipped his chin. **We need to go soon before he blows our cover. He's looking regal, not subservient.**

Chapter 33

On the **Firebrand**, Traxen pulled Rachel onto his lap and embraced her tightly. His tail wound around her ankle and his hands stroked her back. He closed his eyes and savored her fingers caressing his face, neck, and shoulders.

"I was so worried we wouldn't get to you in time," she whispered. "Imagining how she might make you suffer terrified and angered me."

"I'm fine. I'm not happy I was so easily overpowered. I let my guard down."

"Hush. Don't feel guilty about that. At least it was because you're a sexy, hot male, not a king." She tugged on his hair. "Kiss me."

Traxen's lips moved over hers. He drank in her taste, glad to have her close. His hands moved lower to squeeze her delectable ass.

"We've broken atmosphere and are en route to **Nova's** location. We should rendezvous within an hour." Tesix steadfastly did not look up from his console.

"Let's go clean up," Traxen said. **I want her naked.**

"We seem to spend a lot of time doing that."

"That's because we spend so much time doing dirty things." He arched an eyebrow. He chuckled when Westov choked on his laughter.

Tesix deadpanned, "Yes, obstacle courses and mines will do that to you."

Rachel's laugh made him smile as he carried her to the private quarters. **I want to hear her joy every day.**

When she asked, he hastily explained that the Interplanetary League was a coalition of planets who combined forces to combat crimes that crossed between worlds. Earth wasn't eligible for admittance because their technology had not yet reached a minimum level, which was one reason why the Svesti guarded their planet until they could do it on their own.

An hour later, having gotten dirty in the best possible way, then cleaned up and dressed in normal clothes, they walked into the **Nova's** hangar bay. The Spymaster met them.

"Canaan Durek has requested an encrypted comm as soon as you're able."

"Let's take off these prosthetics, then we'll comm him."

"I take it we're headed home, then."

"Yes." **It'll be good to be home.**

"I'll meet you on the bridge." Rachel squeezed his hand and pecked him on the cheek before walking away.

"Was it a successful trip?"

"I believe so. It's one strange planet."

"I look forward to hearing about it."

"Sire," Canaan's serious face greeted them. "You need to return and make an appearance."

"Uncle, we're on our way now. What is going on?"

"We found Frulix."

"You don't look happy about it."

"We inserted a tracker in Sproid without his knowledge and 'allowed' him to escape. We followed his signal to where Frulix hid. When the guards found him, it was…gruesome."

"Gruesome? Did my guards not follow procedure?" Traxen crossed his arms.

"They weren't the issue. Frulix brutally murdered his nephew and his healer. It looked like a blood bath in that room. He has no memory of the events."

Traxen frowned.

"That makes no sense."

"It gets worse, Traxen. When the healers examined Frulix, they found a brainwashing upload in his implant with the phrase 'Take action now.'"

"Wait, someone was controlling him?" Rachel interjected.

"At least to some extent, yes. For how much or how long, we don't know. Devik and Lady Emmy are working on decrypting his comm and other tech now."

"That means there's another player involved." Tails flicked all over the bridge at Rachel's observation.

"You need to meet the king's flitter and take your rightful place. Your guidance is needed now, and you must be visible to the Council." Canaan tapped his tablet. "I've sent the coordinates to Hossix."

"This is a distinctly unsatisfying situation," Traxen said after the comm ended. "I had hoped to take my time wringing every bit of info from the traitor. And to discover he might not have memory of his deeds is unsettling."

"Much of what he did, he should recollect. Mantoor couldn't have had his brainwashing done for more than a month before he snapped, which means the same is most likely true for Frulix. The events on the **Invictus** and most of what occurred on Costonia should still be rattling around in his brain." Rachel rubbed his forearm. "We'll discover what happened."

"You're correct, **belgella**. It's just frustrating."

"Let's go home, Traxen."

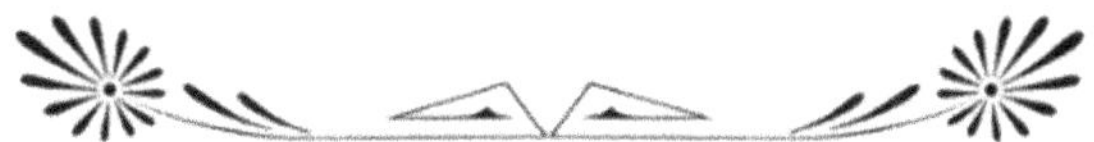

Sitting in his bed after a very long day of discussions, strategy sessions, and catching up on what he missed during their trip to Rumaska, Traxen and Rachel ate a snack of fruit and nuts paired with Estalan liquor.

"To a successful trip for bremmite." Rachel clinked her glass on his.

Traxen sipped. His eyes drifted over her lithe body in a silky nightgown. **I don't care what the Council thinks. I can't throw away my chance at happiness.**

"True mate with me," Traxen said. He held his breath.

"Are you sure? We haven't known each other that long." Rachel caressed his face, her fingers tunneling into his beard.

"I know I want you in my life forever, **belgella**."

"It's a big commitment."

"Yes, it is. Be my love. Be the mother of my children. Be my queen. Be my mistress. Be my pet. Be my everything." **Goddess, please, I've never needed anyone as much as I need her.**

"You know the queen thing is not a plus, right?" Her blue eyes twinkled at him as she took his glass from him and placed it on the side table along with hers.

"I know. Be my mate anyway."

"Yes, I'll true mate with you." They kissed.

So many of their sexual encounters were wild and frantic. But for this occasion, he treated her with reverence and adoration. Slowly he peeled her clothes from her body, kissing and licking her soft flesh as he exposed it to his gaze and his touch. She sighed.

Traxen breathed, "I love you. I will always love you. With you sharing my life, I am happier than I've ever been."

Tears escaped the corners of her eyes and trailed into her hair. Her fingers traced his cheek.

"I love you, Traxen. You've restored my trust, not only in others, but in myself. I can't think of anything better than to be by your side forever."

His tail stroked her calf while his hands caressed her body. Laying her gently on the bed, he played with her breasts—sucking her nipples and nipping at her flesh. Listening to her gasps and moans, Traxen gently licked his way to where her heat emanated hottest. Circling her clit with his tongue, he took his time. Her aroused scent had his erection throbbing. But until he pleasured her, he wanted nothing for himself.

He inserted two fingers into her and pumped. His tongue played with her sensitive nub, and he felt her orgasm building as her cunt squeezed his fingers. He curled them and found that spot inside her that made her crazy with lust. Her hands tangled in his long hair and gripped him to her.

"Yes," she screamed. "Right there."

Her thighs clenched around his ears. Her fingernails digging into his scalp, her scent, her heat, her wetness all imprinted on Traxen's mind. **I'll never forget this. The beauty of our true mating. When she chose Traxen the male, not Sovex the king.**

 After she came, he lined his cock up and slowly pushed into her soaked channel hissing at how good it felt. Their fingers entwined seeking to meld everywhere their flesh touched. He gazed into her eyes as his hips slowly moved. Her hips met his.

He rumbled low. "I will love and honor you every day. I'll seek your wisdom. I'll never betray your trust. Thank you for being you. Thank you for loving me."

Tears flowed unchecked from her eyes, and she smiled tenderly.

"You are the best person I've ever known. You make me happy. You make me laugh even when you frustrate me. My heart is full. I look forward to being yours. Forever. I'll support you. I'll advise you. I'll protect you, and I know you'll protect me. True mate with me."

Enthralled with the beauty of the moment he leaned forward, but primal needs overtook him. He thrust faster as her rippling cunt tightened around his cock. His fangs elongated and sunk into where her neck met her shoulder. She screamed in ecstasy, then bit him on his shoulder. White heat roared through him, his cock vibrated, and his vision blurred.

"The other women didn't tell me about a vibrating cock. Did you know about it?"

Shaking his head, his loose hair cocooning their faces, he kissed her damp forehead.

"No. I never read any reports that mentioned it."

"I hope it's not a one-time occurrence. I could get used to it," she said breathlessly with a grin.

When they recovered, he gathered her to him rolling to his side. Their hands restlessly stroked and caressed each other. Peace settled deep within him. **We'll have this every day of our lives.**

"Traxen," she said quietly. "Look." Her fingertip lightly outlined his clan marking, which was now gold. He smiled.

"You have one too. It looks beautiful on you. We are fated mates. I was afraid to hope."

She laughed merrily.

"I'm so glad I took the chance and the leap of faith to be with you. I love you."

"I love you, Rachel. Today and forever."

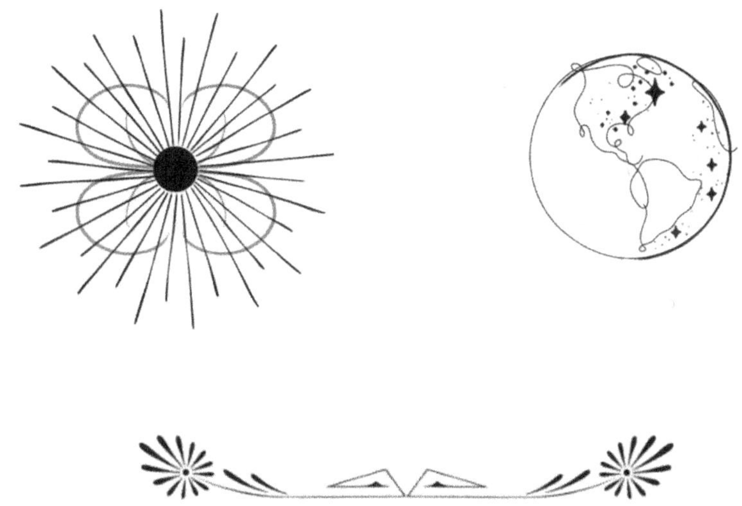

The next day in the office, Xeliv informed Traxen that the Wing Raiders wanted to talk. Traxen pulled Rachel onto his lap and opened the channel to Captain Makai.

"How may I help you today?"

"I think I have something of yours," the Jalaxian said.

"I'm sorry, what are you talking about?"

A Svesti male came into view. Rachel gasped and leaned forward.

"Jevax? Is that you?"

Traxen looked closer at the reddish bronze male with short dark hair. Small scars dotted his arms and part of his face. His brown eyes appeared confused. **Goddess, it is him. He's alive.**

"Is that my name?"

Rachel's eyebrows raised, but Traxen responded.

"Your name is Grulen Jevax and you are a warrior in the Svesti military. We have been looking for you."

Jevax stared at them.

"I don't know you. I don't even know who I am."

A human female with dark hair snuck under his arm which Jevax wrapped over her shoulders. She peered at Rachel suspiciously.

"How do you know him?"

"He's my friend."

"Is that all?"

Rachel smiled.

"Yes, that's all. I'm with him." She motioned to Traxen with her thumb.

"Good. Can you help Jevax?"

"Of course. Bring him home to Costonia," said Traxen. "By the way, it's nice to see you again, Lady Morgan."

"Thank you, King Sovex. We'll be there shortly." She disconnected the comm.

Rachel turned to him and arched her eyebrow.

"I suspect there's a story here."

Traxen grinned.

"You'd be right, **belgella**. I can't wait to tell it to you."

Recap

Races thus far

Human - Enough said.

Svesti - Warrior Race. About seven feet tall, skin in various shades of bronze, semi-retractable fangs, tails, and retractable claws. Ruled by a King. Honorable race protecting many regions of space from the Zuvgran, including near Earth. Most Svesti females died or were rendered infertile thirty Earth years prior due to a virus released by the Zuvgran. Plural is Svesti.

Crestillian - Reptilian Race.

Durelian - Mercenary Race. About seven feet tall, orange skin, three bulbous black eyes.

Ermipa - Mining Race. About four feet tall, furry, round head, oval eyes.

Estalan - Sybaritic Race. Known for its quality liquors and drugs.

Frezzian - Mercenary Race. Adverse to personal risk. Considered dishonorable.

Jalaxian - Warrior Race. About seven feet tall, blue skin, fangs, retractable claws, and tail. Considered honorable. Many work as mercenaries after the Zuvgran decimated their world fifty Earth years ago.

Mostiffian - Mammalian Race.

Nulorian - Mammalian Race.

Pellotian - Avian Race. Green skin and wings.

Praxite - Mammalian Race. Lavender skin and tails. Females have three breasts.

Romittel - Mammalian Race.

Rumaskan - Mammalian Race. Female-dominated. Pink skin, cat-like ears, retractable claws.

Straxian - Mammalian Race. Brown skin.

Wrestikan - Mammalian Race. Four arms and red skin. Home planet was Himita Prime.

Zuvgran - Warrior Race. About seven feet tall, gray skin, fangs, claws, and horns. Ruled by an Emperor. Dishonorable race that invades planets to strip them of their resources and take the inhabitants as slaves. Considered violent. Plural is Zuvgran.

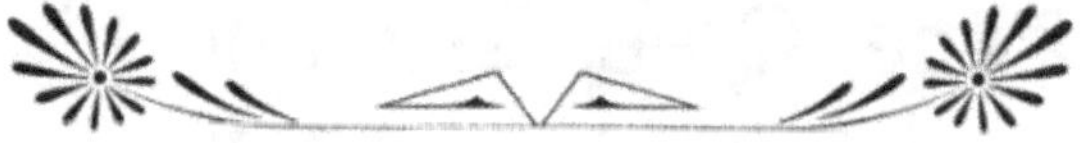

Planets and Space Stations thus far

Earth - Really not the center of the universe as humans might believe.

Costonia - Svesti Home World.

Crestillia - Crestillian Home World. Zuvgran-controlled.

Dianthia – Costonia's moon.

Gladdeus – Gambling world known for its fighting pits and slavery.

Himita Prime - Wrestikan Home World. Zuvgran-controlled.

Ladorta – Ladortan Home World.

Millus - Unoccupied planet outside of Costonian galaxy.

Nulorn - Trading planet halfway between Pellotia and Talonka Six.

Pellotia - Pellotian Home World. Zuvgran-controlled.

Praxis - Zuvgran-controlled.

Romitte - Zuvgran-controlled. Closest planet to Lestanus system.

Rumaska – Female-dominated planet known for their bremmite mines and male subjugation.

Straxis - Agricultural and trading world. Sixth planet in the Lestanus system.

Talonka Six - Mining world closer to Costonia than Earth. Fourth planet in the Lestanus system.

Theron - Space Station approximately one quarter of the distance from Earth to Costonia.

XB9428B - Uninhabited planet, home to a Zuvgran lab.

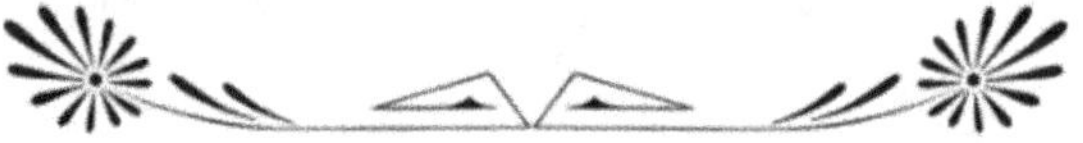

Svesti Houses

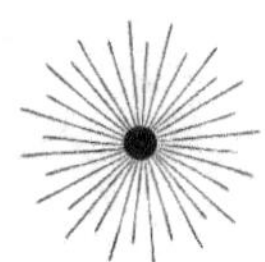 **Davelk** - Ruling House of Costonia.

 **Binova** - Primarily merchants.

 **Fresida** - Primarily educators and scientists.

 **Glixon** - Primarily merchants.

 **Kreliz** - Primarily scientists.

 **Midnar** - Primarily agriculture.

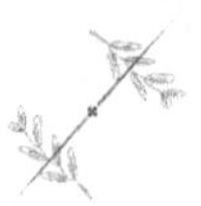 **Nuxar** - One of the two Houses that strictly adhere to the old ways of worship.

 **Ruxila** - Primarily agriculture.

 **Srotix** - One of the two Houses that strictly adhere to the old ways of worship.

 **Troliv** - Primarily merchants.

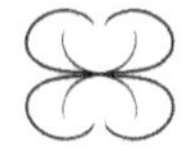 **Vramel** - Primarily warriors and educators.

 **Yula** - Many Svesti healers come from House Yula.

 **Terran** - New human clan marking.

Characters

Humans

Rachel Llewellyn - British, MI6.

Lin Chang - Chinese, botanist.

Emmy Norton - Australian, hacker.

Natasha Petrov - Russian, medical doctor.

Talia Sullivan - American, U.S. Ambassador of Interplanetary Relations.

Ava Taylor - Canadian, chef.

Svesti

King Traxen Sovex of House Davelk - King of the Svesti.

Arinna Brexis of House Midnar – Traxen's grandmother.

Lieutenant Triv'n Brauvix of House Kreliz -

Communications officer on the **Invictus**.

Lieutenant Hozan Crulex of House Yula - Science office on the **Invictus**.

Yan'n Dralix of House Troliv - Warrior.

Rostrox Dresiv of House Troliv – Weapons shop owner in Trezoura.

Canaan Durek of House Ruxila - Vared's father, House Ruxila representative in the King's Court, manages the family estate. Also Main Agricultural Advisor.

Commander Vared Durek of House Ruxila - Commander of the space cruiser, **Invictus**, the flagship of the Svesti military. First cousin to the king.

Pluvi Frulix of House Srotix – Council member.

Hil'n Glopiz of House Nuxar – Council member.

Bavin Hossix of House Binova - Royal Guard.

Merix Hunnek of House Nuxar - Head of aquiponics area on the **Invictus**. Rank - Major.

Grulen Jevax of House Midnar - Warrior.

Gal'n Kalix of House Binova - Security officer.

Besix Kloir of House Kreliz - Warrior.

Jespan Kragen of House Yula – Royal Guard.

Oriba Lunex of House Binova – Headmaster of the Warrior Academy. Rank - Commander.

Rexus Markham of House Yula - Healer on the **Invictus**. Rank - Captain.

Nerid Mantoor of House Glixon - Warrior.

Yistax Minnet of House Troliv – Council member.

Reesa Naturu – Head cook at the palace.

Madix Previv of House Fresida – Royal Guard and Talen's brother.

Talen Previv of House Fresida - Warrior. Head Cook on the **Invictus**. Madix's brother.

Wanon Reccix of House Midnar – Council member.

Ash'n Rivezt of House Yula - Head healer on the **Invictus**. Rank - Captain.

Narilla Rivezt of House Yula - Council member, Main Medical Advisor, Master Healer, Ash'n's grandmother.

Klero Rovex of House Glixon - Warrior.

Nerob Sinoaz of House Troliv - Healer on the **Invictus**. Rank - Captain.

Aldis Sovex of House Davelk – Traxen's grandfather.

Grissa Sproid of House Kreliz – Lerix's mother.

Lerix Sproid of House Kreliz - Warrior.

Lieutenant Devik Tolvex of House Vramel - Head security officer on the **Invictus**.

Pex Tolvex of House Vramel - One of Devik's older brothers.

Rassix Tolvex of House Vramel - One of Devik's older brothers.

Solen Tolvex of House Vramel - One of Devik's older brothers.

Clen'n Vepiv of House Nuxar - Warrior and medic.

Lieutenant Leriv Volax of House Kreliz - Supply Master on the **Invictus**.

Lieutenant Gat'n Wrox of House Fresida - Head engineer on **Invictus**.

Drikon Wurvez – Merchant, Karid's father.

Lieutenant Karid Wurvez of House Binova - Head tactical officer on the **Invictus**, second in command of the space cruiser.

Brestov Xoriv of House Fresida - Security officer.

Wexan Yanz of House Srotix – Royal Guard.

Saletta Yemez of House Ruxila - Ronan's mother.

Ari Zunnax of House Davelk – Spymaster disguise.

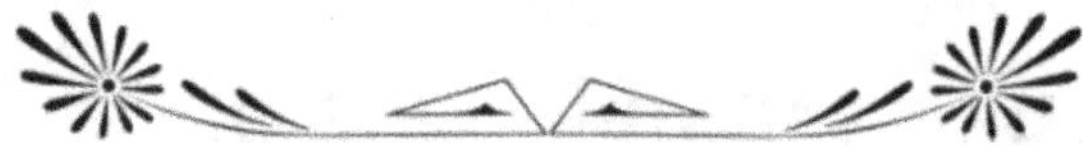

Wing Raiders

Captain Makai - Leader of the Jalaxian mercenary group, Wing Raiders.

Crax - Jalaxian Wing Raider, specialty is weapons.

Kara - Human female in the Wing Raiders, specialty is technology.

Lezon - Jalaxian Wing Raider, specialty is medical.

Rain - Human female in the Wing Raiders, pilot.

Tren - Jalaxian Wing Raider, engineer.

Yaz - Jalaxian Wing Raider, pilot.

Zuvgran

Largon d'Ayen - Jorn d'Olorg's best friend and surrogate father to Ronan.

Jorn d'Olorg - Ronan's father.

Emperor Prigon n'Tuli – Zuvgran emperor.

Commander Rufen d'Urfan – Interim leader of the Zuvgran.

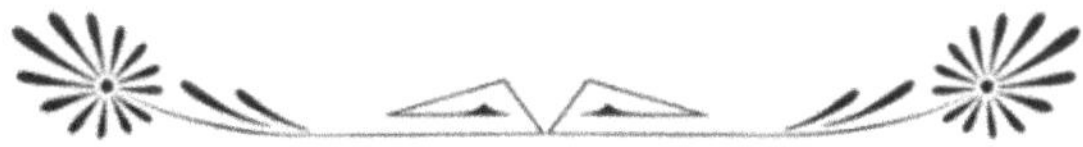

Rumaskans

Mistress Akka – Planetary communications worker.

Mistress Hower – Hotel owner.

Mistress Linoro – Fishery owner.

Mistress Lyet – Senior member of the Rumaskan Ruling Commission.

Mistress Overly – Bremmite mine owner.

Mistress Pitman – Bremmite mine owner.

Mistress Relim – Planetary communications supervisor.

Mistress Summi – Fabric manufacturer.

Mistress Thespa – Bremmite mine owner.

Ryost – Mine worker.

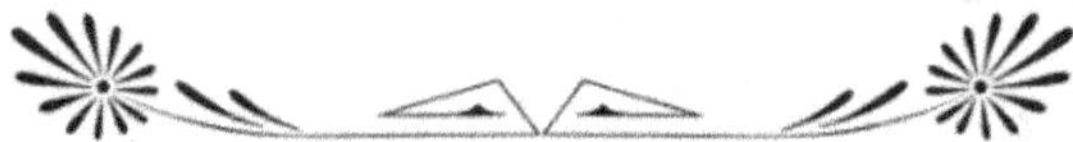

Other

Ronan d'Olorg -Svesti-Zuvgran hybrid. Son of Jorn and Saletta.

Marris d'Olorg -Svesti-Zuvgran hybrid. Ronan's sister.

Annika - Pellotian-Zuvgran hybrid.

Brenos - Pellotian-Zuvgran hybrid.

Kito Dresine - Wrestikan. Shop owner on Nulorn.

Flitos - Pellotian-Zuvgran hybrid.

Gromm - Wrestikan-Zuvgran hybrid.

Herrah - Wrestikan-Zuvgran hybrid.

Manx – Jalaxian body servant to a Rumaskan female.

Molla - Jalaxian female.

Rina - Pellotian-Zuvgran hybrid.

Overseer Roho - Ermipa on Talonka Six, head of the Veba

Mine.

Talos - Pellotian teacher.

Yostal - Mostiffian-Zuvgran hybrid.

Zela - Crestillian-Zuvgran hybrid.

Svesti Words thus far

Bataavi - Cherished one.

Belgella – Beautiful warrior.

Bloniv - Spice similar to Earth's turmeric, but grows in tube-like clusters.

Brellia - Small, rumik-filled pastry.

Bremmite – Crystalline ore.

Caliana - Beautiful female.

Cold season - Comparable to Earth's winter in the northern hemisphere.

Crek - Fuck.

Drelix - Spice similar to Earth's ginger, but grows in tube-like clusters.

Estrecaro - Beloved grandson.

Forliza - Flower similar to Earth's jasmine, but with purple petals.

Harvest season - Comparable to Earth's autumn/fall in the northern hemisphere.

Horicar - Vegetable with a texture similar Earth's carrots, but shaped like blue potatoes.

Hot season - Comparable to Earth's summer in the northern hemisphere.

Kirani - Female feline found in the wild. Similar to Earth's lioness.

Leringa - Fruit that has a hint of spice when ingested.

Lobile - Purple tuber, cross between Earth's potato and sweet potato.

Lunar - Month.

Maxiem - A large animal that resembles a hybrid between Earth's ox and cow. Used as a source of meat, milk and beasts of burden.

Mentok - Similar to Earth's myna bird, but larger and with plumage reminiscent of an Earth's peacock. Chatters incessantly.

Milara - Small brown bird with periwinkle/white chest and underside of wings. Known for its cunning.

Naroon - Large furry animal, similar to Earth's ape, with blue fur. Gregarious and known to be silly in their family groups.

Pertiza - Creamy yellow sweet yogurt made from maxiem milk.

Picana - Little one.

Plostiv - Meat similar to Earth's chicken.

Pyrix – Bearlike animal on the planet Ladorta.

Raralumia - Rare light.

Renewal season - Comparable to Earth's spring in the northern hemisphere.

Ristern - Ermipa organ that filters dangerous gases.

Rulah - Small, furry animal similar to Earth's cat.

Rumik - Meat similar to Earth's ground beef. Comes from maxiem.

Sedapi - Vegetable similar to Earth's celery, but white.

Shurlix - Similar to Earth's tomato, but yellow.

Sibella – Vegetable similar to Earth's onion, but tubular in shape.

Solar - Year.

Tempika - Green berries that taste tart, but also sweet.

Trezoura - Capital city of Costonia.

Trulet - Similar to Earth's oak tree, but with dark blue leaves and orange bark.

Valadium - Steel-like ore when tempered is one of the hardest substances known in the universe.

Valli – Purple fruit similar to Earth's pears.

Wimma - Blue citrus fruit similar to Earth's lime.

Woolah - Red flower that blooms on Costonia during Harvest season.

Yeddom - Orange bean-like vegetable that tastes like Earth's asparagus.

Young – Baby/infant.

Youngling – Child.

Yuffa - Plant similar to Earth's aloe, but with orange ball-like leaves.

Other

Ermipa

Ristern - Extra organ that filters out air impurities.

Pellotian

Annum - Year.

Rumaskan

Wutta – Flaky fish delicacy.

Zuvgran

Grak - Fuck.

Author's Note

As the sixth book, **Traxen** marks the end of the first major storyline arc of the series. Now that we finally know who the traitor is, we can move on. Readers have asked me for more Svesti stories, so I'm not done yet. One of their stories overlaps with the Wing Raiders, but I need to tell a few of the Jalaxian tales first.

My plan for 2024 is to begin a new series with the Wing Raiders to bring us up to the present where the overlap occurs, then more Svesti Fated Mates books. Eventually, all of the Wing Raiders will find their mates.

Some of my favorite characters will be making appearances in future books. As humans continue to interact with Svesti, and possibly the Zuvgran hybrids, more possibilities exist for love to find a way.

I probably shouldn't admit this, but I don't know what will happen as Earth and Costonia increase contact with one another, the Zuvgran's attempts at empire expansion, and the hybrids reach adulthood. I'm looking forward to finding out.

I am certain of one constant—love will continue to make the stars shine.

- Wavy

Thank you for reading Traxen and Rachel's story. If you enjoyed this book, please leave an online review where you purchased it. This lets other readers know whether they might enjoy it, too!

If you'd like to hear about Wavy's other books, you can sign up for her newsletter or find her social media links at wavymartin.com.